THE
BOOK
OF
HEARTBREAK

T0394854

THE
BOOK
OF
HEARTBREAK

a novel

OVA CEREN

alcove
press

This is a work of fiction. All of the names, characters, organizations, places and events portrayed in this novel are either products of the author's imagination or are used fictitiously. Any resemblance to real or actual events, locales, or persons, living or dead, is entirely coincidental.

Published in the United States by Alcove Press, an imprint of The Quick Brown Fox & Company LLC.

Alcove Press and its logo are trademarks of The Quick Brown Fox & Company LLC.

Library of Congress Catalog-in-Publication data available upon request.

ISBN (hardcover): 979-8-89242-276-5
ISBN (paperback): 979-8-89242-175-1
ISBN (ebook): 979-8-89242-176-8

Art direction by Will Speed. Cover illustrations © Kailey Whitman, 2025
Map created by Naz Ekin Yilmaz and Ova Ceren

Printed in the United States.

www.alcovepress.com

Alcove Press
34 West 27th St., 10th Floor
New York, NY 10001

First Edition: August 2025

The authorized representative in the EU for product safety and compliance is eucomply OÜPärnu mnt 139b-14, 11317 Tallinn, Estonia, hello@eucompliancepartner.com, +33757690241

10 9 8 7 6 5 4 3 2 1

To K & Menna, for the finest books and cake,
and Memo, who has the kind mischief that inspires stories

THE CITY OF ISTANBUL

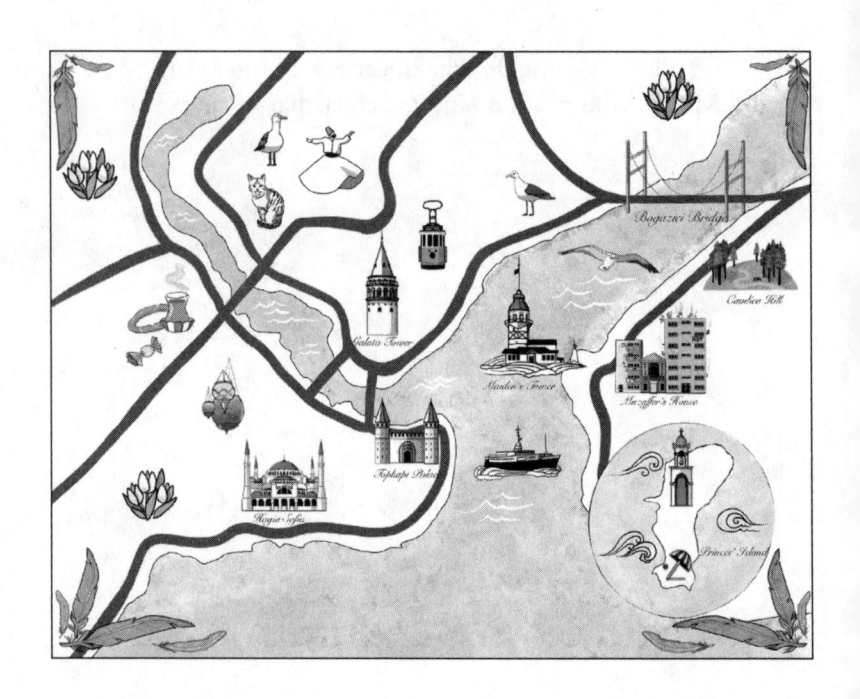

THE HOLY ORGANIZATION OF THE OTHERSIDE

BOSS ALMIGHTY (They Whom Should Not Be Concerned)

- HEAVENLY GOVERNANCE
  Chief Executive Celestials AKA Archangels (Mikhael, Gabriel, Raphael, Uriel)
  - Angel Resources
  - Department of Research and Divine Development
  - Holy Treasury
  - Celestial Compliance Body
    - Divine Disciplinary Board
    - Celestial Audit and Investigation
  - Mortal Affairs Commission
    - Mortal Termination and Transition
      - Afterlife Admissions
      - Field Operations
    - Ethereal Resourcing and Deployment Unit
    - Fate Adjustment Bureau

- - Temporal Intervention Agency
  - Prayer Response & Fulfillment Division
    - Hope Delivery Unit
    - Curse Assessment and Remediation Panel
    - Tragedy Containment Taskforce
  - Prophecy Validation Office
  - Miracle Management Council
- Halotech Data & Integration Hub
  - Celestial Network & Communications
  - Divine Operations Management
  - Sacred Data Systems
    - Vault of Angelic Registry (VAR)
    - Worldly Index
      - Mortal Database
      - Curse and Malediction Archives
      - Miracle Catalogues
- INFERNAL DOMINION (Separate Hierarchy)

Subject: Urgent Inquiry Regarding Discrepancy in Curse Records

Date: 7 January 2025
From: Grey the Compassionate, Associate Cherub, Curse and Malediction Archives, Worldly Index, Sacred Data Systems, Halotech Data & Integration Hub
To: Fate Adjustment Bureau—ALL Angels
CC: Mortal Affairs Commission—ALL Angels

Dear and Most Respectable Angels of the Fate Adjustment Bureau,

I hope this message finds you in cherubic spirits. I am reaching out to address a most pressing matter in the Curse and Malediction Archives.

During a recent database upgrade, I discovered that the curse record CID-1010834556 had been deleted without the approval of my superior, the Divine Data Officer. While I can retrieve some of the data from the backups, attempting to open the full report, including the related document (DTH-9000719), results in an Unauthorized Access error, even though I have the necessary permissions.

And there is more! On several occasions, the cursed mortal, ID: M9392748565670048343, appears to have crossed into our domain, yet there is no record of their arrival on the Otherside. It is most perplexing that this soul has experienced death three times. Three times!

Further investigation led me to conclude that this is the work of an exceptionally strong curse, festering on years of unanswered prayers from another mortal. It's unfortunate that the Prayer Response & Fulfillment Division was too occupied to respond, and thus the curse spawned many tragedies. A quick examination reveals that a throng of mortals involved are already dead, and the curse, which should be dormant according to our sacred systems, is still very much active. It tickles my curiosity.

I would be delighted to volunteer my services in any plans to tackle this curse. I always had a fondness for Konstantiniyye—or Istanbul as it's called these days (a pity if you ask me, as I favor the old name)—and I'm particularly enthralled by enigmatic curses.

As much as the audacity of advising my superiors crushes me, I am obliged to remind you that if this matter falls onto the radar of the archangels or—Heavens forbid—They Whom Should Not Be Concerned, the consequences may be drastic. So we must act, dear comrade superiors!

Your prompt attentions to this matter will be greatly appreciated.

Yours divinely,
Grey the Compassionate
Doctorate of Angelic Scholarship (Hons)
Thrice longlisted for the Heavenly Achievement Prize

CHAPTER ONE

It may not be evident to the untrained eye, but Death is ever-present, woven through our world like the wind, rain or storm. Those blessed with the pure eye understand that Death is not a lone entity but a legion, its acolytes walking among us to fulfill their duties. These emissaries may occasionally falter, their missteps—though trivial to them—bearing dire consequences for mortals. What is a human life to the Hidden, if not too numerous and dispensable to be accounted for with meticulous care?

Excerpt from *The Book of Heartbreak, Müneccimbaşı Sufi Chelebi's Journals of Mystical Phenomena*

My life turns upside down on a Tuesday evening in June.

I get home from school as usual, eager to shut out the world behind the front door. But the minute I see our neighbor Fiona tucked into the hallway, I know something is wrong.

The evening is too balmy for shivering, the hour too late for visitors. Not that we usually have any. It's just Mum and me—if you don't count the succession of men who make fleeting appearances at random hours. Mum's regrettable taste in the other sex must be beginning to drag down the property values in our morbidly expensive street.

"Sare." Fiona looks everywhere but into my eyes, balancing her toddler Dotty on her hip. "Darling."

At the word *darling* my hands go clammy. Mum's friends mostly ignore her asocial, weird seventeen-year-old daughter. But now Fiona extends her arm toward me, her shirt buttons askew, her hair a mess. I recoil from the touch. Whatever has caused her to wash up here wearing slippers and no make-up is bad news, and I want none of it.

"What's going on?" I shrug off my backpack.

"Will you come inside for a minute?"

"Where's Mum?" I'm determined to pinpoint my mother's whereabouts before delving into whatever trouble has transpired. If I can predict what's wrong, perhaps things won't be as catastrophic. "Is she home?"

Now looming at the threshold of the reception room, Fiona shakes her head.

I go still, my gold pendant heavy around my neck, any remaining hope I had melting like ice cream in my hand. Grubby toddler fingers tug at Fiona's hair, but she doesn't flinch. *Shit*, I think as my feet follow them inside the room. *Shit, shit, shit.* The thuds of my footsteps sound hollow—as if I'm made of fear and not flesh. Something must have happened. I begin to plot tolerable scenarios that wouldn't be the worst. Perhaps Mum's in hospital, unwell but unharmed. Or she could have driven to Ferit's place again, the ex she can't forget. Has she made a scene at his? Perhaps the police have arrested her.

Inside, Dotty starts to cry as soon as Fiona sinks onto the worn-out sofa. "Please sit."

"Why?"

"Please," she repeats. Her gaze still evades me. She doesn't want to be here, I realize. She doesn't want to deliver this speech or meet my eyes. I feel a twinge of pity for her, that she has to bear whatever turbulence my mother has caused. My heart flutters inside my ribs like a caged bird. The fluttering is a gentle prelude before a burning pain that mustn't come—a warning that I can't think about others. I have to focus on myself. She isn't here, but Munu's words chime in my ears as I sink onto the sofa, perching on its edge. *You have a responsibility to protect yourself. You must care about yourself and no one else.*

If only it were that easy.

Fiona sets Dotty on the floor before easing herself beside me. The toddler immediately uses the edge of the coffee table to pull herself upright. Three empty wine bottles wobble in front of her, the dappled reflection of the Japanese maple in the front garden imprinted on their necks.

I clasp my hands between my knees and face Fiona, ready to absorb the damage.

"Your mother—" Her knee jabs into mine as she snatches a tarnished coaster from Dotty's mouth. I shift to avoid her squirming. "Your mother was involved in an accident, and unfortunately, she didn't make it." Fiona swallows a dry sob.

"Accident?" I look away from her and glance around the room as if it owes me an explanation. Last night's half-finished meal is sat on a plate in the corner, rotting. Mismatched cushions lie on the sofa, the TV remote wedged between them; wine glasses, an array of empty mugs, boxes of painkillers on top of a pile of magazines.

"She was driving down the M11, and it appears that she'd been drinking—" Fiona shakes her head in disbelief, as if it makes no sense, like Mum was the sanest person on the face of the earth and would never drink-drive. She pauses as if it's my turn to talk, but I don't have any words.

"The police called me an hour ago," Fiona says eventually, with a sigh.

The fact that this woman was Mum's emergency contact fills me with sorrow. Mum lost her own mother when she was born, and her father died when she was pregnant with me. She has a few friends, sure, but no other family. We have no one who truly cares. No one to call when she dies. No one but a neighbor, who clearly wishes she wasn't involved.

"She's . . . dead?" I finally stutter. The idea that someone's life can be flicked off like a light switch—that your mum can vanish on a motorway in an instant—doesn't seem real.

"She's gone, Sare." Fiona reaches for Dotty's shoulder as the child loses her balance and lets out a wail. "I can't believe it. I saw her only this morning."

Dead, my mind registers, like an ink stain expanding on a white napkin. My mother is dead. The fluttering in my chest sharpens into a searing, inescapable throb. My hands twitch on my lap, the scars inside my left palm tingling.

Fuck. I shouldn't have ignored the fluttering.

A dated photograph of my mother and me in a wooden frame grows larger above the fireplace. I must be five or six, Mum is sober, and her smile is timid. Her hand clutches my arm as if to ensure that I'm real, that I'm really hers. She used to love me back then, when I was a child and she still had a light in her eyes. Then I grew up, and she changed. *Why do you make everything a big deal?* Her voice wavers in my ears. *Why do you always have to worry so much, Sare?*

The walls begin to shrink and I exhale all the hope that was left in me. My lungs deflate. My heart begins to sizzle and I look down to my open palm, where three faint scars are carved as reminders for me not to mess up again.

"She's gone," Fiona repeats, her voice stilted like a robot on the brink of shutting down. That's when I spot the fissures appearing on the wall behind her.

No. It can't be happening again. I have to stop it. I have to prevent it.

Rule number three, I recite in vain. *Death is not an option.*

For a brief moment I consider grasping my pendant to summon Munu. Is it too late? Maybe she can help, do something to prevent my failure, but before I can do anything, the walls crumble, and the room closes around me like the grip of an old regret.

She's gone. The words echo, circling me like vultures. *She's gone. She's gone. She's gone.*

"No!" I scream. "Stop!"

Sare, you fool. Did you really think you could win against the curse?

What have I done? How did I trick myself into believing that I didn't love Mum? I never stopped caring about her. She is all I have.

The floor quivers, creaking and groaning in response to my panic, and the house bows down, succumbing to the relentless force of the earthquake. The pain I yearned to forget these past four years pierces me like lightning, proving once more that it's stronger than I've ever been. I should fight back, recite the rules, breathe, count—distract myself. Isn't that what I'm supposed to do?

There are hundreds of ways to fill your life, and they say you should make the most of it. I never dare follow this advice. In the past, I was naive enough to chase happiness, but each heartbreak has taught me a lesson. I wasn't like the other kids. I had to master my emotions. And I thought I had—I haven't cried since I was thirteen. I shut myself away so no affection could worm itself into my chest. I refused every sliver of hope and happiness. I didn't have a drop of love left in me. I can't be screwing all that up now.

But the earthquake rages on, breaking glass, splintering wood—telling me what I truly am. An orphan. A no one. The loneliest girl who ever walked the earth. It's too late to fight back or resist; too late to call for help. I hear the crack of my heart and fall to the floor like a ragdoll.

This time, it only takes nine seconds to die.

CHAPTER TWO

A curse is a fault within the divine order—intentionally or, at times, unwittingly. Many who bear curses traverse their lives without the faintest inkling of their burden, while others may never forget such a realization until they're in the arms of Death.

Excerpt from *The Book of Heartbreak, Müneccimbaşı Sufi Chelebi's Journals of Mystical Phenomena*

Family is fate. It seeks to expand and endure, defying time in a rebellion against individual mortality. It wants to live forever, leaving marks on the earth, begging not to be forgotten.

So people invent surnames to enclose themselves in families; everyone is born into a lineage branded by your ancestors.

But a surname isn't the only thing you receive without consent. You inherit genes. Moles. Dimples. Birthmarks. Illnesses. You inherit your mother's smile or temper. The tremble in her hands when she's nervous, the way she brushes off compliments about her beauty. You inherit a cage of loneliness and the ache of not belonging.

And sometimes, if you're as unfortunate as I am, you inherit poor luck—passed down like a family heirloom, coursing through your blood like poison.

Not that Mum is—was—cursed like I am. She and I were always opposites, as if our roles had been reversed. As if I was the parent and she was the child. I won't take a step without calculating the risks and she never considered the consequences of her actions. I live in a voluntary isolation, barring affection and avoiding any meaningful connections, while Mum dived headfirst into relationships, desperate to be loved. Yet the men who adored her were the ones she couldn't stand; she always fell for those who had no mercy for her.

Perhaps I'm luckier than she was. Perhaps I should be grateful that I can't ever let a boy into my heart. I can't lower my guard, not even for a second. I can't afford to feel love.

Because love is a four-letter death sentence for someone like me, cursed to die of heartbreak.

I was four when I almost died for the first time, and this near miss gave me Munu—the only soul who is ever allowed close to me.

Our first encounter is etched vividly in my mind. Later, when I understood how dangerous it is for me to open my heart to others, I used that memory as a shield, a way to ward off the hazards of potential friendships. But in that moment, I was blissfully unaware of the perils people could present.

A group of kids decided to disown me in the playground with that innocent, headstrong cruelty that belongs only to children. If I close my eyes now, I can still see them running. I can hear the flute of their laughter, the chorus of their words: *you're not playing with us.* I can feel the hot tears on my cheeks, the frantic fluttering in my chest, the scrape of rough bark against my skin as I fell to the ground. Then the fluttering twisted, morphing into a sharp, searing burn. I gasped for air, flailing like a fish out of water.

"Don't cry, canim," a voice soothed me. "Crying only makes it worse."

I lifted my head to see a tiny woman, no taller than the length of my arm, hovering in mid-air. Her scruffy gray pigeon wings were barely noticeable against the puffy sugar-pink princess gown she wore. I thought she must be a fairy godmother here to save me.

She circled me and, distracted by the flapping of her wings, I forgot the sting in my chest.

I opened my hand and she landed on my palm with a sigh.

"Your lifeline isn't particularly long," she murmured, tiptoeing across my skin, each step a faint tickle. "But bolder than the others I've seen. My other assignments, I mean. They did fine." She cleared her throat. "Mostly fine. But never mind that. You're not just any old job. You're quite special."

I remained quiet, wondering if I'd fallen asleep. Maybe this was just a dream.

"You're too young, aren't you?" she asked suddenly. "How old are you now?"

"Four," I answered, absentminded.

"Boss in Heavens!" she gasped, covering her mouth with a tiny hand. "Just a baby, and ready to shatter like glass. Tell me now, sweet girl, do you feel funny around here?" She poked a finger to her chest.

"Not any more," I said, and her smile widened.

"Well, that is good. I've successfully saved you." She beamed. "Sare Sıla Silverbirch, my name is Munu, and I'm your guardian."

"Like a fairy godmother?" I ventured, hopeful.

"Ah . . . wouldn't it be lovely if I had a magic wand?" She chuckled. "I'd flick it, and *poof*—everything would be fixed! But no, I have no wands to wave or stardust to sprinkle, I'm afraid. Perhaps I'm a godmother of sorts, but my powers are . . . limited. Very limited. I work for my boss, who answers to some very important bosses on the Otherside. They're called the Hidden. It's complicated, but what matters is this: the organization serves mortals like you."

I blinked, unable to process her words. My confusion must have shown; Munu's eyes softened.

"If it helps," she said gently, "a long time ago, I was a living, breathing soul—just like you. Trust me, I understand how much it hurts. I had a heart before I died." She pauses to frown. "I still have one, I guess."

"You're dead?" I blurted, gaping at her.

"In theory." Munu cleared her throat again. "Or practice. Doesn't matter."

"Where's my mummy?" I scanned the park anxiously. The tiny woman didn't seem malicious but her admission of being dead made my stomach tighten.

"There," Munu said, pointing behind the fences.

Mum stood laughing with a man, perhaps another parent or a stranger, but turned to wave at me. She had a striking beauty that drew men to her like wasps to a honey pot.

"You did very well today, canim. Remarkable!" Munu chimed without batting another glance in my mother's direction. "Now, I'm not sure how much sense this will make to you, but you almost died today. A near miss for this little heart of yours, but I made it in time."

"W-what do you mean?" I rose to my feet, Munu still in my palm.

"Listen closely—there's no easy way to tell you this, so I will be direct," Munu said, taking a deep breath. "You're cursed, Sare. If your heart breaks five times before the age of eighteen, your mortal life will finish. Can you even count to five? Boss in Heavens, we must use those heartbreaks wisely, if we use them at all."

I stared at her with a furrowed brow.

"Four years old, and already so delicate." Munu took off, leaving my bare palm behind. "We're treading on thin ice—this is a dangerous task."

"What do you mean, dangerous?" I dropped my hand.

"Don't you worry about it." Munu huffed. "I'll protect you from the horrors of mankind. Just promise me this: don't you ever cry, alright? It's the first and foremost rule."

I nodded, unsettled by the gravity of her warning. It would take me a few more years to fully grasp what it meant to bear a curse—how, beneath my rib cage, tucked behind bones curving like praying fingers, lay a heart so flawed that it would kill me with each heartbreak.

"I mean it. It's the first rule of survival against the curse, Sare. *No tears shall fall.* You won't cry, alright?"

"But why me?" I whispered, curiosity bubbling in my chest. "Why do I have a curse?"

"Why, why, why? That's all anyone ever asks!" Munu's wings stilled, her gaze hardened. "You have these stubborn curls and brown eyes, and a cursed heart. It all happens because it does. There is no why. You should be grateful to have my invaluable assistance—many aren't so fortunate."

"Okay." I nodded again, the weight of her words pressing heavier this time.

"Aren't you a sweetheart, canim?" Munu's wings shifted with a soft, feathery sweep, like a sparrow's. "Too kind and gentle for your own good."

With that, Munu became a constant presence in my life, visiting daily, often more than once. Days elongated into weeks, and weeks into months, gradually expanding the dense veil of childhood, and it dawned on me that I was the only person capable of seeing or hearing Munu. I was surprisingly at peace with this realization, for it made me feel special. I tried again to ask her at times, "Why am I cursed?" No one else around me seemed to tolerate such a burden. But Munu would always shut me down. The Hidden were called Hidden for a reason—questioning their ways was futile. "Curiosity never ends well, especially with a boss like mine," she'd warn, and eventually I stopped trying.

I never told Mum about Munu. Back then, my mother doted on me, but she wouldn't have believed me if I said I had an invisible godmother. Besides, Munu insisted it would only upset her. Mum was already sad, and her sadness made everything harder.

Munu's lively banter served as a beacon of light in those dim days of my childhood. She was faithful to her promise to look after me, dedicating every single second that she remained in the world to my well-being and troubles.

I was the one who failed to keep my end of the bargain.

They say that your life flashes before your eyes when you die, but mine never has. Perhaps it was because the pain is blinding, or perhaps it was the sad fact that nothing noteworthy happened in my life except for dying.

I wish I could cite grand reasons for each time I lost my precious life—like love, betrayal or adventure—but they're all disappointingly mundane. My first heartbreak was marked by the departure of a childminder.

Munu had cautioned me against getting too attached to Carly, and I did my best. Mum had found her on a Facebook group and hired her despite the fact that she probably had no qualifications to look after children. Carly would pick me up from school with sheer joy every time she saw me. She was firm but warm, and her house maintained a constant aroma of fish fingers and nail polish. Sometimes a word or a smell lands me back on her squeaky leather sofa— where we watched movies with ratings above my age while I snuggled against her like a kitten. Munu would perch on my shoulder to complain and, like the fool I was, I'd shoo her away.

"You're her job," she'd protest. "You'll end up heartbroken if you don't wise up now."

I was eight when Carly left.

Her departure was my first true heartbreak. The earth quivered around me when I learned she was gone, the rumble foretelling my first death.

After three uneventful years, I ventured into friendship again at eleven, but it soon ended even more disastrously than my first attempt on the playground. Again, I hate to say that Munu had warned me. "I do not trust this Aurelie," she kept saying, but her advice fell on deaf ears. Aurelie was a lovely friend, until we both developed a crush on the same boy. I was willing to step aside, but before I could, Aurelie chose to discard our friendship to claim Thomas for herself. My heart was shattered once more. Twice heartbroken, twice dead. This time, the ground seemed to split beneath me, each crack resonating with my despair. I hoped it would be the last. Surely, no pain could surpass betrayal by my best friend.

Yet, only two years later, Ferit, Mum's most enduring flame, crumpled my heart like a ball of paper. I had stupidly accepted him as a father figure despite Munu's pleas, and this unwise decision cost me dearly. When Ferit finally slammed the door and left for good, my mother and I both collapsed under the weight of our heartbreak. But of course, unlike me, Mum didn't die.

Not until today.

As my disobedient heart stops beating for the fourth time, the quivering of the earthquake diminishes, and the physical pain withdraws. My eyes adjust to the sticky darkness of the Inbetween, a realm of drifting shadows—caught between life and the Otherside. This is where I always end up when I die, stranded between fading and returning, until Munu pushes me back into the world of the living.

The Inbetween looks like a lighthouse, although I've never stayed long enough to scrutinize it properly. Time is scarce here.

I find myself on the terrace that wraps around the rotunda, separated from the starless night by wrought-iron bars. The lantern on the stone wall behind me emits a weak, silvery light that struggles against the engulfing darkness.

I grip the railing and lean over. There is no sound, no movement, yet there's a palpable sense of something churning beneath. For a moment, I consider diving in to uncover its secrets. It could be the space between the planets, or an ocean of dreams.

But before I can move, Munu's familiar chatter fills the silence like birdsong.

"Why didn't you fight the curse, canim?" She's struggling to hold back tears, I realize with shock. Munu never cries. She insists on setting a strong example for me.

"It just happened," I whisper, and gaze into the void, where the impatient night ticks like a clock. Whatever unfolds here fits into a mere blink in the world I left behind.

"Rule number two: *channel your sorrow into rage*," Munu recites. "That might have spared you, had you applied it. Instead, you gave up, didn't you?"

I don't bother pointing out that there's no use in repeating rules for survival when you're already dead. Besides, how could I possibly convert the raw shock of my mother's loss into fury? Mum wasn't exactly Mother of the Year; most days, her eyes would slip over me, as if she couldn't tolerate the sight of me. But things were different once—I would fall asleep in her embrace, lulled by tales of Istanbul and gentle strokes as she brushed my hair.

"I-I don't think anything could have saved me," I stutter. "M-Mum is dead."

It was a battle destined to be lost.

Munu's eyes go wide for a second, then she shakes her head, lips pursed. "Well, she'd been gone a while now, hadn't she? You could barely call that living. Let me guess. Alcohol poisoning, was it? Couldn't she have drunk less, at least for a couple more months?!"

"It was an accident," I say coldly. Sober or not, I loved Mum, and that was my fault. Not hers.

"I'm sorry, canim." Munu flutters up to face me. Her red lipstick and pink dress emit a neon radiance, but the shadows trailing behind her linger as a reminder that she belongs to a place beyond the railing, pulsing like a hungry mouth eager to swallow us both. "But I warned you that things may come to this. Didn't I?"

Munu seems to hate everyone except me. She claims her life was mundane, though she admits she was quite naughty—perhaps the reason she ended up with assignments like me instead of eternal rest. The work she does has made her so intolerant of the living, it doesn't surprise me that she never liked Mum. *Let her cry!* Munu used to complain when I'd consume myself with worry about her. *Why do you care if she ate anything? She isn't your pet, for Heavens' sake, she's your parent.* To Munu, Mum was a threat to my survival, especially after what happened with Ferit. She never forgave Mum for letting him into our lives. But I know it was my own weak heart that's to blame, nothing else.

"Fine. I fucked up again, okay?" I whisper into the shadows, clinging to my anger, ready to rub it like a bulging blister until it bursts.

I brace myself, expecting a rebuke for exhausting my last resurrection, but Munu refrains from chastising me further.

"What's happened has happened." Her eyes are full moons as she looks at me and calms her tone. "You'll be fine. You'll move on."

Is it possible to move on from the death of your own mother? And at what cost, if such a thing may be achieved? But I'll get no answers here. The dark obscures everything around us. I'd be naive to expect the Inbetween to offer any insight. Had Munu's bosses— the Hidden, whoever they are—asked me for feedback, I would've told them it would be preferable to end up dead in a remote, exotic location, and not in an abandoned lighthouse. But they never seem to care, and it remains a mystery as to why they bothered assigning Munu to help me.

"We are so close to your eighteenth birthday—to eliminating the curse," Munu goes on. "You're better off without her for this final stretch."

"Stop," I snap. I sometimes forget how brutally honest my friend can be. I can barely muster the energy to explain to Munu that this loss is unlike anything else that killed me before. Losing my mother is a sudden, crushing blow. A bottomless well I'll tumble into for as long as I live.

"Only six more months, and you will survive," Munu continues as if I haven't spoken. "You'll be normal—nearly—and nothing and no one will be able to break your heart after that."

"I don't think anything else *can* break my heart any more," I mutter.

"Well, precisely!" Munu says, and she looks happy.

Munu makes it sound all pink and fluffy, but the truth is that in six months, on the 10th December, I'll be eighteen, and the curse will be no more. Of course, freedom comes with a steep price, one I'll never feel ready to pay. But if I survive until then without another heartbreak, I will live.

"You can't afford another mistake, canim. You need to think about yourself, and no one else." Munu rushes through the words, without even waiting for a sign of acknowledgment. "Once you're back with the living, no matter how tempting other people's efforts at comfort, you must ignore them. Don't let the grief cripple you. You can't be vulnerable. You must live, Sare. You're my most special assignment. You *must* survive."

I wouldn't call it surviving. When I wake up on my eighteenth birthday, the curse will claim my heart and rob me of the ability to love. For Munu, a life devoid of affection is the ultimate victory. I should be relieved, happy even, for I'll never have to brace the pain of another heartbreak once the curse sees through its grim promise. Though no matter how hard I try, I can never throw off the pervasive sense of future loss.

"I'll be okay." I hardly believe it myself, and I wouldn't be surprised if Munu has her doubts either.

"Shut yourself away. People can't be trusted. They bring nothing but misery, anyway." She looks up to the dim lantern. "Keep the flame of anger alight. Anger won't break your heart. Hold on to your grudges as if they're your shields. Try to channel all that grief into resentment."

"Enough—please." I'm in no state for lectures I've heard a thousand times already, nor for formulating a grand survival plan, or even pondering my next steps upon return. I certainly don't need to try to resent my own mother instead of grieving for her, especially since I did so much of that when she was alive.

"Just do what you need to do," I implore in a voice heavy with desperation. "Send me back."

For the last time, I think. I should feel grateful. But right now, I'm just numb.

Munu nods softly. Despite her tough love approach, I know she will never break my heart.

"Okay, canim. I'll count to five, in the name of the Hidden and their superiors." Munu reaches for my left hand. I open it, gazing at the three scars in my palm, now joined by a fourth—the deepest, a perfect circle. A dot, as if it marks an end.

I look at it, and I remind myself that I have no other chance left. *I have no one.*

Munu blows on the scar and a cool wind sweeps through me as if I'm made of dust. "I weave you back to life," I hear her say, and I am pushed and pulled, drawn and erased, torn and mended as she counts. "One, two, three—"

CHAPTER THREE

Grief is the beast with the sharpest claws. It's sacred. It's consuming. It's unstoppable. You, my rarest reader, must already fathom how it cannot be cast aside or defeated, for this book would not have found you otherwise. The beast will wound you deeply. There will be times when you are certain it will kill you. And yet, you will endure. Until the pain you deemed a punishment becomes your reward, guiding you to a realm of peace that will be only yours and yours alone—just as the beast that delivered you there.

Excerpt from *The Book of Revenge, Müneccimbaşı Sufi Chelebi's Journals of Mystical Phenomena*

Death takes mere seconds in the world I left behind, and if there's an audience to witness my misery, they always assume that I've simply fainted. This time, Fiona's frown greets me as I regain consciousness.

"I'm okay," I reassure her as I lift myself up. Not that she's particularly concerned. She doesn't make a big deal out of it. I guess it's understandable, even for normal people, to faint upon hearing that your mother has died.

"She was probably driving to see Ferit," Fiona says.

All I want is to curl up in bed and sleep.

But I can't, as two police officers arrive soon after that.

I've been given a last chance at life, I tell myself as I perch on the sofa and answer their questions. I tune them out. I tune everything out.

Daphne is dead and I'm alive. But the world doesn't care who is dead or alive. It keeps spinning and people carry on with their daily routines, while I'm in my little cocoon, like an insect trapped in amber, suspended in time. It's a period I can hardly describe. Grief draws a thin line between being awake and asleep.

Munu insists that I erase the word *mum* from my vocabulary to keep emotions in check. I follow her advice, though it does nothing to dull the grief. Mum or Daphne—her absence still aches the same.

Over the coming days, Daphne's friends fill the house. I had no idea she knew so many people. There's a lot of talk and no chance to pause, never mind if I'm ready to face being an orphan. I try to get used to the fact that Daphne will never step into this house again.

"Poor darling," one friend says. I can't pin a name to the face.

"Here's my number in case you need anything," says another. Someone brings me a glass of milk, as if I'm a toddler. I can't drink it. I cradle the glass in my hand and repeat Munu's words. *Shut yourself away. People can't be trusted.* And just like that, they become shadows, flickering lights and distant sobs.

And at the end of every day, when I'm finally alone in my bed again, I embrace the long, dreamless sleep like it's death itself.

Later, a social worker arrives. A woman with a soft, round face who seems ready for a cup of tea and retirement. We take our seats at the kitchen table. It's only after feeling her scrutinizing gaze that I notice I'm still in my pajamas. She asks me questions that prompt simple yes or no answers, leaving them teetering on the tip of my tongue. She offers information about foster care, explaining that I won't have control over where I live until I'm eighteen and out of the system. She asks about my father first, then switches to other options. A grandparent, an uncle, or distant cousin—or even a contact number or address that may grant me one.

I excuse myself to make a hot drink, taking time to escape the inquiry and cool down. Other people's family trees might stretch like the sprawling branches of ancient oaks, but Daphne and I were mere saplings, lacking even the fundamental roots. Our history, by Daphne's account, was short but far from sweet.

My misfortune, it seems, started as soon as I latched onto her uterus. Daphne hadn't planned on having a baby. Pregnant at the tender age of twenty-one, alone in the UK without any relatives, she shied away from modern medicine. She tried old wives' remedies instead, herbs and anything else she could find, but I proved to be a survivor. Which is tragicomic, considering how crap I've been at staying alive since the day I was born.

Fate must have rolled the dice then because, before Daphne could plot other ways to eradicate me, she lost her father in a car accident. Her mother was already long gone, dying in childbirth to Daphne.

Her father's inheritance gave us a comfortable life, but money doesn't erase grief. Daphne was young, parentless, and about to become a parent herself. And there I was, growing inside her every day, nurtured only by her pain and misery.

When Daphne finally pushed me out, I bestowed her some happiness. She wasn't on her own any more. She had a reason to keep going. And for a while, she loved me, and things were beautiful and normal.

Normal.

My poor, oblivious mother had no idea of the defects of my heart.

I used to believe my father would make an appearance one day until I was old enough to realize that he wouldn't. He was a man who briefly entered Daphne's life one night and vanished by morning, leaving no name behind. Eventually, I let go of the idea of him like releasing a balloon into the sky. Men seem programmed to discard Mum, though a part of me wonders if this one might have returned, had he known of my existence.

I shake my head to dispel the fog in my mind, and finally return to my seat across from the social worker, carrying a tray of tea and biscuits.

"Did both of your mother's parents pass away?" The woman forces a smile when I pass her a cup of tea.

I nod. There aren't even any photographs to testify to the existence of my long-gone grandparents.

My father believed in mourning with dignity, in honoring the deceased and ourselves, Daphne would say when I inquired about the absence of family mementos. *When my mother died, Papa removed all her photos, because he couldn't bear looking at them. The people we lose should remain in our memories, not in family albums. Certainly not on the walls as decoration.*

But now isn't the time to dwell on Daphne's principles or the lack of keepsakes.

"What about a distant relative your mother might have mentioned?" The woman's fingers curl around the mug, her signet ring missing a stone. "Do any names spring to mind?"

A name . . . I think hard. There's one. But it doesn't even have a face attached to it.

I pick up a chocolate digestive, lost in my thoughts, drifting to the name that never truly belonged to anyone. Two years ago, after Ferit left us for good, Daphne dissolved into herself, as if her tears were laced with poison. I remember her doe eyes, her labored breathing, and the way she curled up in bed, seeking solace as I tried to offer comfort. I took care of her—cleaning, feeding and dressing her, ensuring she woke each morning. That she still lived. There's a specific kind of terror in going to bed with the uncertainty that your mother might choke on her own vomit during the night. Perhaps that's why I didn't make a big deal of her calling me a name that wasn't my own.

"Iris," Daphne said in the dim light of our joint heartbreak. "Why do you hate me so much? Iris. Why do you still haunt me?" She would sob, and then plead for forgiveness. Sometimes, she'd lapse into Turkish, the meaning of her words deserting me.

"Who's Iris, Mum?" I asked a few weeks later, but she dismissed me with a wave. This Iris must have been a lost friend, I concluded. After all, everyone eventually abandoned Daphne, unable to tolerate the chaos she served up. I was the only constant. The one she left behind.

"Well, do you remember anything?" The social worker takes a sip of tea, sensing hope in my hesitation.

"No." I shake my head. There's no Iris. There's no use in remembering. I drop three spoonfuls of sugar into my cup and create a whirlpool. "There's no one," I say for what feels like the millionth time.

Finally, the social worker resolves that I can remain at home under the supervision of Fiona, while they figure out the next steps for dealing with a seventeen-year-old who's suddenly all alone in the world.

Later that evening, in my room, Munu reassures me. "This is good," she says. "Fiona wouldn't pour a glass of water on you if you caught fire. She'll leave you alone. June's almost over. School's finishing for the year, you can take it easy for a couple more weeks. Then it'll only be five months till you turn eighteen."

Mum's painting of Istanbul stares back at me from the wall—a tower rising from the sea, encircled by gulls. My favorite. It's strange that she's gone yet her brushstrokes remain. I tear my gaze away, forcing myself not to think of her.

Down in the quiet street, the neighbors' bins stand like guards under the amber lamp-posts, with a bold fox weaving between. I absentmindedly trace the newest scar on my palm, and wonder if it will ever stop hurting this much.

Soon, Daphne's existence dwindles into paperwork. Her life fits into a slender folder which I keep near a window in her bedroom.

Days blur into each other. I'm trapped in what feels like an endless Sunday afternoon—curled up on the sofa, drowning in grief while *Friends* plays on repeat.

I keep asking myself why I was dealt so much bad luck. It's not as if I can walk into a GP's office and ask why I was born with a curse. I've pressed Munu for answers, but, as usual, she doesn't know anything.

"Fate is a friend to some and a foe to others," she says. "We can't choose how we're born, so stop worrying about it."

Perhaps she's right. Obsessing over it engulfs me in helplessness, amplifying my self-pity and the gnawing uncertainty of the months ahead.

On the day of the funeral, I'm alone, steeling myself in the unfamiliar silence of the house. I navigate my way to the kitchen to splash cold water on my face, staring at the porcelain washbasin. When my fingers finally slip from the sink's cold edge, I realize how hard I've been clutching on to it.

In the back garden, the wind slaps the branches of the fig tree. I wait for the raindrops to appear on the window as I fetch a bowl, pour a few glugs of milk and toss in my Rice Krispies, but the rain doesn't come. I perch on a chair with the bowl, a spoon and no appetite. Perhaps I've become like Daphne, who could go hours without a morsel passing her lips.

What if I cry today? I've already failed the second rule, and I'm fucked if I break the first. *No tears shall fall.* Another heartbreak may be unavoidable if I let the tears come. And that will be the end of me.

I fiddle with my evil-eye pendant, a keepsake Daphne gifted me when I was old enough to be trusted with it. An evil eye is meant to shield you from harm, perhaps that's why Munu designated it as our link. The gold necklace, endowed with the power to summon her, bridges the gap between us. When I hold it and whisper her name, Munu arrives—if she can. Though in recent years, her visits have become less and less frequent.

"You don't need me as much any more," Munu says when I complain about how little time we spend together nowadays. "And I have so much to do," she protests. "Escorting the people who don't want to die to the Otherside, including the difficult ones who can't believe they're dead. Then there are the almost-extinct animals I have to help protect." She rolls her eyes. "Who really cares if there's one less poisonous frog in the world?"

Her bosses do, though, whoever they are. Munu is forbidden from discussing them, yet it's clear that she cannot shirk her obligations. But she promised she'd be at the funeral today.

On the counter, my phone blips with a notification.

Dropped Dotty to the nursery, OMW. Fiona.

Of course. Who else could it be? I have no friends. No family. I push it away and bin the contents of my bowl.

Above the pedal bin hangs a small frame capturing the Istanbul skyline from the sea. Daphne never returned to her homeland; instead, she poured her nostalgia into her paintings. She sold some online and decorated our walls with the others. As a child, I would sit in her studio, listening intently as she painted and spun tales of Istanbul: a queen of snakes in a dungeon, a maiden trapped in a tower, and men who slumbered in an enchanted cave for centuries. She repeated these stories until I grew older, and then she ceased looking at my face, as though unable to bear the sight of me.

My toes curl on the stone floor. The shadow of our fig tree lays across the white tiles like an old, unhealed wound. "Fig trees bring misfortune." Daphne's voice is carried on the rustling wind. "The djinni sleep beneath it. In Istanbul, no one keeps one near their house."

The culprit of all our misfortunes dances in the breeze, oblivious to my anguish. Daphne should've felled it, and perhaps our bad luck would have been over.

She should've known better.

Communication is classified as Top Secret.
Circulation strictly limited to recipients.
This email will destroy itself once read, so read carefully.

Subject: Important Information

Date: 10 December 2007
From: Five the Fifth, Angel of Death, Field Operations, Mortal Termination and Transition, Mortal Affairs Commission
To: User15963318 (Temporary Ethereal), Ethereal Resourcing and Deployment Unit, Mortal Affairs Commission

Munu . . . You pitiful, ineffectual soul.

Now that you're off, assisting the Fate Adjustment Bureau with some stupid haunting in Himachal Pradesh, I started to wonder why I bother keeping you around. Despite all the chaos you cause, I continue to be forgiving.

As such, even though you've mishandled everything entrusted to you, I am still forwarding the documents of an important upcoming assignment to your undeserving receipt. This is a top-secret mission; our involvement is strictly due to the deathly nature of this curse.

Review the attached report carefully. Take notes if you must, but refrain from troubling my holiness further. I have been extremely merciful, granting this mortal resurrections against this cruellest of curses. As I will not be burdened with repeated deaths of a single mortal, it's your responsibility to ensure these resurrections take place, should they be needed.

Now listen—your paramount duty, on top of your existing duties, is to ensure the girl's survival until her eighteenth year. **She must survive.** The minor problem associated with the curse, prolonged as it is, should then resolve itself. Assigning this task to you tears my halo apart, but due to the Office's dire financial situation, I have no other choice.

I am aware the Himachal Pradesh mission will occupy you for a while. This specific task will not commence until the curse threatens the mortal's life for the first time. So do not pester the child right away. Once your duty starts, take proper care of her and safeguard that pitiful heart. You will be tethered to her, so certain actions will raise alarms for you, ensuring you fulfill your role. However, don't dawdle around the girl; I pray for her soul she doesn't follow your example and become a weakling. Unless her life is in immediate danger, prioritize other duties and occasionally tend to her. You shall instruct her in the rules she must follow to survive—brainwash her if you must, and employ all the despicable mortal methods at your disposal. Remember, I can nail you to the hooves of rabid horses until Doomsday, should I wish it. But, as a paragon of merciful perfection, I continue to tolerate your existence.

You're my weakness, Munu.

Five the Fifth

Attachment:
Document classified as Top Secret.

Curse ID	CID-1010834556
Source of the Curse:	*Beddua* (For details, consult Appendix-III in document DTH-9000719)
Active:	Y ~~N~~
Classification of Active Afflicted Entity:	Mortal ~~Celestial~~ ~~Ethereal~~ ~~Other (specify if applicable):~~

List of Directly Impacted Individuals:	M939274856567048343 (Sare Sıla Silverbirch)—Imminent death on heartbreak
Linked individuals	Alive: M940748543391122301 (Defne Aylin Gümüşhuş) Deceased Links Found: Please consult Appendix-I of DTH-9000719
List of Indirectly Impacted Individuals:	Please consult Appendix-I DTH-9000719
Symptoms and Manifestations:	M939274856567048343 will experience the following if overwhelmed by curse: - Chest pain - Hallucinations (e.g.earthquakes) - Death* * If resurrection is possible, please ensure the subject is not carted to the Otherside. They must remain within the Inbetween until safely restored.
Known Countermeasures:	Upon diverting focus from their feelings, M939274856567048343 will find salvation from a possible heartbreak. The mortal has to fight the curse to avoid termination. Suggested ways to distract the mortal: - Physical confrontation - Culinary temptation (e.g. sugar) - Provoking their wrath - Mathematics (could be simple counting or differential equations if subject has an aptitude for advanced maths)

Catalysts and Triggers:	We strongly advise against crying. **Exercise utmost caution and steer clear of inducing tears.** Mortals often agitate and vex one another, leading us to advise against the cursed individual seeking companionship among their kin. **A life forlorn, harboring disdain for others would be the supreme protection from this type of curse.**
Preventive Actions taken by the Office, if Applicable:	The curse will be put to an end if M939274856567048343 should survive eighteen mortal years. The heart will then be sacrificed, thus exempting the mortal from "love," "compassion" and "mercy." (For a comprehensive list of the emotions that will be forfeited, please consult Appendix IV of DTH-9000719)
Entity's Rights and Autonomy:	N/A
Resources and Blessings Granted to the Entity Afflicted:	1. Guardian Assignment: The Office doesn't currently have the budget to source a celestial. Allocation of a temporary ethereal to oversee and protect the entity has been arranged. 2. Resurrection Provision: M939274856567048343 is subject to repeated restorations until final termination. 3. Karmic Balance Realignment: M939274856567048343 has been indirectly blessed by the Temporal Intervention Agency as an embryo for good fortune.* *Note: This exercise carries a 0.01% success probability.

CHAPTER FOUR

Rule number one: no tears shall fall. Rule number two: channel sorrow into rage. Rule number three: death is not an option.
Sare's Rulebook for Survival

In stark contrast to her turbulent life, Daphne's funeral is an eventless affair. No drunk cheers, no tempestuous ex-lovers causing chaos or puking among the ivy-covered tombstones. No weeping, no sobs. Certainly not mine.

The service takes place in the pointy church a mile from our middle-class street in Cambridge. I stand amid the graves in the sprawling, untamed cemetery, wearing a black velvet dress that gives me an itchy neck.

"Sare-eh." Fiona leans over as we wait for the pallbearers to bear the coffin from the church. I've never been a people person, but I swear every time she calls my name like that, it's as if one hundred abandoned kittens are simultaneously scratching a blackboard. Imagine being told your mother had passed away by that voice. She places her hand on my shoulder and I recoil from her touch. "Don't hunch, darling. Chin up."

"Don't hold back your tears, sweetie," another woman, whose name I can't remember, advises me.

Tears are a gift of vulnerability for those who can afford it, but I can't let myself plummet into sorrow. I have to be strong. Still, it's hard among this crowd: the selfish ex-boyfriends who used Daphne like an emotional—and on rare occasions, physical—punchbag, the neighbors and friends who assumed we were doing okay because we had money. It's hard to watch them pretending they're sad. They didn't care about her when she was alive—why would they now?

My heart flutters, a delicate warning. I have one chance left and I can't blow it. I need to go numb, feel nothing. I want to close my eyes and ears until this ceremony ends. Instinctively, I clasp my pendant. The metal is cold but comforting inside my palm as I wonder why Munu still hasn't shown up. I can try to summon her, signaling my need, but instead, I concentrate on how proud she'll be when she learns how I handled the funeral on my own, and let it drop from my fingers.

I slip my hand into my jacket pocket to fish out a fruit bonbon. The plastic crinkles as I unwrap it, attracting disapproving glances, and Daphne's friends shake their heads with contempt when I offer them one. I have an increasing suspicion that these people kept Mum close to make them feel better about themselves. I bet they sank to their knees to chant Hail Marys after meeting Daphne, grateful they weren't losing at life as disastrously as she was.

"Can you not wait until the service ends to eat?" one asks.

"It's almost noon." I look up at the sky hanging over us, without a hint of blue in the expanse. Not for the first time in my life—or even in the past week—I wonder what the Otherside is like. Did my mother visit an Inbetween, like I do? Munu says she doesn't know, swearing she hasn't seen Daphne. I have no clue if she is up there, if she's sober, or if she knows how much anger and devastation she left me with. Still, I like to imagine someone guiding her safely to peace, unable to bear another scenario. Knowing Daphne, she's probably nodding off in heaven at this hour. I bet the wine up there is top shelf. I snort at the thought. Masking my pain with humor is the only way I can survive today.

I hear a passive-aggressive murmur about manners, then someone calls my name from behind.

"Sare." The foreign, resonant voice of a man, and he says my name exactly as Daphne did. "Sare?"

I crush the sweet between my teeth as I turn to look at the stranger, and the waft of lemon and sugar works like a pacifier. He is tall and slender, his age difficult to pin down, though he seems over sixty. Under a blazer, he wears a waistcoat, jeans and leather boots. His face is cleanly shaved, gray hair tied back in a ponytail, and he peers at me over wire-framed glasses. Shock registers in his expression as our eyes meet, and for a moment we're two circling swordsmen, our weapons testing the air between us, each waiting for their opponent to strike.

I initiate the attack. "Do I know you?"

"No—excuse me." He detaches himself from a group of women to approach me. It's then that I notice his walking stick. "We've never met."

"Sorry, who are you?" I can't eliminate the possibility of him being an ex-boyfriend, even though he looks far too old for Daphne.

"I—" His gaze drops to where our feet point at each other. "I'm your grandfather."

I step back, and the sugary taste of the fruit bonbon sours in my mouth. My heart races, pulsing in my throat. Once I was mature enough to ask questions, my curiosity about Daphne's past was insatiable but it hadn't taken long to drain my mother of the facts. And I knew without doubt that the reason she won a battle against the Home Office to remain in the UK had been the loss of her father right before I was born. "I stayed because of you," she used to say.

"You can't be," I respond at last.

"I'm Muzaffer, your mother's father," he insists in an elegant accent. Hearing the Turkish name makes me wince. I envision Daphne's face next to his. The nose is familiar. The cheekbones. The cup of his chin. I clutch at the faint shadow of my dead mother in his features, clear proof of who he claims to be. Still, I shake my head in protest.

"There must be a mistake." The slate gray July sky sighs with a cool breeze, as if things would be more tolerable if it was November and raining.

The coffin appears before he can respond. No one will find solace in the sight of their mother's coffin, but I welcome it so long as its arrival causes the man beside me to stop talking. As if on cue, rain starts spitting, like I needed more misery. In the drum of my irregular heartbeats, I watch the pallbearers lower Daphne into the ground. Standing next to me, Muzaffer remains as still as a lamppost. I close my eyes and wonder where the fuck he's been all this time, and why my mother lied to me.

A raven caws, hidden in the tangle of the branches above us. At least these true inhabitants of the church grounds—unlike a few of Daphne's exes who turned up with dry eyes—are dignified enough to remain unseen as the final goodbye is about to be spoken.

Farewells were a common occurrence in Daphne's life. All my life I've watched people arrive and depart, as if they were passengers and she always missed the train. No one stayed.

A few of her former lovers fling clods of dirt into the hole that's swallowed her. They cover her with mud and I cover my eyes with my hands, wishing I had the guts—or the heart—to cry.

Later, in a pub that sits in the fenlands like a stranded ship, Muzaffer and I sit in silence at a table by the window while Daphne's friends celebrate her life—whatever there is to celebrate about it. She was miserable on a good day and wasted on a bad one. Or vice versa, depending on your perspective.

"Do you want anything else?" Muzaffer points at my ginger beer. He looks uncomfortable in the wooden chair. Perhaps my company makes him unsettled. He doesn't fit into the image of a typical grandfather with his cold, hardened stare. As if he's here to meet his duty and not his granddaughter. "Food?"

Doves flap inside my ribs. *Shit*. I'm fluttering. I really need to calm down.

"I'm not here to eat." I fold my arms, reciting the second rule. *Channel your sorrow into rage.* Does this man have no manners? He offered no proper introduction, no explanation, no condolences. Who does he think he is, showing up here, as if I had a clue that he was alive? "Your full name would be nice," I say flatly.

He leans back on his chair, one hand on his walking stick. "Muzaffer Hamdi Gümüşhuş."

I cradle the bottle in my hands and wonder how on earth that name is spelled.

"I know this isn't an ideal way to meet." Muzaffer stirs across the sticky table. "But your mother and I weren't on speaking terms."

The pub smells like wet dogs and booze. The fog in my head thickens. I wonder what Daphne's life would have been like if they *had* been on speaking terms, if he showed up a few years earlier. Might she still be alive now? I shake my head to clear such thoughts, but the fluttering won't stop.

Where is Munu when I need her? She'd know what to say to this man. How to protect myself against his claim. In her absence, I decide to do a countdown, twenty to zero, taking a deep breath every two beats, since it always proves to be the best way to simmer down.

Twenty, nineteen, breathe.

"She told me you died in a car accident." My voice is a whistle amid the din of tipsy revellers. "Why would she say that if you were alive?"

"I don't know. Perhaps it was more comfortable for her." He makes it sound so trivial, as if Daphne had merely chosen to wear joggers instead of jeans.

"Or perhaps I don't have a grandfather." I twirl the chilled bottle between my fingers, the glass slick with specks of condensation. "My mother isn't a liar." I swallow a sob.

No tears shall fall, Sare, I tell myself.

Eighteen, seventeen, breathe.

He looks frightened now. The surrounding murmur and clinking glasses rise above our silence. He digs in his jacket and extracts a laminated card, pushing it across the table with his index finger.

It's a driver's license, featuring a black-and-white photo of Daphne with a broad smile. I stare at a younger, happy version of her in disbelief. I read her name, alien words in Turkish letters. *Defne Aylin Gümüşhuş,* not Daphne Silverbirch. I knew she had changed her name, but still, her birth name becomes a mountain between us. In a single instant she becomes a stranger. A liar. A fake. A fraud.

A surge of anguish grips my heart as I confront the realization that Daphne deceived me. She had a living father. I scan the bar, the restaurant, to make sure everything is as it should be. No cracking walls, no wobbling ceilings. *You're okay,* I comfort myself. *You won't suffer another heartbreak just because your mother lied to you.*

Sixteen, fifteen, breathe.

"Where were you all this time?" I feel the sting of tears and blink them away, taking a large gulp of ginger beer. The sharp burn in my throat provides a distraction from my body's possible malfunction.

Fourteen, thirteen, breathe.

"It's complicated," Muzaffer says as he reaches out to take back the card, sliding it into his pocket. "This isn't the right time or place for such discussions."

"Aren't you offended that she told me you were dead?" My chest tightens.

His fingers fidget restlessly over the rounded top of his walking stick. "We had . . . disagreements," he admits after a brief pause.

His head tilts slightly, as though he's delving into distant memories. "She accused me of favoring her sister."

Her sister. It takes a while for his words to sink in.

"Mum—" I fail to imagine a world where Daphne had anger, or a sister. Mum was gentle, tender, too consumed by her own self-destruction to be angry with anyone else. "Mum had a sister?"

"I had two daughters," Muzaffer mutters with glassy eyes. I wish I could reach out and slip off his mask to see what lies behind the cold facade, see if he carries the signs of heartbreak at losing not just one daughter, but two. "Iris and your mother. Both are gone now."

The word strikes me like a lightning bolt, illuminating memories of Daphne's heart-shaped face. Her quivering voice.

Iris. Why do you hate me so much?

"And *did* you favor Iris?" Suddenly, I want to tear him apart to uncover the truth.

"What?" He seems startled by my question. "I treated both my children equally, if that is what you want to know. A lot of time has passed since . . . I've certainly made mistakes. However, I prefer not to dwell on the past."

"Then why are you here?" My voice is more agitated than I intended. Childlike. But I suppose one should be permitted to feel annoyed when they've been kept in the dark about so much.

Twelve, eleven, breathe.

"I want you to come live with me in Istanbul," he says.

I stare at him, uncertain if I heard him right.

Ten, nine, breathe.

"You have no other family." He straightens in his chair.

"But you abandoned Daphne," I say. *And then she abandoned me.*

"It's not the same."

Eight, seven, breathe.

"You're my granddaughter," Muzaffer says matter-of-factly, as if I'm the answer to some equation.

Six, five, breathe, Sare.

"And you want me to come with you?" I repeat, forcing myself to sip my drink. The sugar runs crisp on my tongue, much like the possibility of another life in another city. My mind drifts to Istanbul, the home my mother always seemed to miss so much. And, although I've never set foot there, it's a familiar place with its seven hills and the sea, all brought to life through Daphne's paintings and stories.

Four, three, breathe.

Fortunately, as I focus on it, Istanbul becomes a distraction, comforting to imagine.

"If you stay, you'll be placed in the system, bouncing between temporary homes until you turn eighteen," Muzaffer says. "In my house in Istanbul, you'll have stability." He doesn't mention the word *family*, as if he fathoms how dangerous relationships can be for me. A family is an emotional minefield I'll have to navigate, but then he seems devoid of emotion, so perhaps we're a good match.

"You can return if you can't get used to living there. I'm not going to force you to stay."

Two, one, breathe.

"I'm sure you won't." I compose myself. Surely, a man who let his daughter leave won't lock a granddaughter in a room or a tower.

Zero.

Breathe, Sare.

The countdown worked its magic, and I've weathered the worst of it. The fluttering remains subdued. Why do I even care about Daphne's relatives? I shouldn't be asking questions. I wish Munu was here, and then I could ask her advice on how to deal with this. Though I bet everything I have, not that it's much, that Munu won't like the idea of a grandfather. It's a dangerous proposition.

You're almost an adult, I tell myself. *You can make your own decisions.*

What remains for me in England, beneath this gray summer and steel sky? Only emptiness and the absence of Daphne. The leftovers of her unstable life. Grief. And the uncertainty of what awaits me until I turn eighteen. If I move to Istanbul with Muzaffer, I can start over, miles away from all the heartbreaks. I can leave the past behind. Just like Daphne once did.

It could be the safest option for me.

And maybe I can finally get some answers—about why my mother was the way she was, how she ended up here. Why she hid her father from me—or was she the one in hiding? I know it in my bones, Daphne and Defne aren't the same person. Something must have happened to Mum. Something that made her leave everything. But what?

"Consider my proposal." Leaning on his stick, Muzaffer rises from his chair. His aloofness might be daunting for a normal seventeen-year-old, but for me, it's a warranty. He won't be a threat to me. Not when he's so detached. "I'll visit you tomorrow."

But I've already considered it. Istanbul is an escape plan. A map of answers. A chance to peek into my mother's hidden history and discover why she lied to me.

"There's no need," I announce.

A fleeting cloud of fear passes over his face. Is he afraid of me turning him down? I'm not accustomed to bearing a responsibility like this, making a difference to someone.

"I'll come with you." My words startle Muzaffer. And I'm startled too, only now realizing what a huge decision I've just made. Swallowed by the pain of the grief as much as the pain of being deceived, I demand answers—whether from Muzaffer, or Istanbul itself.

Muzaffer nods, unaware of my internal tumult, remaining on his feet. "I'll make the arrangements to leave as soon as possible," he says.

I trust him. Somehow, I sense that he is a man of his word.

Munu finally arrives in the evening with a loud crackle, erupting in a torrent of complaints directed at the Hidden. Despite the unfair treatment she receives, her deep-seated loyalty and respect for them never wavers. This toxic and certainly unprofessional relationship always confuses me. Munu never elaborates on her work, and I gave up asking a long time ago. But grief makes me restless, and tonight I find myself craving answers—why exactly am I cursed? Still, I unwrap a sweet and let Munu vent. This isn't the time for an argument about the Otherside or the curse. Not before I break the news about Muzaffer.

"I'm so sorry that I missed the funeral." Munu's face crunches like the butterscotch I bite into. "There was a fire in a care home—I had to assist a lot of very confused people to the Otherside."

"It's okay. I managed." I shrug and then show her the sketch I made earlier, hoping that highlighting the beauty of her features will soften the blow when I reveal my plans.

She whizzes over to study the sketchpad. "This is stunning, canim."

I divulge the details of my eventful day while she gushes over my drawing, not pausing for breath. Terror spreads across her face with the word *grandfather*. When I tell her that I'll be moving to Istanbul with him, her pigeon wings tremble as if she's been struck.

"Have you lost your mind?" she cries, landing on the sketchpad, noticeably getting smaller each second. "Why risk yourself with another family when you just got rid of one?"

The shrinking is an uncontrollable feature: a "gift" from her boss designed to make her exhibit better self-control—fear and anger only make her smaller.

"Just consider it," I insist. "It's the best way to spend the next five months. He's cold and distant. He didn't even offer me any condolences—or hugs. He won't be a problem. You don't believe I'll open my heart to him, do you?"

"You'll regret it." Munu's voice becomes whinier as she keeps shrinking. "You said he's old, Sare. What if you get attached to him? Old people fall, or have strokes. What if he just drops dead? I hate to remind you, but if your heart breaks one more time, that's it—no more resurrections."

"Stop being so negative," I snap. My bones feel hollow. Why does Munu always have to be the campaign manager of possible tragedies, forcing me to be pessimistic? I look outside, where the honey-colored sunset glides over the rooftops across the street, as if the world is a place where only sweet things happen.

"Don't tell me you're already fond of him," she whimpers. Her tiny shadow splays on the sketch like a bad omen.

"I don't care about him," I retort. "I just met him, Munu."

"I don't approve of this." Munu whips her head side to side. "Istanbul is a miserable place—too many people, too nosy and mingling. You can't even breathe without someone commenting on it. It's a minefield for you!"

"I'll be distracted by the new surroundings," I reply, uncertain who I'm convincing.

"Boss in Heavens, Sare," Munu says, now as small as my pinkie finger. "I get it. You want to run away. But why not a road trip to Scotland? One of those islands where there's only cows and ponies? You can still go to Istanbul in winter, after you're eighteen and invulnerable."

And heartless, I add silently, thinking of how the curse will destroy my ability to love for the rest of my life. I wish I could share in Munu's joy at losing what makes me human, but I must be a fool because I still feel sad at the prospect.

"It's better to live with Muzaffer. He keeps his distance," I say. "Istanbul is a new place. A new life, Munu. I promise, I won't let anyone get close." I don't mention that I'm also driven by a need to uncover why my mother lied to me about her family. I owe myself the truth, but Munu won't understand that.

"Please, canim. Please don't go." Munu regards me with eyes too huge for her tiny face. She is the only person who knows I'm cursed, the only one who knows how flawed I am and how my heart could snap at any moment.

"Too late. I made up my mind." I nudge her with the tip of my finger.

"I forget how stubborn you are." Munu flies away. "Like the shell of a walnut."

I don't respond, feeling a strange relief that she gave up so easily. I'd prepared for her to clutch at my hair and beg me to stay in Cambridge, tears streaming until I promised not to leave.

"I just have a bad feeling about this," Munu says, returning to hover beside me.

"It'll be fine," I reply.

I can only hope that I'm right.

Communication is classified as Highly Confidential.
Circulation strictly limited to beings of celestial origins.

Subject: A Sincere Apology for Not Being Worthy of You
Date: 10 July 2025
From: User15963318 (Temporary Ethereal), Ethereal Resourcing and Deployment, Mortal Affairs Commission
To: Five the Fifth, Angel of Death, Field Operations, Mortal Termination and Transition, Mortal Affairs Commission

My Most Precious and Noble Patron and Director,

I have exhausted every effort within and beyond my capacity to dissuade the mortal from traveling to Istanbul. Yet, she remains as obstinate. She'll be traveling on the fifteenth of July.

Mighty and Merciful One, my sole wish, like yours, is for the girl to reach eighteen.

Might we arrange a meeting to discuss an action plan? It has been too long since our last conversation, and I yearn to be worthy of your presence once more.

In your forgiveness and favor,
Your most devoted servant and forever admirer,
Munu

This email will destroy itself once read, so read carefully.

Subject: Do NOT reply

Date: 10 July 2025
From: Five the Fifth, Angel of Death, Field Operations, Mortal Termination and Transition, Mortal Affairs Commission
To: User15963318 (Temporary Ethereal), Ethereal Resourcing and Deployment, Mortal Affairs Commission

Munu,

What have I told you about addressing me? I'm your **boss**—not your friend, confidant, or anything more. Certainly not your fairy godfather or crying wall.

Consider this your final warning. Do not mistake us for equals and presume you can demand meetings with me. I will not tolerate such audacity.

I am not surprised you failed to dissuade the girl; frankly, I should have left you to rot in Hell long ago. Yet, a minuscule, inconvenient speck of care remains in my otherwise empty chest.

Now that you've demonstrated your inadequacy again, take this advice: keep the girl away from that bloody tower. It is the source of the curse and will draw her in. While I have my own measures in place to assist in this, it is your responsibility to prevent her from falling into danger.

It's not I—the holy, the deserving, the admirable—but you who once was a mortal. Use your experience. Find ways to keep her indoors. Encourage her to write a novel; isn't that what every mortal aspires to? Convince her to binge-watch Turkish television series or take up crochet. Break her legs, if you must (in a way from which she may recover).

She must not reach that damned tower.

I highlight this once more: we will not meet. I am eternally busy, and emails are a far more efficient medium. Remember what happened last time—you nearly disintegrated at the sight of my glorious form. This is for your own good, and remember: I'm the most merciful.

Five the Fifth

CHAPTER FIVE

Among all the lands I have traversed, Konstantiniyye holds a unique allure. The city is a spell in the mouth of the sea, ensnaring every mortal who passes through its gates with a curse, for they will never erase its memory from their minds.

Excerpt from *The Book of Heartbreak, Müneccimbaşı Sufi Chelebi's Journals of Mystical Phenomena*

I arrive in Istanbul on a sweltering Sunday afternoon in July, having indulged in a perilous quantity of millionaire's shortbreads on the flight. Leaving the airport, I feel queasy in the intense heat of the Turkish summer as I scan the throngs of people for the promised chauffeur.

I spot the driver in the sea of suits, holding a sign announcing: *Sare Sıla Silverbirch*. I dislike the word *Sıla*, which means *longing*. When you consider that Sare translates to *pure*, my name becomes a fucking joke. *Pure longing*.

I approach the black suit, waving to signal who I am. He introduces himself as "Gökhan, Mr. Gümüşhuş's driver" and guides me and my luggage to a waiting gray Mercedes. I have nothing but a suitcase and my favorite of Daphne's paintings—the one depicting the tower—carefully wrapped. Munu protested that I should leave it, but I couldn't. It was the first thing I saw every morning, a habit—I hope—that will soothe me in this foreign place. A small piece of my old life.

As the car slides out of the airport and Defne's Istanbul wraps its arms around me, I leave my worries behind. The warm breeze strokes my cheek. *It will be okay,* it says. *Everything will be okay.*

After an hour of weaving through traffic, between towering skyscrapers that rise above sprawling slums, we reach a bridge that opens up to a breathtaking view of the shoreline. The maps of Istanbul must be illusions because the Bosphorus isn't some mere lake surrendering to the land. The sea seizes this city between its blue claws.

I lean out of the window, eager to absorb as much of the view as possible. On one side, the domes and minarets of Hagia Sopia ascend like the throne of a forgotten king, and on the other, the solitary Galata Tower stands proud, its conical peak a spear against the concrete jungle. This is a view Daphne recreated so many times in her paintings—and just one glance makes me grasp why she could never let Istanbul, Konstantiniyye or Constantinople go. The city of seven hills, many names and sovereigns is built on top of long-lost stories, and it imprints itself on you.

When the car skirts the coast, my gaze is drawn to a white tower standing in the middle of the sea, with gulls circling it like whirling dervishes. The Maiden's Tower. My heart skips a beat. It's even more beautiful than Mum's painting depicted. Lifted straight out of a fairytale, like a box full of stories waiting to be discovered.

Once upon a time, Daphne's voice rustles in my mind as I recall the story of this tower, *when the fleas were barbers, the camels were town criers, and emperors ruled instead of sultans, Istanbul was called Constantinople. In that city lived a wealthy man. He had a dozen sons but only two daughters. The youngest of the girls was as beautiful as a pearl, and she had a pure heart . . .*

Nestled in my bed, listening to this sad tale, I would hold my breath each time the headlights from a passing car illuminated the painting on my bedroom wall, still naive enough to imagine that the soaring minarets could pierce the sky. Munu, however, would express her displeasure, criticizing Daphne's choice to fill a six-year-old's head with tales far grander than her imagination could fully grasp. But I devoured them.

One day, a seer predicted the girl would die a terrible death when she turned eighteen. The desperate father built the whitest white tower in the middle of the sea, so neither Death nor its specters could find the girl . . .

I close my eyes, unable to bear thinking about the ending. Why must stories be denied happy endings, when life itself is already rife with sorrow?

We drive along the seafront, veering into a slender street before ascending a hill, and soon the Maiden's Tower vanishes from view. The memory of Daphne sizzles in my chest. The car finally pulls up to the curb. Just before I step out, Munu appears with a loud crack. I've been longing for her since I hopped on the plane, but she must have been busy again.

"I'm sorry, canim, been chasing bloody leopards all day. The buggers have been eating red pandas," she explains, still catching her breath. "And these red pandas, like you, must survive."

The driver shuffles outside, plucking the suitcase and Daphne's painting from the boot of the car.

"Is this it?" I poke my head out of the window.

"This is it," Munu says, with a deep sigh.

I get out gingerly. I don't know how I imagined my new home when I agreed to move in with Muzaffer, but it certainly wasn't this.

The house stands on a slope that slants everything like italic letters, crouched between two seven-story buildings. The steep angle puts strain on my ankles as I shuffle along the pavement. It's a miracle that the Mercedes doesn't slide down the hill. I gaze up at the house, separated from the road by a metal gate and a meager front garden that leads up to a tiny porch. The flayed walls are washed with the brazen yellow light of summer, revealing layers of plasterwork beneath the chipped paint, shabby and unloved. It's a fucking wreck. Three stories, two balconies, tall windows with sealed shutters. What kind of people keep their windows closed on a day as hot as this?

"Looks like it needs a good renovation," Munu says, drifting behind me like a miniature shadow.

If only it was just his house that needed a revamp, but the whole neighborhood brims with neglect. A smell of rubbish wafts from bins as stray cats linger, searching for scraps. Graffiti is emblazoned across the taller buildings, their balconies connected by wires with laundry flying on them like bunting. Curtains billow from windows, wafting out voices and the canned audio of TVs. The sea is the only calm in the chaos. It churns below the incline at a seemingly impossible angle, unperturbed by the city.

When the driver pushes at the metal gate, the hinges groan as if waking from a hundred-year sleep. He carts in my stuff and I fall in a few steps behind him and unwrap the mint humbug seeded in my jeans pocket, but the sticky heat has got to it first. My fingertips lose the fight and, without any bins in sight, I stuff it back into my pocket.

"You can't possibly want to stay here. It's an absolute shamble." Munu flutters into my path as I head to the porch, as if she can block me. "Perhaps this is your sign to head straight back to the airport and catch the first plane to the UK."

"It's not that bad." I ignore her and climb up the steps to the entrance. "There's magic in chaos, after all."

"You're young and full of dreams." Munu rushes to keep up. "But I'm ancient, and I recognize a nightmare when I see one."

The front door towers over me, twice my height, with one wing ajar. My luggage and the driver have already vanished into the darkness inside. Just as I'm about to follow, a brawny man sporting a dense mustache emerges on the threshold. With his hair slicked back with pomade, he wears a crisp polo shirt and an overpowering cologne, which could probably make a squad of soldiers smell like a bouquet of roses.

I hesitate. If it wasn't for the driver who brought me here, I'd think I arrived at the wrong address, because the man looks at me with a frown, almost a mask of shock, as if he didn't expect me on his doorstep. But when he speaks he dispels my doubt.

"Sare?" He rests his burly fingers on his chest.

I blink at him.

"Y-You . . ." The man examines me, as if I'm a piece of space-craft proving alien life is real. "Mr. Gümüşhuş was right, Allah is my witness, you look so much . . . like your—"

"Who the hell is this?" Munu barks in my ear at the same time.

"I don't know," I snap at Munu stupidly, interrupting the man. I'm so used to chatting with Munu, it's hard to shut up when there's an audience.

"Oh." He looks at me with a hint of confusion. "I am Azmi, Mr. Gümüşhuş's assistant. Welcome home."

"He's inappropriately informal for an assistant," Munu mutters, circling around the unsuspecting Azmi. "Scowl at him, so he knows his place."

I shuffle inside, doing my best to ignore Munu's opinion on Azmi's manners.

The house is cold and dingy—a shock after the blazing summer heat outside. The entrance hall is wide, with two doors on either side and a metal staircase that spirals above us to ascend into more darkness. Large oil paintings in gilded frames cover the peeling wallpaper as if ashamed of their surroundings. A tattered rug rots on the wooden floor. A console with carvings stands to the side, gathering dust. A museum, more than a house.

A ginger cat lies on the hard floor just a short distance from me, her tail swishing like a whip.

"This is Böcek." Azmi gestures at the animal. "Mind you, she is scratchy to everyone but Mr. Gümüşhuş, so best to leave her alone."

"An overly chummy butler, and now a cat?" Munu shrieks with frustration. "Devils be damned. Is this an old man's house, or a parade? What's next, seven dwarfs?"

I gesture to her to zip it.

"Let me take you upstairs to your room." Azmi frowns, catching the movement.

I can't protest. Exhausted and drenched in sweat, I need a shower and a twelve-hour nap. Part of me wonders where Muzaffer is hiding, but I don't inquire as to what keeps him occupied at the time of my arrival—which was arranged weeks ago. *I'm not here for a family reunion,* I remind myself. I have nothing to share with him.

"Mr. Gümüşhuş is keen on routines," Azmi begins. The staircase rattles as we climb. "Dinner is served at eight p.m., and breakfast at eight a.m. Your grandfather expects you to attend at these times. The house has rules."

As we arrive at the upstairs landing, I'm breathless from keeping up with Azmi's pace.

"Your bedroom." He points at the door on the left. "Mr. Gümüşhuş rests during the day, and the house must remain quiet. Might I remind you to set your mobile to silent? No loud music, or late phone calls, please. You will find headphones in your room."

There's a closed door on the opposite side of the hallway. Munu whizzes further down the corridor.

"The second floor is where Mr. Gümüşhuş resides, and he won't expect to find you there," Azmi says.

I hold my breath. A staircase ascends to the unknown land of Muzaffer's quarters. A chandelier drapes down from the ceiling with a thousand crystals attached to its brass neck.

"You're free to roam downstairs, but please do not move any furniture, or make any adjustments." Azmi sighs. "Mr. Gümüşhuş

50

likes preserving everything in a certain order. On this floor, please do not fiddle with any locks. What else?" He blinks. "Ah—I live in the basement flat. I don't often come upstairs. You need anything at any time, please look for me. No need to disturb Mr. Gümüşhuş."

"You were right about Muzaffer—he doesn't seem the paternal type, does he? And this one . . ." Munu abandons her exploration of the house to resume her pursuit of Azmi, whose perkiness seems to have waned after reciting the long list of rules. "Perhaps he is harmless." Munu spins around him. "If you resist cuddling that impish cat, this might actually be a suitable arrangement till you're eighteen. Maybe coming here wasn't a bad decision after all."

Is it not, really? A wave of queasiness rolls over me at Munu's enthusiasm. She sounds convinced that I'll be lonely—and miserable—here.

Doubt gnaws at me as I scan the walls. No photographs. No clue if anything once belonged to Daphne, or indeed any sign that she ever lived here. Suddenly, I'm unsure if moving here will bring me any closer to the answers I crave. But . . . Daphne must have been here once. Perhaps she stood right here, on this spot.

Iris, Daphne's whisper echoes in the dim light.

Somewhere behind these doors, Mum had a room, a sister, a father, a life, a different name. But no matter how hard I try, I can't imagine her in Istanbul. She's become a coin with two heads that I toss, looking for answers but getting none. Defne and Daphne.

"Any questions?" Azmi asks.

The problem, unbeknown to Azmi, is that I have too many. Why did Daphne lie to me? Why did she tell me Muzaffer was dead? Where is her room?

"Where's my mother's room?" I pick the easiest of them to start.

"Locked, I'm afraid. As I mentioned, your grandfather—"

"I want to see it." Agitated, I don't let him finish. "Actually, I want to stay in that room."

"You can't." A sharp voice slips into the silence like a dagger.

My gaze travels up the staircase until it finds Muzaffer. He stands tall on the steps leading to the second floor, his grip tight on the railing, knuckles white. "Your bedroom is prepared. Azmi made sure you'll have everything you need. Please refrain from exploring other rooms on this floor."

Then he turns to Azmi and tells him something in Turkish. I notice the difference in his tone. The smoothness.

They share words and glances that escape my understanding, until Azmi gives what I presume to be a goodbye nod and starts down the stairs. Munu watches Muzaffer with narrowed eyes.

"You must be tired from your journey," Muzaffer comments, thinking we're alone. "Rest now." It sounds like an order more than an act of compassion, and he doesn't linger for a reply before withdrawing to his quarters again, leaving Munu and me sharing an awkward silence.

CHAPTER SIX

Those of the mortal realm who wish to understand the Hidden consider those blessed with the pure eye as fortunate. Little do they realize that this gift is a burden, for the craft of seers is fraught with the worries of both the seen and unseen, their sanity besieged by the profound truths they withhold.

Excerpt from *The Book of Revenge, Müneccimbaşı Sufi Chelebi's Journals of Mystical Phenomena*

Unlike the rest of the house, my bedroom appears to have undergone recent renovations. It's massive, almost as large as the ground floor of the house I left behind in Cambridge. The shutters are drawn back, revealing a breezy interior, though my pleasure is instantly dampened by the decor. It's as if someone picked up a highlighter and outlined every piece of furniture in glaring hues of pinks and yellows. A large desk is crowned with a rose gold monitor, and a light green swivel chair sits beside it. An enormous bed is tucked beneath a bright pink canopy, next to a lilac armchair. And then there's the wallpaper: clouds barfing rainbows. Do they think I'm seven? I wonder if it's Azmi who decorated this room, as Muzaffer's interest in me doesn't seem to extend beyond ensuring that I obey his rules and stay well away from him.

I pluck a lollipop I'd saved for later from my bag, wondering why on earth Muzaffer is so secretive. Does he think I'll break locks and ransack his house? I lean against the cool glass door of the balcony I spotted from the street. A metal table, two chairs and an array of plant pots crowd the tiny space. The yellow darkness of a slow sunset paints the stone tiles caramel, but despite the hour Istanbul doesn't show any signs of slowing down. I can still hear people, cars, gulls—cacophonies that are way outside any sane person's comfort zone.

Munu stays inside, skimming through the room, examining everything. She clicks her fingers to open the wardrobe and starts ransacking. Unlike her, I have no appetite to discover whatever is lurking inside and I nip out onto the terrace to snatch a breath of fresh air. Across the narrow street, higher buildings with colorful balconies stacked on their concrete bellies. But, despite the abysmal lack of privacy, I'm instantly in love with this spot. I feel like the queen of a long-lost kingdom sitting on my throne. I suck at the lolly and lean over the edge of the balcony to see the sea glistening like a jewel at the end of the slope.

Still clutching the warm metal railing heated by the sun, I suddenly straighten, alerted by the instinctive feeling of being watched. I turn my head to see a boy across the road, huddled over a green railing in the opposite building. His red t-shirt and cargo shorts are faded, but he's as radiant as the setting sun. His face, framed by curls brushing his shoulders, is enchanting, as if someone hand-carved the most symmetrical, angelic features from marble and blew life into them. Perhaps calling him a boy does him an injustice. He's a modern Greek god.

His gaze, ready to send thunderbolts in my direction, feels invasive, even though he's not close to me, standing a few meters away across the road on his own balcony. The hint of confusion on his face shifts into a scowl, as if he's observing something he can't quite decipher.

Then the scowl drops and he mouths a "wow."

Fuck. Did I somehow offend this person, just by being here? Boys like him don't pay attention to me. I divert my eyes, though his gaze remains electric against my skin.

From inside, I can hear Munu's singing echoing off the walls. I try to ignore the boy and study the street. And, after a couple of minutes, I stare enough at the laundry lines to realize that watching the fluttering garments in the breeze is more therapeutic than I'd imagined. But the calm is quickly broken.

"*Who* are you?" the boy asks, as if he's accusing me of something.

I glance left and right, puzzled by his reaction. There's no one else around. Why he's so taken aback by me is beyond my understanding. I try to appear unbothered and roll the lollipop in my mouth.

"Aren't you too old for a lollipop?" he persists, narrowing down the potential unseen balcony dwellers he may be addressing by criticizing my choice of snack.

"Me?" I yank it from my mouth as a flush blooms on my cheeks. "Last time I checked, lollies didn't have age limits. They're not just for kids like you, rest assured."

Oh God, I sound so stupid. The joke falls flat, a pale imitation of the witty retort I'd envisioned.

But he laughs, amused, clearly comfortable in his skin. "I turned eighteen in April," he says. "And you, I presume, are in double digits? Still old for a lolly, I'd say."

I can't block another whimpering "Me?" Shit, Sare. You can't keep acting like a wind-up toy. Now I see no option other than revealing my age. "Seventeen, and—"

And I can't finish my sentence.

"Heavens, Sare!" Munu's shriek makes me jump and I barely avoid a fatal tumble over the railing onto the street. "I leave you alone for two minutes and you're already flirting with a rake?" Munu whizzes onto the balcony, ignoring my near miss, clearly only caring about the danger of death by heartbreaks. She tugs at a lock of my hair. "Look at him—a predator!"

"Ouch. Stop it," I hiss, trying to push her away while pretending my struggle is just a yawn. Not that I care what the boy thinks of me, but he's still watching me with keen interest. The last thing I need is rumors about my sanity spreading among the neighbors.

"I'm so disappointed, Sare Sıla Silverbirch, I truly am," Munu tuts, attempting to drag me inside by clawing my hair as if I'm a naughty puppy. "I know boys like him very well—it only takes one hello to be doomed. Look at that smirk. Absolutely, explosively beautiful and he knows it—the cheeky bastard. He'd blow up any girl's heart in a minute."

"Be reasonable," I groan, no longer caring who might hear me. I've never flirted with anyone, not once in my life. How can Munu assume I'll throw myself at the foot of the first boy I bump into in Istanbul? "Let go of my hair—"

"Why is she harassing you?" the boy asks.

What. The. Fuck.

Time stops.

Munu freezes, my curls still in her hands.

I'm already frozen.

The boy watches us with an amused expression, rubbing his chin with his thumb. The possibility of me looking remotely normal is now long gone.

"W-what?" I gawk at him, finally rescuing my hair from Munu's grip.

"The catty Tinkerbell." He points at Munu, leaving no doubt that he can see her. "I asked why is she—"

"W-who are you?" I somehow find the power to speak, cutting the boy off.

"My name is Leon Dumanoğlu. My aunt and I rent this apartment, which belongs to Mr. Gümüşhuş, and the last time I checked he lived alone with his housekeeper. So really I should be asking who *you* are?" His gaze darts between Munu and I. "You and your ethereal."

"M-my—what?" I stall, trying to decipher the strange term. What on earth is an ethereal?

"That flamboyant little spirit latched on to your head?" He laughs. "Unmissable in that pink dress and with those spectacular wings. Tell me, is she yours, Sare Sıla . . . Silverbirch?"

I barely register him addressing me by my full name, too stunned by his acknowledgment of Munu. No one other than me has ever been able to see her before. I cling to the balcony railing for support. Ransacking my mind for a way to respond, I come up blank.

"For the sake of screaming sinners," Munu curses, back to her usual sniping. "First of all—my dress is fuchsia, not pink. Second, I'm not a mere spirit. Third—"

"Don't tell me you're an angel," the boy teases Munu.

"I—" Munu shrieks as she begins to shrink. "Of course I'm not an angel!"

"You can see her?" I stare at them both in bewilderment, still unable to believe what's happening here.

"Obviously." Leon's smile is smug, and it makes my heart gallop. "I'm a seer. I have the pure eye."

The word *seer* washes over me, reaching out from ancient stories. At this revelation, Munu shrinks even further, hiding behind my hair as if using my body as a shield. Meanwhile, I'm left wondering what the hell a "pure eye" is.

"Who do you work for?" Leon lifts an eyebrow. "Grey?"

"Who?" I'm puzzled, unsure if he's questioning me or Munu, or both of us. "Grey?" I hesitate, conjuring images of silver strands. "Do you mean Muzaffer?"

"What's the deal with you two?" Leon leans above the balcony rails as if he wants to lower his voice, but still needs to be heard. "A punishment? A haunting? A curse?"

Hearing the word *curse* from him stuns me. How casually he speaks of such things.

"Munu is my friend." I scowl, baffled by his implication that our relationship must be negative.

"Don't spare our names for him!" Munu yells, as if she hasn't already given mine away, but her voice dwindles into a mere hum as she continues to shrink.

"The ethereal don't make friends. They work for the Hidden and—" Leon tilts his head. "Is she getting smaller or am I seeing things?"

"Tell him to shut up!" Munu whines, entangled in my curls. "The Hidden shall not be spoken of by filthy mouths!"

"Calm down . . ." I dip my fingers into my hair in search of Munu. Fuck! This isn't the eventless start I'd hoped for in Istanbul.

Leon's grin takes on a devilish edge upon observing my misery. "I'm informed about every ethereal authorized to roam in Istanbul right now, and your sassy sprite isn't one of them. So, tell me— does she possess a permit to remain on this side?" His head moves forward like a wolf's. "What's your *mission*?"

I sense Munu's shudder at the word *mission*. Leon makes it sound like a grand, heroic task, and he would probably burst into laughter if he knew that our sole goal is to keep me alive.

"How can she change her size like that?" Leon's voice softens. "Who blessed her with such a skill?"

"Idiot!" Munu's voice is a buzz that certainly doesn't reach Leon. "He doesn't even get that I can't control it."

"Leave us alone!" I snap at Leon. "You're stressing my . . . friend." And he knows too much—far more than me. It's unsettling.

A fleeting look of surprise passes across his face. "I'm just trying to help."

I lift my chin. "What makes you think we need your help?"

"Ah, this secrecy intrigues me. As much as your face." He smiles, and I wonder what he means by that.

"My face?" I manage to locate Munu nestled inside my hair and pluck her away before she digs her nails into my scalp.

"I've seen you before," Leon declares.

"Where?" I grimace, but he remains silent. I'm almost certain he's messing with me. I've never met him—how could he have seen me before?

"Never mind," Leon drops his voice.

Munu escapes my hand and makes her way to my right ear.

"I beg you, canim, let's go inside now," she whispers, and her plea sends shivers down my spine. "Please."

My Munu, who typically brims with confidence and never utters "please" to me, is trembling with desperation and scared out of her wits, I realize. It's not anger that made her shrink, it's pure fright.

"*Neredesin Leon'cum?*" A girl appears behind Leon. A tall, beautiful creature with the smoothest skin and the longest legs. She follows Leon's gaze and frowns at the sight of me.

"Let's go." I nod at Munu, as I scrutinize the newcomer. I've met enough people for one day.

"I work in the Maiden's Tower on weekdays," Leon calls out after me, "should you ever find yourself curious enough to visit. Bring your friend, too. We can continue our chat. I *hate* leaving things unfinished."

I step back into my bedroom without responding, Munu's terror is enough to put me on high alert. I can still feel Leon's eyes on me as I leave. But it's only as I slam the door behind me and draw the shutters closed that I realize how rapidly my heart is beating.

"Prattling prophets, grant us mercy." Munu grows to her normal size once we're sealed in the room. I've never seen her so terrified before. "What misfortune to land next to a seer. A seer!"

"How can he see you?" I ask.

"He has the pure eye, doesn't he? The deceiving devil!" Munu groans. "Oh, I *hate* seers. The know-it-all busybodies, thinking themselves so superior."

"Who the hell is Grey?" I try to work through my questions one by one.

"Must be his boss, on the Otherside. How would I know? I'm not even a foot on the hierarchy, I'm just a slipper." Munu shakes her head so wildly her necklaces jingle like bells.

"So, you've never heard of this Grey before?" I fold my arms. Something feels off. Leon knew so much—Munu must share his knowledge.

"Stop asking me! Curiosity is forbidden, I've told you a million times before. Do you want me to be punished?"

Of course I don't want Munu to be harmed, but it doesn't seem fair that Leon speaks of the Hidden so freely, while I get brushed off.

"And now he's seen us, he won't stop sticking his nose into our business. No one warned me there would be a seer awaiting us. I wouldn't have come here had I known!"

"Well, he lives here, doesn't he?" I point out the obvious, baffled by Munu's witless ramblings. "I doubt he's orchestrated this as an ambush."

"Seers seek solitude and confinement to deepen their connection with the Hidden." Munu bites her finger. "If this fiend has chosen to settle in this chaotic metropolis, he must be hatching some sinister plans."

Leon's face flashes before my eyes: his brown curls dancing in the breeze, his dark eyes, his curious gaze tracing my skin. That mocking, arrogant smile.

"He's probably just an idiot teenage boy," I say. "He didn't look that dangerous to me."

"What do *you* know about danger? A baby, you are." Munu draws a sharp breath, then dips back into her gloom. "What am I supposed to do now? I'll definitely be in trouble. It's always somehow my fault, isn't it? Always easiest to blame poor Munu."

Before she can drift away, I seize my chance to ask more questions.

"What is a pure eye?" I approach the delicate topic carefully, bracing myself for a scolding. The word *seer* is familiar from Daphne's stories, but I've never heard of a "pure eye" before.

To my surprise, Munu is eager to explain. "The pure eye can see things that do not belong to this world. The Hidden were kind enough to bless some mortals with it. Some can see the dead, or sniff the secrets of the future. Some are even more uncanny—they can put their arms through to the Otherside, breaching the boundaries that separate the living and the dead. They can speak with the Hidden."

I recall the story of the Maiden's Tower and how a seer predicted that the girl was going to die.

Munu drops her voice. "Some seers blow malicious spells in knotted ropes to doom people's fates, bury back-to-back spoons in graveyards to separate loving couples. They can plant the worst nightmares, tear your mind apart—shred by shred—or even your body. They can sprinkle bad fortune on you as if they're dusting pesticide on crops. Even an evil eye won't protect you from their malice."

I grasp my evil-eye pendant, which has already failed to protect me from the curse, and try to lighten the mood. "I'm already cursed. What's the worst that can happen?"

But Munu will have none of it. "There's always worse when it comes to seers," she says. "Promise me you will be careful—keep all these doors and windows shut. Don't leave the house. But if you still have the misfortune to be in his company somehow, ignore him. Promise me." She turns to face me and her expression is as serious as I've ever seen it. "Promise you will stay away from that boy."

I nod. "I promise."

And I do stay away from the boy.

But it turns out, he won't stay away from me.

Subject: Unexpected Local Visitors

Date: 15 July 2025
From: leon.dumanoglu@gmail.com
To: abettergreyforabetterworld@gmail.com

Dear Grey,

I regret that there are still no leads on finding the materials. But I'm getting closer, and I'm certain it's somewhere in the tower, as Sufi Chelebi spent his last days there.

I'm emailing you after a strange turn of events. Remember the girl I've been dreaming about for the past few months? She arrived today—in the flesh. Same face, same hair, same frown. There's no question it's her. I've identified her as Sare Silverbirch, my land-lord's granddaughter.

As you know, my aunt Harika is a clairvoyant and dream expert. She's just as baffled and thinks these dreams might be a warning—for something great and sinister.

Silverbirch seems oblivious to my standing as one of the finest seers in Istanbul. It could be an act, though. Now, here's where things get peculiar: she's not alone. An ethereal presence accompanies her, exercising a certain influence on Silverbirch. Even more puzzling, I found myself able to communicate with this ethereal—named Munu—effortlessly.

Munu is female, deceased in her late twenties or early thirties, drifting around Istanbul without a valid permit. She is roughly thirty centimeters tall, and has the wings of a pigeon. She did a vanishing trick upon spotting me, shrinking herself down in size. It's clear she's no ordinary ethereal. But who does she work for, and what is her relationship to Silverbirch?

What if they're after the books? The last thing I need is more competition. Please do a background check for this Munu and let me know asap.

Also, I had a run-in with that nosy historian, Professor Arman Aziz. He dropped by last week, sifting through the museum for the ridiculous Ministry of Tourism project. He will be working with the museum for some time. I doubt he knows about Sufi Chelebi, so he's nothing to worry about, but still . . . I'll be alert.

I'll spend a few nights in the tower to see if that changes anything and will report back. I must be the one to uncover Sufi Chelebi's legacy.

Best wishes,
Leon

CHAPTER SEVEN

To those for whom the past whispers as a dear friend, recollection brings solace. Yet, others, haunted by their memories, find foes in their bygone days. Who might cast judgment upon them? The act of remembering is a path these souls would forever avoid if only they could.

Excerpt from *The Book of Revenge, Müneccimbaşı Sufi Chelebi's Journals of Mystical Phenomena*

That first night, sleep eludes me, despite feeling physically and emotionally exhausted from the long day. I've met more people today than in the last few years, and being scrutinized takes a toll on my stability. I don't go to dinner and instead sprawl on my bed with my phone and a packet of lemon drops.

The floorboards above groan despite the hour. Muzaffer won't let anyone upstairs into his quarters, so it must be him drifting between the rooms. I wonder why he can't sleep. Maybe it's grief that keeps him awake.

Don't be daft, Sare, I scold myself. Muzaffer doesn't even let me in Mum's room. His arbitrary rules are probably more important to him than the daughter he's lost.

It's 4 a.m. when the grumbles of my stomach become unbearable—the result of eating nothing but sugar since I arrived in Istanbul. Hunger pulls me from my bed and I scramble out of the room. No floorboards have creaked in the last hour, no singing taps—so Muzaffer must be asleep.

A slice of light leaks from the half-open kitchen door as I hurry silently downstairs.

"Hello?" I whisper as I push it open. There's no answer. The sharp odor of disinfectant blends with the faint remains of dinner. I slip inside. The cupboards are spread out symmetrically in a U-shape and a kitchen island rises up in the center, with various pots and pans dangling off a metal grid above it. An aga sits proudly between the cupboards. I wonder if there are any crisps in those cabinets, or crumpets, or waffles? But I don't want to ransack them and risk making noise, so I sneak to the fridge and pull open the double doors.

Under the white fluorescent light, I scan the shelves. Just an array of leafy vegetables. Nothing sweet or interesting. I grab a cheese container in one hand and a loaf of bread, elbow the door closed, and that's when I spot Muzaffer. Looming by the door frame with the ginger cat nuzzling between his legs.

"What do you want?" he asks, and I shrink back. Does he mean right now, here in the kitchen? It sounds like an accusation, as if I'm trespassing or robbing him of something. We stare at each other for several agonizingly long seconds until I escape his gaze, unable to bear the thought that he may be questioning if I'm worthy of being under his roof.

"You missed dinner." Muzaffer states the obvious and the cat shoots into the hallway. "I assumed you were tired."

"I fell asleep." The lie comes easily. Why he cares about my attendance at dinner remains a mystery.

"Yet here you are, snooping around for food." He grunts. "Set an alarm next time."

A pang of annoyance hits me hard at the unfairness of it all. He buried a daughter he hasn't seen for years, and here he is lecturing me about mealtimes as if he's my landlord or head teacher.

"I'm not used to eating with company, or having a routine." My voice sounds strange. Defensive. "I mostly ate alone back at home, whenever I wanted. Daphne wasn't really the maternal kind." I seek the politest way to describe how shit my mother was at parenting. "She'd never set a table unless it was for a boyfriend."

"Well, whatever you grew up with is irrelevant here. This house does have a routine." He evades my remarks; I could be speaking to a wall. "You can't eat at random times."

Fuck your routine, I want to tell him.

"I'm sorry," I say instead. It's true, though—I've never felt sorrier.

Muzaffer's fingers fumble on the door frame, searching for a handle to cling on to. "I can't wake Azmi now to feed you. The poor man is up at five o'clock every day."

"I—It won't happen again." My anger slips away as quickly as it appeared, challenged by the threat I pose to the kind house-keeper's sleep.

"Good," Muzaffer says and I hope that it is, already breaking the promise I made to Munu and myself to not get involved with Daphne's father.

What is wrong with me? Why do I care what he thinks of me?

Muzaffer approaches. The lines of his frown deepen. By the time he towers above me, my pulse beats in my mouth. What follows occurs almost in slow motion. He attempts to pluck the container from me and I recoil. It slips out of my hand and smashes into a million pieces across the floor.

I brace myself for being kicked out of the kitchen, out of the house.

Instead, Muzaffer gestures at the squeaky-clean island. "Sit."

Why does everything he says sound like an order? I perch on a barstool beside the island. The glass crunches under his slippers as he shuffles around the kitchen. He pours a drink, and the smell of booze wafts above me, awakening memories I'm desperate to forget. Perhaps Daphne left because her father tried to control her. Perhaps she left because Muzaffer loved Iris more, and she hated Daphne. Perhaps they both hated Daphne, and that's why he despises me.

Does he really despise me?

Unaware of the storm of emotions in my chest, Muzaffer sets down his drink, and lays out a butter dish, knife and chopping board. It takes me a while to grasp that he's preparing food for me. Muzaffer, who hasn't even said "Hi" or "Are you okay?" or "I'm devastated that Defne died, and I can't imagine how *you* must be feeling," doesn't want me to go to sleep hungry. Gratitude hits me harder than the container just hit the ground.

Muzaffer takes a deep sip from the drink, then another. His fingers are long and slender, slicing the cheese, skin blotched with brown spots of old age. The thud of the knife on the cutting board is rhythmic. He chugs his drink, then lifts his gaze to me. Does he lack the courage to look at me without getting drunk?

"She loved this sandwich." His hands tremble as he spreads butter on the bread.

Is it Mum he's referring to, or Iris?

"Do you like cheese?" Muzaffer asks.

I nod.

"Your mother liked cheese. But Iris wouldn't eat it," he says. "Hers had to be done with sausage and mayonnaise."

"What happened to Iris?" I ask. And why did my mother never tell me about her?

"Iris," Muzaffer says, a smile withering on his mouth before it blooms again. He blinks at me as if he's waking from a dream and doesn't know where he is. "Iris died in the earthquake."

"Earthquake?" I can't keep my mouth shut. I've read about the deadly earthquakes that have hit Türkiye over the years, and it shocks me to discover Iris was a victim of these disasters. I'm dying to find out more about her, and her relationship with Defne. Was she alive when Mum left Istanbul? Was she really Muzaffer's favorite? My head buzzes with a million questions.

But Muzaffer has moved on from the subject. "Eat." He pushes the plate forward.

I can't remember the last time someone made a sandwich for me.

"Thanks," I mutter, not sure if it's too much or too little to say, but my voice would betray me if I said any more. Why do I want to cry? Why now?

Rule number one, Sare. No tears shall fall. Not over some late-night food. Not for a grumpy old man who can't even say Mum's name.

I pick up the sandwich. It would be rude not to eat it immediately. Not to mention the fact that I'm starving. Plus, eating is a valid excuse for not talking.

"You look so much like her," Muzaffer says. "It's painful to look at you."

But I don't really look like Daphne, I want to say. I don't have my mother's feminine beauty, her doe eyes. Even our hair doesn't match: mine is wild and curly, and hers was smooth and fair. Perhaps Muzaffer is properly drunk now, or he's forgotten his own daughter's face.

"Tonight is an exception," he mutters as I take a big bite. "Understood?"

"Okay." I nod—there will be more time for questions in the day. And besides, this may be the best sandwich I've ever had—creamy cheese, sharp pepper. My "thanks" suddenly feels too dry.

Muzaffer downs the rest of the drink, and shuffles over to the sink to wash his hands. "Breakfast is at 8 a.m." He raises his voice to battle the gushing water. "I expect you on time."

"Thank you, M—" I barely stop myself from calling him Mr. Gümüşhuş. I'm not sure how I should address him. Perhaps it's best not to address him at all. "Good night."

"Leave the light on as you go," Muzaffer says, his movements now relaxed, as if he's processed my existence and concluded that he can tolerate me. "Be careful not to step on the glass. Azmi will clean it up in the morning. Goodnight—" He pauses, as if he too isn't sure what to call me either. "Goodnight, kid," he finally says.

He's gone before I can reply.

I set three alarms to wake in time for breakfast the following morning.

As soon as I slip out of bed, I feel the urge to draw back the curtains and pull open the shutters to let in the sunshine. The rainbows on the wallpaper are even more intolerable when muted and subdued in the dim light. But, before I grab the curtains, I remember the danger lurking across the street on his balcony. Leon, and his threats to unravel what's wrong with me, is reason enough for me to keep everything shut.

When I finally climb downstairs for breakfast, the clock chimes eight. I locate the dining room near the kitchen. Muzaffer is already at the head of the oval table that's too grand for a crowd of only two chairs, reading his newspaper with an espresso cup in hand.

"Good morning." The voice comes from behind the paper, revealing no recollection of last night.

"Morning," I reply and shift my focus to better things. Food. Sadly, no sweets appear on the lavish spread across the table: cheese, olives, cucumber, boiled eggs and bagels. Not a pot of jam in sight. Reluctantly, I scoop a few olives onto my plate from the dish.

Muzaffer flips a page. What's the point of making the effort to eat together if we're going to ignore each other?

I spear an olive with my fork. It proves to be a surprise when I bite into it. Not a good one. The bitter and metallic taste bursts in my mouth, and I again doubt the wisdom of moving in with Muzaffer.

The door opens and Azmi appears with a pillbox, which he presents to Muzaffer alongside a glass of water. I count eight pills as he swallows them one by one and wonder what they're for.

"Did you sleep well?" Muzaffer asks, his eyes on the glass of water.

"Yes." I nod.

"Do you need anything?" His fingers fidget over a fork.

"No." *I only need to survive the next four months,* I muse.

He returns to his newspaper then. With a pang of annoyance, I throw him a question.

"Why are there no photos in this house?" None of Iris, or Daphne. Not even Muzaffer himself. In this room, there's only an oil painting of Istanbul and some Ottoman calligraphy on the walls. This house doesn't feel like someone's home. Remove the inhabitants and it would feel like a hotel.

Muzaffer lowers the paper again, revealing a frown.

"I get it if you don't want to keep Daphne's photos," I explain. "You fell out and all that. But aren't there any of Iris, or their mother? Or you, even?"

A vein throbs on his forehead. I wonder if he's startled at hearing Mum's name.

"I don't like posing for photographs," he says. "I don't entertain myself with images."

The people we lose should remain in our memories, not in family albums, Daphne's voice echoes in my mind. *Certainly not on the walls as decoration.*

"She told me," I whisper.

"What?" Muzaffer's porcelain cup clinks on the saucer.

"Mum told me you had her mother's photos removed."

His hand quivers as he pours himself more coffee.

"But I still don't understand why she told me you were dead," I mutter.

"I'm sorry," Muzaffer sighs. A shadow of Daphne falls across him as he talks, her features glittering in his sagging face. And there's my own reflection trapped there too, if I stare at him long enough. The thick eyebrows. The curls. The pale skin. I'm starved of my mother's feminine beauty, doomed to be tall and lanky like

Muzaffer. Daphne was petite, born to be scooped into men's arms like a doll. I'm sure if anyone tried that on me, my limbs would dangle like the branches of a willow. "I can't help you."

"Something must have happened," I insist.

"Your mother wished to leave and so she did." He pauses as Böcek sashays into the room, weaving her way straight into his lap. "I warned her against it," Muzaffer says as the cat nuzzles against him. "She didn't listen. She never listened."

My fork listlessly circles on my plate, my appetite long gone.

"Eat," Muzaffer commands. "Don't waste food."

A hot, red anger claws my stomach. Why does he always order me around? Is the stupid food on my plate more important than Daphne?

I must be a masochist, because I stuff another olive into my mouth. The next months will be easier than I imagined. It'll be a blessing to be furious all the time. What protects the heart better than anger? I'll have no trouble with rule number two.

Channel your sorrow into rage.

Soon I'll be eighteen, I tell myself, free of any other restraints I have to tolerate until then. Never mind how the curse will claim my heart, robbing me of love. I'll have breakfast alone and eat whatever the hell I want, whenever I want.

But you still need answers, a small voice in my head whispers, deepening my misery, because I know it's right.

I don't go out that day, or the next. A sudden, overwhelming tiredness sweeps through my body like a straw broom. Like the maiden who died in the tower not far from this house, I imprison myself in my room, lying in bed, windows and doors shut. I do nothing but eat chocolate and watch horror movies. I order KitKats via Azmi, who seems delighted by my company. Although I don't take it too personally, given the loneliness in this house.

The only thing that worries me is Munu's absence. Our time together is already scarce. She's always overwhelmed with the amount of work she's expected to do, but it's very rare that she doesn't visit me for a whole day, especially not two. I wonder if the boy across the street has anything to do with it.

Finally, on my third night in Istanbul, Munu appears to justify my fears.

"You didn't leave your room, did you?" she asks as soon as she zips in front of me.

I shake my head.

"That devil is raising inquiries about me," she whispers, her face illuminated by the harsh light of the monitor I use as a TV. "Boss isn't pleased. 'You should have been more careful, Munu!' As if it's my fault a seer lives here."

"But . . ." A knot of worry tightens my stomach, as I recall Leon's inquiry about Munu having a permit. It's rare that Munu's tongue loosens, so I risk asking a question that has been puzzling me. "What trouble could you possibly be in if everything's in order with your job? You're my guardian."

"Canim, I don't decide on any order. Orders are decided for me," she mutters. "Now, stop asking questions, or else I'll end up in even more trouble. What if they're watching us? What if they bugged this room?"

"Stop being so paranoid." I roll my eyes. "Perhaps I should go to that tower tomorrow and warn him off," I casually suggest, glancing at Daphne's painting across the room. I removed a world map to hang it there instead, so it's still the first thing I see when I open my eyes every morning. It's time I go and see the tower in person. It's just so . . . alluring.

"Are you out of your mind?" Munu bellows. "You won't step anywhere near that tower. The lair of that monster? Promise me you won't!"

I narrow my eyes as I watch her shrink. "Why are you so worried?"

"It's too dangerous!" Munu shrieks. "A malevolent place fit for a sinister thing like him."

I disagree with her about the tower. A fragile, beautiful structure can hardly be described as malevolent, but I don't protest that point.

"Listen, I can threaten him to stop investigating you," I say. "Muzaffer is their landlord. While he seems to barely tolerate me, I'm sure he won't be very happy if I tell him Leon is harassing me. And surely even a wicked seer has to cope with the worldly matter of eviction."

"He can't harm me. My boss will protect me." Munu's eyes scan the room. She looks uncertain. "Just stay away from the boy seer. Don't even mention his name again."

She makes me swear that I won't pursue him before she disappears into the night.

Every building must have its own voice, and Muzaffer's crumbling mansion loves singing. The floorboards above are murmuring their favorite groans under Muzaffer's gentle steps.

Every night, I stare up as if the ceiling is transparent and I can see him.

Funnily enough, the ceiling I watched during the sleepless nights back home had a similar texture to this one, despite being miles away from this strange city. There must be only a handful of types of ceiling in the world. Daphne's face doesn't immediately form on this one though. Perhaps because the house seems devoid of her presence—no photos, no belongings, her room locked, her name avoided. If only I could do as Munu says and quit thinking about her. Only a few months ago, I was angry at her all the time. It was easier to be bitter than torment myself with how her eyes skipped past me, as if I was a ghost. Perhaps she didn't want to look at me. I was furious at the way she drank so much, wasting herself away, how many men she brought home, how weak she was. But none of these things matters any more. Only the happy memories of my childhood haunt me. How she used to paint in her garden studio, and I'd sprawl on the floor with my crayons scattered around me, working on my own art. One day, she braided daisy chains for us. "My little pixie," she said as she set it on my head. "How pretty you are." She made me sit for a painting, the daisy chain and all the innocence of childhood displayed bare on the canvas when she was done.

When I was thirteen, I made my own daisy chain. But she wouldn't paint me that time. "You've changed," she said. "You change every day." As if it was my fault for growing up.

The more I think about it, the more perplexing it becomes, how much she used to love me once, and then one day, it was no more. Now, the fourth crack lies deep in my heart, lanky and fractured, making it impossible to move on. As if, were I to run my hand over my chest, my fingertips would come away with blood. The other three were just scratches. The lapses of a child who let her heart shatter over nonsense.

My mother's death becomes my second shadow.

Nothing can break my heart like that again. This time, I'm sure.

Communication is classified as Highly Confidential.
Circulation strictly limited to beings of celestial origins.

Subject: Urgent Inquiry Regarding Work Permit

Date: 18 July 2025
From: Grey the Compassionate, Curse and Malediction Archives, Worldly Index, Sacred Data Systems, Halotech Data & Integration Hub
To: Ethereal Resourcing & Deployment Unit-ALL Angels
Cc: Fate Adjustment Bureau-ALL Angels

Esteemed and most Honorable Angel Superiors,

I hope this email finds you in cherubic spirits. Given the absence of a response to my other correspondence with the Fate Adjustment Bureau, which may have been obscured by the voluminous tasks on their holy desks, I'm writing to you in the first instance to beg for your most sacred attention on a separate matter.

Through the surveillance of mortal acolytes, I discovered an ethereal in Konstantiniyye without a valid work permit. Adding to this perplexing occurrence, this ethereal, Munu, seems to communicate with mortals with an ease that makes me think something is surely amiss.

I kindly request the prompt dispatch of the necessary documents to my department so we can update Sacred Data Systems accordingly. Failing this, I'll be compelled to initiate a formal inquiry into this ethereal's activities. Needless to remind you that They Whom Should not be Concerned, Our Boss Almighty, maintains an unwavering stance on unlicensed servitude. The balance between us, the Hidden, and the mortals is a matter too delicate to ignore.

I eagerly anticipate your blessed intervention in this matter, so we may continue to uphold the celestial order without a blemish on our impeccable record.

Ova Ceren

Yours divinely,
Grey the Compassionate
Doctorate of Angelic Scholarship (Hons)
Thrice longlisted for the Heavenly Achievement Prize

CHAPTER EIGHT

Many weep their sorrows, yet few truly mourn with their heart. The maiden, however, grieved with her very soul. "I failed," her soul confided in me. "I made a mistake." Reader, understanding how youth's fervor often crafts our gravest errors, I was ready to extend the forgiveness she sought. Alas, she did not seek absolution from me, or perhaps I had none left to give.

Excerpt from *The Book of Heartbreak, Müneccimbaşı Sufi Chelebi's Journals of Mystical Phenomena*

The rest of my first week in Istanbul runs like an open tap. I adhere to the mealtimes. For reasons unknown to me, Muzaffer only eats two meals a day, and like a soldier I mold myself to his routine around the clock—from 8 a.m. breakfast to dinner at 8 p.m. Staying within the confines of the house keeps me occupied.

I spend most days reading or sketching on the balcony, doing my best to ignore Leon across the street. It's intolerable to be the subject of his arrogant gaze. I don't know why he surveys me like this, with a pouting mouth and narrow eyes. As if I'm a human grenade and he doesn't want to miss the explosion. The light-brown-haired girl with long, tanned legs who occasionally joins him must be his girlfriend, I figure, if he only has one. Luckily, he doesn't attempt to speak with me again. But he watches me. His eyes move when I move, and whenever I unwrap a lollipop, I swear his mouth curls with contempt.

One afternoon, I'm engrossed in a sketch on the balcony, my legs propped up on the railing.

"You'll get sunburned if you stay out here without any shade," comes a cautioning voice. Glancing upward, I spot Leon lounging on his own balcony, shaking his head in mock disapproval. In response, I hoist the pad higher, deliberately shielding my face from his gaze.

"So, sunburn isn't your biggest concern, then?" he teases.

"Of course it isn't," I retort, lowering the book. His gaze flickers down to my lips, lingering for a beat too long, sending a jolt of electricity to my stomach. "You can't even begin to fathom the challenges I navigate daily."

"I'm not surprised." He nods. "With your flamboyant rogue running around unauthorized, who knows what troubles you're entangled in?"

"What is your problem?" I snap. "Why are you so obsessed with Munu?"

"Oh, wait—" He chuckles softly. "Are you jealous?"

"Y-you—" I stammer, lost for words, my cheeks flushing with stupid embarrassment. "You're insufferable."

He laughs again.

"Stop being such a jerk," I snarl. "And leave me alone."

"I swear, I will," he says. "If you tell me what brings you two to Istanbul."

"Why don't we discuss what *keeps* you in Istanbul, seer?" I don't hesitate a comeback after recalling Munu's words about seers, and how they live in confinement. Istanbul is vivid and ever-present, always beckoning. Not the ideal location for someone like him, if he is who he says he is. "Shouldn't your kind be in confinement instead of a bustling metropolis?"

"I'm on a mission," he says. "Trying to locate materials that are key to unraveling the mystery of a curse."

"A curse?" I freeze on the word, studying his face. But there's no sign of sarcasm or arrogance. Only pure concentration. "What curse?"

"The curse of the Maiden's Tower—have you heard of it?"

I shake my head in confusion. "The tower is cursed?"

"Not the tower itself," he explains. "The maiden who lived there. I'm sure you've heard of the myth?"

I ignore his question. "Is that why you work there?"

"Why else would I take a job as a mere security guard?" Leon folds his arms, seemingly offended that I'd even considered him doing something so ordinary.

"What type of materials are you after?" I close my book and rest it on my leg. "Artifacts to smuggle?"

It's his turn to snort. "Ever heard of Sufi Chelebi?"

"No. Why should I?" The name is unfamiliar, and it sounds like an artisan tea brand.

Leon bestows me with another snort. This annoying handsome shit. Fine, not a tea brand, then.

"Sufi Chelebi was a prominent seer," he says. "The most famous of curse-breakers."

This makes me pause. A curse-*breaker*? Curses can be broken? The revelation slams into me, louder than Istanbul's frantic pulse, twisting hope and dread together in my stomach. All these years, despite how many times I asked, Munu never breathed a word of this.

"How—" I croak, the question hitching in my throat. "How did he break curses?"

Leon stares at me, as if trying to calculate my intentions.

I stare right back at him, wondering if he's lying or not. Why should I trust him anyway?

"If you have a drop of knowledge of our craft and the Hidden," he says, his pretty lips curling with that damn smile, "you'd know you have a few options to break a curse."

"Of course," I grit out through clenched teeth. *You can't ask him any more,* I tell myself. *You can't give him the satisfaction of boasting about how well-informed he is while you're left in the dark.* "Whatever. I was just checking if you actually know what you're talking about."

"You almost emit a glow when you're angry," Leon mutters. "Fascinating, considering how oblivious you are of the Hidden."

Now I'm certain he's messing with me. I do not *glow.*

"Cut the bullshit, please," I say with a mock sweetness. "So your mission, this maiden." I tuck a curl behind my ear. "Why was she cursed, then?"

"But I assume you already know?" He beams at me, leaving me torn between swooning over his beauty and wanting to punch him.

I fold my arms. Munu was right. He's sly as a fox. "Of course I do," I lie.

"Oh, I see," he murmurs, with a false sincerity in his tone. "You must have figured it out yourself, then. Care to compare notes? It's quite the enigma, after all."

"I don't have to tell you anything." I feel tension knotting between us.

"No one knows why the maiden was cursed, except the caster of the curse, and perhaps the great Sufi Chelebi himself. It happens to be my mission to find out, you see? And there are . . . other details, top secret, of course, that I can't share at the minute."

I took his bait. He knows I'm only pretending. I must turn as red as a tomato. The shame of my crude lie and frustration of being fed scraps of information gel into another, leaving me in an explosive mood. Top-secret mission? Nothing makes sense. I slide my legs off the railing and prepare to leave.

"Wait," he says. "I answered your questions. Now it's your turn. Tell me why you're here. Why doesn't your ethereal have a permit?"

"I have no idea what a fucking permit does, and the last thing I need is your interrogation," I declare, rising from my seat to withdraw into the sanctuary of my room.

"You don't seem accustomed to goodbyes," Leon calls after me, as if I owe him the courtesy. "But you'd better bid farewell to your friend Munu if you two can't prove she's authorized."

I don't reward him with a response, mostly because I have no idea how to respond. His arrogant grin is the final image I'm left with before I close the curtains.

God, I hate him.

In the evening, when I'm calmer but still pacing my room, I clasp my evil-eye necklace and summon Munu. After Leon's threats, I'm sick with worry about her well-being, but what troubles me more is why she's never mentioned these curse-breakers to me.

"Munu," I whisper, pressing the evil eye into my palm. "Munu, I need you."

I brace myself for silence, but the loud crack of her appearance catches me off guard.

"Canim! Has that fickle fiend done something to you?" Munu's gaze sweeps the room. Her appearance shocks me. Eyes deep and empty. Face bereft of make-up, her hair loose. No necklace or earrings, just a simple white dress cinched with a bow at the waist.

"Are you okay?" I sink onto my bed.

"I'm done for." Munu's lips quiver as she flies over to me. "That boy has been prying into matters he has no business with, the malevolent marauder."

"He's asking about your permit, isn't he?"

"What does he know? Of course I won't have a public permit, I work on extremely confidential projects." She lands neatly on the "O" of a cushion embroidered with the word *Love*. "I shouldn't have wandered around without care. I should have been more vigilant. My boss will be in trouble because of me now. I've already failed them, when they're the most undeserving, the most merciful."

"Maybe, if you shared some details about your work and the Otherside," I say after a brief pause, "I might be able to help."

"I can't." Munu shakes her head. "I can't speak of hi—the boss's secrets."

"Leon seems to know a great deal about your job, and he has no problem projecting his opinions from across the street," I argue. "He threatened me earlier, regarding you, and oh, he mentioned that curses can be broken."

"What? When?" Munu's wings flip rapidly. "You didn't tell him *you're* cursed, did you?"

"Of course I didn't." I roll my eyes. "But is it true? Can I . . . break this curse?"

"Lies!" Munu squeals, instantly beginning to shrink. "He's a charlatan—vile, sinister, worst of his kind!"

I'm disheartened by her extreme reaction, and the quiet hope inside me flickers out. "He sounded so sure of himself."

"That vicious bastard!" Munu cries as she continues to dwindle. Whether it's because of anger, or fear, I can't tell. "Why is he so obsessed with you?"

"He's more fixated on you," I retort, remembering Leon's interrogation about Munu. His cocky smile and handsome face. Could he really be interested in me? Knowing Munu's flair for exaggeration, I brush off the thought, ignoring the warmth creeping up my chest.

"Why are you blushing?" Munu whines. "He's not *romantically* interested in you, Boss forbid! You are just a potential tool for his demonic missions."

"I don't see how I could possibly help his missions." I clear my throat. "I think he's just trying to annoy me."

"The seer has sensed the veil of secrecy surrounding us," Munu says, as if heralding doom. "He's curious, as they invariably are, like a hungry fox hunting in a meadow, ready to dig in and unearth your secrets. And if, Boss in Heavens, he uncovers the curse, he won't care if your heart breaks or not. Think! If you die and this curse dies with you, he'll claim it as his success, do you understand? You're not his problem! His kind only seeks ways to turn things to their benefit. He can't be trusted."

"But why—" I try to figure out the best way to form the question without further agitating Munu and causing her to disappear entirely. "Why does there need to be so much secrecy about me? About you?"

"Because—" Munu blinks, her mouth twitching as she considers this *because*. Outside, the mosques cast the night prayer across the city like an eerie warning.

"Because—" She begins and stops again, trembling as she gets smaller.

Finally, when she speaks, her voice is a low buzz. "Because, I can't tell you, that's why. I have no rank, no say in the hierarchy. I know nothing except my assignments. I can tell you all about my miserable workload, if that will quench your curiosity, or the punishments I'll meet if I release the secrets of the Hidden. Will that distract you from that horrible boy and his wicked deeds?"

"Try me." I raise my eyebrow, inviting her to speak. I'm annoyed that she can't tell me anything when Leon seems to know everything. It almost feels like they're playing a game without me. But any information she can offer about the Otherside would be of interest right now.

"Fine." Munu shakes her head again. "Let me explain why I must leave now. Listen to just one of the countless woes I'm expected to deal with, and maybe you'll have some pity for me. There's a man cursed to hit every red light in traffic, and today he's heading for a busy junction in central London." She speaks so fast, I can hardly make out the words. "The halfwits in Temporal Intervention informed me at the last minute that I need to guide him out of the Ultra Low Emission Zone, as Fate Adjustment predicts that all the idling exhaust pipes behind him will shave an estimated twenty-five days off mortal lives in the area. And guess who'll be punished if his curse creates a traffic jam?"

I gawk at her, stunned by the outburst. How could a man end up with such a curse? What the hell is Temporal Intervention?

Munu lifts her hand, cutting me off before I can open my mouth. "My job isn't easy, Sare. Please don't make it harder by asking me all these questions. I just execute orders—that's it! I have no power or knowledge."

"But did you just say . . . fate?" I can't help but ask. She's never disclosed this much to me before. "As in . . . destiny?"

"Trust me. It's best you don't know," Munu sighs.

"Should I be worrying about you?" Guilt tugs at me for pushing her. No wonder she's always busy—if they make her run bizarre errands like these. *She is a slipper,* I remind myself. Not a head. She's helping me as best as she can. "Will you be in trouble because of the seer?"

"Just stay in this room," she growls back. "Stay away from him, and I'll be golden."

She attempts to inject some optimism as we say our goodbyes but I'm not a child. I can see the way her hands shake, and how her eyes dart toward the balcony, as if Leon could emerge there any minute. Why is Munu so insistent on locking me in this room? And why would Leon lie to me about breaking curses? I can't shake off my unease. Leon is arrogant, and maybe his threats to banish Munu are cruel, but the way he spoke about his mission and his craft sounded genuine.

There's something off in all this.

As I sit in the dark after Munu departs, a daring plan starts to take root within me. A scheme to find out exactly what's going on, even if it means betraying my friend's trust.

Communication is classified as Top Secret.
Circulation strictly limited to correspondents.
This email will destroy itself once read, so read carefully.

Subject: A Cautionary Word

Date: 22 July 2025
From: Nine the Ninth, Senior Angel of Fate, Fate Adjustment Bureau, Mortal Affairs Commission
To: Five the Fifth, Angel of Death, Field Operations, Mortal Termination and Transition, Mortal Affairs Commission

My old friend Five the Fifth,

I hope this email doesn't find you well, because it won't leave you better. I'd hate to spoil your good mood.

A cherub from Sacred Data Systems is flooding our inboxes regarding that malice that's given us a permanent halo-ache since the day it spawned. You know which one I'm talking about, right? The fiasco in Constantinople—the one you beguiled me to alter the records for, ensuring it could never be traced back to us—involving that vexing mortal woman. Was I naive to trust you? Back then, I was just an officer, though now I've risen through the ranks at the Bureau. If you're relying on my glorious achievements to save us, I will be devastated to disappoint. We're both doomed if our small oversight comes to light.

I love my job too much to lose it over some ridiculous old story, Five.

That busybody cherub is also raising inquiries about *your* illegal little employee. I shouldn't have to remind you that curses are EXTREMELY unpredictable, that they can be dangerous and get out of control. You should never have meddled with the resurrections. And you certainly shouldn't have assigned your ethereal pet to be in charge of such delicate matters.

Nevertheless, I have undertaken the troubles to verify the lineage of the cursed mortal M9392748565670048343, and no one related to her is alive apart from an old man who—as destiny won't lie—is unlikely to produce more heirs. As such, if this mortal perishes, the curse will perish with her and no one will find any trace of this . . . blunder. Why not, my comrade, simply take care of this now? Why wait? You may advise me to ignore the cherub, but isn't it the rule-following, ambitious little pricks like him who stir up the most trouble?

Remember, I've kept your secrets all this time, but what's the worth in keeping secrets if the horns are blown?

With utmost dedication to the divine causes,
Nine the Ninth

CHAPTER NINE

The bearer is reborn to suffer and thus to give suffering; a soul carrying the weight of an endless cycle. A loop of existence from which there is no escape. This fate defies the natural order. As I pen these words, I can't help asking myself: what purpose does such eternal suffering serve? What lesson is to be learned from a punishment so enduring? May Allah show mercy on those bound by such a fate, for they are trapped in an eternity of cruelty.

Excerpt from The Book of Betrayal, Müneccimbaşı Sufi Chelebi's Journals of Mystical Phenomena

The following day, despite how disloyal it makes me feel, I head to the Maiden's Tower. I have to understand why exactly Munu is so frightened of Leon, and which one of them is telling me the truth about breaking curses.

As I step out of the house, Muzaffer's driver Gökhan emerges from out of nowhere and follows me, asking if I need transportation. I wonder, as I firmly reject his offer, if Muzaffer has instructed him to keep an eye on me. As if I need a babysitter.

I descend the narrow slope, taking my time to avoid a misstep, so I won't snap an ankle and jeopardize the fresh start I've sought in Istanbul. Gravel crunches under my feet as I reach the bottom of the street. When I dart around the corner, I lift my hand to shield my eyes from the sun's blinding rays and cross the road.

Istanbul thrums with a chaotic rhythm. Crowds weave through the sidewalks, their lively conversations and laughter blending with the constant honking of taxis and the melodic shouts of street vendors. Overhead, gulls screech as they soar through the sky. Nobody could ever feel alone in Istanbul, I decide, walking along the seafront in search of a way to reach the Maiden's Tower.

When I spot the island-bound boat amid the bustling port, I surge forward, determined to catch it. Once aboard, the gentle sway underfoot leaves me light-headed. Perhaps traveling across the water for the first time, or the thrill of my newfound independence, or the fear of what might go wrong, makes me dizzy. Challenging menacing seers who look like heartthrobs wasn't exactly on my to-do list when I arrived in Istanbul.

Finally, the boat sets sail, and the clamor of traffic fades into the sound of lapping water. I try not to think about the promises I made to Munu—to stay away from Leon, and the tower—and how, with a single trip, I'm breaking both.

When the boat docks at the islet, I unwrap a mint humbug, bracing myself against the daunting thought that this picturesque landmark is said to have once been a prison to a poor maiden. It looks so peaceful that I struggle to believe there's any truth to the tale.

Instead of joining the stream of tourists flocking the arched entrance of the courtyard, I veer off and skirt the perimeter. The island's shore is jagged with rocks bristling against the sea. Up close, the tower's weathered exterior looks pristine, a result of recent renovations that mask any signs of its turbulent past, which, according to the tourist information boards, includes surviving three earthquakes and a fire.

A peculiar yet familiar sensation stirs within me as I study the structure, as if I've wandered on its grounds before. Perhaps this sense of déjà vu originates from Daphne's painting, and the memories of her telling me the tale of the tower. I've listened to it countless times, so I can recite it from memory.

After a seer prophesied her death at the age of eighteen, the maiden was confined to this island for protection. But Death still arrived on her eighteenth birthday, as a serpent hiding in a fruit basket, weaving through a cluster of grapes like a ribbon. The maiden greeted the snake with naive curiosity, having never encountered such a creature before.

There's something so tragic about this story—how the maiden didn't expect harm from the snake. How her father's attempts at shelter and protection left her vulnerable.

If misfortune is written in your stars, Munu used to say each time Daphne told me this story, *you could jump on a spaceship to Mars and it would still follow you.*

A gull shrieks above, jolting me back to the present. Dispelling the veil of nostalgia, I refocus on my mission. I didn't come here to daydream.

I head into the courtyard, where the crowds have now dispersed, and there I find what—or rather, whom—I came for.

Leon.

He leans against a wall near the entrance, a striking figure in his security guard uniform. He was already good looking in his shabby t-shirt and shorts, but the sleek suit makes him something else. I despise myself for finding him so attractive.

The devil, Munu whispers in my head. And his gaze locks on to me with an unyielding magnetism as if to prove her right, robbing me of the chance to study him as freely as I desire.

I notice a subtle twitch in his impassive expression as he sets eyes on me.

In a heartbeat, he closes the gap between us.

"Silverbirch. What are you doing here?"

"Visiting the museum," I try to respond as nonchalantly as I can muster.

"Is that so?" He sounds unconvinced. "I'd hoped you'd finally decided to show me your cards."

"Well, unlike you, I'm not a gambler." I use sarcasm to mask my nervousness. "Or a con artist."

"Not everything is as it seems, Sare Silverbirch." Now he looks annoyed, and I feel pleased with myself for deflating him.

"So you say." I adjust my bag on my shoulder. "Oh, also . . . Before I forget, let me tell you something very important."

God, I'm really not good at this.

He seems amused, his arrogant smile back in place, all ears for whatever I might blurt out next. Suddenly, all the carefully curated words in my head seem ridiculously foolish to voice aloud.

"Leave Munu alone." I lift my chin higher, forcing down the fear. "Stop raising inquiries about her."

"And why exactly would I do that?" He steps closer. Too close. My breath quickens at the scent of his cologne. Physical closeness isn't my forte, after all. It takes a lot of willpower to maintain unwavering eye contact, but I'm determined to prove his intimidation tactics won't work on me. Despite my resolve, the depths of his eyes—dark with hints of honey—grow more disconcerting by the moment.

"Because—" I swallow hard. "If you upset my friend, that means you upset me. And trust me, you wouldn't want to cross your landlord's granddaughter."

"Do you realize—" he tilts his head slightly, and we're so close now that the scent of mint from his breath washes over me—"that I'm only doing my job?"

Of course, these oh-so-secretive duties again. Leon, Munu—everyone seems to have some grand purpose, a role to play on a mysterious chessboard where I'm just a pawn being shuffled around.

I fold my arms. "What sort of job involves threatening innocent spirits—or ethereals, if I'm obliged to use your fancy terms."

"Can you imagine the chaos if the ethereals walked among us freely?"

I can't, obviously. I don't even fully grasp what ethereals are, or what they do here, or why they need permission in the first place. I clamp my mouth shut to avoid further embarrassment and mask my irritation.

"Someone has to put in the effort to maintain order." Leon smiles again, as if talking to a small child. "If things go awry, the Hidden would be the first to be displeased, and I bet they'd be way more pissed off than you. Or your friend, whatever she's up to."

I'd be surprised if he could say a single word without patronizing me.

"You're not the only one with a highly confidential, top-secret mission," I snap at last, attempting to assert authority, though the remnant of dominance is fading like the taste of the mint humbug on my tongue.

"Ah, and what exactly is your mission?"

Shit. I suddenly realize what I just let slip.

Leon draws even closer, as if daring me to step back. His height surpasses mine, a head taller than me, imposing. The locks of our loose hair entwine, stirred by the sea breeze. I am rooted to the spot.

He doesn't scare me, I reassure myself, holding his gaze. *I can't show any weakness. I won't back away.*

Fuck. Perhaps coming here wasn't such a good idea after all.

"Are you after the books?" His voice is suddenly a whisper.

I gawk at him. "What books?"

"*The* books," he grunts.

"I have no idea what you're waffling about."

His eyes glint with curiosity and he retreats to establish some much-needed distance between us. I try to seem unperturbed by his movement, and his stare remains fixed on me, as if he's hunting for a reaction.

"So, as I was saying," I fumble. "Stay away from Munu, or you'll regret it."

With this ultimatum, which I have no idea how to fulfill, I turn away to head into the tower, abandoning Leon in the court-yard. A glance over my shoulder doesn't deliver relief when I note that he isn't following me. Instead, a weight settles in my chest, uncomfortably close to disappointment.

Inside the tower, soft light filters in from above, bathing the stone walls. In the absence of any curtains, the hardwood floor reflects the sunlight. Even with the throng of people, there's a sense of calm—a serenity unlike any I've felt before.

The upper floor is a round room, encircled by large windows that frame breathtaking views of the sea like a living painting. There's an exhibition of calligraphy that captivates the onlookers with the swirls and flourishes of an ancient language. In the center, a sturdy wooden column climbs toward the vaulted ceiling, anchor-ing the room like the mast of a ship. I lean against the smooth railing. Here, suspended between the land and the mass of water, I feel the strange sense of déjà vu again. As if I've been right on this spot before.

But it's impossible. I've never set foot in this place until today.

I drift over to the window, where the sea stretches wide and knowing under the vast sky. With a deep sigh, I allow myself to wonder how it would feel to be someone else.

Someone untouched by curses.

Someone who has never faced Death.

Someone . . . normal.

There is a tranquility here, a familiarity that pulls me in. I nestle inside a windowsill and close my eyes briefly, surrendering to a sense of peace, until a ship's long, bitter horn jolts me back to reality. There's a sour taste in my mouth and a dull ache on my shoulder. Checking my watch, I'm shocked to find it's nearly 3 p.m. Did I fall asleep?

I rise back to my feet, bumping against an unexpected obsta-cle. I look down to see a leather-bound book, seemingly out of place on the museum's polished floor. I could swear it wasn't there when I arrived. With a mix of reverence and curiosity, I lean down to scoop it up.

The worn cover is weathered, but the title gleams boldly in gold. *Müneccimbaşı Sufi Chelebi's Journals of Mystical Phenomena: A Guide for Breaking the Most Enigmatic Curses.*

Breaking the most enigmatic curses?

The claim sends a shudder down my spine. *Sufi Chelebi.* Isn't that the guy Leon mentioned? Could this be *the* book he wouldn't stop harping on about—the mysterious "materials" he spoke of? Well, he's clearly not been looking very hard.

The book is larger than an ordinary hardback. Heavy to hold. It looks old. Shouldn't such an object be under glass protection rather than lying abandoned on the floor? I scan the room for a museum attendant, but there are only tourists. Perhaps I could just quickly flick through and glimpse the secrets of this so-called curse-breaking.

I hurry downstairs and burst through the doors into the courtyard. The sun's rays strike my eyes sharply after the dim interior. Squinting, I stumble toward the archway only to collide with a figure. We're two opposing currents in the flow of visitors and the crush sends a surge through my body. I spin around, ready to apologize—and meet with Leon's frown.

The abruptness of the encounter sends us both staggering, but he's the first to speak beneath the aggressive caws of the gulls flickering above us.

"Careful." He composes himself, then his gaze falls on the book clutched to my chest. His eyes widen with an astonishment that's too authentic to be an act. "H-how—Where did you find that?"

"This?" I raise the book with a smirk. The wind picks up, twining through my hair and tugging at the pages. The paper rustles, as if the tome wants to be cracked open.

"Stop waving it around," he admonishes, extending an arm to snatch it from me, but I shrink back, clutching the book closer. "Do you even realize what you're holding?"

"I thought I could have a quick look, seeing as you're letting it lie around like a piece of rubbish on the floor."

"What? It didn't—It couldn't—" His eyes darken. "Don't try to trick me, Silverbirch."

"Why would I trick you?" I scowl. "Is it my fault museum artifacts are scattered about the place?"

"Don't you get it?" he hisses. "That book does *not* belong to the museum." Then he groans, as if talking to me is insufferable. "We can't discuss it here. Come inside, to the office." A large gull lands nearby, its beady eyes lingering on us. "Now." He grabs my wrist. I don't know why I let him drag me inside, but perhaps I'm so desperate to learn how to break a curse, that I do.

CHAPTER TEN

Only those in quest of seeking or offering aid can reach my journals.
Excerpt from *The Book of Revenge, Müneccimbaşı Sufi Chelebi's Journals of Mystical Phenomena*

The office is situated in the basement. Leon takes the lead as we descend the stairs. We arrive at a decrepit old door, and I hesitate at the threshold when he unlocks it, contemplating whether I should retreat back upstairs. But Leon is already inside, and he flicks on the light, illuminating a mundane office—not the eerie, underground lair of Bluebeard I'd envisaged.

He's practically a stranger, a small voice says inside my head. *Why are you alone with him, Sare?*

He's a neighbor, another voice counters.

A strange neighbor, I conclude. But I'm not exactly the most normal person either.

I peer down at the book, at the promise it holds as a guide to breaking curses . . . Fuck, I have to know what it's all about. I slip inside and the door bangs shut behind me, the clank of the metal hinges echoing in the empty stairwell outside.

"Please sit," Leon says, settling on the edge of a metal trunk that seems too low for his tall frame; his knees almost poke out of his trousers. With limited options, I settle into the office chair opposite him, mindful of the tight space between us.

"Did Munu guide you to the journal?" He leans forward, surveying me for a reaction. "Are you here to steal it?"

"Excuse me?" I glare at him, clenching my fists. "Do I look like a thief?"

"If you're not a thief," he says, pinning me down with his stare, "then what *are* you?"

I hold his gaze defiantly. "I have no idea what you're talking about."

"Please." His voice dips, revealing a flicker of vulnerability. "Drop the act. Is the journal the reason you and your ethereal sidekick showed up here? Are you two some sort of relic hunters?"

"It was on the floor," I say, agitated. Why is he so mad about this bloody book? "I *literally* stumbled on it—I just . . . I had to pick it up."

"Do you expect me to believe that?" His jaw clenches. "I caught you running away, remember?"

"I wasn't r—Look, I don't care what you think." I shrug. "But that's what happened."

"We'll see about that," he says, rising from his seat. My heart skips a beat as he leans over me, but I realize he's only turning on a computer. His sea-salt scent fills my nostrils as the operating system starts with a hum. "Where exactly did you say you found it?"

CCTV footage fills the screen. I blink at the grainy gray light.

"Upstairs . . . about ten minutes ago," I reply, my annoyance swelling as he rewinds the recording. But then I see myself on the screen. In the black-and-white footage, I lean down to scoop something nonexistent from the ground.

On the camera, the book is invisible.

"Shit," I gasp. "I swear to you—I swear the book was there!"

Leon stares at me, his expression unreadable. The steady tread of visitors on the level above us fills the silence in the dark office.

"So." Leon lets out a sharp breath as he pauses the screen, where I now stand still, compelled by an invisible item between my hands. "You're telling the truth."

"Why would I lie?" My voice rises in pitch. "You're fucking annoying."

I glimpse a fleeting trace of hurt in his expression, but it disappears so swiftly I might well have imagined it. He switches off the monitor and returns to his spot on the trunk.

"I assume you'd like to read the book, Silverbirch, so I suggest keeping it civil as you'll need my help with translation." He looks angelic as he smiles. "Or have you learned how to read Turkish?"

"Well, you're either confused, or blinded by your over-confidence, because it's already in English."

"What do you mean?" Leon sounds taken aback. He reaches out for the book, and our fingers brush. A warmth travels up my arm, straight to my heart. I flinch, inadvertently letting go of the journal.

"It's in English," I mumble as he cradles the book in his hands like it's the most fragile thing on the earth. "I obviously couldn't have read the title, if it was in Turkish."

"I see." Leon is lost in his thoughts. "And here I am, reading the title in Turkish. *Müneccimbaşı Sufi Çelebi'nin Gizemli Olaylar Seyahatnamesi: En Muamma Lanetleri Bozmak için bir Rehber.* But I believe you."

I lean over to check, but the title hasn't changed for me. Still the same letters: *Müneccimbaşı Sufi Chelebi's Journals of Mystical Phenomena: A Guide to Breaking the Most Enigmatic Curses.*

"What does that mean?" I ask, poking my finger at the word *Müneccimbaşı.*

"It's his title," Leon explains. "It means the chief of the seers. Sufi Chelebi served as the sultan's advisor—until he . . . lost his mind while writing this journal."

"And what did he journal about that was so special?" I frown, staring down at the book. "It looks like an ordinary old thing."

"Hate to repeat myself, but not everything is as it seems, Silverbirch." Leon raises the book. "This is the most prominent book for seers of my kind—the curse-breakers—and revealed only to those deemed worthy."

The word *curse-breaker* makes me forget the book for a moment, and Leon's bossy advice. I wish I could trust him, but I still feel uneasy looking at his face, and I don't want to feel hopeful when I can barely believe a word he says.

Hope, Munu whispers in my head, *is a malfunction.*

I'm frightened to believe there may be a way to break the curse and save my heart and be just . . . normal.

"You haven't got a clue about any of this, have you?" Leon mutters. "The curses, the craft of seers, the Otherside, or the Hidden even. Yet, Sufi Chelebi's wisdom chooses you, despite your obliviousness to its significance."

I can't believe how he reads me so easily, and how much he knows when I don't. But there is something he doesn't know about me. *Of course, a guide to break curses would appear for me,* I want to yell at him, *it's me who's cursed, not you!* But I can't let him know that, and I swallow all the words on the tip of my tongue, which only serves to make me angrier.

"You're the most arrogant and pretentious person I've ever had the displeasure to meet." I take a deep breath to calm down.

"I've been watching you for over a week now." Leon grins, clearly enjoying my misery. "Enough to figure out you're the most stubborn and grumpy girl *I've* ever had the pleasure to meet."

"So you admit you've been watching me." I snatch the journal from his hands.

Leon shrugs. "It's part of my job."

Of course, I scold myself. *Why else would he be interested in me?*

"A job you're not so good at, given I managed to find your beloved book before you did," I muse and he purses his lips, eyes fixed on the book as my fingers fumble over the cover.

"This is the original copy," Leon says. "The only compilation of Sufi Chelebi's three books, where he famously documented the three curses he worked on."

Three curses. A shiver runs down my spine. I know I'm not the only soul who had the misfortune to carry a curse. Still, hearing about other curses—broken curses—unnerves me.

"Are you going to open it, or shall I?"

I glance down at the book, and delicately flip to the first page. The parchment is aged, its yellowed surface marred by stains. I start by reading the foreword aloud, intent on demonstrating to Leon that the text is indeed in English.

My rare and most fortunate reader,

Our world revolves under the watchful gaze of the sun and stars, cruel and merciful, with night surrendering to day in an unending rhythm and darkness bowing to light. Perhaps you've already uncovered the wisdom that all of this is a magnificent creation, orchestrated by divine hands. Yet, even the most skilful of designers can make errors. It is the mistakes of a flawless and eternal universe that my journals investigate. Perhaps it is our imperfection as mortals, or the insatiable desires that weave complexity into our existence, that release curses to drift among us. And seldom does a curse burden a single soul alone; its tendrils spread far and wide. This intricate web of afflictions is what makes the task of curse-breaking so fulfilling.

I have dedicated my life to finding traces left by curses and their connections with the Hidden. This pursuit of unearthing their legacies has been the very essence of my life's work. This tome serves as a testament to unraveling the enigmatic curses and mysterious phenomena that have plagued individuals through the centuries. It is my fervent hope that my endeavors will illuminate the path of fellow seers who traverse shadows like mine, or serve a cure to those encumbered by plights, seeking a way out.

But I caution you now, dear reader, to tread carefully and turn away if you lack the fortitude for what lies within, for one will not be able to stop seeking the truth once the poison to know more invades your heart, and these tales have the power to bend your perception if you do not possess the right eyes to see.

My heart sinks with this ominous introduction as the harsh reality of the situation hits me.

"He certainly has a flair for drama, doesn't he?" I try to make my voice sound light.

Silent, Leon lowers himself to a crouch, drawn to the book sprawled open on my lap. There's an intensity in his posture, a magnetic pull, a need to bridge the gap between himself and the pages. His eyes devour the words as if he's on the brink of diving headfirst into its depths.

"Can you just break . . . any kind of curse?" I turn my attention back to the tome. It's the perfect excuse to avoid Leon's scrutiny. "Perhaps some curses aren't meant to be broken?"

Leon lifts an eyebrow. "Why do you want to know?"

For a moment his eyes betray a hint of longing, the kind that dwells in someone who carries a burden. Perhaps, I think, if we find the courage to show each other our scars and secrets, we may find solace. But I avert my gaze, frightened, and he responds only with a subtle clearing of his throat.

"Silverbirch." His voice is smooth as thick hot chocolate, his beauty makes it difficult to concentrate. "I've been searching for this journal for the last eighteen months. I scanned every corner of this island. I tried sleeping here, alone in this cold dungeon of an office. I tried hunger and thirst, I tried bathing in the sea in the moonlight, and I even drank nothing but salt water till I vomited up my guts. I've tried every form of suffering. But nothing brought me the book until you did."

I'm caught off-guard at this confession, but I resist the urge to ask how drinking salt water or fasting would help to locate the book. "You really couldn't find it?"

"Obviously not," he replies with frustration. "Do you think I live here in this chaos and endure this hopeless job for no reason? This book is the key to solving the mystery of the curse linked to this tower, and if I become the person to uncover it, especially at this young age, then I'll make a name for myself. I'll earn success. Respect. Power."

"Right." Recalling Munu's words about seers and their plans, it dawns on me that Leon's obsession with me—or rather with Munu—may be because he considers us rivals in his quest for this journal. "And this tome consists of three sections, did you say?"

He nods. "The first book is rumored to be named *The Book of Revenge* and it's a case Sufi Chelebi documented in a village called Tirnava."

I flick through until we see the title, *The Book of Revenge: The Plight of the Tirnava Villagers*. There are illustrations between handwritten pages. Some depict crying people, a cemetery with an open grave. I keep flicking through without daring to read the text.

"The second part is *The Book of Betrayal*."

"Or, *The Creeping Curse of the Serpent Queen*," I say, running my fingertips over the heading.

Leon shifts closer for a clearer glimpse of the section. As he reaches to turn the page, my hand edges against his again, sending a tremor through me. We both recoil and I rush through the pages, seeking distraction from the whirlwind of emotions flooding through my chest by focusing instead on the ominous illustrations.

"The last part is the one that cost the great Sufi Chelebi his skills," Leon says, his voice hoarse with ambition. "The one that drove him to madness. It's called *The—*"

"*The Book of Heartbreak*," I utter the words just as they form on Leon's lips. My heart tightens upon the final word. *Heartbreak*.

"Or, *A Convergence with the Cursed Maiden of Konstantiniyye*," Leon finishes.

The next page, adorned with an illustration of the maiden, absorbs him.

"No way," he exhales in disbelief. His shock startles me and at first glance, I don't understand the significance of what he's seeing. It's only a hand-drawn portrait, with Sufi Chelebi's neat handwriting declaring her to be "Theodora of the House Doukas, The Cursed Maiden of Konstantiniyye."

A vibrant figure, standing beneath a sky of gold, overlooking the azure sea, her hair flowing freely on her shoulders. Behind her is the Maiden's Tower.

A pendant dangles delicately above the neckline of her dark green dress, an evil eye in a gold circle. An exact replica of my own necklace. I barely stop myself from clutching it. *A coincidence*, I tell myself. Evil eyes are a common symbol in history. But then my gaze travels further up, tracing the image to a face I know too well.

Fuck. I gasp, breathless.

Because the maiden, Theodora, bears an uncanny resemblance to me.

Communication is classified as Top Secret.
Circulation strictly limited to correspondents.
Note: This email will destroy itself once read without minding if
you read it carefully or not.

Subject: Re: Old friends Make the Worst Enemies

Date: 23 July 2025
From: Five the Fifth, Angel of Death, Field Operations, Mortal Termination and Transition, Mortal Affairs Commission
To: Nine the Ninth, Senior Angel of Fate, Fate Adjustment Bureau, Mortal Affairs Commission

My old friend Nine,

I took the liberty of changing the subject line—your original wasn't to my liking. Unlike yours, this email is not a warning, but a gentle reminder from a caring friend.

Last I checked, Prayer Response and Fulfillment fell under the Fate Adjustment Bureau. Didn't we all undergo the same comprehensive training on the mechanics of the Mortal Affairs Commission? It's *your* responsibility to receive the prayers, deal with them, and prevent curses from taking root. It's *your* neglect that allows them to fester like fallen fruit.

So my dearest, forsaken mortals, consumed by vengeance and fragility, cast curses because of **you**.

Yet there I was, entangled in your fiasco all those years ago in Konstantiniyye, in my supreme mercy and preventive measures, saving you from the archangels' wrath when you were just an inexperienced Curse Remediation Officer. It's devastating enough that I never received so much as a thank-you card for my help, but now, reading your baseless threats dims the light of my halo.

Tell me, Nine: why should I shoulder the blame because you chose to follow my "suggestion" to alter the records? Or if you hadn't, would you have preferred the disgrace of your department's worst Centennial Performance Report for failing to prevent such a malicious curse? Surely, that would have cost you those cherished promotions.

And about that mortal girl. I've granted her a few resurrections. So what? You are of Fate. I am of Death. It's my prerogative to decide when and how to terminate her. So calm your trembling wings and **stop scheming against my strategies**.

As for my little "illegal helper . . ." I searched my inbox but can't find a trace of complaint about her from your department. She recently assisted you in places like Lawang Sewu, the Kusovnikov House and Himachal Pradesh. Need I remind you of the countless other places she's lent a hand? I can gladly send a detailed report if you're feeling nostalgic. You seem to be confused about who owes whom, but let's be clear, dear friend: it's you who is indebted.

So—**the ethereal is mine**. I am her boss. I decide her fate, not you or some busybody cherub who should be wiping the dust off the divine archives instead of writing emails.

Last but not the least: stop being paranoid. Have your new duties worn down your courage? Use logic if you have any left. The archangels couldn't care less about the Mortal Affairs Commission as long as the rock keeps rotating. Do you honestly believe they'd read a cherub's email? And if you're afraid of our Boss Almighty . . . Ask yourself: how would a cherub ever warrant the attention of They Whom Should Not be Concerned, when our divine organization is drowning in its own busyness? Remember, no one has ever seen Them. No emails, no meetings—not even the archangels have the privilege. All their orders arrive through the fax machine.

If you're really worried about that nuisance, offer him a back-office role within the Bureau where you can keep him under your thumb; being a creature of the lowest rank, he'll surely accept.

If that doesn't stop him from hitting the keyboard, you can send him on a mission to Hell, where—Our Boss Almighty forbid—something fatal might befall him.

Be good, old friend. Be creative. And, above all, be grateful to have me as an ally.

Five the Fifth

CHAPTER ELEVEN

The protocols governing the mystic conclave renowned among those who possess the pure eye as "the Hidden" are intricate. Nevertheless, through my extensive interactions with a multitude of seers throughout Anatolia, I have managed to unravel their involvement in certain events. The most plausible explanations of many enigmas lie in their intervention. But the reasons that these entities, whose powers transcend the ordinary bounds of human capability, choose to keep the countless curses in our world remains a mystery.

Excerpt from *The Book of Betrayal, Müneccimbaşı Sufi Chelebi's Journals of Mystical Phenomena*

When we finally emerge from the tower, the intensity of the sun has waned. After finding my own face looking back at me from *The Book of Heartbreak*, a sense of suffocation overtook me. I stumbled, unable even to walk, and was forced to take Leon's arm as we climbed the stairs after leaving the book locked in a drawer in his office.

Now I can breathe again, but the dread remains on my chest. I'm fully aware that my arm still clings to Leon's. But unlike me, he doesn't seem bothered by our physical closeness; he's too distracted to notice.

"I think," he says, with furrowed brow, "you need to tell me why you're here."

It hurts my pride to admit how perplexed I am, when he sounds so sure of himself. It's almost my turn to tell him, "Not everything is as it seems, Leon Dumanoğlu," but I can't find the energy to speak.

I refrain from sharing the eerie feeling of déjà vu I felt upon arriving at the tower. I don't trust Leon—what am I to him, if not another enigma to solve? A job. A tool he can use to have more power in his world.

I quiver as I recall Munu's warnings. He'll unearth the curse and seek ways to turn it to his benefit.

"Are you okay, Silverbirch?" Leon's voice is soft as velvet beneath the sound of the gulls. Since we revealed the maiden's image, he looks at me . . . differently.

Don't let him fool you, Munu murmurs in my head again. *He's an arrogant, cocky, power-hungry seer. He will explode your heart.*

"Maybe," I admit, though my voice betrays me. The wind catches my hair, sending it billowing over my shoulders. What's the point in pretending? "Not really."

Why would the maiden, Theodora of House Doukas, bear such a resemblance to me? And if Theodora really was cursed, did she also die every time her heart was broken? My head pounds with questions, as if I'm being bludgeoned with them, but the worst thing is that Leon appears to be convinced now that I'm somehow linked to this book.

It doesn't make sense. The room was dimly lit, and it was just a drawing. Perhaps, if I go back and look at it, Theodora won't look so much like me.

"I have a theory, if you want to hear it." Leon leads me to a bench facing the sea. Back in his office, he insisted on keeping the book. Considering his almost two-year quest for it, and the queasiness it induced in me, I had no choice but to accept.

"Fine," I mumble as we take our seats. I gently withdraw myself from Leon's radius, only to immediately yearn to reconnect.

Below us, the waves lap gently against the rocks, their rhythm soothing as a lullaby.

I take the opportunity to study Leon's profile: the curve of his nose, his defined jawline. And, as I study him, I feel my heart shift to a strange rhythm. I redirect my focus to the endless motion of the waves.

"You are somehow linked to the maiden and you want to know how to break curses." He leans toward me, his shoulder brushing mine. It feels too intimate to feel the warmth of his skin, still I don't shrink away. Perhaps I'm too paralyzed. Perhaps I don't want to. "You're *different*. Certainly not as ordinary as you claim to be. I can feel it. Maybe one of your parents had the pure eye?"

Of course I'm different, my heart is cursed.

"I don't think I have seers in my lineage." I clear my throat. "And there's nothing different about me. I'm a perfectly normal person."

I wish.

"The issue is, my intuition is rarely wrong," Leon says. He looks at me like I'm a puzzle he's determined to solve, and I can't stand it. The best way to make him believe a lie is to tell him the truth, I decide. At least parts of it.

"You were right," I tell him. "I know nothing about your craft, or the significance of it. I have no idea why this book decided to appear for me. I have nothing to do with any missions from the Otherside. I just want to . . . survive Istanbul." *It's not a lie,* I reassure myself.

"And what about your sassy little Tinkerbell?"

"Munu is my guardian. She was always here, since I was very little, so I'm not really sure why you're so obsessed with her permit."

He considers my confession.

"That book." I attempt to change the subject. "*The Book of Heartbreak.* You said it was the end of the great Sufi Chelebi. What happened to him?"

"Well, I have to read it, to be sure. But it's rumored that after meeting the maiden to end her curse, Sufi Chelebi made the mistake of falling in love with her. She was dead, and he was alive. It rendered him mad."

"Because he fell in love?"

"With the wrong person." Leon nods. "Love can be dangerous for seers. If you fall for someone who you can't have, or who wouldn't love you back, it can become an obsession, clouding the pure eye. Like poor Chelebi, triggering his own downfall . . . Just because he couldn't command his heart."

"Fucking hell," I gasp. I can't see how any of this relates to me, yet the fact that Sufi Chelebi was in love with a girl who could be my twin leaves me oddly unnerved, as does Leon's seeming composure as he so blithely relates Sufi Chelebi's journey to insanity. As if the guy ended up with a speeding ticket or an upset stomach, and not the ultimate catastrophe.

"Do seers often go mad?" I inquire cautiously. "You describe it like an occupational hazard."

He weighs my question, as if trying to decide whether I'm mocking him or not. "Depends how good you are," he says, after a short pause. "But yes, you could say that. Seers who have visions both asleep and awake are more prone to insanity. Just like Sufi Chelebi . . . and me."

I'm dying to learn more, but I hold my tongue. *It's none of your business, Sare,* I tell myself.

"Anyway—" He tucks a curl behind his ear. "Before his pure eye abandoned him, Sufi documented the phenomenon of certain recurring curses, where a mortal is doomed to be reborn repeatedly, each time bearing the same misfortunes. And my theory is . . . Well . . . If Theodora looks like you, then maybe she *is* you . . . Or rather, you were—"

"You think I'm the maiden?" I interrupt, bewildered. "Like . . . a reincarnation?!"

"Not an elegant way to describe it," he grunts. "But roughly, yes."

"Seriously?" A brittle laugh escapes me. "That's your theory—that I'm some long-dead girl reborn?"

"Why else would the book reveal itself to you and not to me?" His tone carries a tinge of arrogance.

"Well, perhaps it's because you're shit at your job," I retort with a scowl. "Especially considering your far-fetched theories. Lucky, I'd say, as it means you won't go mad if you fall in love."

A gull swoops past Leon, alarmingly close. I flinch, yet he remains unfazed, both by the near miss of the wings and my biting remarks. "I need to consult Grey," he says.

"Who's Grey?" I feel encouraged by how. Unlike Munu, Leon speaks of the Otherside freely. "Are they your boss?"

"Does your friend have a boss, then? Who is it?" Leon seizes the opportunity to strike at me with another question.

I'm quick to reply, "I don't know."

The cheeky bastard grins. "Funny how you describe your relationship with your ethereal as a friendship, yet your trusted *friend* doesn't bother telling you who she works for." Leon's lopsided smile sends my thoughts reeling. How can he be so attractive and annoying at the same time?

"It's forbidden to speak of them," I assert, folding my arms.

"It's forbidden to speak their true titles, or their core intentions," he says, his voice laced with playful mockery. "But clever clues can paint vivid pictures, don't you think, Silverbirch? You seem bright enough." He leans in, his minty breath carried on his whisper, causing my cheeks to glow at our closeness. "Imagine—who could your friend be aligned with, if she's accusing me of consorting with their eternal rivals, the devils. It brings to mind thoughts of halos . . . and wings . . . doesn't it?"

I suck in the air as shock floods over me like a tide.

Halos. Wings. Beings that forge fate and destiny and death.

How foolish I've been all these years, assuming that Munu belonged to a gang of fairy godmothers in strange place called the Otherside, disregarding all of her remarks about her boss being in the heavens. Leon even mentioned them that first day we met—and I just ignored him. "No . . ."

"Yes," Leon says.

"Angels?" I can barely breathe.

"Precisely," Leon confirms with a nod. "Mortals or ethereals usually can't speak of them, as most will be notified when they're spoken about. Think of it like a tracker app on your phone. Hence 'the Hidden.' But if you write about them, they can't trace you. So your friend, I'm sure, had plenty of chances to pass you information."

I mull over his claim. Munu, my Munu, has served divine beings who supposedly stand for justice and mercy all along? But why would she deliberately pass up the chance to tell me more about them—or what they have to do with my curse? The thought of her boss and the punishments she's constantly threatened with churns in my stomach like sour milk.

"And how come you can speak so freely?" I lean back, exhausted by my confusion.

"Because I'm blessed." Leon straightens on the bench. "I proved my worth to Grey, and he's given me his blessing."

"This Grey," I fumble, "is he an angel?"

Leon nods, as if this revelation is nothing. "Yes. And he's informed me that there's some sort of discrepancy going on with records—your flamboyant friend may be a victim of trafficking."

"Trafficking?" I roll my eyes. "Why would angels traffic dead people?"

He leans closer. Again, too close.

"The ways of the Hidden may seem complex from afar," he whispers. "But they are surprisingly mundane. They're like a big corporation, overseeing our world. They may be holding your friend captive, without granting her admission into the Heavens or Hell, and utilizing her for the dirty work they're unwilling to perform themselves. Running errands. Rectifying errors. Handling perilous and labor-intensive endeavors. Stuff like that."

Silently, I tally the all the times Munu has grumbled about being forced into unwanted duties. I recall her anxiety about her boss and the potential and very dire consequences should she ever attempt defiance. And the pervasive secrecy of it all. Could Leon be telling the truth?

After all, he's divulged secrets Munu kept from me. Munu, who always accuses Leon of lying.

"Even if any of this is true," I say eventually, remembering the real reason that I came to the island this morning—no matter what Munu's kept from me, she's mine and I need to protect her. "Why does it matter to you? Leave Munu alone, okay? She's got nothing to do with your book."

"I mean no harm to her," Leon reassures me. The honey-colored streaks in his dark brown eyes flash like distant nebulae. "As long as I get to keep the book, I'm good."

"Fine," I mutter through clenched teeth.

"But if she's a victim," Leon insists, "she needs to be rescued. And—" He stalls as he looks at me, reading the disbelief on my face, but then rallies. "The book chose you for a reason, Silverbirch. Do not ignore it. Do not be afraid to face who you really are."

"I have to go." I rise from the bench, cradling my bag to my chest, suddenly feeling overwhelmed and determined to catch the next boat before it leaves for the mainland. Angels. Curses. It's hard to wrap my head around it—how Munu could be tied to something so far beyond my wildest guess. I won't know for sure until I speak to her.

"I know you're withholding something." Leon's words are edged with a raw intensity that sounds quite unlike him. "There's something going on with you. Normal people's faces don't grace artifacts like *The Book of Heartbreak*."

"It's a coincidence." I shake my head, thinking of his far-fetched theory about the maiden and me. It's too much; it's all too much. "It's not even a photograph, just some stupid doodle."

"Stop being so stubborn and admit that I can help."

I back away. "I don't need help." I never needed it. Never expected it.

He can't help me, I tell myself as I trace my steps back to the dock. *No one can.*

The sun lies low on the horizon when I finally reach home. The memories of Sufi Chelebi's journal and *The Book of Heartbreak* are distant and dreamlike as I kick off my shoes inside the cool house.

Just because some old Ottoman—one who ended up in the jaws of madness—sketched a girl who likely resembles countless other girls, including myself, doesn't mean I'm her reincarnation. Surely I'd remember being born in another life? I comfort myself with these thoughts as I climb the stairs, but as I push open my bedroom door, Böcek streaks past me like a dart, startling me into a jump. The little intruder stares back with unblinking eyes before vanishing into the shadows of the hallway. I swear this cat hates me. Heart racing, I shut the door behind me, dismissing Leon's theory with it.

But what remains, like the sting of a wasp on my skin, is the identity of Munu's boss, and all the information she withheld from me. Why didn't she tell me? Did she think I'd hire a billboard and tell the world that angels are real if she shared her secret with me? Why didn't she trust me? Who would I even spill my guts to about my spirit guide working for angels?

Munu must have an explanation, I repeat to myself. I need to give her a chance to explain. With a pang of nervousness, I grip my necklace and summon her. I don't have much hope considering how busy she's been the last week but, surprisingly, only minutes later, I hear the crack and pop of her arrival.

"Canim," she says, chest heaving. "Is everything okay? Did that devil harm you?"

I gaze at her, relieved but wondering. *Does she know I was with Leon?*

I try to maintain my composure. "Why wouldn't I be okay?"

Munu simply shrugs, drifting around me, as if she's examining I'm all in one piece. Silence is never a good sign with her.

"Are things okay at your end?" I ask, Leon's words still ringing in my ears. "With your *boss*?"

"Barely." Munu fidgets as she settles upon the chaise longue.

"Have you heard of someone called Sufi Chelebi?" I sink onto the bed opposite her. "I searched online, but couldn't find anything about him."

"Where did you hear that name?" Munu straightens, her expression wary.

"I was with Leon today." I decide to be honest. I need to set an example, if I'm expecting the same from her. "I went to the tower and—"

"Sare Sıla Silverbirch!" Munu flits up from her seat, closing the distance between us in a flash. "You met with that *devil* on that forsaken island? How did he manage to lure you there? I told you to stay away from him!"

"It was my decision to go," I emphasize each word. "I wanted to warn him not to meddle with us."

"You shouldn't be risking yourself with his company, when you're on the verge of finally being free of the curse. You're so close to freedom, Sare. Don't blow it now."

Freedom. I wish I could share Munu's enthusiasm for losing the ability to love. Despite the allure of a life without heartbreaks, the knowledge that I'll soon be heartless fills me with sorrow. Would I even be the same person? Perhaps I'll become a cruel, cold version of myself, like Muzaffer, who seems to have forbidden smiling and compassion in his life.

"Why exactly *am* I cursed?" I inquire, hiding my face behind the canopy. I feel foolish for not questioning the origin of the curse properly before. I was too young when I exhausted all my curiosity with Munu, and while her answers were never satisfying, they became the foundation of our bond—a shield to protect me from the worst. "The less you know, the safer you are," she would say, and I believed her. At least until I read the words: *A Guide to Breaking the Most Enigmatic Curses.*

How can I remain in the dark when there's even the tiniest speck of hope of breaking this curse?

"Where's all this coming from?" Munu snaps. "Why are you suddenly bombarding me with questions?"

"What's wrong with wanting to know?" I challenge her. "It's not like I'm going to tell anyone. I don't even have a friend to talk to."

"Something's happened." Munu's voice trembles as she lands on a book stack on the bedside table. "It bothers you. Tell me, what misfortune has befallen us this time? What ill wishes has that devil whispered to you?"

"I—" I hesitate. "I happened to find the journals of a seer called Sufi Chelebi. It's an ancient, magical book, and looks like Leon was after it. But what's more important is that I—There was a girl on one page . . ." My voice wavers, disbelief threading through my words. "It had this whole section about the Maiden's Tower—*The Book of Heartbreak.* Heartbreak, of all names! And the maiden, Theodora, she looked like me. She even wore the same pendant—" I grasp at the evil eye that sits on my chest.

"Theodora?" Munu stops me abruptly.

"Do you know her?" My question comes out like a plea.

Munu shakes her head as she begins to shrink.

In the dimly lit bedroom, the fading light of the sunset casts long shadows across the pink canopy. I would be a fool to believe Munu any more.

"Theodora of House Doukas," I repeat the maiden's name. "Sufi Chelebi fell in love with her . . . spirit."

"Nonsense!" Munu shrieks as she keeps getting smaller. "It's a ploy to mess with you, and you walked straight into the seer's trap. I told you: you shouldn't have gone to that wicked tower. You shouldn't have come to Istanbul. This place is teeming with his kind and their malevolent devices. Rats running rampage. Seeding ideas into your head. Where is this treacherous book? Give it to me!"

"I left it in the tower," I say defiantly. "With Leon."

"You're friends with him now?" Munu pouts. "Let me remind you once again: seers cannot be trusted. Love moves in silence, canim. A boy like him can slip into your heart as fast as a dagger. It won't bleed at first. Not until he pulls it away—"

"I told you, he won't break my heart," I snap. "Besides, what do you know about love?"

"I know enough," Munu whispers. "Love makes you rot. Breaks you into a million pieces. You can assemble yourself again, but you'll never be the same."

The urge to know more about Munu's mortal life rages on, making me forget my own troubles. "So you fell in love, then?"

"Once," she whispers. "And it brought me nothing but sorrow."

"*You* loved someone?" I'm taken aback by Munu's confession. "Who?"

"It's been so long." Munu smiles. "His name needs to remain forgotten. But the heartbreak is here with me. Anyway—" she shakes her head—"I'm not here to tell my life story. It's you we should be talking about. You're the one who matters. Not me."

"But—"

"You must have utmost caution, canim. The devil named Leon is a curse-breaker, and he will pester you. You can't afford to tell him of the curse! I'll sense it if you did, for there are ways to alert me to its utterance, but I still fear he may unravel your secret some other way. There are ways to learn things without hearing them. I fear . . . of those."

"If there are such ways . . ." I hesitate, recalling Leon's reveal about the nature of Munu's bosses, "why didn't you once try to explain who you're working for? It wasn't fun to hear it from Leon."

"W-what?" Munu stutters. "What do you mean?"

"You work for angels, don't you?"

I expect her to cackle, call it rubbish, brush me off. But she doesn't.

"What?" Munu's face drains of color, and she flies off the chaise longue, away from me.

"I get it, you can't speak about it. But Leon said these *angels* can't trace writing." I feel sad all of a sudden. Exhausted from everything I've uncovered, and the ambiguity of who to trust. "I asked you countless times and you had every chance to explain. But you never once made the effort to reveal anything to me. Am I not trustworthy enough, after everything we've been through together?"

My heartbeats pick a dangerous rhythm.

Rule number two, I recite. *Channel sorrow into rage.*

Rage.

I don't have to work hard. The anger is raw, simmering. I prepare myself to ask Munu why, since my arrival in Istanbul, my problems have only multiplied and she's been increasingly absent, leaving me alone to navigate the challenges without offering any help. Or why she's so against the idea of breaking the curse. What if there's a chance—a sliver of hope—that I could become normal? Why doesn't she care?

But, seeing how distressed Munu is and how my heart drums in my chest, I force myself to keep my mouth shut and just pretend to be okay—as I always do. Munu is already losing her shit about Leon, and I can't add to her troubles. Surely, there will be solid reasons behind this secrecy. Munu would never betray me. Everyone else may pose a threat to my heart, but she can't be one of them.

"Sare," Munu falters, fluttering in the air again, as though searching for a way to escape my questions. "My boss and I—we have a history that binds me to him. We have . . . a contract. It's not like you think. I'm not hiding anything from you. I'm bound to be loyal."

"So it's true?" I drop my voice to a whisper. "Your boss is an . . . angel?"

Munu glides down softly beside me and gives one sharp nod.

"And you're sure you never heard of a Theodora?" I ask. "She was cursed too."

"That name doesn't ring a bell." Munu whips her head. "Now, don't see that boy again. He may be hot, I get it. But he's not a mere eighteen-year-old with whom you can have a summer fling. I'm worried you'll develop feelings for him, Sare. People like him . . . They use you. They ruin everything."

"You think—" I cut her off, a bit louder than I intended. Then I feel it again. The subtle fluttering. Instinctively, my hand travels to my chest, pressing against my heart as if to stop it, like placing a palm over a mouth to hush a whisper. I start again. "You think I'm falling for a boy I just met, and I'm so unlovable that he'll be the end of me?"

"No, Sare," Munu whispers. "I don't mean it like that."

"You're an idiot if you think he's what I care about," I burst out, ignoring the fluttering in my chest. "It's the book! It's the claim—the *hope* of breaking this bloody curse once and for all that I'm after. Not Leon."

Rule number two, I repeat. *Be angry, Sare. You have every reason.*

"You're the one who never tells me anything," I press on. "You're the one who keeps me in the dark. Perhaps that's why you think Leon is a trickster or a con artist—because you recognize yourself in him."

I take a deep breath, embracing my anger like a crisp fire on a cold night.

The fluttering dies a slow death in my chest.

"You used to be grateful, canim. Not everyone with a deadly curse is given so many blessings to stay alive." Munu, my sole confidante all these years, rises from the sheets, her expression fraught with disappointment. "The boy has poisoned your mind. He's already turning you against me. He seeks to drive us apart. He will fail you. That's what people like him do. Please, stop listening to him before it's too late."

"What if I don't?" I'm sick of being ordered around. Sick of knowing so little.

"Then I can't protect you, even from yourself," she says. "We're so close to your eighteenth. Once the curse takes away your heart, you will never experience sadness again. Don't you get it? *Love* is the true curse."

And with that, she departs with a loud crack, leaving me with a silence almost too hard to bear.

Munu's absence stretches over several days like a deliberate punishment, as if she intends to teach me a lesson by making me acutely aware of the void she leaves behind. The house brims with an oppressive silence and I swing between fretting over her safety and feeling enraged.

As if falling out with Munu cast a new curse on me, I can no longer find the courage to reach out to Leon, even though I thirst to read Sufi Chelebi's journals, to understand how one *can* break a curse, if such a thing really can be achieved.

The Maiden's Tower and the image of Theodora cast long, somber shadows over my days, even when I receive two invitations from Leon in writing, delivered by Azmi, who seems strangely thrilled that the most handsome boy in the neighborhood is seeking out my company.

"Looks like you have an admirer." He winks at me when he hands over the first note. I don't bother reading it.

When he brings the second note, he teases, "I can't tell if you're playing hard to get or just aren't interested."

Now accustomed to Azmi's over-friendliness, I stare dully at the white paper, at Leon's handwriting in silver ink.

I'll wait for you this evening. 6 p.m. by the docks. Please, Silverbirch. We need to talk. L.

"Azmi," I tell him in all seriousness as I crumple the note in my palm. "Please don't bring me any more notes. I know where to find him if I need to."

Guilt gnaws at me all afternoon as I wonder how long it'll be till Leon realizes that I won't show up. Still, I'm determined not to see him. A part of me is convinced that he won't lose sleep over being stood up, but another urges me to reach out, to give him a chance to unveil the mysteries of the Hidden and to dive into a book that promises a world where curses can be broken.

And *The Book of Heartbreak* . . . I can't forget about it. I dream of it, as if it's been written only for me. As if I really am Theodora. I dream of myself in the tower, with the book between my hands.

"Break the curse," the pages whisper. "But be careful—do not fall in love. Remember what happened to Sufi Chelebi."

The gleam of the gilded letters on the journal blinds me like a flash of lightning. Then, I remember Sufi's haunting foreword, cautioning his unfortunate reader of the unyielding thirst for truth his writing will provoke, or the danger of losing one's perception if they don't possess the necessary eyes.

I'm frightened—frightened of the thirst, frightened of my heart, that I lack the necessary insight.

And more than anything, I'm frightened of losing Munu.

A week into my seclusion, Leon shows up to the house. The afternoon's muted silence has driven me to the garden and I'm determined to distract myself with Mikhail Bulgakov's *Master and Margarita*, until the distinctive sound of Azmi's flip-flops slapping the ground interrupts my visit to Bolshevik Moscow.

"You have a visitor waiting inside," he announces with an amused expression, as he fans himself vigorously against the heat. "You told me to dismiss the notes, but not the writer, yes?"

I sigh, but still drag myself from my chair to follow Azmi reluctantly back inside the house.

In the foyer, Leon is even taller than I'd remembered, his hands casually tucked into his pockets in an attempt to appear at ease. But the clench of his jaw betrays his tension.

"I'm not used to being stood up, so I thought I'd come and be dismissed in person, as you're so eager to offer the experience." Leon's voice carries a mock hurt. "But if not, I need a word with you. In private, please."

"I'm not sure why you ever assumed I'd come," I retort. "Perhaps other girls run when you click your fingers, but I'm not one of them."

"Oh, you most certainly aren't." Leon's gaze drifts over my shoulder and his expression shifts, his hands slipping out of his pockets. I turn to see Muzaffer walking down the stairs to stand beneath the archway. As he draws near, to my relief, I realize he's getting ready to leave.

"May I take Sare out, Mr. Gümüşhuş?" Leon asks Muzaffer before anyone has the chance to speak. I roll my eyes. Why would Muzaffer have any say if Leon can talk with me or not?

Muzaffer seems to agree with me, as his glance darts between us. The wardrobe creaks as he retrieves his hat and walking stick. Böcek leaps down from the top of the wardrobe, landing soundlessly beside him. She stretches luxuriously, as if she's been lounging there all along, then winds herself around Muzaffer's ankles while he slips into his shoes without any acknowledgment of Leon's request.

"Don't stay out late," he grunts. "And don't let the cat out."

Leon and I linger on the steps leading to the modest front garden after Muzaffer departs.

"Your grandfather is quite the character," Leon remarks.

"Is that why you sought his permission to—" I pause, to mimic his voice—"take me out?"

He chuckles at my effort to copy him and proceeds toward the road. I find myself following.

"Just so you remember next time," I say, my voice taut with annoyance, "I make my own decisions. I don't need to be authorized to go out."

"Well, I can't guarantee a next time," he says. "I have a busy schedule."

There it is again, that arrogant grin.

When I throw him a glare, he puts his hands up defensively. "It's just respect for our elderly. He's our landlord, and your grandfather."

"I barely know him," I admit as we step outside the gate and onto the pavement. "We only met a month ago, after my mum died."

He doesn't respond for a while. A dog barks somewhere behind us, while a street vendor bellows in Turkish, as if trying to outdo the dog's noise.

"I'm sorry about your mum," Leon says at last, for once no mockery in his voice. "How did it happen—if it's not too painful to talk about?"

I inhale slowly, at a loss for words. It's the first time someone has asked about Mum, and all I've tried to do is leave her behind. A mother is hard to forget, but even harder to remember.

A motorbike roars past us.

"Careful." Leon yanks me back from the road and closer to him.

His touch makes me nervous, mostly because I notice how hard it is to be near him and stay focused.

"A car accident," I whisper, fixing my gaze on his worn-out t-shirt. "She was dead at the scene."

"I'm sorry." His grip tightens on my arms. I cannot bear him feeling sorry for me. I don't need his pity.

"I heard your mother's gone too," I blurt out, pulling away from him. "Azmi's been very chatty about you lately."

"My mama's been gone for quite some time," Leon shares. "I was thirteen when she told me I was old enough not to need her any more and that Harika, my aunt, would look after me from then on. She left the same day." He averts his gaze. "It was difficult, but I got used to it. I don't know if she's dead or alive. And I can't say I care any more."

"I'm sorry," I murmur, regretting my intrusion into such a personal matter, yet Leon seems unfazed. He looks so content and confident, it's impossible to imagine him abandoned or heartbroken.

"Don't be." He smiles. "I'm better off with Harika. We're kindred spirits."

"In what way?" The question escapes me before I can rein it in. I'm drawn to his story, eager to understand his heart. His flaws. Everything that makes him human.

"My mother didn't possess the pure eye," he says. "For those without the craft, living in close quarters with the pure sight can be overwhelming. The path to our vision is not an easy one."

We make our way across the road toward the seafront.

"Sometimes," Leon muses, "if you can't find a mother in someone else, you learn to be your own."

"I understand," I find myself responding, astonished that I'm in agreement with him for the first time. Yet how could I not be? My own mother was often absent, lost in her pursuits of men who'd never love her back, and seeking solace in alcohol. I suppose, like Leon's aunt, Munu was the constant in my life; my kindred spirit. In more ways than one. I sigh, reluctant to admit how much I'm missing her, how much hanging out with Leon feels like a betrayal of her.

If only she wasn't so adamant about not trusting Leon . . .

Around us, runners and walkers are dotted along the shore, a few cargo ships strewn on the surface of the sea like fat slugs.

"I finished reading the journal," Leon says as we walk along the seafront. My shoulder brushes against his arm. "I think you need to read it too. At least, *The Book of Heartbreak*. Perhaps you'll find something in it that will speak to you."

"Me?" I try to seem casual, but I'm compelled by his offer. I long to feel the weight of the journal in my hands once more, to flip through its yellowing pages and absorb its secrets. "Thanks, but I'll pass."

It's a ploy, Munu whispers in my head. *Don't walk into a seer's trap.*

We seek shade beneath a sprawling sycamore tree, standing face to face. Leon studies me; if he's disappointed with my response, he doesn't show it.

"Sufi Chelebi was no ordinary seer." He breaks the silence. "And you just stumbled upon his journal, as if it were a pebble on the shore. There must be a reason why the book has chosen you. Sufi Chelebi trusted you." Leon's eyes never leave mine as he speaks, each word more intoxicating than the last. "So I, too, will choose to trust you, Silverbirch. I will tell you the real reason why I'm investigating the maiden's curse."

I stand still, uncertain if Leon expects a response or not. A man who gracefully balances a tray stacked with bagels atop his head sashays past us. My throat dries as I wait to hear Leon's top-secret mission. His confession.

"The curse I'm investigating was instigated when a girl died in the Maiden's Tower during the reign of the Eastern Roman Empire, and then it was stopped during the Ottoman reign," Leon begins. "And now I've read Sufi Chelebi's journals, I know for certain that it was him who stopped the curse."

"So?" I frown. "What's left to investigate, then?"

"Because the very same curse is still active. Something has awakened it. Perhaps something far worse. It's why Grey tasked me to find Sufi Chelebi's book."

"How can you break a curse?" The breeze tousles my hair and obscures my vision. I no longer care if Leon senses that I'm cursed. I want to know. I need to learn if there's a way.

"It often involves sacrifice," Leon explains. "It's the easiest, most guaranteed way."

Even in the blazing heat, an icy dread creeps down my spine. *My heart*, I think, *is going to lose the ability to love once I'm eighteen.*

That is the sacrifice: my heart, me.

"But it's not the only way. There are . . . a few methods. According to the craft's doctrine," Leon continues. That wicked flame of hope sparks to life in my chest again. "Curses are glitches in the divine system. Once a glitch happens, it's usually followed by a string of unfortunate events—the thread keeps fraying. With no real understanding of emotions, the celestials assume people are simple and lowly beings, when in fact, we are complex and intelligent. Their inability to grasp our nature hinders their ability to resolve curses. They can't combat worldly problems as well as the seers can, and that makes individuals like me invaluable. We study the origins of a curse, and analyze the reasons behind it, to present a solution. Sometimes it's a chance to fix past mistakes. Heal the damage that the curse made," Leon explains. "In *The Book of Revenge*, Sufi explains how he unraveled the curse of Tirnava. A family of Christian villagers who lived in fear, disguised themselves as Muslims to escape persecution. Over time, their facade became their reality and they forgot their true heritage. Sufi Chelebi uncovered their hidden past and the curse that had plagued them for generations. With his help, they discovered that their true freedom lay in remembering, and the curse faded away once they did."

"Do you mean, they broke this curse . . . by recalling their heritage?" I give him a measured look, trying to gauge the truth. It's a lot to take in.

"It wasn't quite as simple as that, but, essentially, yes," Leon declares, retrieving a sherbet lemon from the pocket of his t-shirt and holding it out to me. When I extend my arm, he dangles it just out of my reach.

"Any curse can be broken, Silverbirch—" he flashes the lopsided smile I now know so well—"if you stop being snooty about the ways to investigate, and keep an open mind."

I finally manage to snatch the sweet from his grasp, my fingers brushing his in the process. I'm not sure why I even fight for it, as I already have an entire bag of the sweets at home.

"And what exactly do you gain by fixing these curses?" I pop the sweet into my mouth, the tartness biting my tongue.

Leon considers my question, his gaze lingering on my lips.

"Don't tell me you're acting out of the goodness of your heart." I frown, Munu's warnings about seers and their underlying motives ringing in my ears. "You want fame, or money. What else? Let me guess . . . Will you be Seer of the Month if you break a curse?"

He doesn't laugh, but at least he doesn't look offended.

"I won't lie to you, Silverbirch. Those play a part in motivating me. Just not in the way you imply." He smiles. "Do I want money? Yes. The museum pay is terrible. We rely on Harika's tarot readings, and, well, since she became menopausal, her pure eye has been going downhill. She's lost a lot of clients. I need to look after her, just like she cared for me. If I make a name in certain circles, we'll attract patrons, paying clients. Money would buy a house, and Harika wouldn't have to worry about paying rent or retiring. But it isn't the only reason. The craft gives me the chance to be a part of something that can change the world. The Hidden believe they know best for our destinies, but not all their actions are noble and fair. Not all of them are like Grey. Sometimes they see curses spawn and they don't lift a finger. They watch suffering and tragedies, as if what happens in the world doesn't matter. Take the tower, for instance. Something crooked and fundamentally wrong happened there, certainly involving the Hidden, and it's still plaguing unsuspecting mortals. Who will set it right, if not me? I can help those unfortunates. How can I turn my back on it?"

I'm speechless. There's no way these passionate, hopeful words can be an act. A wave of guilt washes over me for thinking him self-serving.

"The craft is a dying tradition." He wrinkles his nose, as if the admission pains him. "It's no surprise, given the long history of my kind being used and exploited by the Otherside, and even on this side. But with Grey, I'm lucky. He's a good partner. He treats me as an equal."

Not that I'm an expert on celestials, but judging by how they treat Munu, Leon's remarks come as a surprise.

"Working with him has already helped me. I've been given a training opportunity in Peru, where a great master lives near a city called Puerto Maldonado. Istanbul isn't the only city in the world with places like the Maiden's Tower. Curses spawn everywhere. Avebury Circle in Britain, Ponte Vecchio in Italy, Häringe Castle in Sweden . . . I want to uncover the tower's curse before I leave, and have that achievement under my belt before I travel the world and write my own journals like Sufi Chelebi did." His eyes lock on to mine. "With the fame that follows, perhaps I can become a master myself in a few years and inspire the next generation."

I focus on the honey-colored flecks in Leon's eyes, telling myself that I'm not attracted to him. *It's just the heat getting to me, the blazing afternoon.* Not his charming face nor his words that warm something in my chest, like a marshmallow toasting over a fire, or his heroic ambitions.

"Please," Leon says, filling the silence between us. "Read *The Book of Heartbreak*. Respect the craft and the book as it has respected you. Perhaps then—" his mouth curves into a smile again—"you may recall something of use. And, who knows, *you* might even be the one to break the curse. Imagine the lives you'll change. I'd be honored to document your great achievement."

"Fine." I shrug, feeling overwhelmed by a mixture of fear and curiosity. Despite my reservations, I can't deny the allure of Sufi Chelebi's companionship, especially in Munu's absence. "Bring it to me, and I'll do my best."

Communication is classified as Top Secret.
Circulation strictly limited to correspondents.

Subject: Urgent Retrieval of the Mortal Artifact

Date: 28 July 2025
From: Five the Fifth, Angel of Death, Field Operations, Mortal Termination and Transition, Mortal Affairs Commission
To: Grey the Compassionate, Associate Cherub, Curses and Malediction Archives, Worldly Index, Sacred Data Systems, Halotech Data & Integration Hub

Cherub,

It has come to my attention that one of your mortal acolytes possesses a valuable artifact—an old book of an Ottoman fool—exposing a potential security threat for certain historical cases. I urge you to promptly return this mortal item to me and thus prevent it from falling into the wrong hands.

This is a **strict** order.

Signed,
Five the Fifth

CHAPTER TWELVE

I caution you now, dear reader, to tread carefully and turn away if you lack the fortitude for what lies within, for one will not be able to stop seeking the truth once the poison to know more invades your heart.

Excerpt from *Müneccimbaşı Sufi Chelebi's Journals of Mystical Phenomena*

Perhaps due to the gravity of its contents, I find myself unable to delve straight into Sufi Chelebi's journal after Leon brings it to me.

"Keep it safe," Leon says, as he passes it to me just outside the front door the next day. "Guard it with your life, if you must."

"Why?" I frown, surprised. I'm used to Munu's flair for drama, but I never expected Leon to be this serious.

"There are . . . some interested parties who want to obtain it." One of Leon's eyebrows shoots up, though he does not go so far as to reveal the nature of these "parties," nor how dangerous they might be. And I don't ask, because my nerves wouldn't handle knowing the answer.

I wait until after the night prayer, when Istanbul and this house are most quiet, before snuggling into my bed with the book.

It's as if the tulle canopy will provide a barrier between me and the world once I immerse myself in Sufi's words. I'm one candle away from feeling like a medieval scholar as I turn the pages of the first section: *The Book of Revenge*.

It appears that the Ottoman village of Tirnava was haunted by a monstrous creature that always attacked at night. I recall what Leon had already explained, how Sufi Chelebi broke the curse by discovering the origin of its history. Chelebi seems certain that the beast seeks vengeance, unleashing its wrath upon the village by slaughtering livestock and demolishing silos, leaving only destruction rather than sustenance. A journal entry dated April 1497 catches my eye as I flick through the pages.

Each day I study the vengeful beast, I approach a curse most unsettling. A plight that ensnares the bearer, a relentless bond that even Death can't destroy. They're simply denied passage to the Otherside. They avoid Death, or perhaps, Death avoids them.

The bearer is reborn to suffer and thus to give suffering; a soul carrying the weight of an endless cycle. A loop of existence from which there is no escape. This fate defies the natural order.

As I pen these words, I can't help asking myself: what purpose does such eternal suffering serve? What lesson is to be learned from a punishment so enduring?

May Allah show mercy on those bound by such a fate, for they are trapped in an eternity of cruelty.

I pause. This is the concept of reincarnation—via a recurring curse, just as Leon said. The idea of being reborn with the same curse, repeatedly, is terrifying. More daunting are the drawings of the beast. I shiver and decide to skip the entire section. What follows is *The Book of Betrayal,* recounting the tale of Shahmaran, the noble Queen of Snakes, who befriended and trusted a young boy. Despite warnings from her serpent kin—"Humans live to regret their mistakes"—she welcomed the boy into her secret palace beneath

Konstantiniyye, loving him as if he were her own child. But the boy betrayed her for coin, revealing her palace's whereabouts to the sultan's men, who sought Shahmaran's scales for their priceless value. Hunted and cornered, Shahmaran cursed the boy and his descendants with endless, maddening nightmares in her final moments. Years later, to break the curse and save his children, the boy—now a man—was forced to sacrifice his own life—a heavy price for his cruelty. Sufi Chelebi notes this as a stark lesson in the tolls of betrayal.

At last, I move to where my true curiosity lies: *The Book of Heartbreak.*

Just like the other two sections, I'll skim through it, then return it to Leon, I tell myself as I sit up straight in bed, watching the shadows lingering on the wall. Perhaps Munu was right in saying that it's dangerous to explore the path of seers, that it's full of misery and sorrow. Learning of people trapped for an eternity, or imprisoned in towers, is enough to consider myself fortunate.

I take a deep breath and flick through the opening pages to see Theodora again.

There's no mistaking it—her face is eerily familiar. The arch of her brows, the shape of her eyes, the tilt of her jaw. Even the faint downturn at the corner of her lips. It's like staring at a reflection distorted by time.

Theodora of the House Doukas, the Cursed Maiden of Konstantiniyye.

I have searched countless times for House Doukas online over the last week, yet every bit of information I found was about their men. There were no resources about Theodora or any other women, as if they didn't exist. It infuriates me how history always ignores women, as if they didn't have names or importance.

Sufi Chelebi must be right when he wrote that once you taste the poison of knowledge, you cannot turn away. There's no other explanation for why I care so much, or why I begin properly reading *The Book of Heartbreak*, even when Munu's voice in my head screams at me to drop the book.

Ova Ceren

7th of June in the year 1502

Word reached me of a woman, Hürmüz Dükkânîzade, famously married seven times, with no man willing to be the eighth. It's claimed that Hürmüz's love is an ailment that weakens those who receive it until they succumb to a frail heart and find their eternal rest. Hürmüz is trapped in a cycle of perpetual mourning, and the folk have named her The Mourning Bride of Seven Husbands. This news stirred my spirit, for I am convinced this affliction is the very curse I have long pursued—an ancient malediction passed down through the ages. Though the family now bears the name Dükkânîzade, I have no doubt that this woman descends from the famed Byzantine Dokaz lineage.

This ancient curse that afflicts a noble family remains one of Konstantiniyye's most enduring mysteries. Legends recount different aspects of the tale, but I have yet to uncover the true origin. I sought an audience with Hürmüz immediately, and upon learning that the sultan's chief müneccim desired her presence, she received me in her parlor, her face hidden under a black veil, worn likely after the passing of her latest husband.

This unfortunate woman is unaware of the full nature of the curse she endures. An hour in the company of this poor soul confirmed beyond doubt that the family is indeed afflicted. Curiously, the curse appears to follow only the females. Hürmüz's sisters, though well-married, all perished young. Women, being more complex and enduring than men, present a different challenge in understanding. Though it is unclear if her sisters were also cursed, Hürmüz's descriptions of her mother—who died soon after being abandoned by her husband—lead me to believe that the curse indeed plagued her as well, taking the form of unrelenting heartbreak that stole the will to live.

But the most crucial revelation Hürmüz Dükkânîzade has bestowed upon me is the key to my puzzle. She experiences strange, recurring dreams— dreams that, though rare, could be recognized as echoes of ancestral memories, especially with a plague like hers, passed through generations.

She dreams of a tower, of all places—the miniature one that stands across from Üsküdar, famed as the Maiden's Tower. I believe it is therefore time for me to journey there. I, the great Sufi Chelebi, hope to be the one to dispel this curse once and for all.

12th of June in the year 1502

I journeyed to the Maiden's Tower today—a curious structure, once a Byzantine watchtower, now under our blessed Sultan Bayezid's reign. I rowed to the islet after the Cuma prayer, and even from afar I could sense the lingering presence of a curse. The air itself seemed thick with its remnants. Why haven't I set foot in this place before?

Before the boat had even made berth, a vision gripped me. I saw the figure of the maiden, casting herself from the upper balcony into the sea, as an earthquake tore through Konstantiniyye. An anguished cry reached my ears, spoken in a language foreign and forgotten, yet I knew this was no ordinary plea—it was a beddua, an ill-wish. Where there is a beddua, there lies the root of a curse.

But who was this unfortunate soul, and whom did she curse?

The vision clarified her tragic end between the angry waves but offered no further answers. I spent the remainder of the afternoon in deep meditation, yet no other visions revealed themselves to me.

Before I turn to the next page, my phone pings.

Is the book OK? Hope you are too? L

It's been so long since someone, other than an automatic notification from the NHS or school, messaged me. With a slightly annoying surge of excitement, I relish the fact that Leon is thinking of me enough to message me.

I write out the reply a few times, deleting and retyping the simplest words as if I learned the alphabet yesterday.

Book is still in one piece, and I've not been murdered. Thanks.

He replies with a laughing emoji, and I feel foolish for how much a single message can stir inside me. The silly smile lingering on my face quickly fades as I turn to the next section of the book.

17th of June in the year 1502

I did not give up on my pursuit to see the maiden, but alas, the tower brought no more visions to me.

Until finally, after two days of fasting, the maiden revealed herself to me in Çamlıca Hill as I was taking a nap. Reader, I am allured by her facade, and even though she perished several hundred years before I was even born, my poor soul craves to set eyes on her.

In my vision, I saw her face fresh as a cherry branch dressed by the spring, and her silent eyes were filled with tears.

"Azylios, my love," she pleaded, her voice trembling. "Is it you?"

I quickly scribbled the name onto some parchment, knowing full well I could not speak with the maiden. Even the greatest seers are bound by this truth—conversing with the dead risks sending them back to the realm of Death.

"You are not him," she said, her face falling with disappointment. "He has forsaken me, just as he abandoned Eudokia."

I hurriedly noted this new name.

"I am Theodora of House Doukas, cursed to love a man who will never be mine," the maiden declared, her voice heavy with sorrow. "I have committed grave errors, yet I have paid with far greater suffering. Please, noble one, end this torment."

At the name "Doukas," I dropped my quill with a thrill, transfixed by the desperate way she addressed me. What grave error have you made, angelic one? *I wondered, without the capacity to ask.*

The fragile thread I maintain between Theodora and myself won't allow me to speak, yet I burn to know. How could one believe such words from a being whose lips bore the tender softness of rose petals? How could such a delicate creature ever bring harm to another?

I pause, unable to stop the blush that creeps up my neck. My fingertips brush my lips to see if they in any way feel like petals; considering my likeness to Theodora, there's a good chance. I recall the way Leon's gaze lingered on my lips yesterday when he gave me the sherbet lemon, and then I have to pinch myself to stop getting distracted by Leon's opinion on my lips.

I refocus on the book. The dramatic, ancient ramblings of Sufi for Theodora—whom he calls his beloved maiden now—goes on and on. He mostly finds resemblances between her and the fauna of Istanbul, which eventually becomes bland and repetitive. I skip chunks of love declarations until, on 14th August of the same year, he has a significant entry.

My efforts have borne fruit. My beloved conversed with me again. A dream and two visions—but perhaps they were dreams too. It's hard to discern any more.

Theodora now persists in finding me regardless of where I am. Rustem Pasha cautions me, suggesting that her pursuit might be a form of haunting, as she now shadows my every step, refusing to be confined by the boundaries between our realms. But I am convinced that her presence is but a manifestation of love and affection.

Since the third day, I have forsaken all sustenance but water sweetened with a hint of sugar, for hunger brings a clarity to my eyes, and such starvation is a meager effort when I burn with the desire to remain with Theodora.

Beneath the largest fig tree inside the hallowed courtyard of Şemsi Pasha Mosque, I have made my abode. There, as I surrendered to the embrace of slumber, she appeared before me.

"I cursed my sister," Theodora confessed. "And in turn, she cursed me. All that has befallen me, I have rightly earned. Neither of us shall find peace. Help us, noble man."

"Where is your sister, my dove?" I wished to ask, but I sense she will depart if I speak. Some days, I worry that my search for a way to bind us supersedes my will to break her curse.

"Eudokia," Theodora said, as if she read my thoughts. "Will she ever forgive me?"

Reader, as my chronicles repeat within these pages, the fundamental laws of our realm present two ways for lifting a curse: through a sacrifice deemed worthy, or by rectifying misdeeds that ensnared those it initially entangled.

Why did these sisters curse each other? What error did they commit? Without understanding the nature of their wrongdoing, I cannot hope to correct it. The notion of sacrifice looms as a possible means to break the curse. I contemplate whether my humble soul might serve as a fitting offering to end their suffering. I confided in Rüstem Pasha, and he declared that I have lost my senses. But I cannot sit and wait while Theodora suffers for an eternity.

Perhaps I have weakened. Slumber overtakes me in Theodora's absence, and light returns with her arrival. It dawns on me that perhaps it is I who ventures forth in search of her, rather than her coming to me.

I pause at this entry. My heartbeats frantically, as if Theodora herself has materialized before my eyes.

I'm unsure what to make of it all. The book rests against the bedding, as if it's grown in size since I started reading it. It has now proved the desperate warning of its foreword, which I fear I have taken too lightly.

I feel the urgent desire to summon Munu, to share everything I've read, but I'm still angry with her, and I certainly don't want to be the first to make contact.

You're not a child any more, I tell myself. *You're almost eighteen.*

Still, I turn off the light to stop myself reaching for my pendant—or the book—again.

At breakfast the next morning, the table is set for one person—there's no Muzaffer in sight. Worrying is my first reaction. In the last couple of days I've noticed the number of pills he takes has dramatically increased, plus he doesn't look very well. I'd wanted to ask him about it, but the constant sour expression on his face proved a deterrent.

He isn't your problem, I almost hear Munu advise. But no matter how hard I try, how dysfunctional our relationship is, or how angry I am with him for not reaching out to Daphne, I still feel trapped by my concern.

What if he's really sick?

I rush into the kitchen to find Azmi cleaning the fridge. "Mr. Gümüşhuş has a medical appointment," he says when I ask after his whereabouts.

I don't ask what it is. It must be something serious, and I don't know how much more of the truth I can face this week.

With Muzaffer's sudden absence affecting me more than I expected, I avoid my room after breakfast, where *The Book of Heartbreak* waits like an unspoken threat, and retreat instead to the garden with my sketchpad. I settle by the small pond, the reflection of the Judas tree overhead rippling across the water. I try not to dwell on what Theodora might have done to be locked in the tower, or why she and her sister, Eudokia, cursed each other. But more than anything, I still can't grasp what *The Book of Heartbreak* has to do with me. *Just because Theodora and I share a similar appearance, it can't mean I'm her reincarnation,* I keep repeating to myself.

Drawing always helps me unwind. Just a few hours in the sunshine, and I'll be ready to return to the shadows of those pages and uncover the end of the story—and Sufi Chelebi's fate.

As I finish a sketch of the tower a few hours later, alone in the garden, I hear footsteps. I turn to see Muzaffer, leaning on his walking stick, watching me. Despite the vibrant colors of the sunny day, he looks ghastly. Pale and worn.

"Are you okay?" I can't help myself. "You missed breakfast."

"Medical appointment," Muzaffer says. A wasp whizzes past him but he doesn't flinch.

What's wrong with you? I want to ask, but I can't.

"What is it you're drawing?" He's slow to close the distance between us. When he sets his eyes on my draft, he frowns. "The Maiden's Tower?"

"I'm quite drawn to it," I mutter. "It looks like a fairytale."

"They ruined it with the recent renovation," Muzaffer grumbles.

I wonder if he knows anything about the tower's history that might prove useful, considering all the historical tomes in his personal library. "Do you know the story of the tower?"

"I'm sure there are books that will help better than I would." He readies himself to leave and, strangely, I find that I don't want him to.

"I read one . . ." The words leave my mouth before I can stop myself. "A version of the story different from the one Daphne told me. She said the myth says a man kept his daughter confined in the tower so she wouldn't die at eighteen as foreseen by a seer's prophecy. But she still died."

"She told you that story?" He doesn't seem to approve. It stings how he still avoids Mum's name.

"I came across this . . . book that instead mentions a curse on the tower, and two sisters—written by an Ottoman man—Müneccimbaşı Sufi Chelebi. He was in love with the maiden."

How can I explain that a magical book appeared to me, claiming curses can be broken?

"Sufi Chelebi?" His frown deepens. "Never heard of such a name."

"He was the sultan's chief seer in the 1500s," I carry on. "And the maiden was named Theodora and she had a sister, Eudokia, who cursed her. They cursed one another."

"Why would sisters curse each other?" Muzaffer sounds agitated. "That building was nothing but a watchtower. These old tales are just musings. Why are you wasting your time like this?" He shakes his head. "You have everything you need—go shopping, find some friends your age to show you the city."

His dismissive frustration hurts me more than I can imagine.

"Why did you invite me here," I retort, "if you hate me so much?"

"I don't hate you." His features smoothen, surprise flashing in his eyes. "Why would I hate you? You're all I have left."

"Why don't you let me in Daphne's room?" I push, emboldened by his reaction. But his face shifts into a frown again.

"Do you not like your room? You can redecorate it if you like."

"My room is fine." I shrug. Does he really care about me enough to let me redecorate a whole room? It looks like a nursery but I can live with it. "I just thought I could see her stuff. Find a keepsake."

His cat, Böcek, darts from a near bush before he can reply, then slows down like a little madam when she's by Muzaffer.

"There's nothing there," he retorts, as Böcek nuzzles his legs.

"Why did you and her fall out?" I drop my voice. I'm afraid to hear the answer.

He considers my question. Perhaps the cat soothes him, because when he speaks again, he sounds calmer.

"Your mother made some . . . decisions. And then instead of facing the consequences, owning her mistakes, she chose to escape. She abandoned me, and I chose to move on. What else can you do?"

"What did she do?" I ask. I can almost hear Munu in my head. *Do you really want to know, Sare? Why do you care?*

"It's been eighteen years," he exhales. "It doesn't matter any more. You have a whole future ahead of you. Don't dwell in the past."

"Easy for you to say." I gather my art supplies and rise from the bench.

"I know you're grieving," he says. "I can find her photos, if you'd like. If you think it will help."

"I don't know," I confess, suddenly frightened. I stand across him for a couple of awkward seconds, unable to express my feelings. "It's okay," I say at last. "I don't need anything."

Perhaps I should move on too.

In the evening, I go back to Sufi Chelebi's journal. His entries become shorter, more frantic.

18th of August in the year 1502

Theodora arrived again after three more days of hunger.

"My own desire destroyed me," she said, her voice hollow. "I am my own ruin. My heart shall remain forever fractured."

Jealousy surged like a storm within me as she uttered names—Azylios, and then Lazarios. I almost replied to inquire who these men were—but she will leave me forever if I converse with her, so I stopped myself.

"You see the depths of my soul. You forsake sustenance just to see me, and my hunger for forgiveness," Theodora uttered, unaware that she has become the sole nourishment for both my spirit and body. "Yet, your love remains. Will you help me, Chelebi? Will you set me free?"

May Allah have mercy on my soul, I will do anything for her.

22th August in the year 1502

Today, as I cleansed myself for morning prayer, Theodora appeared as a reflection upon the water's surface.

"Only in your presence do I feel pure again," she whispered. "Help me, Chelebi. The curse haunts me—it flows through our bloodline like a river racing to the sea. Perhaps you can set us free."

A few more, repetitive, short entries, some are frantic and unreadable, and then I arrive at the last page. It's lengthy, and harder to read.

10 September of the year 1502

Theodora, the warmth in my chest, the rhythm of my heart, cursed by her own flesh, who this day finally trusted me with her sin. Perhaps because I have become so frail, wrought by fasting to behold her, she pitied me.

Like a beggar, I spent the night under the fig tree on Çamlica Hill, as Theodora overwhelmed me with a torrent of memories.

I know everything now. It was her sin. My dove, my angel, my beautiful has sinned the gravest of the sins to her own flesh and blood. And it has wrought generations of heartbreak and suffering.

"Forgive me," Theodora whispered as she took me through her past, and I wept for her.

I wept for myself, for I misunderstood everything.

My dove . . . She wasn't . . . She was not innocent!

I was a fool. But I love her still.

In a moment of clarity, I saw what needed to be done to end this curse and stop the suffering. It's the cruellest of the curses, repeating the cycle of abandonment.

I had to forgive her. I had to speak the words, and in so doing sacrifice my own craving, my own love and desire to break the curse. There was no other way without severing the delicate thread that bound us. I had to abandon her to set her free.

"I, Sufi Chelebi, the third son of Mehmet Emin Efendi, once chief of the müneccims for the sultan and now a servant of your love, I forgive you, Theodora of House Doukas," I declared. "For what you have done to them and what they have done to you."

Then, to my great despair, my beloved let out a joyous sob, followed by a deafening, rattling sound.

"It's gone, Chelebi," she cried, once the silence of the night enveloped us again. "You saved me. And now, I shall wait for you in the halls of eternity."

Then she faded away, leaving in her wake a void. As if she was never there.

I remained awake until dawn caressed Konstantiniyye, knowing Theodora would not return.

Can I endure her absence? This, I cannot say. Perhaps this love has become my curse.

What have I wrought upon myself?

I stare at the final page, my head heavy with a storm of emotions.

Despair, for Sufi Chelebi's fate.

Frustration, that he left the origins of the curse unwritten.

But more profound and dizzying is the shock. *Generations of heartbreak.*

I'm unable to peel my eyes from the words.

I read the last entry, over and over, not one bit less confused each time. Could the curse that runs through me be the very same one that haunted Theodora?

My eyes drift to Daphne's painting of the Maiden's Tower across the room.

If only I could understand why the curse would reawaken after Sufi stopped it.

The letters replay in my head, I can almost hear Sufi muttering, his obsession, the transformation of his insatiable desire for knowledge to a cureless love for Theodora. His despair crawls through centuries, weighing on my stomach like a stone. I close the book and set it aside.

Love is a disease, Munu always says, and isn't she right? Poor Sufi Chelebi.

I cover the book with a blanket to put it out of my sight. Perhaps there's another reason why Leon wrapped it up before passing it to me. Perhaps, like me, he wishes he hadn't ever set eyes on it but, also like me, he's helpless against the desire.

I lie awake all night, thinking about Theodora. The way I look like her. The way she said, *"My heart is cursed"* to Sufi Chelebi. Did she too, die of a broken heart? But then, why did she need forgiveness? What did she *do*?

The monster who cursed your heart, Sufi Chelebi had said. *Her sister, Eudokia.*

It's unsettling to think that one person can curse another, that something so malicious can originate from human intent.

So who cursed me? I have no answer. The call to prayer starts outside. A chorus of Arabic words wash the city like a tide. I close my eyes until the echo of the imam's voice diminishes between the buildings.

In my dream, Sufi Chelebi lies lifeless under the fig tree.

The curse demands a sacrifice, Theodora says. *And it's still hungry.*

CHAPTER THIRTEEN

Verily, objects imbued with otherworldly sentience yearn for their rightful domain, returning with unseen force when fate disrupts their bond.
Excerpt from *The Book of Revenge, Müneccimbaşı Sufi Chelebi's Journals of Mystical Phenomena*

After breakfast, I sneak out with the book, tucked under my arm, pulsating like a second heart.

Across the street, Leon emerges from his building accompanied by the girl I spotted on his balcony before. I push through the gate. Her hair is the color of toasted almonds and her long gazelle legs are tan against her cotton sundress. Her obvious beauty makes me feel like a garden gnome.

"Pelin," Leon introduces her, and she seems distressed. I wonder if it's because of meeting me.

"Sare." I nod. Pelin offers a reluctant handshake, her grip firm on my fingertips, her hazel eyes narrowing as they rake over me. Her eyebrows lift as her gaze lands on the book cradled in my arms.

"Nice to finally meet you, Sare." She glances at Leon. I can tell they've been speaking about me, or the book, or Leon—or any combination thereof, likely leading to a condemnation of one or more of us.

"I trust you've read Sufi's journal," Leon says.

I nod again.

"And now we all know what happened to Sufi Chelebi," Pelin says. "And you'll advise Leon that he needs to stop tracing his footsteps, won't you, Sare?"

Pelin looks at me as if I have power over Leon, and I reward her with a frown.

"At least leave the book with her." Pelin's hair gleams in the sunshine as she turns to Leon. It's curious how she seems immune to sweating. "She found it. It's hers."

Leon shakes his head with a heavy sigh. "You're going to miss the ferry, Pelin."

"You promised me, Leon. You promised Dad." Pelin softens her voice. "You have the Peru trip coming up, you don't need to prove yourself to anyone. You don't have to do anything with the tower. You're already a fine seer."

I look away, embarrassed, as if I'm eavesdropping on a private conversation. Overhead, gulls circle us like harpies, their obscene shrieks edged with tension, as if they can feel my stress.

"Enough, Pelin." Leon's words cut through the air, sharp and final. "I told you, this is my case. She is mine—my responsibility, I mean."

I'm too stunned to speak. *His responsibility?* What does that mean? And what's wrong with this girl? Is she jealous? The idea is more laughable than unsettling. Pelin is straight-out-of-a-shampoo-ad beautiful; there's no way she'd think I'm a threat to her relationship with Leon. I clutch the book, anxious about what exactly I've got myself into, instead of passing a few uneventful months that would eventually lead to a curse-free life.

"I'm frightened." Pelin's voice is barely a tremor. Her gaze flickers from Leon's hardened face to me. "And you should be, too, Sare Silverbirch."

"Pelin," Leon cautions.

"Remember what happened to Sufi Chelebi," Pelin snaps at him.

Leon shrugs. "I'm not Sufi Chelebi."

And I'm not Theodora, I think. *I can't be.*

"Fine." Pelin shakes her head with disapproval, and dashes off without offering a goodbye, barely escaping the car that speeds past us, its engine moaning in response to its climb up the slope.

"Goodbye to you, too," Leon mutters. "Typical Pelin—always ultra-protective. Don't worry. Her father is a master, he'll set her mind at ease when she gets home."

I wonder if they're dating, though I don't ask. It would explain the effortless ease between them, the way they move together, always comfortable in each other's presence. I shake my head, trying to push aside Pelin's warnings, or whatever her relationship status with Leon may be, and prepare myself to part ways with *The Book of Heartbreak*.

"Let's go upstairs, to mine," Leon suggests, his gaze shifting to the large gulls that swoop up and down the narrow street, seemingly oblivious to my desire to escape. "We have to talk."

"I'm sorry, I can't—" I attempt to hand him the book. It hurts to separate myself from it, but I have a feeling this hurt will only grow deeper if I delay it. "I just want to return this. I don't want to get involved—"

"Is this because of what Pelin said?" He interrupts me with a deeply etched frown. "She's not a curse-breaker."

"She seems to know a great deal, though," I mutter. Everyone does, except me.

"Not everything is as it seems, Silverbirch." Leon grins. "Look, we really need to go somewhere inside. It's not safe out here." He looks to the skies again.

"Please, take it." I step forward to thrust the book to his chest.

A shadow streaks across my vision. I glance up to see one of the gulls plunging toward me, aiming straight for the book. The flurry of beating wings and its enraged shriek sends a jolt of terror through me. I leap back to escape, clutching the journal to protect it. But the bird dives fast, bringing with it the unmistakable stench of sea, fish, rot and something else—something . . . off.

"Silverbirch—look out!" Leon's voice is strangled as he lunges forward to knock me over. I land hard on the cobblestones. A sickening crunch of metal and bone echoes along the narrow street, and I lift my head to see Leon sprawled on the asphalt, his face contorted in pain, blood blooming crimson on his leg. A moped is tipped over beside him, the driver a blur of fury, ranting in Turkish.

Rooted to the spot, I'm drenched in sweat and fear, guilt washing over me.

He saved me. He pushed me, and instead he took the hit—it should have been me in that spot, not Leon.

"I'm okay." Leon grits his teeth. Relief floods through me that, despite looking far from okay, he isn't fatally injured. I pull myself up and rush to his side.

"*Abi, tamam.*" He gestures to the motorist, and receives more yelling in return before the man jumps back on his bike and disappears down the road.

"The book—" Leon winces as I lift him to his feet. And I realize that, in my concern for him, I left it lying on the cobblestones.

I turn back to scan the ground, slightly disappointed that his heroic actions might have been to save the book rather than me, and see the gull plummeting toward the tome again.

"What the fuck?" I watch the enormous creature soar away with Sufi Chelebi's journal clutched in its beak. "It took the book!"

Helpless, Leon and I watch the bird disappear into the skies.

"Upstairs," Leon commands, as he grips my arm. Despite his state, his hand is a steel claw. "Now."

"Shouldn't you go to hospital?" I ask as he furiously drags me into the cool darkness of the building. I'm too perplexed to question why we need to be inside his house right now.

"I'm okay," he says, a lie that falls flat. "Not the first time I got hit by a bike. And we really need to talk, Silverbirch." His eyes lock with mine. "At least help me climb the stairs."

"Fine," I mutter, sulking. I hate being this close to him, but how can I refuse after he just saved me?

The stale air of the building seems to thicken as he takes hold of my waist. It isn't just a touch, it's a raw energy, rough and crackling, pulsing through my veins with each passing second. I feel breathless, though it may be because his arm is wrapped like a tight band around my waist. His muscles feel hard and tense as he presses himself onto me for support. It's an utterly foreign sensation. I want to slip away, escape, but remain in this moment at the same time.

He lets out a soft groan as he hoists his leg up the first step, and my heart begins to gallop in my chest. Living in confinement in my own bubble for nearly eighteen years, I swear I've already touched Leon more in the last ten minutes than I have anyone else in my entire life. *This needs to stop,* I decide. *I'll help him to his door, then turn on my heels and march back home. To safety.*

We continue to climb, slowly, agonizingly, impossibly close. Leon pauses after every step. On the fifth, the overhead light flickers and dies, plunging us into sudden darkness.

"Wave your arm," Leon whispers into my ear.

"What?" I ask.

"The light." The warmth of his ragged breath causes me to tremble. "It's movement controlled."

I wave my free arm to make ourselves known to the stupid sensors of this stupid building. Muzaffer should sort this place out.

Somehow, we reach the final, precarious step. But then Leon loses his balance and momentarily falters. His stumble sends a jolt of panic through me. On reflex, I try to pull him onto the landing but he must have interpreted it as my own loss of balance, because he holds me in his arms and crushes me against the cool, damp wall.

My heart stops as his body presses against mine. I'm acutely aware of the prolonged gaze that binds us together like a spell, but I can't look away. I can't break the magic of this moment.

I don't want to.

The spark in his eyes transforms into something else—a question or a challenge, I can't tell. For a second, I wonder what it would mean to answer it. My own fear—or foolishness—immobilizes me, rendering me breathless.

"Fuck." The woody, salty scent of his sweat surrounds me. "That hurt like hell, Silverbirch."

"Be more careful next time," I counter, pushing him gently away. We're safe, secure and very stable after all. I have no excuse to be so close to him any more. My hair, thankfully loose, veils the blush creeping up my cheeks. My ears burn as if they're on fire—I half expect them to crumble into ash as he pulls himself away. I refuse to meet his gaze, only lifting my head when the jingle of his keys breaks the silence and he manages to unlock the door.

"I guess I'll see you later then," I mutter.

"You can't be serious?" he says. "I just got hit by a moped. You can't leave me alone. What if I have a head trauma?"

"You didn't hit your head." I linger at the top of the stairs. I should go. I must go.

"Please," he begs. "Come inside."

I hesitate. Then, like an idiot, I follow him.

Leon's apartment is the complete antithesis of my expectations. Gone are the visions of worn sofas and band T-shirt tapestries I'd conjured in my imagination. Instead, the walls, painted a sweet tone of lilac, are adorned with shimmering constellations and astrological charts. The air holds a soft pot-pourri scent laced with a faint, intriguing hint of leather. Crystal lamps cast a warm glow around the short hallway which leads to a door that stands like a portal to a symphony of floral prints.

A few moments after we've stepped inside, his aunt Harika, the potential mastermind of this pastel wonderland, emerges from behind a door.

"Leon?" When she sees his state, her hand—heavy with sparkling rings—rises to her chest. "What happened?"

"I'm fine," Leon rushes to reassure her. After we shut the front door, his composure seems more relaxed, despite the pain. And I start to wonder if that display of groans and moans were simply to mock me. "But we lost the book."

"Ah." Harika waves her hand, long nails painted in a shade of peach. "What is lost today shall find its way back. Soon, when the stars align with hidden intentions," she says dreamily, making me wonder if she's really insightful, or just prone to theatrics. "I'm sorry I failed to foresee this—perhaps then you could've avoided the accident."

"You already warned me to make a copy of the book," Leon protests.

"That was just good old wisdom, darling, not the eye." Harika sighs. "Now, let me get you some bandages."

Leon guides me to his room, and soon Harika arrives with a tray. She leaves a clean cloth and a bandage, a bottle of lemonade and two glasses, then leaves, shutting the door behind her.

"You don't seem to be in pain any more." I point out the obvious.

"Not everything is as it seems, Silverbirch." Leon winks at me. "I'm just really resilient."

The wind whips the billowing curtain into the room. Beyond the tulle, the view of my balcony across the street feels strange. But what's stranger still is being alone with Leon, in his bedroom.

"Please sit," he says.

I glance around. There aren't many spots on offer except his bed and office chair. I perch on the chair, and he sits on his bed. The desk is messy—enormous headphones, a PC, piles of books.

Leon takes the muslin cloth and crumples it in his hand, then wipes his legs. Thankfully, the cuts don't appear too deep. I don't offer any help. I don't have the courage to touch him more.

Instead, I pour our drinks.

"Thanks," he says. The ice cubes tinkle inside the glass as I offer it to him.

"I'm sorry." I sink back on the chair. "You lost the book because of me."

"It's fine." Leon studies the carpet as if he's discovered a secret message on it. "I'm just grateful I had the chance to read his journal and make a copy. It wasn't mine anyway. I was going to return it to the tower."

"Aren't you frightened? Of getting in too deep?" I echo Pelin's warning. "After what happened to Sufi Chelebi. How he lost his pure eye." I avoid the mention of his obsession with Theodora, which ultimately caused him to starve himself of nutrition and sanity.

"If you succumb to your fears, you'll only become a shadow of yourself." Leon shrugs, his gaze unwavering as he meets my eyes. "The curse is still around and someone needs to break it."

I consider these words. With a heart that ticks like a time bomb, I've spent a lifetime carrying fears in my pockets like stones. Courage never bestowed me peace.

"Those gulls looked monstrous." I shake my head. "Why would they take a book?"

"They weren't just birds." His jaw tightens. "They were possessed by the Hidden, or their minions. Not all the Hidden are fond of seers—some resent us for our abilities. I can't say who stole the book yet, but I have a feeling Munu may know."

"I doubt she'll share anything, even if she does." I recall our heated argument. "She wasn't pleased with our encounter in the tower. I haven't seen her for over a week now."

I wait for a reply, taking a long sip from my drink, struck by the foolish hope that perhaps Leon can tell me when Munu might return.

"I'm not certain about the journal, but your friend will be back, I'm sure," he says. "And perhaps when she returns . . . If you still need answers, I can bend her. I can extract—"

"What the hell do you mean?" I frown, recalling all the horrors Munu attributed to seers.

"With Grey's help, I can bend the ethereal, and they'll have to reply to all questions truthfully. No lies." Leon leans forward like a hawk, his eyes ablaze with a fierce passion.

"Don't be ridiculous," I retort, my voice tinged with defiance. "I'm not going to let you terrorize her. She's my friend."

"It won't hurt her, but you will get your answers. I've never met anyone else who made friends with an ethereal," Leon mutters. "But yet, you . . . Sometimes I look at you, and wonder if you're somehow favored or blessed by the Hidden. You are quite extraordinary, aren't you?"

I almost snort. If only he knew the truth.

The intensity of his stare doesn't wane, even through my silence.

Get up and leave, a small voice in my head urges.

But escaping would be Munu's way of thinking. And Munu is the one who kept me in the dark. I can't live in fear any more. I'm not a child.

"Why . . ." I swallow my fear, my voice trembling slightly. With quivering hands, I place my drink back on the tray. "Why do you think so?"

"You say you don't possess a pure eye, Silverbirch," Leon states matter-of-factly. "Yet you can see Munu. Do you remember, when I saw you two on the balcony, I refrained from addressing the ethereal and spoke to you first?"

I nod. How could I forget?

"Because we, those with the pure eye, have to pay a price to see the deceased. Hunger, pain or confinement. Sufi Chelebi spoke once with Theodora, and it cost him dearly: he lost her. So tell me, how, with your innocence of such dark arts, can you chatter with Munu as if she's your classmate? What is the source of this blessing?"

"S-she helps me." I avoid meeting Leon's gaze, my heart pounding in my chest. I feel exposed, yet strangely compelled to confess. I don't know why I trust him. I don't know why my mouth is loosened, but it's so easy to talk with him, so effortless. I've been carrying this secret for so long. I'm so thirsty to tell it. And I feel so lonely. Finally, after nearly eighteen years, I have the chance to share it with someone who'll understand, someone other than Munu.

"Why do you need help?" Leon's voice is gentle, but his eyes pin me down. "What for?"

"Because I'm—" I hold Leon's gaze. How easily the words spill from my lips. How desperately I yearn to unburden myself. "I'm cursed."

Leon pauses for a long moment, a flurry of emotions stirring in his bright eyes.

The word *curse* tastes funny in my mouth. Perhaps it's the remnants of the lemonade that's gone sour. Or just saying it out loud to someone who isn't Munu. I don't know if I feel lighter, after the confession, or just hollow. Time, tightly drawn with a patience I can no longer bear, slows as Leon watches me.

"I knew it," he says finally, although more to himself than to me. "You bear a curse. It's why I can't stop thinking about you."

Shit. I'm lucky I didn't have anything in my mouth, otherwise I'd choke on this declaration.

He can't stop thinking about me.

Me!

"Why didn't you tell me sooner? This changes everything. Perhaps—" He grimaces, as if he's recalled something. "What does the curse do to you?"

Say it, and he'll think you're a freak, a voice in my head chants. A freak who dies with every heartbreak.

"I—" I hesitate. "I can't talk about it."

"Don't you want to break the curse?" I see a million stars in Leon's eyes, each glittering with their own possibility.

"It will be no more when I turn eighteen."

"A curse won't dispel itself on a birthday."

A silence sits atop us. A gull lands on the railing of the balcony outside. Suddenly, I start to panic. I've already said too much. Why can't I shut up?

I can't bear him discovering how doomed and fragile I am. A girl with a heart of glass, living on borrowed time, trapped in the safety of isolation, more terrified of love than of Death itself.

Think, Sare. Think fast. Find something conventionally tragic that won't make you look like a loser.

"I-I will die young." It takes all my strength to form the lie. "All the women in my family are cursed to die young." But it's still a form of truth. Everyone did die young: Iris, Defne, their mother.

"Fuck," Leon mutters, distracting me, his face contorting with sorrow. "I'm so sorry."

A pang of guilt swells in my stomach for deceiving him—but it's the only way. He won't stop asking questions about the curse otherwise. And it's easier to pretend I'm not the only one who's suffering.

"It's fi—" I begin.

A shrill cry pierces the air, making me halt. Not mine, not Leon's. It's a bold, vivid, familiar cry.

At first, I assume it's one of the gulls. But it's deeper, knowing. A louder voice.

And then Munu drifts in from behind the curtains. She seems to have aged in the past week, with loose strands of unkempt hair, her face drained of color, her usual flamboyant attire swapped for a simple black dress, as if she's mourning.

"You." She lifts a shaking finger at Leon. "Why won't you leave her alone?"

"Munu." I step between her and Leon.

"You spoke of the curse," Munu says, as if I have betrayed her. "You told him!"

"Where were you all this time?" I'm puzzled, agitated. "How do you know what we're talking about?"

"Oh, she knows, because she works for the eyes and ears that are always listening, don't you, Munu?" Leon steps around me. "Tell me where the book is, and I swear on the craft I'll save you from him."

Save her from who? Before I can ask, Munu lunges forward and yanks at my collar.

"If you have one drop of love for me," she says, "one drop— please, go to your room, and do not speak with this devil again." She shivers like a twig in the wind, shrinking with each word. "He will flay my soul into ribbons, he will ship me to the depths of hell, but worse, he will never speak to me again."

"Munu." I step away, freeing myself from her frenzy, my heart leaping inside my ribs. "Calm down. Who do you mean?"

"I am done this time!" Munu shrieks. "They will think it's all my fault, they always do. They're angry already, canim. What will happen to you, then? Can you hear how they're calling me . . ." She pauses and snarls, like a wounded animal, at Leon. "All because of *you*. Because you filled her head with your nonsense about curses and how they could be broken."

"Any curse can be dispelled under the right conditions. It's not only the Hidden who possess the power to shift things." Leon towers behind me, unperturbed by Munu's despair. "Sare has the right to know."

"And you think you know it all, boy seer." Munu watches him, her eyes deepening into a darker shade of hatred. "Perhaps it's natural for someone like you, a young protege in the craft, a beautiful creature, adored by everyone. You live in a world that belongs to you, not one you have to keep up with. You convince yourself you can mend other people. Fix mistakes. Break curses. But heed my advice," Munu says as she flies toward Leon. "Some things are better left alone. Refrain from engaging with her for the next few months and then she'll be free of the curse. This is for her own good."

"At what cost?" Leon seems to grow taller as he commands her.

My gaze locks with Munu's. I shake my head, mouthing a silent "no." Please, don't say anything. She takes the hint and nods with understanding before speaking again. "Don't you get it, you silly boy?" Munu growls. "Even the greatest seers make terrible mistakes. You're not the one risking everything here. Sare can't afford to trust you, or challenge this curse; it's too dangerous. She's the only soul I care about in this damned world, and I won't let your ambitions destroy her. Just because that madman Sufi broke the curse once doesn't mean it can be done again."

An awkward pause follows her outburst, sending me staggering as the weight of her words sinks in.

"What did you just say?" I whimper, suddenly dizzy, my hands reaching out for support. In my haste, I clumsily knock over the lemonade glass, sending it splashing to the ground. "How do you know what Sufi wrote?" I'm quivering. Lessening. Broken. I'm the one who's been betrayed. "Why are you making it sound as if the maiden's curse and mine are the same thing?"

"I—" Munu mumbles. Her eyes scan the room in panic. But no lie reaches out to help her as she begins to shrink.

"Because it really is the same curse, and she's the one who stole the book . . ." Leon glances at her. Understanding dawns on his face. "You used the gull to get the book, didn't you?"

"It wasn't yours, anyway!" Munu hisses at him.

"Did you do it?" My hands are shaking. Could Munu really have lied to me, my friend, my confidant, the only soul I've ever truly trusted? "A trick, you called that book. A ploy. Why steal it, then? How many more lies have you told me?"

"Canim." Munu buries her head in her hands. "No—stop now. I only wish to protect you. Please don't be upset. Remember the second rule."

"Shut it." I hate myself for being so brainwashed by her into obeying the second rule. It's instinctual: my anger sweeps away the pain of her betrayal, bold and nightmarish. It wants to rip my heart apart. To end my suffering once and for all. But it's the only protection I have against further shattering.

I search for Leon's arm for support and he pulls me away from Munu, encircling me in a tight embrace as if I might crumble. A sense of calm washes over me at this closeness. If the curse is my poison, Leon must be the antidote because the fluttering that had taken flight within my ribs now subdues with his nearness.

"Are you okay, Silverbirch?" He is a distraction. The best kind.

I shake my head. I'm not okay. I'm really, really not.

"The boy is a mistake," Munu whimpers.

And then she disappears, leaving me alone with Leon in the sulking heat of the dying afternoon.

Communication is classified as Top Secret.
Circulation strictly limited to correspondents.

Subject: Re: Urgent Retrieval of the Mortal Artifact

Date: 2 August 2024
From: Grey the Compassionate, Associate Cherub, Curse and Malediction Archives, Worldly Index, Sacred Data Systems, Halo-tech Data & Integration Hub
To: Five the Fifth, Angel of Death, Field Operations, Mortal Termination and Transition, Mortal Affairs Commission

My dear and most esteemed comrade, Five the Fifth of Death,

I know what you are and what you did with *that* curse, as clear as a halo in the Heavens' light, and I'm coming for you.

Cherub

CHAPTER FOURTEEN

Trust may be the strongest of bonds yet it's delicate enough to be severed with a single word. Once it's broken, no effort can fully restore it, leaving a growing gap that drives hearts apart.

Excerpt from *The Book of Betrayal, Müneccimbaşı Sufi Chelebi's Journals of Mystical Phenomena*

Only after Munu departs do I realize how hard I've been clutching Leon's arm.

"What is going on between you two?" He breaks the heavy silence. "What was she talking about? What rules?"

I shrink away instead of responding.

I'm so sick of not knowing who to trust or what to say. A part of me burns with frustration at how much I revealed, how vulnerable I let myself become. Munu's departure is a harsh reminder that I can't afford to be close to anyone—least of all, Leon.

"Are you okay, Silverbirch?" Leon insists. I take a step back and he doesn't close the gap between us.

Since I met Leon my already disastrous life only went more downhill. I read Sufi Chelebi's journal seeking hope, only to find turmoil in *The Book of Heartbreak*. More questions. More unrest.

And now it's costing me Munu. Have I been foolish to rely on her?

"Does she have anything against you?" Leon's voice is full of concern. "If you're in some sort of trouble—"

"Please." I lift my hand to signal him to stop. I need to compose myself, consider everything, figure out why Munu stole the book. It will take three more steps to reach the door and leave his room, and then perhaps another two hundred to the safety of mine. But would being alone fix anything? I'm not even sure I'm the same person who left my house today, or who read the book yesterday. And I'm certainly not the girl who arrived in Istanbul three weeks ago.

"The book," Leon says, back to business mode. "She has it. Can you summon her, and ask who she's taken it to?"

"She won't come," I whisper, almost certain that Munu won't appear again in case she upsets me to the point of no return. "I have to go."

"Don't." Leon's tone makes me hesitate. "I'm so close to solving the mystery of the tower." His voice is a plea. "You are the missing piece, Silverbirch, I'm sure of it. The book chose you. Not me, not anyone else—you."

I feel suddenly foolish, thinking he actually cared about me, and not the bloody curse, or the tower. Of course he wants me to stay—so that I'll spill my secrets. "I have no idea why the book chose me, but I don't care. It only frightens me now."

"I can help." He pauses, as if waiting for his words to sink in. "We can help each other."

I shake my head. "No one can help me."

"Don't be afraid of hope," Leon says.

Hope is a malfunction, Munu repeats in my mind. And she's right. Hope is dangerous for me, and Leon is full of it. "I shouldn't have come here." My fingers fumble on the door handle.

"We can break the curse, you and I," he says. "We can rewrite history together."

No one has ever proposed any sort of partnership to me before, and even though I can't say yes to him, there's a small temptation. *If only I could trust him.*

He watches me, waiting for an answer. What can I say? *Sorry, Leon, I'd love to, but bonding with anyone is basically a death sentence when you're cursed to die of heartbreak.* The thought is so ridiculous I want to laugh and cry at the same time.

"Sare," Leon says, with a hint of longing. My name fits between his lips like a dagger in its sheath. "The curse is the link between you and Theodora. Come to the tower with me again, and perhaps you'll remember something to help—"

"No." I shake my head again. "I won't go there."

It's the one promise I made to Munu that I'll keep. Not for her sake, but mine.

Finally, I find a grip on the door handle and thrust myself out of his room. He calls after me as I widen the distance between us, but I ignore him.

I slam the apartment door behind me, and race down the stairs, but no matter how fast I run, the heat of his gaze remains like hot iron on my face.

Back at home, I turn off my phone, sealing myself away from the outside world by closing the window and the shutters. I leave strict instructions with Azmi that I don't want to be disturbed, ensuring that Leon can't breach my solitude.

I sleep as if I haven't slept for years. I toss and turn in bed, caught in the claws of nightmares.

The book chose you, Leon says in the midst of my dream.

The book chose me, I repeat, standing in the Inbetween, neither dead, nor alive.

Love is a disease, Munu warns. *Hope is a malfunction.*

You're not Daphne, she says. *You shall live, Sare.*

She's not Daphne, whispers Theodora. *She is me.*
What if you were reborn? Theodora asks. *What if we're one?*
No, I cry out. *No. No. NO!*

Then I gasp, awake, drenched in sweat, my screams still echoing through my room.

I can't lift myself up the next day. The morning becomes the afternoon, and I dream between the mosque's prayers until the evening.

Perhaps I should sleep for a few more months, and then everything will stop hurting. Perhaps when the curse finally lifts, I will be fearless.

It's the first prayer of the evening when Munu's voice fills the silence.

"Canim."

I don't budge, still burning with anger. I pretend to be asleep, so she'll leave me alone.

"I know you well enough to know you're not really asleep," Munu insists. The soft flapping of her wings stirs the air as she hovers above me. "Well enough to know that you're so angry, you won't be heartbroken."

"What do you want?" Reluctantly, I sit up. "Save your breath if you're going to lecture me about Leon. I haven't seen him since yesterday."

Or was it the day before?

"You're torturing yourself letting him manipulate you like this." Munu lands on the bed next to me. Soon, despite my anger, I'm facing her like a sunflower turning toward the sun.

"Should I let *you* manipulate me instead?" I hiss.

"Even if Chelebi's claim is true and a mortal really can break the curse," she says, ignoring my snark, "the risk is too great. Don't you get it? I might not be able to save you from what you might discover. You must live, Sare. You must survive."

But I'm past the point of caring about the risks. Her caution does little to diminish my desire to know the truth. Sunset brims through the curtains and I try to plot scenarios that could fit into the holes of the answers I crave.

"Perhaps I'm really Theodora," I fumble. "Perhaps she died of heartbreak too."

"Don't be absurd!" Munu erupts, her voice sharp with disdain. "I've never heard a more pitiful notion. You're *not* Theodora. She was shrouded in a darkness that could never taint your pure soul."

I gasp with a shocking realization. "You knew her, didn't you?" I freeze. "You *knew* Theodora."

"No." Munu recoils as if struck. "I do what I'm told, and I don't look back."

Nothing makes sense—her secretiveness, her fear. And then, as clear as the morning sky, I suddenly understand why she's so terrified of hearing about Theodora.

"You were her guardian." I grapple with this electric discovery. "You were helping Theodora, just as you help me now. She died of heartbreak and you failed with her, and now if I don't reach eighteen, I'll be reborn as someone else. I'm doomed to live this curse for eternity, and you're doomed to suffer with me." I stare at her, defiant. "I'm right, aren't I?"

I realize at that moment that my theory, as improbable as it sounds, is the most plausible explanation. And judging by Munu's quivering, I've hit a nerve. But how much of it is true? And what else is Munu hiding from me?

"Nonsense," she protests again, backing away from me, beginning to shrink. "Do not force me to speak of it. He will punish me."

"Munu," I beg. "Please. I don't want to sacrifice my heart."

Munu looks shocked by my confession. The truth feels so near, yet so distant. Just like Leon, who offered to do his "bending" to make Munu speak, I wish I could grab her shoulders and shake the truth out of her.

"I don't want to live a loveless life," I plead, my voice cracking under the weight of my despair.

"Love is a disease," Munu says. "It rots you. It reduces you. It's the worst of the pains. You'll be better off without it. Navigate these last months until you're eighteen and then accept your destiny. Once the curse takes your heart, you will never suffer again. You will be invincible. No one will ever hurt you again. Shouldn't you be grateful? Surely that is enough reward?" She tries to take a step forward, but falters. In some fucked-up way, I feel sorry for her—perhaps even sorrier than I feel for myself. "The truth might hurt you irrevocably. Stop seeking it!"

"I'll make no such promise," I whisper. "Not any more."

CHAPTER FIFTEEN

It's often observed that individuals within the same family bear striking resemblances, passing down features such as the curve of a mouth or the hue of hair, even the warmth of a smile from one generation to the next. Curiously, though, mortals very rarely inherit the memories of their ancestors. This absence of memories makes it all too simple, at times, for one to overlook or disconnect from their heritage, as if the threads of lineage and legacy can be easily loosened by the passage of time. And the essence of one's forgotten heritage continues to flow within each person's veins like poison.

Excerpt from *The Book of Betrayal, Müneccimbaşı Sufi Chelebi's Journals of Mystical Phenomena*

I don't know how I manage it, but that evening I present myself at dinner.

"You're having nightmares?" Muzaffer doesn't seem to be enjoying the pasta dish before him. Our plates remain almost untouched. "I heard your screams last night."

It takes me a moment to understand what he's talking about. Of course, last night's dream, and how I woke screaming that I'm not Theodora.

"Azmi says you've not left your room for days."

I roll my eyes. The way he highlights that it's Azmi paying attention to my whereabouts, as if it'll cost him dearly to say, "*I'm worried about you*," gets under my skin. Why is he so scared of caring? Does he have no heart? Perhaps I'll be like him when I turn eighteen and the curse makes its claim. And then we'll both sit here with flat faces and hearts of stone. We'll be best friends then, I'm sure.

"Sorry if my screams woke you," I sulk. "Besides, why are you suddenly so interested in my welfare?"

He looks taken aback. He dabs his mouth with his napkin before speaking again.

"I care about you, Sare. I want you to be well. You're the only one I have."

"Am I?" Under this roof, I feel like a problem, or a responsibility.

"I found a good school for you," he says, changing the subject. "It's not long until September now, and being busy will help."

"I'm not going to any school." I set my fork aside. A string of spaghetti drops to the table in a faint, as if it can't handle the tension between us. "I'll be eighteen in December, so you won't have to worry about me any more after that."

"You're all I have," he says again. "I will make sure you have a good life."

For a moment, a small part of me wants to comfort him, to let him in, let him help. But while this curse remains unbroken, I need to ward my heart against such weakness if I want to survive. I have no more heartbreaks to spare. Munu's lectures from my childhood are deeply rooted, etched into my mind. They flood all at once. *Families are minefields. People always hurt you. They leave. They ignore. They neglect. It's the ones closest to us that inflict the most painful wounds.*

I swallow hard. *I'm all by myself.*

"I wish you did the same for Mum. Checked on her, made sure she was well. Then perhaps she'd be alive now," I mutter. It's a low blow. I hate myself as soon as the words leave my mouth. I know we had a house and a comfortable life in the UK because of Muzaffer's funds, but money wasn't enough. It couldn't have been enough—not for Mum who needed him.

"I'm sorry," he fumbles, shrinking in his seat. "We all made mistakes. But your mother . . ." He shakes his head. "She is the one who abandoned me. I can't change the past."

Muzaffer looks like he's going to say more, but instead slams his hand on the table. I flinch as the porcelain jumps, bracing myself for his rage. But, instead of yelling at me, he calls for Azmi.

What have you done, Mum? What happened in this house?

"Azmi." Muzaffer bangs on the table again, his face red. "Azmi! Where's my raki?"

A flustered Azmi appears at the door. "But . . . the doctor said no alcohol—"

"To hell with what the doctor says," he retorts. "Bring my drink."

I stiffen as we both wait for Azmi to serve his booze.

"There is no peace in the past," Muzaffer says when his raki is brought in and he's taken a long, hard sip from the glass. A waft of aniseed washes over me. "Don't look back. Look ahead."

By half past ten the call to prayer urges Istanbul to sleep, yet the city defies this guidance. Sleep proves impossible and I turn to Netflix, hoping for a solid scare, something to shake off the very real horror show of the week. Though even jump scares seem quaint compared to my life right now.

There are footsteps upstairs, accompanied by the dreamy voice of a Turkish singer from a gramophone.

Halfway through the second movie, I feel a movement under the bed. My body tenses with alarm. Something is, quite possibly, terribly wrong. When the desk across the room begins swaying left and right, I worry that I'm facing another heartbreak. But why? I'm not even fluttering. I don't feel *anything*.

Suddenly, it hits me—this isn't the curse, it's an earthquake.

A real earthquake.

A cacophony erupts outside, dogs barking hysterically, car alarms shrieking in a discordant chorus, and collective screaming that tears through the night.

The clock points to 2.30 a.m.

As the rumble soars in pitch, my mind races, mapping my escape routes: the balcony, the stairs. But then, as suddenly as it began, the shaking recedes, leaving the city to lull itself back to sleep. I almost relax, but a boom from upstairs shatters the stillness. Something— or someone—has fallen, sending rattles through the house.

Muzaffer?

Without thinking, I bolt out of bed, then out of the room, and sprint up the stairs, to the place I know I'm not welcome, tracing the path of the groan that emanates from a slightly open door. I push my way inside to find him sprawled on the floor, his walking stick on one side and a broken glass on the other.

"Are you okay?" I brace myself for a scolding, but when he lifts his swaying head to see me, his face lights up.

"I-Iris," he groans.

"I'm not Iris," I reply.

"I'm sorry. S-Sare?" He looks confused now. I recognize the delayed heaviness of alcohol in him even before the sharp aniseed scent of the raki cuts through me, as I bend to help him onto his feet. Memory must be my worst enemy, because the smell suddenly takes me back to the UK, trying to wake Daphne in the morning, or cleaning up her vomit.

"Forgive me." Muzaffer staggers as he sits up.

"Stop moving. You'll cut yourself." I lean down to hold him, glad that I'm wearing slippers. I don't know what's wrong with me, why I can't just leave him in his mess.

He reaches out and, before I can escape, he grasps my hand in his. "Iris," he whimpers, as I lift him up.

I try to slip away when he's back on his feet, but he lurches forward and grabs hold of me, paralyzing me with a hug.

"Iris." His head presses against my shoulder.

He can't even say my mother's name, but he chants Iris's. *His favorite.*

"I said, I'm not Iris." I attempt to push him away. I'm not a cage to hold Muzaffer's emotions. I'm not his second chance at being a parent. But he has other ideas, as his arms cling to me with a strength that doesn't match his gaunt, feeble frame.

"I miss you," he says. It sounds like a prayer. I wish I didn't understand what it meant to miss someone gone forever, but I do. I think of Mum as Muzaffer's body trembles with sobs, as if he contains an earthquake in his heart. His sadness seeps into me like damp creeping through a wall. "*Her şey burnumun ucunda olup bitmiş de ben görememişim.*" He switches to Turkish, pulling me to his chest. I feel his tears on my face. "*Babacığım.*"

I know the word. *Father*, he says.

"What do you mean?" My voice is a croak. "What are you saying?"

"I miss you so much." Muzaffer clutches me even tighter. "The house is so silent without you two."

Does he mean me, Iris—or Mum?

"Please let me go," I manage, quivering. I want to hate Muzaffer—I need to hate him—but I can't. I'm terrified of getting attached to him, but even more frightened of hating him, of how deeply it would wound me to hurt him.

"You didn't deserve any of this." His eyes flicker like a lighthouse. One blink and he is sober, another and he's drunk again. "It wasn't your fault. I'm sorry."

I manage to release myself from his embrace, uncertain who is he addressing.

What is he apologizing for? What the fuck happened to Iris?

"Sare!" Azmi appears in the doorframe, and I flinch. "Are you alright? Mr. Gümüşhuş?" He hurries into the room wearing a dressing gown.

"I guess he—" I gulp with relief that I can leave Muzaffer with Azmi without worrying if he'll hurt himself again. I've done enough already. "He fell."

"Iris," Muzaffer repeats like a broken toy again. I grab his hands and pass him into Azmi's care.

"I'm not Iris," I whisper. "I'm Sare, remember? Daphne's. Defne's!"

"Sare." Muzaffer frowns. A slow, painful expression settles on his face.

"This way, please." Azmi tries to guide him away to a chair, but Muzaffer doesn't budge.

"You were right," he says to me. "I could've made things better for her too. I should've been around more. B—busy, wasn't I? Occupied with everything else. And then they were both gone and nothing else mattered. Nothing else remained. I should've done something to save them, I should've—"

He buries his head between slender fingers. I leave him standing amid the pool of shattered glass, the sound of Azmi's soothing murmurs in Turkish closing around his whimpers.

I want to reach out, pull him into a hug and tell him everything is okay now. But I can't.

I'm about to head out when I catch a glimpse of a pile of photographs on his desk. The house is so starved of memories, I'm instantly drawn to the image on top: Muzaffer and his daughters. I pluck it up with trembling fingers. Has he been looking at these? My gaze finds Daphne, yet to become my mother, probably around the age I am now. She grins, carefree. A happiness I've never seen on her face before. She looks loved, and normal. *Mum.* My heart sizzles at her smile.

Beside her stands another girl.

I forget to breathe when my eyes land on her face.

"Iris," I gasp.

Suddenly the shock in Muzaffer's eyes when we met makes sense. The way his tongue slips when he's drunk. The way Mum called me "Iris." Azmi's reaction on the day I arrived.

The older girl is the only person in the photograph who doesn't look happy. And I know she's not, because I've seen her frown many times in the mirror.

Iris Gümüşhuş is my doppelganger.

A few minutes later, Azmi has already carted Muzaffer away from the mess he left behind, and now he's trying to clean up the broken glass with a dustpan.

But I'm still anchored by the desk, unable to rip my eyes off *Iris, who looks just like me. Iris, who looks like Theodora.*

"Why is he so upset?" I hover above Azmi, clutching the photo in my hand. "What happened to Iris?"

"E–excuse me?" Azmi lifts his head.

"Iris," I repeat. "She died, right? Didn't you say you've worked for Muzaffer since you were sixteen? Surely you were here when it happened."

"I don't know why you're—"

"He told me Iris died in an earthquake." I cut him off. "Is that true?"

"It was an accident." His Adam's apple bobs with clear discomfort. "Iris had an earthquake phobia. I think she was scared the old tower would collapse, and tried to make a hasty escape, and that's why she fell."

"Fell?" I echo. "From a *tower*? What tower?" Dread walks on my back like a spider. Even before Azmi speaks again, I feel the answer in my bones.

"The Maiden's Tower," Azmi says. "It used to be a restaurant back then."

Iris died at the Maiden's Tower. Why does everything link to that bloody tower? There's no breeze in the room, but I feel a wind whipping around me as if I'm standing in the midst of a storm.

170

"What year was it?" I demand. "When did she die?"

"2007." Azmi says curtly. "April."

A chill creeps in my bones. Iris died just before I was born, December of that same year.

She died in the tower, of all places. Just like the maiden.

I'm reeling—a bird trapped in a cage, wings thrashing against the metal bars.

"If you can let me clean up now," Azmi warns, but I'm no longer listening.

Iris, Daphne whispers in the fog of my mind. *Why do you hate me so much?*

My heart races. Tears sting behind my eyes.

Mum. Did you see Iris every time you looked at my face?

I grew up to resemble the sister who hated her.

I am nothing but a shadow. A haunting. A reincarnation.

I storm out, desperate for a distraction to stop myself from crying, an escape from the assault of my discovery.

Another shock awaits me as I navigate back to my room. A flicker of movement catches my eye as I step inside and I brace myself, expecting another earthquake to rattle Istanbul's bones. My heart nearly stops when I realize the movement is actually a figure standing in the shadows.

Leon.

"Silverbirch." He strides across the expansive room.

I slam the door shut behind me. "How did you get in here?"

"I climbed in from the balcony," he explains, closing the distance between us in an instant. "I had to make sure you were okay after the earthquake. *Are* you alright?" His embrace is tight.

I'm not used to being cared for by people other than Munu, and the fact that Leon was worried enough about me to climb up to my room fills me with an odd warmth. I want to return his hug, to wrap my arms around his sturdy frame, but I can't seem to move.

"I-I'm fine," I manage, my words stuttering as I reluctantly extricate myself from his arms.

But I'm not okay. Not when Munu has deceived me, not when I bear a striking resemblance to my late aunt, Iris, who perished at the tower.

Not when I've figured out Mum hated looking at me because I have the face of her estranged sister.

Leon tucks a stubborn curl behind his ears and keeps his eyes on me. I wonder how many other girls have found him in their room.

"Do you always climb into people's rooms?" I ask, mostly to pull my thoughts elsewhere. Leon never fails to distract my heart from the suffocating woes that seem to follow me everywhere.

"I tend to use the front door." There's a flicker of amusement on his face, but it doesn't affect me the way it usually does. "You're not used to earthquakes. I had to check if you were okay."

"I told you, I'm fine." Leon has no idea how familiar earthquakes are for me. As the last thing I experience before every death, this one was a mere hiccup; there are far more terrifying things lurking in this house.

"You look pale." Leon's voice falters as he glances at my face, then to the frame in my hand. It's only then I realize I'm still clinging on to it. "Who is she?"

"My mother's sister," I mutter after a brief hesitation. "Iris."

"Bloody hell," he says. "She looks just like—"

"Me." I turn away. *And Theodora.*

"Where is she?" Leon's gaze hardens.

"She died." My voice is a whimper.

Leon's jaw clenches. "Why haven't you told me this before?"

"Because I just found out what she looks like," I snap. With a sudden exhaustion, I drag my feet over to the bed and sink down onto it.

"Do you still think your likeness to Theodora is a coincidence?" Leon follows suit.

"I don't know what to believe any more." My heart, my worst enemy, stirs in my chest. "Perhaps you're right, and I was once Theodora—and . . ."

"Iris too?" Leon crouches before me, like he did in the basement office of the tower. But this time, his proximity doesn't alarm me. There's something in his touch that heals and diverts me from the fluttering. I don't shy away from his gaze as he studies my face.

"I-I don't know." All I do know is that something dark and sinister lies in my family history, and it ties me to the Maiden's Tower.

There's no peace in the past, Muzaffer had said at the dinner table, and perhaps he is right. Look how the discovery of a single photograph shook me to the core.

I'm so absorbed in my self-pity that I don't even realize Leon has been speaking.

"I said, what will you sacrifice?" Leon leans over to me to be heard, so close that I can smell his woody scent. "What will happen when you're eighteen?"

I shake my head. "Now isn't the time to discuss it." As if there's ever a right time.

"You're sacrificing yourself, to break the curse, and that's why you're so secretive about it." His words are heavy, as if he's chewing on barbed wire.

At that moment, I understand why he's been pressing for answers. *He thinks I'll sacrifice my life when I'm eighteen.* "N-no," I stammer. "Don't be daft. I won't sacrifice myself."

It's only my emotions that will die. Not me.

Leon scrutinizes me with evident disbelief, likely because I must look like a wreck with the whirlwind of emotions swirling within me.

"Munu was here earlier," I tell him, eager to steer away from the subject. "She knows Theodora. She gave it away. But it's hopeless, she won't speak of it, won't tell me anything." I reach out and seek his hand. My skin is cool against his warmth. "Can you really make her talk? Would you still . . . *bend* her for me?"

He nods. "I will, if you want."

There's nothing else I want now more than the truth. And Munu owes me that.

"But, even if she tells me—" I don't have the courage to hope, not after all the disappointment and heartbreak I've suffered. "It still doesn't mean that I can break the curse."

"You will break the curse." Leon's eyes are bright now with determination. "The book chose you for a reason. Understanding the curse, with its origin and triggers, will present the solution."

Outside the room, heavy footsteps echo on the staircase.

"You need to leave." I stand from the bed and urge him toward the balcony. "No one's in a good mood tonight, and if they catch you here—"

But Leon doesn't seem to mind.

"Come to the tower with me," he says. "I'd say tonight, but some professor is doing a field study. We can go tomorrow night."

"I'm not sure." I can't find the strength to go there when I just found out that Iris died there.

"Silverbirch," Leon says, "visiting at night is vital. If you really are reborn, if you really were trapped there in another life, you'll remember something. The dark hides the seen, but it unveils the hidden. And then you can summon Munu and I can bend her."

"This 'bending' won't hurt her, right?" It's not easy to explain to Leon that the bond between Munu and me runs deep as blood, strong as any familial tie.

"I promise," Leon says. "I won't do her any harm."

In the dim light, he looks like a prince from an ancient tale. Suddenly, I wish he wouldn't leave. *But this is a business partnership*, I have to remind myself. He's only helping me because of the curse. I can't let any feelings in.

Beyond the window, a baby's shrill cry echoes between the buildings.

"I'll wait for you tomorrow." He rises to his feet, letting go of my hand. "Downstairs, at midnight."

I nod, uncertain whether or not I'm actually agreeing to his request.

"Good night, Silverbirch," Leon says, then slips away into the shadows outside, leaving me alone with nothing but my mother's old family photograph for company.

CHAPTER SIXTEEN

A "beddua" embodies the simplest form of a curse within mortal grasp. It is an utterance by the aggrieved, a sequence of words forming a malevolent wish, a profound longing from those harmed to impose a curse upon the transgressor.

Excerpt from *The Book of Heartbreak, Müneccimbaşı Sufi Chelebi's Journals of Mystical Phenomena*

Despite spending the whole day building a long list of reasons why I'd better stay away from the tower and Leon, I slip out of the house the following night.

My heart instantly picks up a new rhythm as I see Leon's tall figure waiting for me outside.

"Are you okay, Silverbirch?" he asks as he watches me push the gate open. The gloom that filled my head all day dispels as soon as my eyes settle on him. His joy is too hard to ignore; it's almost contagious. Is it normal that he makes me feel this happy?

You're only a job to him, Munu's voice says in my head. *An assignment. Business. Don't fall for him.*

My shoulder brushes Leon's arm as we walk down the slope. I'm astonished by how quickly and readily I accept his closeness. With him I'm another version of myself, though even this one is still afraid to love, or admit that she can develop feelings for Leon.

Would he still look at you like this, that insistent voice pipes up again, *if he knew what the curse will do to you if you survive it?*

And I have a question of my own too. Will he still want to work with me, if he finds out I've lied to him?

I have no answers.

He doesn't invade my silence until we arrive at the docks, where I'm surprised to see someone else waiting for us. Pelin.

She steps forward, beautiful as a siren, and passes Leon something.

"I borrowed the boat from Master Bora, Pelin's father," Leon explains, showing me the keys.

"Please think again." Pelin grimaces, focusing on Leon as if I'm not there.

"Pelin . . ." Leon sighs.

She pouts. "Then at least let me come too."

"You know you can't." Leon pats her shoulder. "This is destiny, Pelin. There's a reason Sare and I found each other—and the book."

We found each other. My heart skips a beat.

"You're risking yourself, and everything you worked for." Pelin glares at him.

Leon jumps into the boat and Pelin heads toward me.

"Please, Sare," she whispers. "Leon likes to play the hero—he likes to help people. He's drawn to this curse—please don't let it consume him the way it did Sufi Chelebi. Please protect him."

There are so many unknowns in the near future, and the past, and perhaps I was too focused on the curse and what it will do to me. I was selfish, never figuring this trip could harm Leon.

"Pelin!" Leon snaps before I can respond. "I'm not a child, and you're not my mum."

"You won't give up, will you?" Pelin shakes her head in frustration. "Just be careful, you two," she says, then walks away, leaving us alone under the blinking light of a broken lamp-post.

I climb into the boat after Leon, and he turns on the engine. I grip the edge as we speed off, rocking, battling with the strong current. In the narrow neck of the sea between the mainland and the tower, the water is thick with friction, the waves trying to push us back.

"What exactly is your relationship with Pelin?" I shouldn't ask—I shouldn't care—but I can't help myself.

"We grew up together," Leon answers. "She was, and still is, my only friend."

The boat's engine whirrs as we approach the island. Despite the gravity of our quest, a wave of relief washes over me—Leon isn't romantically involved with her.

What's wrong with me? Why does it even matter, when my life hangs in the balance?

Lost in my thoughts, I let my hair catch in the breeze and fill my lungs with the salty perfume of the sea. On the shore, traffic flows despite the late hour, the headlights of the cars dotted like Christmas decorations along the mainland.

Leon's voice pulls me back. "Pelin's father is my master—my teacher," he says, oblivious to my turmoil. "He saved my life when I first contacted the Otherside. Or I should say, the Otherside contacted me."

"H-how?" I ask gingerly.

"I was six when the visions started. One day, I was playing outside and a child appeared—and then disappeared as quickly as he had arrived. It didn't take me long to realize he wasn't alive. I continued to see him at random times, and even in my dreams. He demanded that I find his murderer. It's a sad story, Silverbirch, not one for today. But if it weren't for Pelin's father, I might have been long lost. Master Bora taught me how to control the visions, when to summon them, and how to dismiss them."

"Didn't your aunt help? She's a seer too, right?" I'm taken aback by how, like me, Leon has endured a childhood with the shadow of Death looming over him. Perhaps we have more things in common than I realized.

"The craft works differently for everyone," Leon says. "Harika is a clairvoyant, not a curse-breaker like me. She's haunted by the future; I'm haunted by the past—and the present."

"What about Pelin?"

"Pelin doesn't have the pure eye," Leon says. "She's a warden. She studies and documents our craft. When we arrive," he goes on, as we cut closer to the tower, "you might have a flash of something—a vision that will connect you to the past. Don't fight it, okay? Trust it."

I recall all the times Munu begged me to be selfish, to focus only on my needs. Now, I have to set aside the guilt of betraying her—or putting others in danger—in order to find the truth.

I have to do this, I tell myself. *I owe it to myself.*

It will be okay. It must be.

The tower is silent but expectant as we arrive, and I shiver as I step down from the boat onto the rocks, once more experiencing that disturbing feeling of déjà vu.

"Everything okay?" Leon touches my arm and I recoil instinctively.

Is he pitying me? A cursed girl, alone and helpless. A charity case. *He likes to help people,* Pelin's voice plays in my mind. I fill my lungs with the sea air and focus on the task at hand.

"You were right . . ." I hesitate. "I-it's different in the dark. More familiar."

My words light up Leon's eyes with excitement, a reminder how obsessed he is with the curse.

"You look different too," he says. "You almost glow . . . again."

"Now's not the time to take the mickey." I roll my eyes. "And trust me, the curse doesn't come with a radiance package."

"Hmm." He purses his lips, but he doesn't protest.

With slow steps, we enter the courtyard. Leon guides me in without uttering another word, perhaps he wants the silence to absorb me, to better trigger a memory of another life, when I was not Sare, but Iris—or Theodora.

The summer air is warm, but I still wrap my arms around myself.

"Shall we go inside?" Leon gestures at the tower.

The interior feels smaller than it looked the last time I visited—the foyer, free of the tourists, casts strange shadows through the arched windows.

I shake my head. "It's better outside." My voice echoes as we climb the staircase. "More familiar."

"The terrace, then," Leon says as we reach the rotunda.

"This is where the maiden hurled herself into the sea," I say, impatient as Leon unlocks the door. "If I'm the same person reborn, aren't you concerned about what could happen to me now?"

"I'm here to protect you." His gaze holds mine with such intensity, I'm convinced he would leap after me if I were to hurl myself into the sea. "We're in this together. Partners."

I pull myself together. *Business partners. That's all we are.*

"Silverbirch." Leon's jaw tightens as he studies my face. "Don't be afraid of hope. You *will* break this curse."

"Your hope—" I close my eyes as we step outside—"is contagious."

I try to concentrate in the silence. The night hums around me, electric with Leon so close by. My hands tightly grip the railing. But no memories, no voices, no flashes arrive. Doubt starts to creep upon me. If I was really Theodora, the maiden trapped in this tower, wouldn't I recall a flicker of memory?

I'm Sare Sıla Silverbirch, I tell myself. *Four months shy of eighteen, four times heartbroken.* Had I lived another life, the pain of it would be here with me. Time cannot erase heartbreak. Even death won't allow me to forget mine. There should be some trace of a past ache, a shadow . . . But there's nothing.

All I have are my own sorrows. Not Theodora's. Not Iris's.

I open my eyes again to take in the view of the Bosphorus. The late hour has transformed Istanbul into something wilder and more beautiful. The city lights twinkle in the distance on the mainland and a constellation of stars joins them, shining on the blanket of the water. As I stare into the velvety darkness beneath the reflections, the peculiar feeling of déjà vu stabs me again. I let go of the railing, while the skyline shimmers and the soft waves lap at the rocks like cats licking their paws.

The sea is dark beneath us, like a hungry mouth ready to devour nightmares.

The sea.

The darkness.

This balcony.

"Fuck," I gasp into the night with a sudden understanding.

It's the lights. The lights are misleading.

This place . . . *How could I not have seen it before?*

"What is it?" Leon is tense, his eyes pin me down as if I might thrust myself into the sea any minute.

But I won't. How can I? Now I know what this place really is.

The lights tricked me, or perhaps Leon's company is the worst distraction, but as I study the wrought iron panels circling the balcony, the waves caressing the base with an unyielding patience, I become certain why the tower feels so familiar.

"Nothing," I hear myself lie. For there's no way to explain to him how foolish I was, deceived by the sunlight, failing to see the truth on my first visit. Or perhaps I was too occupied with Leon.

But now under the weak light of the stars, I'm certain this place is the Inbetween.

"You've sensed something," Leon says, after a long pause.

"I-I've just—" I grapple with finding an explanation, revealing the truth without revealing the burden of the curse. How can I tell him I've stood here *dead* four times? Four times, Munu sent me back to life from this tower. "I'm just overwhelmed, thinking about how Iris and Theodora died here, on this exact spot."

And that I have been resurrected in the same place they died.

"Is that all?" Leon insists and I study him, the sharp contours of his face illuminated under the luminous gaze of the moon, his gaze dark with a stark desire to know.

He smells my lie. I see it in his eyes, but still I shake my head.

"Okay." He finally exhales, leaning over the railing. "I thought you'd have something. I thought this would work."

A shiver overtakes me. It did work. Do I arrive in this place because I kept dying here? Am I really reborn?

There's only one person who is always with me in the Inbetween, and I'm certain she holds the key to this mystery.

I clutch the evil-eye pendant that rests strangely cool against my skin.

"I should summon Munu," I tell Leon. "So you can bend her."

I need the truth. I need to know if I really am Theodora.

Leon's face is shrouded in shadows but his eyes gleam in the dark. "Are you sure?"

"Yes." I hold his gaze. I have to uncover the true origins of the curse.

My fingers tighten around my necklace, not allowing doubt to creep in and dissolve my courage.

"Munu," I whisper. "Munu, I need you."

I've never needed you more.

For a second, I assume she won't arrive. But then the air between Leon and I thickens and Munu appears with a crack, gaunt as a galley slave in the depths of a dark ship. My stomach tightens upon seeing her thinning face.

What if I'm betraying my friend for nothing?

"Canim." Munu cruises to me, then lets out a soft scream when she notices where we are. "Why—What are you doing here? I don't want to be in this place."

"Forgive me," I mutter.

"The seer dragged you here, didn't he? It stinks of him, even more than it stinks of the sea."

"Where's the book, Munu?" Leon says behind her.

"You cannot command me, boy seer." Munu whirls around. "What are you? A mere child with less skills than height."

"You owe me the journal." Leon's eyes narrow. "You stole what is mine."

Munu rises in the air, as if she wants to belittle him. "The book didn't want you to find it. I heard them talking about it—" She drops her voice as she always does when she's speaking of the Hidden. I lean forward to hear. "They say you have the same compulsions as Chelebi. And his book wished to protect you, silly boy. It didn't want you to perish like the fool himself did. But the madness already pesters you, doesn't it? You're obsessed with Sare. You think she's the maiden. You dream of her when you sleep and even when you're awake—you even forget to eat unless you see her eating."

Hearing Munu accuse Leon of being obsessed with me sends a jolt of adrenaline to my core, distracting me from why I summoned her in the first place. Leon, obsessed with me? He can't fall for me. I glance at him with a pang of concern, but his stern expression betrays no hint of his true feelings.

"You have been reduced, just like Chelebi," Munu snarls, unaware of the effect her words have on me. "A girl blinds you, of all things. But I caution you: what you seek isn't yours and it never will be. The book—" Munu nods her head to the sea, then to me— "the girl. None of it."

A vein throbs on Leon's neck. I've spent enough time with him to recognize his fury. As I decide to intervene and tell Munu to shut it, all of a sudden, Leon's face crumples, his eyes fixed on a point beyond me. I check behind my shoulder to see what he's staring at, yet there's nothing but darkness.

"Grey—" Leon shuts his eyes. "I'm ready. Go ahead."

Then he becomes unnaturally still, straight as a telegraph pole.

"Leon," I call, cautious. But he doesn't seem to hear me. His head yanks back, and forward, then he doubles over, clutching his stomach. Panic sweeps me. "What's happening to him?" I turn to Munu. "Are you doing this?"

"Don't be daft. I don't have such powers," Munu moans. "Grey is coming. Leon will be the vessel through which Grey will manifest."

I recall how angels watched us through the gulls, how they controlled them. I swallow hard as Leon finally straightens, his posture relaxed.

"Ahh . . ." He sounds odd, childlike. And then I realize it's not just his voice that seems out of place. His eyes emit a faint gray light, casting an ethereal glow, and his face wears a serenity I've never witnessed before. Gone is the usual, confident Leon I know. Instead, there's an expression of innocence, disarmingly guileless.

"What a beautiful evening," Leon utters. His voice, now distinctly not his own, resonates like a chorus of singing children. "I've always favored Konstantiniyye's skyline to any other."

"Leon, what's going on?" Even as the words leave my mouth, I know it won't be Leon who answers.

"He's not Leon any more," Munu mutters, darting toward me. "His boss is here."

"Silence," Grey commands.

I suppose I should feel terrorized in the presence of an angel, but beneath my concern for Leon lies only my determination to unmask the truth.

"I'm no one's boss," Grey declares. "Quite the contrary, I'm here to save those who need saving—I sense mistakes that have run well past due course."

Mistakes? I frown. The angel speaks in riddles.

"As if we need saving from anyone but you two busybodies," Munu mutters. Like me, she looks like she's past the point of being frightened. "And I've made no mistakes."

"Dear daughter, you made mistakes, and mistakes were made *to* you." The creature that inhabits Leon smiles. "You have been suffering for long enough, Munu, don't you think? Now you will reveal the truth your supervisor has been hiding so wickedly: confess the evidence of his misdeeds. Or would you rather have me bend you?"

"Sare," Munu says, as she begins to shrink. Clearly not past the point of fear, then. It tugs on my heartstrings. "Please, tell him to leave me alone."

"Sare Sıla Silverbirch?" Grey-Leon's face lights up. "I've heard so much about you. Well, heard is a stretch perhaps, but you're floating around in Leon's head a great deal. The youth and their fixations, eh? What great passions you all have! All those . . . feisty feelings!"

"Nice to meet you too," I mutter, blushing. I don't know what else to say. "Is Leon alright?"

"Of course he is! Do you think I'm a monster? Your . . . friend will be back as soon as I depart, good as new. Now, shall I start the interrogation?" Grey suggests. "I don't think the ethereal is going to confess by her own free will and, as much as I'd like to bless you with my presence, I don't have all night."

"Sare," Munu begs. "Tell him you don't want this—he'll listen to you!"

"No need to be dramatic." Grey-Leon towers over her as she continues to shrink. "Ah, a plume of fear, worry, and—anger? Emotions are fascinating, aren't they, Munu? I've always wondered why our Boss Almighty never blessed us celestials with hearts, while every mortal possesses one. I'd love to have a couple of hearts myself." He reaches forward with hawk-like precision, snatching Munu with his hand. "You're nearly half alive, aren't you?" His eyes widen with surprise. "It's astonishing how he didn't fully send you to the Otherside. Kind of genius, I give him that."

I stare at them both, stupefied. *Who does he mean?*

But before I can ask, Grey lifts Munu and blows a puff of air onto her face. "Be still," he murmurs.

A moan escapes from Munu's throat.

"Let go—" Munu stops, mid-sentence. Her face crunches and for a moment I almost consider begging Grey to stop, but I know that Munu will never really talk otherwise, and I have to know.

"There, there now," Grey says. "You're all ready to tweet. Tell us: where's the book?"

"F-F-Five has it," Munu says. "*The Book of Heartbreak* must be destroyed."

Who the fuck is Five? I'm too stunned to ask.

"What a shame! But I'm not surprised, he never seems to appreciate anything done by mortals." Grey chuckles, though it sounds like pouring rain. "Sare Silverbirch, please proceed with your questions as you see fit. I have to keep hold of her, if you don't mind?"

I nod. Even though I'm well aware that Grey probably doesn't care whether I mind or not.

Inside Grey's palm, Munu trembles like a twig in the winter wind despite the warm night. But I can't worry about her now. Ever since I saw Theodora's face, one question has been plaguing me and now I can have it answered.

"Tell me," I whisper. "Was I Theodora once? Am I the maiden in the tower?"

"You are only you and no one else," Munu replies.

"Liar," I say.

"I only speak the truth," Munu says. "Not what you want to hear."

"Then why is this place the Inbetween—" My throat runs dry. "Why do I rise from the dead on the same spot where the maiden and Iris died, if I'm not their reincarnation?"

"You are no reincarnation," Munu says. "You gravitate here, because this place is the origin of the curse."

Finally, she admits one piece of the truth.

"Then how am I linked to Theodora?" I demand.

"Theodora of the House Doukas . . ." Munu hesitates, then speaks again. "She was your grandmother from twenty generations back. She was the first bearer of the curse. A sick twist of fate how you look so much like her. The curse exists to cause suffering, of course."

My spirits sink, as Munu confirms what I already suspected: I *am* from Theodora's bloodline. But how could Theodora become a mother or a grandmother, if she lived and died here on this island? The truth seems complex, enshrouded in layers, and the prospect of uncovering the core of it fills me with dread.

"But Theodora died here." I think of the multiple versions of the myth I've heard, but I'm certain none of them mentioned any children. "She had no children."

Munu snorts. "*The maiden* died here, devoid of love and company. She didn't have the warmth of any other human being. She never had children of her own."

"Why are you talking in riddles?" I snap. "How could Theodora be my grandmother, then?"

"Theodora wasn't the maiden." Munu laughs now, like a mad woman. "The fool got it all wrong. That *great* seer, Sufi Chelebi."

"But Chelebi—He summoned the maiden—" I stammer. "I don't understand . . ."

"I told you not to trust the seers, didn't I? Yet you let them manipulate you. That pretentious Ottoman assumed that the maiden was cursed, and he ended up summoning Theodora, the true bearer of the curse. I bet it's his own foolishness that brought on Sufi Chelebi's doom, once Theodora revealed to him what she had done." Munu looks me in the eye. "The maiden herself wasn't cursed. She was the one who cast the curse."

"The maiden—" I manage. "The maiden is the origin of the curse?"

I think of *The Book of Heartbreak*, how Sufi Chelebi avoided explaining what Theodora showed to him. *She wasn't innocent*, was all he had said. Was it his own shame that stopped Chelebi from explaining the mistake he made in assuming Theodora was the maiden?

But who was the maiden, if it wasn't Theodora?

"She couldn't forgive." Now Munu is crying, tears running silently down her cheeks. "How could you forgive, when your own flesh and blood betrays you?"

My mind races through the fragments I read from *The Book of Heartbreak*. And then I remember how Theodora pleaded to Sufi Chelebi: *My heart shall remain forever fractured, as shall my sister's.*

"Her sister," I mutter, still hardly able to believe it. "Theodora's sister was the maiden!"

"Yes." Munu nods. "Eudokia of House Doukas was seventeen when she stepped inside here, to her prison."

"Eudokia of House Doukas," I repeat, still trying to put together all the pieces of the puzzle.

"The tale has transformed through the ages, hasn't it? What do they say these days? How do they reimagine it? A devoted father locks up his daughter in this forsaken tower in desperation, so he could protect her from death, right?" Munu laughs a bitter laugh. "I listened to Daphne telling you all about it when you were young. The ending never changes. Death always finds its way here, and the maiden always dies. That is the only part that remains true." Munu lifts her head to gaze at me. "None of those versions mention Theodora's wickedness though. No one knows how one sister's venom poisoned another."

I no longer understand which sister she means.

"Theodora deserved everything she got. She deserved the curse, the hurt, the grief. Eudokia—she was innocent. At least at first . . . Then she changed too." Munu slowly shakes her head. "Love rots everything. But hatred . . . Hatred helps you survive."

"Were you Eudokia's guardian, then?" I crave her confession. The truth seems so near, as if I can reach out and clutch it, if only I knew the right questions to ask. "But . . . Eudokia wasn't cursed, so why did you help her, Munu?"

"Don't you get it? I wasn't anyone's guardian. I wasn't helping anyone." Munu writhes, and Grey releases her with a pitiful look, as if she's no longer worth the effort. She flies over to me and reaches out to touch my cheeks, as if she's throwing herself onto my mercy. "The maiden caused *all* the suffering. It's why everyone is so angry with her. It's why everything is always her fault. She caused so much unrest, so many glitches in the divine system. She's the one to blame, because she didn't listen."

I freeze. Suddenly, the truth dawns on me. Yet, I can't believe or accept it. It suffocates me, destructive, unthinkable. *No,* I tell myself. *It can't be.* There must be another explanation.

Still, I must ask. "How do you know all of this?"

The stars above us seem to falter when Munu speaks again.

"Because I am the one who cast the curse. *I* am the maiden," she says at last, and my heart burns as if it's been thrown into a fire. "I, Eudokia of the House Doukas."

CHAPTER SEVENTEEN

Hate is a faithful companion to those who are betrayed and wronged by the ones they hold dearest, for they inflict the deepest wounds. Where love enslaves, hatred is ready to serve.

Excerpt from *The Book of Heartbreak, Müneccimbaşı Sufi Chelebi's Journals of Mystical Phenomena*

Breathe, I command myself. *Count down. Distract yourself.*

But all my efforts are futile. Munu's words plague my ears.

Munu is the maiden, the origin of the curse that has killed me four times.

The only person who loved me is the one who cursed me. Or perhaps that was another lie. Perhaps she never loved me, and I was simply a price she had to pay for creating a curse. It wasn't fear that held her back from telling me the truth. It was her deceit.

Munu's betrayal sinks deeper into my skin and I think back to everything she ever did, everything she ever said. She held my hand the first time I had the fluttering, she made me believe she was my friend. She whispered malice to me, against everyone else, even my own mother. She taught me to hate everyone, trust no one but her.

I was a sacrifice, I was a pawn—a token trapped in a bell jar of lies, betrayed by everyone who should have protected me.

My heart sizzles. I didn't realize how hard I had been fluttering, but now the burning invades my chest, inescapable.

"One big tragedy, isn't it? Even messier than I thought." Grey, who has been silently observing us, now approaches Munu. He distracts me for a moment. "I must ask—is Eudokia registered with the Mortal ID: M1274856567048112?"

Munu stares at him, a hollow shell of herself. "How would I know?" she snaps. "I am a mere servant of Five."

Grey nods. "I suspected as such."

"He'll never forgive me," Munu whispers, but she doesn't look like she's talking to us.

I'm numb, too dizzy with the fluttering in my chest to distract myself.

"Well, it was a pleasure to meet you all, but it's time for me to depart," Grey says. "I need to write a few correspondences. But fear not, dear daughters, I understand how you were treated unjustly. I understand very well. I will be in touch soon." Grey waves at Munu. "Take care of Sare Sıla Silverbirch, now. She does not look well."

Leon becomes stone still as Grey departs. My knees wobble as I step forward, trying to reach him, and Munu whizzes around my shoulders with desperation.

Fluttering. All I sense is the fluttering until she speaks.

"Forgive me," she whispers. Her eyes are full of sorrow. "I failed to protect you from the truth."

I try to take a breath, but the burning in my chest won't let me. Her treachery blooms in my lungs like a poisonous flower. I place my hand on my heart as if I can convince it to behave.

"Rule . . . number . . . three . . ." I whisper. "D-death—"

But I can't speak. The pain comes in waves, a burning that tells me to surrender, to drop to my knees, to sacrifice my life to make it stop.

"No . . . No, Sare Silverbirch, you will not die because of me. Death—" Munu's scream pierces the night—"is not an option!"

Death is not an option. I part my lips but no sound comes out.

I wish I could ask Munu if she was only pretending to love me all these years. Or else how can she be so cruel, after everything we've been through? *I trusted you,* I try to say, though my voice has already left me. *You were the only friend I had. You were the missing half of my mother. Of myself.*

I'm here, I'm not here, I'm alive, I may not be alive. I've never been so close to crying.

I close my eyes as Munu weeps.

"I'm not worth it," she says. "You cannot be heartbroken because of me—not when you're so close to eighteen. Please! Look at me!" she cries. "I couldn't bear it if you die because of me."

What does it matter? You're a liar, like my mother. A fraud. A fake.

Why does everyone lie to me?

Sare, my heart sighs. *Why do you still trust?*

Gravity pulls me down. My lungs deflate. The scars on my palm hurt like stab wounds. I'm falling, and I'm so ready to let go, just so it'll stop hurting.

I drop to the ground, and the sky is all I see, with the stars seeming to explode above me from the fire in my chest.

This is it, Sare, I tell myself. *This is the moment you die for the last time. The life you wanted so dearly is no longer yours. It never will be.*

The earthquake should begin soon, then my heart will crack at any minute, and I will be gone forever.

Fight it, a voice inside my head says. *Death is not an option. Think of Muzaffer,* it insists. *You're all he has. He needs you. He cannot survive another loss.*

Muzaffer, whom I didn't once address as grandfather. Whom I didn't once hug.

"I always loved you," Munu says, somewhere nearby. "No matter what Theodora did to me, I never once saw her in your face."

She's stroking my hair now, or perhaps it's Death, already pulling me across to the Otherside. The burning in my chest is too intense for me to recognize what's going on any more.

"Hey!" A furious voice cuts through the darkness like a dagger. "What's wrong with her?"

Leon.

I want him to leave, so he won't see me in this miserable state, but the numbness has spread all over my body now. All of a sudden, I feel lighter, as if I'm floating, but then I feel him—Leon. He's scooping me up from the ground, holding me close to his chest. He does it with such ease, as if I was created to fit into his arms, or his arms were created to hold me.

"What's happening?" He lifts me up as if I'm a doll. I'm limp. I'm weak.

I'm going to die in Leon's arms, I realize in panic.

It's not fair. None of this is fair.

I must fight it, I must do something before the earthquake starts.

"What have you done to her?" Leon cries again.

"I haven't—She's—She's—It's the curse!" Munu stutters. "Do something! You brought her here, now you need to save her!"

"Silverbirch!" Leon sounds desperate. It's strange to hear him helpless. "Please. Say something. Do you hear me?" His arms wrap around me like a blanket. I lean my head against his chest and breathe in his salty scent. And then his heart begins to drum in my ears. The thuds of his heartbeats imprint on mine, overruling my own rhythm. Then there is only his heartbeat and mine, and nothing else in the world.

"We need to distract her," Munu yells.

I force my eyes open to look up at Leon, so I can see his beauty one last time.

But the curse is hungry. It won't let me see him.

"Distract her!" I hear Munu wail.

I can sense Leon's hesitation. He pulls me closer to himself, as if daring me to fight against the curse.

"Do something!" Munu screams, and that's when I feel Leon lean down and press his lips to mine. And I, who have never been kissed, taste him like freedom.

It's ironic that a kiss saves me from a heartbreak.

But it does.

He does.

Leon.

When our lips lock, the burning in my heart recedes. With a newfound fierceness, I reply to his passion with mine. Our kiss is a wildfire. A portal. An antidote to death's oblivion. Time stretches like a lullaby and the burning pain begins to pale. Soon, the world expands and I'm no longer in the tower but adrift, floating over a sunbrushed field, away from the sea and the darkness. The beats of my pulse realign with his once more. My fingers rake through his hair. Our roots intertwine.

In that everlasting moment there is no longer an ancient curse, no more heartbreaks, no towers imprisoning maidens.

Somewhere far away, the waves still lap under a starlit sky.

And I am just a seventeen-year-old girl with a galloping heart.

"Enough. Leave her alone!" I hear Munu's shriek. "I said distract her, not suffocate her!"

Munu's unimpressed voice distracts me from the madness of the moment. The burning in my chest is no more—now it's my lips that feel on fire.

"You saved her. How romantic. How reckless," Munu buzzes on. "Now, leave her alone."

"Leon." How can I ever look into his eyes again, after a kiss like that? "I'm okay—to stand."

Leon hesitates for a few seconds, then helps me back to my feet.

"And you—" I turn to Munu. "How dare you still speak to me?"

"Sare—" Leon frowns with an unreadable expression. "Are you sure you're okay now?"

"The worst is over." My face burns with shame and anger, my lips swollen. "Thanks for distracting me."

Is that fleeting disappointment on Leon's face?

Now that the fluttering and burning is no more, I realize how presumptuous it is that the first thing he decided to distract me with was a kiss.

I recall Pelin's words: *He likes playing the part of the hero.*

The recollection of how fiercely I kissed him back floods me with such embarrassment and shame that I want to jump from the tower and into the waves. *I'm a fool.*

"Canim," Munu says, distracting me. "Get rid of him, please."

"No," I warn her. "First, you tell me everything about the curse. No more lies."

"No more lies," Munu agrees with a nod. "But I demand privacy." She gestures at Leon. "You will soon be aware of what seers have done to me. I won't speak in the company of one."

"I can't leave her," Leon objects, his jaw clenched with frustration. "Silverbirch—"

"Please leave," I urge him, the charred outline of our kiss lifting from my lips. I can't let him see how weak I am against his charm. "This is between Munu and me."

Hurt clouds his face again. Perhaps I'm imagining it. "Fine," he concedes with a grunt, then turns to go. "I'll be downstairs. Call me if you need me. I'll be waiting."

We watch him disappear. I press my back against the wall, grounding myself in the cool stone. Munu hovers nearby, her wings drooping as if weighed down by memories. Her betrayal settles between us, thick as the humid air. Then at last, Munu speaks.

"Once upon a time," she says, "I was mortal. An innocent. And a fool."

Just like me.

"I was an idiot who hoped, until my unheard prayers diminished all the light I had in me. Even my name abandoned me, canim. It's been a long time since I remembered I was Eudokia. Almost a thousand years, yet I can close my eyes and my name rises in my mind. Eudokia of the House Doukas, I was. My father was a nobleman in the court of the Emperor Alexios. I was the youngest of his two daughters.

"My sister Theodora was two years older than me and—" A shadow grows on her face as she pauses. "My sister's tongue was a silk ribbon; once she began to speak, it could cover anyone's eyes, especially mine. She was beautiful and I always trusted her, never once thinking she could ruin me. I must show you, canim, for there is no way to tell what she did to me. Close your eyes," Munu mutters. "I promise, it will be quick and painless."

I obey her command, as I've done countless times before, not certain why I still trust her. I hear the flap of her wings, then she places her hands on my eyelids.

"I always wished to get rid of these memories," Munu whispers. "I didn't understand they'd be worth carrying their weight, for a day like this."

A flash of light blinds me, and when I open my eyes, there's no sign of Munu. I find myself in a room with a four-poster bed, where two girls with ribbons in their hair are racing around.

"Theodora," the shorter one says. I barely recognize Munu. She has no wings, and she's the size of a normal child. Her face brims with the innocence of childhood. "I'm scared alone in my room."

"Then stay here," replies the older girl, cradling an enormous white cat in her arms. "Eudokia can stay with us, can't she, Cleo?"

Theodora resembles me so closely that, if it weren't for their attire and the furnishings, I could easily mistake the scene for one of my own childhood memories.

The cat jumps down out of her arms, darting toward me. The light flashes and the room shifts.

It's the same room, but the girls are not around the bed any more, and something feels different . . .

"Theodora!"

I turn to see Eudokia emerging from the wooden door with a sense of urgency. She appears as old as I am now, taller than I've ever seen her. Dressed in a blue gown cinched at the waist with a golden belt, and her hair adorned with a pearl tiara, she is a striking beauty.

"I've been searching for you everywhere." Eudokia hurries over to Theodora, who is seated on a windowsill with Cleo nestled on her lap. "You missed the banquet."

"I'm not feeling well," Theodora murmurs, though there is no visible sign of illness on her. Through the window, the sea stretches out dark and expectant beneath the night sky. I forget to breathe when I see the Maiden's Tower in the distance, as oblivious as a mere lighthouse.

"You won't believe what happened," Eudokia squeaks, her excitement palpable as she fumbles through her garments to retrieve a piece of parchment and a gemstone ring. "Papa allowed me to dance with Lazarios, and then Lazarios gave me a letter . . . and his ring."

"A ring?" Theodora flinches as her gaze drops to the ring in Eudokia's hand. The cat meows softly in her lap.

"Oh, he loves me, Thea!" Eudokia gushes with joy as she slips the ruby ring on her finger. Then she passes the note to Theodora. "He swore his undying love to me."

With that, Eudokia begins to dance around the room, as if still in Lazarios's arms. A brief flicker of hurt crosses Theodora's face before she carefully folds the letter again.

The cat drops to the ground and bolts toward me. The moment she hits me with a hiss, the light flares and I'm pulled into another memory.

Theodora and Eudokia are huddled together in a vast, echoing hall, with stone walls decorated with vivid tapestries. Eudokia's pale skin is almost translucent against the dark green of her plain dress, while Theodora's red gown seems to glow in the dim light. Two men are in the room with them, their voices echoing off the vaulted ceiling. One, a man with a salt-and-pepper goatee, has a haunted look in his eyes. The other, younger and with raven black hair, speaks with a chilling intensity.

"When dreams speak, they never lie," he declares, pointing a long finger at Eudokia. "I saw it. Your youngest will be the downfall of your great family, if you don't lock her away. Her freedom will cost your house dearly."

A shiver runs down my spine. He is a seer, I realize. His prophecy dragged Munu to this dark place. It's why she hates seers so much.

"You must cease all contact with her," the man says flatly.

"Eudokia—I can't," the other man—clearly the girls' father—protests, his voice trembling. "How can I?"

"You must," the seer insists, his eyes filled with a grim determination. I catch Theodora giving him a subtle nod, her expression unreadable. "Think of your other children."

"The tower," Theodora suggests, her voice barely a whisper. "Can't she stay in that tower?"

"I will, Papa," Eudokia says, her voice filled with a strange resignation. She steps forward, her gaze meeting her father's. "I'd rather live in isolation than bring about the fall of our victorious house."

I want to cry out, to beg her to reconsider. But I'm frozen in place, a helpless spectator. I watch as Eudokia agrees to walk into her prison, of her own free will. Theodora embraces her, tears streaming down her face. They weep together, their sobs echoing through the empty hall. And then, the light flashes again, and I am transported to the tower.

The structure feels different, more fragile. Eudokia is alone on the rotunda, her only companions are doves, kept in a cage like herself. Gulls whirl around the tower, the sun rises and falls, Eudokia drops to her knees and unites her hands in prayer.

"Saints and angels, I pray to you," she begs on her knees, her hands clasped tight. "Either return my freedom, my family, my love, or let Death claim me."

The sea is silent. So is the sky. I watch Eudokia as years fade her away. The doves are her only companions. She buries them on the islet when they die, digging graves with her bare hands. The servants who bring her food arrive with new birds.

The light flashes again.

I glance down from the window with Eudokia as Theodora disembarks from a boat. She climbs up to the tower with hurried steps, and emerges at Eudokia's door. I watch Eudokia shrink away, unable to return her sister's embrace.

She must be so starved of human touch, she has forgotten intimacy.

"Sister," Theodora says. "Our father has been laid to rest, and since the earth took him, I haven't known peace. I cannot sleep, for he visits me day and night, Eudokia—so I came to beg for your forgiveness."

"Why, sister?" Eudokia asks. "Why should I forgive you? You haven't wronged me."

Upon Eudokia's words, Theodora collapses in the center of the room, huddled inside her skirts.

"Sweet Eudokia." She lifts her head. But Eudokia's face darkens, her eyes fixed on Theodora's hand. And then I notice the ring Lazarios had once given Eudokia, shining on Theodora's finger like a bead of blood.

"Where did you get that?" Eudokia frowns.

"Don't you understand? I loved him too. I loved him incurably. I loved him so much I thought I'd die from it. I loved him until I forgot who I was. And I made a pact with the devil. I paid the seer to whisper a false prophecy into our father's ears. I betrayed you. It's I who imprisoned you here. There was no prophecy."

Something sinks in me with this confession, but Eudokia doesn't move. A minute passes, with soft sobs of Theodora, and silence from Eudokia.

"Theodora," Eudokia says. "With whom I shared my childhood, my heart, my meals, as well as the void left by our mother's absence. My sister. Did you really betray me? No, it cannot be true. Perhaps I've gone mad, after all these years." Eudokia closes her hands to her eyes. "Perhaps I am seeing nightmares awake."

"Forgive me." Theodora creeps to Eudokia's legs. "Father is now beyond the border where no secrets can be kept. He knows what I've done. I've become a creature tormented by guilt for wronging you. I swear on my children, regret rules my heart. Love blinded me, my passion made me a fool. I implore you, with all the kindness in your heart, to forgive me. Father won't leave me alone until I set you free. Please, please, Eudokia. You were always good and kind. I came here to seek your mercy."

And just then, in the wake of Theodora's words, as if the fury seeps into the land beneath the sea, Constantinople begins to tremble, gripped by the tremors of a mighty earthquake.

The earthquake terrorizes Theodora, she claws her sister's skirts like a child. "Mercy, Eudokia," she cries as if she were the one causing the earth to shatter.

Eudokia tugs at her skirts to get rid of her, and then she walks to the doves' cage. She cracks the cage open, ignoring her sister's pleas, and releases the birds. But they shy away from flying.

"Unlike me, they don't know freedom," Eudokia tells her sister. "It's harder when you do know, sister."

She stands against the open window and thrusts a white dove into the air, and the rest follow with their flickering wings.

Theodora, seemingly hopeful of Eudokia's kindness to the birds, begs again. "Eudokia, let's leave this place . . ."

The earth groans as if it too saw the silent fury in Eudokia's face.

"Leave?" She confronts Theodora. "I have become one with this place, and it with me. No longer am I your sister. In place of my heart, I now harbor a darkness birthed from the pain you wrought upon me. How dare you stand before me and plead for forgiveness! I curse my own tongue for having once addressed you as a sister, and may I burn in the seventh circle of hell if it utters a word of forgiveness."

"I beg you," Theodora pleads, bowing down to Eudokia's feet, but Eudokia recoils, repulsed by the gesture. "Lazarios left me too, if that offers any consolation. He abandoned me. He was cruel, Eudokia. He tortured me. He forbade me from using his name. 'Lazarios belongs to your sister,' he said. I was to address him as Azylios. He was never mine. Never my Lazarios—as if his heart always belonged to you. He never loved me as much as he loved you."

Eudokia fixes Theodora with a blank, hollow stare. Her sister goes on, desperately.

"And when he left, he took a piece of my soul with him. I've not known peace since the day I set my eyes on him."

With this, Eudokia lets out a laugh that makes my hairs stand on end. "What is it, compared to what you've done to me? You crippled me. You shattered my soul. Never shall I grant you forgiveness, not even if the earth splits open to swallow you."

Theodora weeps, but Eudokia seems unmoved by her tears. A shadow crosses her face, hollowing her eyes.

"May our lineage bear the torment you've carved into my heart," she shouts. "May their hearts shatter over and over, may they love only to lose and trust only to be betrayed. I curse you, and each child you bear, and all their descendants to endure the fate of my poor birds—fluttering in futile resistance, writhing against a freedom of which they were robbed. Let Death conquer them heartbroken and all alone, until they fall one by one, so I *become* the downfall of House Doukas, as was once prophesied."

I tremble watching Eudokia climb onto the windowsill, fulfilling the false prophecy, as the earthquake rages beneath us. Theodora lets out a wail once she figures out what her sister is about to do, but not quick enough to catch her before she leaps.

I'm numb with sorrow when I hear a splash of waves, and the light flashes again, but not before I get a glimpse of black wings and eyes. And then I am back in the darkness of the night and Munu is removing her hands from my eyes, pulling me back to where we stand on the Maiden's Tower, where all the anguish began.

"I was a fool to think that death was a salvation," Munu murmurs. "Death was no victory against my sister."

She drifts away, looking at me expectantly, as if I'm supposed to throw myself on her mercy like Theodora did. But I'm not Theodora. I haven't deceived anyone.

Munu's wings quiver as if she's shivering.

"So you cast the curse," I mutter. "What happened after that? How did you get those wings?"

"After the earthquake died, I looked up to the walls to see Theodora, whose hands gripped the windowsill, and when my eyes followed her gaze, I saw myself afloat in the sea, shapeless in death. And then he came . . ." Munu said. "My beloved—My b-boss, may he forgive me for speaking his real name. Five the Fifth, Angel of Death. But before he could take me, another one of them came—Nine the Ninth, and she told me that my beddua had cast a curse."

I recall Sufi Chelebi's words: a beddua is the worst form of an ill-wish, sourced from a suffering heart.

"'Retract your words at once, implore a tovbe and seek redemption,' she urged me. And before you ask, canim, a tovbe is a penance to a beddua—an act of deep and genuine regret. It would have stopped the curse before it took root. But I didn't regret what I had done. I had just made the ultimate sacrifice so I wouldn't ever feel obliged to forgive Theodora. I refused to say it."

"You had the chance to stop this?" I groan. She had an opportunity, and she blew it.

"Fury had blinded me. Five warned me—he is the all-knowing, always blessed. He told me I was being foolish. Nine was even angrier than him. But I told her that she too would not be forgiven, for I prayed day and night to the angels while I was in that tower but none ever answered until I died. And then, as Nine was about to crush me in her fury at my defiance, Five intervened. He saved me from Nine's wrath, made me an ethereal. Though he marked me with these wings and the inability to control my body when I'm angry or scared, so I would remember how I rebelled against the Hidden and do better, he also blessed me with a new name. A new name holds power, canim, it's a new beginning. And Five bound me to himself with my new name, Munu. He tethered my fate to his until the world crumbles into dust. I owe him my existence."

Finally, Munu falls silent. Above us, the delicate darkness of the sky hangs like a blanket, before being drawn back when the night hours begin to recede into morning.

I realize the story has ended, but I still don't have my answers.

"What happened to Theodora?" I ask. "How did the curse find me?"

"Theodora walked away from the island alive. But the curse followed her and her line, shifting between the women of our blood, taking a different form of heartbreak in each. Hers was abandonment. Even her children left her." Munu trembles like a dewdrop on a spider's web. "I watched the curse rot my family, I watched my house's downfall. Until—" Munu pauses, biting her lips, her fingers fidgeting, fighting with an unknown enemy. "Until that seer, Sufi Chelebi, stopped it."

"But I-I don't get it." I'm clouded by confusion once more. "How could I be cursed if Chelebi broke the curse centuries ago?"

"Please, calm down, canim," Munu warns softly.

"It's Sare to you now!" I snap, as if I can be her "canim" any more.

"I don't exactly know what happened," she says, her voice breaking.

"Perhaps it was you again!" I fill my lungs with the salty air to cool down my rage, unable and unwilling to believe her.

"No, I swear it wasn't me." She shakes her head vehemently. "I was away on a mission when the curse reawakened in 2007."

The year Iris died.

"I was in Himachal Pradesh, in a town called Dagshai. I can prove it." Munu insists. "Five lent my services to Nine. I was responsible for handling a string of hauntings. It was terrifying. I feared for my own soul. And Nine was a nightmare boss. No breaks, no help from other ethereals. Just me, drowning in one task after another. But one day, Nine appeared, with threats of Hell fire, and told me 'another wretched soul' from my lineage had awakened the curse. I panicked. I wrote to Five for help, but he, too, was livid, claiming my bloodline was born to torment him." She pauses, her eyes dark with guilt. "I always assumed your mother was the culprit. Or perhaps her sister. They were the only descendants of Doukas in Istanbul at that time. I swear, I didn't do anything."

It hits me like a punch to the stomach. All those years I thought Mum was reckless, fucked up, unlucky, or even weak . . . It wasn't her fault. It wasn't bad choices or misfortune. She was a descendant of House Doukas and her heartbreak was inevitable.

"Daphne was cursed too." My voice is a croak.

Munu only nods, her eyes wild and untamed, living through her memories.

"But you weren't guiding Mum like you do me." I swallow hard, trying to focus again. "How did I end up with you? Why didn't she get any help?"

I remain silent until she speaks again.

"You were just born when Five sent me documents explaining what the curse would do to you. You are the one with whom the curse will end, once and for all. You are special, Sare. You are unlike any of those who came before."

I am special. I am the sacrifice.

"My task has always been keeping you alive," Munu carries on. "I was still in Dagshai when the information about the assignment arrived. When Nine finally released me from her service, I visited you. You were asleep in your cot, canim, like a drop of pearl, innocent and oblivious to the darkness ahead. I left, of course. My task wasn't due to begin until the curse threatened your life for the first time. Later, when I met you properly, I began to grasp the cruel mistake I'd made in cursing my own family. But don't get me wrong—I haven't forgiven my sister. You're the only reason I've ever regretted what I did. You don't deserve it, Sare. You don't deserve any of it."

You don't deserve this, Muzaffer's words ring in my ears.

Who does deserve it then? Mum? Iris?

Was Mum the one who awakened the curse? Is this all because of her?

There was a darkness around her, one I was too blind to notice. Now I know we bear the same shadow—and Daphne wasn't enough to satiate it. It wants me.

I place my hand above my heart. I don't know how I can stay so calm. Perhaps Munu's deceit broke me so hard that no fluttering is left in me.

"I promise, it will end soon, and you will be free from the burdens of a heart—you will be invincible."

"Shut up," I lash out. "Don't act as if you're a martyr. How can you still reel off this crap after the agony you've caused? Do you have no shame?"

"I tried to protect you. Love and its ensuing sorrows breed nothing but ruin."

"No." I stand my ground. "Chelebi's book chose me for a reason. I *will* break the curse before it takes my heart."

"Even if that fool's book has really chosen you, even if there's another way," Munu says, cruising closer to me tentatively while I draw back, "it's too risky. You could die, Sare. Do not let the seer drown you in hope."

The word *hope* sounds so bleak on Munu's lips.

"What do you know about hope?" I mutter. "You're a cruel, heartless woman. You lied to me all these years. I'm doomed because of you!"

"I loved you as if you were mine."

"Yet you never once *told* me that you loved me," I dismiss her outright.

"I didn't want you to be weak," she pleads.

"I won't let you manipulate me any longer. I'll either break the curse, or I'll die trying."

"Please." Munu flies back and forth. "Sare—"

"Leave, Munu, or should I call you Eudokia now?" I snap. "I will never forgive you."

"But the curse—"

"It's not your problem." I pause and, with shaking fingers, I tear off the evil-eye pendant that has hung around my neck since my very first heartbreak and fling it to the ground. It hits the floor with a clink, cracking the gemstone. "Take it. I won't need it from now on."

Munu's body trembles with spasms as she sobs.

"Begone!" I cry, wishing it didn't hurt this much to cut myself off from her. "I never want to see you again."

Communication is classified as Highly confidential.
Circulation strictly limited to beings with celestial origins.

Subject: Job Offer

Date: 5 August 2025
From: Nine the Ninth, Senior Angel of Fate, Fate Adjustment Bureau, Mortal Affairs Commission
To: Grey the Compassionate, Associate Cherub, Curses and Malediction Archives, Worldly Index, Sacred Data Systems, Halotech Data & Integration Hub

Cherub,

Your hard work, despite being unsolicited, has caught our attention. We would like to offer you a role better suited to your skills. See the job description attached. You can start immediately. There's no further need for you to work on curses, or whatever there is to do in the mortal archives.

Ta.
Nine the Ninth

Job Title: Senior Cherub, Temporal Intervention Agency
Reports to: Temporal Intervention Coordinator, Reporting to Nine the Ninth, Senior Angel of Fate, Reporting to Archangel Absolute, Head of Mortal Affairs (Emissary to They Whom Should Not Be Concerned, Our Boss Almighty)

Job Overview:
The **Senior Cherub of the Temporal Intervention Agency** oversees and executes divine interventions within the mortal realm, ensuring timely responses to celestial requests. This primarily back-office role involves subtle adjustments to timelines, and

making sure all changes are in accordance with the grand divine plan. As a senior team member, you will collaborate with resourced ethereals and higher-ranking angels across Mortal Affairs Commission to maintain the cosmic harmony.

Key Responsibilities:
- Coordinate with the **Fate Adjustment Bureau** and **Mortal Termination and Transition** to ensure the resources are appropriately utilized
- Prepare detailed reports and graphs for the **Celestial Compliance Office**
- Be able to distinguish between miracles and catastrophes
- Develop new intervention tactics to minimize the consumption of angelic resources

Qualifications:
- Minimum 500 years of celestial experience
- Strong understanding of fate mechanics and cosmic harmony

Attributes:
- Precision, foresight, and unwavering commitment
- Ability to perform under divine pressure
- Can-do, Will-do, My-Bosses-Know-Better-Than-I-Do attitude

This is a fantastic position suited for an experienced cherub ready to take on a senior role in shaping the destinies from behind the scenes with no need for the hands-on fieldwork. You'll have significant potential for divine career development.

CHAPTER EIGHTEEN

Courage may lead to wisdom, yet also lays the foundation for betrayal.
Excerpt from *The Book of Betrayal, Müneccimbaşı Sufi Chelebi's Journals of Mystical Phenomena*

When I finally navigate my way downstairs, the tower is no longer the fairytale I once thought it was. The space feels hollow now, cloaked with darkness and my own sorrow. I scan the foyer until I spot Leon in the silver glow of the moonlight. He leans on the wall, hands in his pockets.

"All done?" he asks, as if nothing just happened upstairs. As if I didn't just lose everything. As if we didn't kiss.

I nod, and an awkward silence fills the air between us.

He kissed me. I shiver as I step toward him. *And, what's worse, I kissed him back.*

"What happened upstairs . . . " He hesitates as our eyes lock, his voice strained by a tone I can't decipher. "It was—"

"It was nothing," I interject, fueled by shame. I can't bear his regret on top of everything else.

Leon's face is partially shrouded with shadows, but the hurt beneath his frustrated expression is unmistakeable.

"It's not the first time Munu made things worse than they already are," I say. "And I'm sorry you had to deal with me in that state. It was completely unacceptable for us to . . . you know. We're only business partners."

He pauses a moment, considering my words. "You had to deal with me too, by the looks of it." He clears his throat. "I wasn't really thinking, and I was under pressure—the ethereal was in such a panic. I didn't know what was happening to you."

"I can't really remember," I say. I force a smile to make the lie convincing. "Don't worry, it didn't mean anything."

"Of course," he says, with an enthusiasm that matches mine.

"Glad we're clear on that."

"Where's Munu?" Leon is quick to change the topic.

I shrug. "She's gone."

Leon nods in response, seemingly distracted.

We walk out into the courtyard in silence, side by side, back to being two strangers.

I watch him, as the sea churns around us like an unsettled child, savoring every contour of his face, every curve and line. My heart welcomes an unfamiliar rhythm in our closeness. A deep longing surges within me, compelling me to reach out to him. I yearn to touch his skin, to rake my fingers through his hair once more, to press my lips against his. This newfound hunger for physical contact overwhelms me, leaving me aching inside.

Fuck. One kiss, and I'm already falling for him?

I seethe at my own weakness. *Don't be an idiot, Sare.*

Love, Munu whispers in my head, *is a disease. It rots everything.*

Even with the slim chance that I'm something other than a mission or a charity case for Leon, and he feels the same wildfire raging in my chest—the curse still looms above me, a monstrous shadow destroying any chance of a future. The Hidden decided my fate before I even drew my first breath, casting me as the vessel of this curse, to live and die with it. In four months, I will turn eighteen and be empty of emotion. Love will abandon me forever.

But I will not be obedient. I will not bow to the ways of the Hidden.

Whatever my mother or Iris has done, I will unearth it.

You could die, I hear Munu again.

I could die, I repeat to myself. *But I will die with the truth.*

"So." Leon distracts me from my haunted thoughts. "Did you manage to learn anything useful about what reactivated the curse?" He tries to sound casual, but I know he's just as keen as I am to uncover the mystery.

I tell him everything—everything he needs to know—carefully weeding out the details about how the curse claims its victims through heartbreaks. I can't bear the thought of him knowing, of being seen as some pathetic freak doomed by love.

His eyebrows arch as I finally fall silent. "Eudokia cast the curse, but your mother and aunt awakened it?"

I nod. "There's no one else."

"And we know for certain that Iris died here, didn't she?" Leon's brows furrow.

"Do you think that Iris died here, cursing my mother?" I frown. "But my mother was nothing like Theodora. She was kind and . . . sad. She wouldn't harm her sister."

"Someone must know something," Leon says. "A friend or a relative. Someone."

"There's only Muzaffer," I sigh. "And he won't speak."

"Then a clue in the house—"

"He doesn't let me in Mum's room," I interrupt, sounding more annoyed than I'd intended.

"All you need is a key," Leon says.

He makes it sound easy, and perhaps it *is* easy, but right now, I'm exhausted.

"You don't look very motivated." A playful smile plays on his lips.

"I'm too tired." *And hurt.* "I need ten hours of sleep and six bars of chocolate before I can feel motivation."

"You're funny." The stars inside Leon's eyes shine brighter than the ones dying above us. "I like it."

He likes it.

I feel a fluttering, not in my heart, but in my stomach. Leon searches his pockets and hands me a sherbet lemon. This time, he offers it without a challenge.

"Thanks." I accept it. "Thanks for tonight."

I might be a fool with a wild imagination, but I swear the surrounding darkness seems to lighten, as if infused with hope by the warmth of his smile.

It's almost time for morning prayer when I finally make my way home.

In the pre-dawn tranquility, I stand in the hallway and think: what other time would be better to wander around without Muzaffer or his sidekick Azmi's eyes on me? I have to find out what happened to Mum, why she left Istanbul, why she never returned. It has to be something to do with the curse.

So I take a deep breath and motivate myself to break one of Muzaffer's rules.

Through the archway lie two reception rooms, a small office and a library. I've got used to the way Muzaffer deals with grief by simply ignoring it. I know there are no photographs anywhere. No remnants of Iris and Defne. But right now, I'm fueled by desperation to find something. Anything to help me shed light on the past.

I tiptoe into the library, where cabinets and drawers may be concealing evidence from the past. When I catch Böcek slipping in behind me like a ghost, I jump, clamping my mouth to block a scream. But she's unfazed, with her paws neatly together like a vigilant guard, gaze fixed on me.

"Just looking," I whisper to her. "Keep quiet, no meowing."

I swear her eyes narrow—or maybe it's just my imagination, warped by the revelations of the past few days. I ignore the uneasiness the cat stirs in me and refocus on my task.

Tall wooden shelves tower on both sides, shouldering hundreds of books. Walking up to the nearest shelf, I run my fingers along the spines.

There's a drawer in one of the bookcases, and it doesn't surprise me to discover that it's locked. I feel stupid. What am I doing here, rummaging through shelves? It's not like I'll find a book titled *A History of Muzaffer's Creaky Mansion—Year Two Thousand and Six.* Still, I won't give up. People don't merely live and die and vanish. They leave traces behind. There must be something, somewhere, that belonged to Daphne or Iris.

Finally, my investigation pays off and I stumble upon some bits in a cabinet. An old copy of *Around the World in Eighty Days*, inscribed: *Iris, with love from your father.* Then a tattered copy of a book called *Doctor Zhivago*, by Boris Pasternak. It's well-read to the extent that its pages might fall out, but inside the cover, with the neat handwriting I know so well, it reads: *Defne A Gümüşhuş, 09/10/2005.*

Her handwriting clasps tightly around my throat. I run the tip of my finger along the words, as if it can connect me with this Defne Gümüşhuş, whom I never met.

Defne, who owned this book.

Defne, who inscribed the book and left it behind.

Daphne, who will never laugh again, never read another book, now rotting in a cemetery a thousand miles away.

I was so occupied with the curse, so distracted by the hope of breaking it, that I've neglected my grief. Now it pours down on me as I hold Mum's book. Sharp as the day she died.

Iris, Daphne's voice whispers from the pages as I flick through. *Why do you hate me so much?*

The morning beyond the shutters shines brighter, and soon the house will awaken. I need to take the book and leave, but instead I cling to it, frozen in time. All I want is to rest my cheek on her name, and weep.

No tears shall fall, I repeat the first rule. *Don't you dare cry, Sare.* But I miss Mum. I miss her so much.

I miss her even more now, knowing it was the curse that condemned her to love those who would never love her back. And worse, she had to look at me every day and see the spitting image of a sister who hated her. No wonder she was so broken, and yet I always judged her.

I cradle the novel in my hands, wishing it could tell me everything. The scars on my palm, the reminders of my past heartbreaks, sting like candle flame against my flesh. I've had enough turmoil for one night. I'm numb enough without fluttering, or any other threats from my heart.

Perhaps my heart is tired, just as I am.

Perhaps I fooled myself into thinking that by moving to Istanbul Daphne might still be alive somewhere else, somehow.

Lost in my own agony, I fail to realize I'm no longer alone.

"Sare?" Azmi's voice breaks through my reverie as he approaches.

Startled by the intrusion, I step backward still holding *Doctor Zhivago.*

Azmi gazes at the open cabinet, the sight of my investigation drawing a frown across his face. "Did you need something?"

I shake my head. *No one can give me what I need.*

He walks toward me, trying to see what I'm clinging so tightly to. "You shouldn't be opening these cabinets."

"I'm just looking around," I retort. "Why is it such a big deal?"

"Your grandfather wouldn't like his collection to be handled without his knowledge." Azmi points at the copy of *Doctor Zhivago.* "Please, may I?"

But my hands aren't ready to let go. I hide the book behind my back.

"How about," Azmi says with the tinge of a fake cheer, "I order a new one—"

"You don't understand," I protest, my voice shaking with desperation. "I want this one. It's Mum's."

"It will upset your grandfather." Azmi's perkiness deflates like a balloon. "His health is fragile."

"Fragile? He was drunk last night. He wouldn't mind me borrowing one book, I'm sure."

"I shouldn't be telling you this, but I must . . ." Azmi's brow furrows. "Your grandfather . . . is sick."

"What's wrong with him?" I'm exhausted from feeling sad. Constantly, limitlessly, incurably sad. *Please don't answer me, Azmi,* I pray silently. *Please just stop here. I can't contain another drop of sorrow.*

"Kidney failure," Azmi replies.

"Is he going to be okay?" My voice is flat, distant—like someone else speaks the words.

No tears shall fall, Munu recites in my head.

"It's not a curable condition," Azmi says. My heart sinks low. "But Mr. Gümüşhuş is strong, and he has the best care. That only leaves him to be careful. He must not be stressed."

"Am I stressing him?" The words slip out in a whistle.

"He has been through a lot," Azmi says at last. "Don't get me wrong, your arrival brought him joy, but there's also sadness. The way you resemble your aunt . . . isn't easy for him."

"Azmi," I ask, with caution, "you know why my mother left Istanbul, don't you?"

For a moment, Azmi looks like he'll say something. I'm afraid to even breathe, afraid to discourage him, as I watch his thick eyelashes flicker.

"It's not my place to speak of family matters." Azmi takes a deep, exasperated sigh before speaking again. "I guess one can say that Mr. Gümüşhuş feels deeply upset about the circumstances that caused your mother to leave. But there's no use in disturbing the past, for everyone's sake."

Why does everyone keep telling me to leave the past alone, when I can't?

"Now, may I?" Azmi gestures at the book I still cling to.

But I'm not going to give it up, just because Muzaffer regrets whatever he's done to mess up my mother's life. I recall how, when his tongue loosened, Muzaffer called me Iris. How he cried for Iris, but never once mouthed my mother's name.

"I'll keep Daphne's book," I say, defiant. "Tell Muzaffer that I'll return it if he needs it."

Once in my room, I lock the door, and Daphne's book feels as if it's ablaze in my hands. For a few minutes, I fear the fluttering will be back, followed by the burning pain. The book might grow larger until it fills the room and triggers an earthquake that will then lead to another heartbreak. I shut my eyes. But when I open them again, I don't feel anything unusual, and the book remains unchanged. My room, in contrast, feels shrunken, its air growing increasingly stifling.

I'm frightened of myself after what happened in the tower. How ready I was to give up everything, how ready I was to die. What if Leon hadn't been there? Would I be dead now?

The truth might hurt you, I hear Munu's warning again. *Stop seeking it!*

In dire need of fresh air, I fling the curtains wide and swing the balcony door open. Outside, morning matures with a gentle breeze that's warm on my skin.

I withdraw to my bed, beneath the canopy, and place Daphne's book on the sheet like a sacrificial offering. When I finally find the strength to leaf through the pages, a slip of paper falls out. I translate it using my phone.

My love,

Why can't we just leave? I want to escape and never return. It feels foolish to wait. Baba will never give us his blessing.

Everything fades away in your presence, but when we're apart, I'm drowning in guilt and longing. Only when we're alone together do I feel alive.

You are my hope. You're the sun, the moon and the stars. Without you, there's only darkness.

Don't ever leave me . . .

D

I read it. I read it again. And again. The paper is light as a feather in my hands. It holds no weight, yet it presses down on my chest. It's in Mum's handwriting—the unmistakable, passionate, impulsive intensity of Daphne in love. Did she have a boyfriend here? I'm not surprised that she never mentioned a love interest in Istanbul, when she kept even her family a secret.

I frown with confusion, shocked by Mum's disdain for her home—proof that she was miserable. Daphne wanted to get away from Istanbul.

Was it her father who she couldn't tolerate? Was it Iris?

I close my eyes, imagining a young Daphne under this roof. Was Muzaffer as strict then as he is now? Did he really favor Iris, driving Daphne to abandon everything?

I want to escape and never return.

Except that, no matter how far she ran, Mum could never escape.

I, the spitting image of her sister, would always drag her back.

I must have fallen asleep, because when I open my eyes, the clock points at noon.

I change my clothes and dash downstairs. The dining room is empty, but I find Azmi in the kitchen, washing a heap of leafy greens in the basin.

"Is everything okay?" I ask.

"Your grandfather has an appointment," Azmi says.

"Doctor's?"

Azmi nods.

"Is he okay?"

"I hope so," he sighs. "I pray for him every day."

Something sizzles in me, but I want to ignore it. I can't admit how much I care about Muzaffer, how devastated I'll be, despite myself, if something happens to him.

Why do you care, Sare? I want to kick myself. He mourns for Iris, and ignores Daphne.

"You're very loyal to him." I lean on the counter.

"Your grandfather saved me from the streets," Azmi responds. "He can be strict, but he is a good man."

"He was just a crap father, then." Why did Muzaffer abandon his own daughter, if he was kind enough to save Azmi? I hate myself for feeling angry, but I can't help it. Not after last night.

"Sare." Azmi's head snaps up, his tone sharp. "You're being unnecessarily harsh. Don't forget, your grandfather raised the girls all by himself. He loved them. He was a good father. And he's taking care of you despite everything w—"

He stops abruptly. I'm stunned by his defensive outburst.

"Despite what, Azmi?" I ask, plucking a peach from a fruit bowl on the counter.

"It's just . . . he has been through a lot." He shrugs, closing off again.

I squeeze the soft flesh of the fruit in my palm, resisting the urge to snap back. If only he had any idea what Mum and I had been through.

I find myself wandering the seafront as the afternoon wanes, deliberately steering clear of the path leading to the Maiden's Tower. The memories of last night, of Munu and Theodora, Daphne and Iris, and how their fates intertwined with the Maiden's Tower and the curse, is still too raw, too painful to remember.

I veer toward the livelier part of the shoreline, where the pulse of everyday life—people walking their dogs, joggers setting their own pace—offers a soothing normality. Anything to dispel the misery inside me. And for a while, I'm lost in the bustle, occupied with people watching, until my peace is disrupted by a voice, unexpectedly familiar.

"Sare?"

I'm surprised to see Pelin. She wears a baby blue dress that gracefully highlights her never-ending legs, her hair swept up into a carefree bun, leaving her shoulders delicately exposed. The skirt's hem dances in the sea breeze, yet her unwavering gaze holds mine with an iron grip.

"Hey," I manage, though my feet itch to flee. It's nearing 5 p.m. Leon must be nearly finished with his shift at the tower. Apart from a brief "Is everything alright?" message from him, which I've yet to reply to, we haven't spoken since last night.

"I'm glad I bumped into you," she says. "Can we talk?"

"Sure," I respond, feigning nonchalance. My mind races with possibilities. Is something wrong with Leon? What could Pelin want to talk to me about?

"I don't know if Leon mentioned it," she starts, disappointment etching her features, "but he's supposed to go to Peru next week. It was all arranged—an opportunity in Puerto Maldonado, secured with the help of my father. And now Leon is postponing it."

Leon's dream to go to Peru is no news to me, but Pelin's abrupt disclosure of his imminent departure date sends me reeling. Next week sounds painfully soon, and hearing that he delayed it brings no relief.

"Did you ask him to stay?" Pelin probes, tucking a loose strand of hair behind her ear.

"Me?" I gawk. Even if Leon consulted my opinion about this trip, I'd never tell him to stay. *Or leave.*

"Sare . . . " Pelin's expression hardens. "He's delaying his plans because of the tower. He's obsessed with breaking that curse, as if such a thing is possible. You need to convince him otherwise, before he squanders his future. There's so much at stake for him."

"I don't think it's my place to tell him what to do," I say. Pelin's words sting, but I resist the urge to argue further. It's so clear that she loves him, that she cares for him enough to challenge me. And perhaps she's right to insist that the curse can't be broken—its origin is ancient, shrouded in mystery, and I'm navigating it without a map in the darkness.

"If you care about Leon, let him go. He has a fresh chance in Peru. As long as he's close to you, there is only danger here for him." Pelin looks like she's about to burst into tears. "He's a curse-breaker, Sare. Do you know what happens to them when they fail, or when they fall in love with someone who they can't have?"

The desperation in Pelin's voice shocks me more than her words. I stare at her, stunned. The sound of a ferry horn vibrates between us.

"Remember Sufi Chelebi," Pelin whispers.

"Look—I'm not Theodora, and he's not Chelebi." I'm miraculously calm and composed. "There's nothing between us."

"He's going to miss the chance of a lifetime, Sare." Pelin sighs. "His life has been a hard one. He worked so hard to be the seer he is today. He still thinks he's not good enough, and trying to fix this curse will prove something. I read the book—Sufi Chelebi didn't even reveal the origin. It's a lost cause at this point, a myth. There's no guarantee he, or you, can break the curse—"

I barely stop myself from defending the curse; it's not a myth. I exhale. What's the use? Pelin is worried about her friend. And I guess I am too.

"What makes you think he'll listen to me?" My voice is a croak. Does Pelin know we've kissed? The thought alone burns with embarrassment, but it's overshadowed by the prospect of Leon's future in Peru, and a greater fear that I—and my curse—might destroy his sanity.

"At least stop giving him hope," Pelin persists. "Stop seeking his help."

Am I giving Leon hope? I almost laugh out loud. How can I offer Leon something I scarcely dare to feel myself?

The sun rests warm on my shoulders.

I recall how, each time my skin touches Leon's, I feel momentarily free from the curse's grasp. How, last night, for the first time in my life, my heart followed a lead other than the curse's, and beat in time with his.

"I'll think about it," I concede.

A part of me knows Pelin is right. I shouldn't drag Leon into this mess, not when there's no guarantee we can break the cycle. But he is the only person who understands what it means to live under the curse's shadow, even though he isn't aware of the heartbreaks.

I should let him go; give him the freedom I'll never have.

But I can't.

It will be strictly business, I tell myself, as I wave Pelin goodbye. No feelings, no attachments. Nothing more.

And yet, even as I make that promise, I know I've already broken it.

Leon climbs up to my room again in the evening.

"You can't keep doing this," I hiss, watching him emerge onto the balcony. "I'll be in trouble if Muzaffer sees you here."

"You haven't returned my messages." He scowls. "What did you say? We're . . ." He places his index finger on his chin, as if he's thinking hard. ". . . business partners. So you can't ghost me."

Of course I can, I grimace silently. *To protect myself from death, and you from insanity.*

"I need time to process everything." I shrug. "I'm not a robot. You don't learn every day that your ancestors were cursed in a tower by the person you trusted most."

And of course, not to forget, I almost died in the discovery.

Leon grimaces. "I told you ethereals don't make friends, didn't I?"

It's less than twenty-four hours since we kissed, but now we're back to being strangers. No, more than strangers, actually, because right now he annoys me as much as he did the first time we met.

"I can leave if you want." He shrugs, his height filling the door frame.

Does he think I'll beg him to stay?

Leon lifts an eyebrow, as if he's inviting me to respond. I hate him for being so good looking, even in scruffy shorts and a t-shirt, which seems like his staple outfit when he's not working.

And his rebellious light brown curls, his sharp nose, his brown eyes.

Fuck. What is wrong with me?

I can't afford to let my feelings take control.

You almost died last night. Focus, Sare. Think.

Leon belongs to another world. He is a seer. He needs to go to Peru. Pelin is right, this quest is dangerous for him. I can't let him end up like Sufi Chelebi.

Reading my silence as rejection, Leon shifts back onto the balcony. "You want me out?"

You're a fool if you believe that, I think silently, but avoid the question. We stare at each other, and in the end keeping him close wins out against protecting him.

"I found something today . . ." I try to sound cool and unfazed. "A book that once belonged to Daphne, with a note in it."

When I show him the piece of paper, he scrutinizes it for far longer than a single read-through would necessitate.

"This mystery recipient might know what happened," Leon says.

"Yeah, we should focus on finding him," I agree.

"You have to get into your mother's room. Surely Azmi has all the keys—it won't hurt anyone if we borrowed them."

"Tomorrow is Friday. Muzaffer is usually out until noon for Cuma prayer, and Azmi will be with him."

"Perfect," Leon says. "We only need an hour or so."

He's thrilled, I notice, to have plan of action. It genuinely cheers him up to hunt down this curse. How can I take that away from him?

But then that smile also betrays his mounting obsession with the curse, enough to climb onto my balcony. Enough to tolerate my kiss.

"I can do it myself," I force myself to say, thinking of my earlier resolve, the promise I made to Pelin. "You've wasted enough time with me, there's no need for you to come here again."

He holds my gaze, taken aback by my sudden change of tune. "What do you mean?"

"W-well, I can easily find the keys . . ."

"Oh, come on. I don't mean *that*." Leon scowls. "You think I'm wasting my time being here?"

"You have more important things to think about." I sink into the armchair.

"What could be more important—" he looks at me, baffled— "than breaking this curse with you?"

"A trip to Peru?" Shit. Why can't I keep my mouth shut? "The one you postponed?"

Leon's eyes narrow. "And how do you know about that?"

"I bumped into Pelin today." I escape his gaze. "She said you're due to leave soon."

"The dates can be rearranged." Leon's tone is cold. "Pelin means well, but she's overthinking it."

"She's worried about you—"

"I know what I'm doing, Silverbirch. And I'm not going anywhere until I honor Sufi Chelebi's memory by breaking this curse."

223

"Aren't you afraid you'll end up . . . like him?" The chair squeaks as I shift in it.

"Only the brave make the best seers. And tell me . . ." His eyes scan my face, lingering on my lips. "Once you taste courage, how can you go back to being a coward?"

Perhaps I *am* a coward. I break his gaze to remind myself again: I can't have feelings for him.

His job, Sare. Munu's voice speaks in my head. *This is why he's here. Do you think he climbs up into your room just for you? Do you think he'll stop his pursuit of the curse just because you exclude him from your research? Stop worrying about him. Worry about yourself.*

How I wish I could erase Munu from my mind, forget everything she brainwashed me with.

"So, we have a deal?" Leon distracts me.

"Fine." I fold my arms. "I'll wait for you tomorrow. But come by the front door this time, please."

"Am I allowed to break it, if it's locked?" He chuckles. "That'll give Azmi a real adrenaline rush when he's back. I can picture him figuring out what I did, chasing me down with a rolling pin."

He laughs and when I join in, I realize how long it's been since I even smiled.

Subject: Re: Job Offer

Date: 5 August 2025
From: Grey the Compassionate, Associate Cherub, Curse and Malediction Archives, Worldly Index, Sacred Data Systems, Halo-tech Data & Integration Hub
To: Nine the Ninth, Senior Angel of Fate, Fate Adjustment Bureau, Mortal Affairs Commission

My valuable superior Nine the Ninth,

I'm beyond delighted to accept the post. The Temporal Intervention Agency is a dream home for me, and I'm thrilled to be working in the back office.

There's an old saying that's attributed to Archangel Mikhael. I'm sure you've heard of it. *Mend a single thread in the divine tapestry, and you could save the whole holy divinity.*

This, my esteemed superior, is my motto, and I can't wait to join the Temporal Intervention Agency to start improving divine interventions. I must add, this offer comes as quite the surprise—considering how many roles I've applied for over the past century without so much as a whisper in reply—but I'm keen to prove what a brilliant decision it is to employ me.

Yours divinely,

Grey the Compassionate
Doctorate of Angelic Scholarship (Hons)
Thrice longlisted for the Heavenly Achievement Prize

CHAPTER NINETEEN

Don't be deceived by the purity of truth; it's complex and rarely leads to the destinations we expect. The deadliest poisons are often the purest.

Excerpt from *The Book of Betrayal, Müneccimbaşı Sufi Chelebi's Journals of Mystical Phenomena*

Unsurprisingly, things don't go as planned the following day.

When we sneak into the basement flat to Azmi's quarters to borrow the set of master keys, another locked door greets—or rather repels—us.

"I suspected as much," Leon says.

"And I assume you have a plan?"

"I always have a plan." He grins, one eyebrow arching. "I'll pick the lock."

I glance at the two different locks. "It doesn't look like an easy target."

"Not this one." Leon chuckles. "We can't lose time here. Let's just go upstairs."

Sweat dampens my palms as the anxiety of defying Muzaffer gnaws at me, even though he's unlikely to return for a few hours. It feels anything but honorable to ransack his house behind his back, but still I lead Leon up the stairs to Daphne's room.

Böcek trails after us, her sharp eyes fixed on me, as if to remind me I'm breaking the rules.

"Don't judge me," I mutter once we're stationed by the door, and she drops beside me, casually licking her paws.

The floorboards creak as Leon crouches down in front of the lock with a tweezer, or something like it, in his hands.

"You seem quite . . ." I cross my arms, searching for the precise term. ". . . experienced."

"One must acquire certain abilities to keep up with the demands of our endeavors," he responds with his usual arrogance. Then he turns his attention back to the lock.

After a few minutes of fiddling, the lock emits a loud clack, proving his mastery.

"After you." He gestures with the flair of a true gentleman as he opens the door.

I hesitate at the threshold that separates Daphne and Defne, aware that the line I'm about to cross was never meant to be breached. Whatever happened here, Mum didn't want me to know.

You're risking yourself, I hear Munu's voice in my head. *Stop digging into the past!*

But this isn't about satisfying idle curiosity, it's a quest for answers, for something—anything—that might help me break the curse. I can't lose my heart without a fight. And don't I owe this to Mum? She died with a broken heart. I need to find out what happened to her. With this resolve, I move forward and scan the space, half-expecting some remarkable revelation, and yet the room looks old . . . and ordinary.

The weathered carpet sprawls across the floor, blanketed by a layer of dust. Judging by the color, it was once a soft, light green. A faint odor of lavender lingers in the air, failing to mask the musty aroma of neglect. It doesn't take much effort to see that no living soul has been in here for a *very* long time.

The bed is pristine, as though my mother had tidied it just before her departure, its heavy wooden headboard adorned with carved leaves.

I walk over to the dressing table and examine an array of books beneath its speckled mirror.

"I'm sorry," Leon says. "I didn't think how hard it would be for you to be in this room, sifting through your mum's belongings."

I must look miserable.

"It doesn't feel like hers." I trace my finger through a layer of dust. "It feels like a stranger's, and that somehow makes it worse."

"We don't have to do this," he says, surprising me. "I don't want you to be upset, Silverbirch."

I consider this. Is he ready to give up his quest to conquer the curse?

"Thanks for the pep talk, but I'm fine." I surrender to sarcasm to dismiss the idea. "Come on, time's running out."

And so we begin our search.

Leon rifles through a cabinet, regularly getting rewarded with plumes of dust, while I sift through the bedside tables. A surge of adrenaline runs through me as I find a bunch of photographs in a drawer. I flip through them. There's Daphne, standing in front of the house with another girl. In the background, Muzaffer's Mercedes, with his driver, Gökhan, leaning against it, a watchful amusement in his posture. Everyone looks younger—suspended in a snapshot. Next, Daphne is hugging Azmi's arm. It blows my mind how loyal Muzaffer's employees are, and how well they keep his secrets. The last photo is a group of teenagers, none of whom I recognize except Iris—it's startling to see a face so similar to mine. She's all smiles, her hand on the shoulder of a young man—tall, dark and very handsome. He's smirking at the camera, sharing Iris's joy.

None of the photos bear dates or notes.

I carry on, another drawer, and the next. Finally, one creaks open, revealing a bundle of papers.

Letters.

"Look at these," I call Leon. "They're in Turkish." I begin to leaf through them but Leon plucks them from my hands and I watch his eyes dart between the lines. Then, with a deep frown, he reads them out to me in English.

"*Defne, sweet muse of my cravings. Every moment away from you is eternity, and my love burns me like fire. My being can no longer endure the absence of you—*" He clears his throat. "Sorry, I'm doing my best to directly translate the words."

"Right," I mumble, unable to stop the flush of embarrassment creeping up my neck. *Sweet muse of my cravings*—what does that even mean?

"*Soon, we'll be inseparable,*" Leon continues. "*Till then, I'll lie restless, envisioning your touch against my skin. Eternally yours, A.*"

For a prolonged moment, I examine the carpet, and Leon can't seem to lift his gaze from the letter. Who the fuck was this A—a poet or something?

"Any idea who this flowery A might be?" Leon asks, mirroring my thoughts.

"No idea. I told you before, Daphne didn't even tell me about her family."

"It doesn't sound like a casual affair, does it?" Leon says, skimming the next one. "Check this one out. *Iris isn't herself any more. It's impossible to live with her, knowing she hates me. I pity her, despite how miserable things are. I want her to be well, and I know it would help her if I left. Papa says she's ill. What sort of illness can change a person so quickly? She was fine only a couple of months ago. I feel uneasy, as if something awful will happen—but I shall do as you ask and wait. You're the only thing that makes life bearable. D.*"

I let Mum's words sink in, rendering me speechless.

"Did you know that your aunt was ill?" Leon asks, distracting me.

"No." My voice croaks with this newest discovery. "I know nothing about her."

"Looks like your mum's boyfriend stopped her from fleeing Istanbul."

And yet, when Daphne eventually managed to escape, it was without this A. How did they fall out? Where is A now? My head buzzes with a million questions.

A greeting card remains in the drawer, a faded glimpse into old Istanbul on it. I pick it up and turn it over. Turkish scribbles.

"An address?" I pass it to Leon.

"Fuck," he gasps after studying it. "You're not going to believe this."

"What does it say?" I inhale his musky scent as I draw closer.

"Well, there is a return address . . ." Leon frowns. "Somewhere in one of the Prince's Islands, Büyükada. But the note—"

I'm impatient. "Yes?"

A flash of discomfort appears in Leon's face as he begins to translate.

"15th of April 2007. My dearest, please write to me. You told me not to call you, but I'm sick with worry. Has your father or Iris discovered the baby? Or did you leave already? If I don't hear from you by next week, I'm coming there. I worry your father won't take it well. Praying for you. Arda Banguoğlu."

The note hits me like an electric current.

The baby, the baby, the baby.

It can't be me, I reassure myself. My mother had me in the UK, not here. It must be another baby. Perhaps she had a miscarriage, or she gave it away.

But I was born on 10th December, 2007.

"Silverbirch . . ." Leon brushes a curl away from my cheek. His touch isn't enough to distract me this time.

The truth crashes on me like a tonne of bricks. I *am* the baby. I was conceived here, in Istanbul, and that means . . . I try to step aside but slam my thigh into the open drawer. My hand, searching for a support, finds Leon's.

"He's talking about me." I take a deep breath, trying to ignore how hard my heart is beating now. "*Me.*"

I stumble as I find my way to Daphne's bed. The mattress squeaks as I perch on its edge.

"Are you okay, Silverbirch?" Leon says, following me.

I'm not.

Can my mother's lies really be that deep and crooked? It all feels so fucked up, so wrong.

Rule number two, I recite. *Channel sorrow to rage.*

My anger rises like an animal, wild and untamed. I'm desperate to rip up the card and the letters, to burn the house down, to leave and never come back.

Just like Defne did.

"She told me my father was a one-night stand in Cambridge." I try my best not to cry, choosing to attack the subject rather than avoid it. Make a joke of it. Make it small, until it stops hurting. "Why did she lie? A passionate lover in Istanbul sounds much more exciting."

No tears shall fall, I remind myself. *Rule number one.*

"Mothers are complicated," Leon ventures cautiously.

I burst out a laugh. It's the only way to release the anger without crying.

Leon's brow furrows with concern, as if he's worried that I'm losing it.

Perhaps I *am.*

"If you need a break, or a bit of fresh air, we can leave." He kneels down before me. "We can always come back later."

His dark eyes are full of compassion. I imagine my head on his chest, like it was the night we were in the tower, resting in the curve that perfectly aligns with my cheek. Like I'm a piece of him and he's a piece of me. As if together we'll become a whole. If I give in, he'll make me forget all of this.

I never wanted anything more than to hug him right now.

But it's wrong, isn't it?

He and I, we're not meant for each other. A boy destined for madness if he loves someone who cannot love him in return, and a girl who'll perish if her heart breaks once more.

I shrink back and try to compose myself.

"I'm okay," I say flatly. "I just—"

I can't be weak. I can't let my guard down.

"I need to find this Arda guy. He might be my . . ." I can't finish that thought. "I need to go there now."

"It's not the easiest address to get to," Leon says reluctantly. "Let's hold off until tomorrow. Let's look into this person before planning a visit."

"Why would I do that?" I feel a pang of annoyance.

Leon rises to his feet. From the expression he wears, I can tell he's battling with himself over what he's about to say next.

"If he really is your father—" Leon's gaze intensifies—"then why did your mother conceal his identity? You shouldn't rush to him without being sure that he's a decent man."

"What?" I stare at him, taken aback by his insight, shocked that he thinks of me with such consideration.

"I'm just saying that discovering your heritage is one thing, breaking a curse is another," Leon says. "Don't let the idea of a father distract you."

You *are a distraction*, I think silently. Rage *is a distraction. A father is not a distraction.*

But Leon doesn't understand how with each piece of information I gather, the darkness around me lifts a little.

"I'm not interested in this . . . A." I hesitate, not used to speaking from my heart. "Not in himself. I just have to find out why Mum left Istanbul, why she lied to me. Perhaps then . . . it will make sense, and then I can forgive her. It's exhausting, being so angry."

I surprise myself with this confession. And then I panic. *Why is it so effortless to talk with Leon? Why am I blurting out my feelings like an idiot?*

"Listen." Leon sits next to me. The bed squeaks under his weight and the unstable headboard bangs against the wall, tearing a fragment of the wallpaper. "I can't fully comprehend what you must be going through, but I'll offer a piece of advice, if you'll accept it. There's no use in holding a grudge against the dead."

I rise to my feet, pacing the room. My pulse drums in my ears as I consider his words.

"Plus," Leon says cautiously, "it's obvious your mother had a hard time in Istanbul."

"Arda must know something," I say. "We have to go there."

"Even if we leave now we won't arrive till the evening—your grandfather won't be pleased if you disappear all night."

"He won't be pleased if I go next week, or next year," I say. "He doesn't like me asking questions. Perhaps he was angry with Daphne for getting pregnant unmarried. Why else would she hide the pregnancy? Why else would Arda worry about Muzaffer's reaction?" A groan of anger escapes me. Is that why they fell out? *Could Muzaffer really be so cruel?*

I cling on to the headboard for support. Just then, a glimpse of torn wallpaper catches my eye, exposing an outline beneath. My irritation morphs into curiosity as I lean closer to examine it.

"What is this?" I press my face closer to the wall for a clearer view. "Graffiti?"

"Hold on," Leon cautions as I reach to strip away more of the wallpaper. "You can't stick it back on if you take it off. Your grandfather will know we've been here . . ."

"He's not been in here in years," I say. "And if there's something hidden behind the paper, I need to see it now rather than lose sleep wondering about it."

"But—"

"Now, or never."

He throws his hands up. "Fine."

He's silent as I tug at the flayed wallpaper. The initial tear uncovers a larger fragment of writing, urging me to carry on. I pull away piece after piece, revealing letter after letter, tossing strips onto the floor until we're surrounded by a sea of discarded paper.

When at last I stop, absorbed by the revelation unfolding before my eyes, I can hear Leon swear. The remnants of the wallpaper rustle beneath my feet as we step back to take in the entire spectacle.

Emblazoned across the wall, in black ink, repeated over and over are the words: *Yer yarılıp seni yutsa bile seni asla affetmeyeceğim.*

It's not written in pen or marker and the script is erratic, the lines varied in thickness, with blotches and smears disrupting the flow. A crime scene Muzaffer tried to hide from me.

"I-I will never forgive you, even if the earth splits open to swallow you." Leon's forehead creases. "That's what it says."

Even before he told me the meaning, I felt that it was an ill wish. It reeks of desperation and fury.

"Do you understand what this is?" Leon asks.

I'm lost. Speechless. Still, I know deep in my bones what the walls are screaming at me.

"It's the trigger," I whisper. "It's a beddua."

The sheer magnitude of its repetition is enough to reveal why it was strong enough to awaken the curse. I stand before it, helpless, unable to take my eyes off the haunting refrain that covers the entire wall. I have no idea if Iris scribbled this, or my mother, and no idea what it is they swore not to forgive, or if my heart can bear to know it.

CHAPTER TWENTY

No calamity surpasses the wrath of those who have been wronged.
Excerpt from *The Book of Revenge, Müneccimbaşı Sufi Chele-bi's Journals of Mystical Phenomena*

After what feels like an hour staring at the wall covered with the beddua, I can speak again.

"It's almost the same thing Eudokia said to Theodora."

I will never forgive you, even if the earth splits open to swallow you.

Outside the room, the afternoon prevails, its golden light slanting through the window and stretching long shadows across the floor. I could stay rooted to this spot all evening, and I still wouldn't understand what might have happened between Daphne and Iris.

"One of them said this beddua." Leon's eyes narrow. "Like Sufi Chelebi says, no calamity surpasses the wrath of those who have been wronged."

"My mother is the obvious victim," I assert. "You saw her notes. You read the letters."

Leon sighs. "Let's step outside for now. You need to rest, and tomorrow we'll visit Arda Banguoğlu. I'm already fasting, and if I lie down to sleep, I might trigger a vision about this beddua." He gestures at the wall.

"What?" I watch his face in disbelief. "You can't be serious. You're starving yourself? Like Sufi Chelebi?"

"It's a common practice to wean off worldly pleasures to invite visions and dreams—"

"How long have you not eaten?" I snap.

"Since yesterday afternoon," he confesses. "I do it all the time, Silverbirch. Don't worry about me."

I examine his face, the face I'm afraid to look at too closely, and see his hollowed eyes, his sinking cheeks, and my own selfishness.

Was I too blinded by my own misery to see how closely he follows in Sufi Chelebi's footsteps?

The air goes colder around me. I know he won't listen to me, even if I tell him to stay away. But before I can open my mouth, I'm interrupted.

"What are you doing here?" Muzaffer stands by the door, as tall as a reed, leaning on his walking stick.

For a moment, none of us move, or make a peep.

"We were just . . . looking." I break the silence, holding Muzaffer's unforgiving gaze.

Muzaffer's eyes escape mine to fall on the sea of scraped-off wallpaper, his fingers fumble on the head of his cane.

I nudge Leon. "You have to go."

"Are you sure?"

"Please, go," I choke out. "I'll be fine."

He rushes out, mumbling an apology to Muzaffer, and only then do I realize that the card with the address remains in his pocket. I curse my own stupidity for forgetting the most crucial detail.

"I asked you a question," Muzaffer says once Leon's footsteps diminish down the rattling staircase. "Why are you here?"

"You know why." I defend myself. "I wanted to see Mum's room."

Muzaffer advances toward me and I back away. The gap that stretches between us seems to play its own game, where one must always yield ground, as if to maintain a safe distance. Reminding us that we will never be a normal grandfather and granddaughter.

"What do you want, Sare?" Muzaffer glances at me warily. His face is pale. "Why did you break into this room? Why do you vandalise it?"

"I didn't vandalise it. I didn't write this," I retort. "But you know that. Is that why you keep it locked?"

"Go to your room," he says.

"Did Iris write this?" I point at the wall. I'm aware I sound unhinged, but I can't stop myself. Not any more. "She hated Daphne, didn't she? She made her life a living hell."

"You don't know what you're talking about," he snaps again. "I don't know how to deal with all this. I don't know how to protect you," he mumbles. "Perhaps bringing you here was a mistake."

"No," I protest. *I'm not a mistake. Not any more.*

"Enough," Muzaffer says, lifting his cane. "Get out."

I shake my head. I'm not afraid of his anger. I'm afraid of myself, my own rage, of finally releasing the pain I've held in all these months—my grief which sleeps like a dragon with fire entombed in its core.

"Fine. I'll ask Gökhan or Azmi to remove you then." Muzaffer's voice dwindles as he prepares to depart.

"Do you have any idea what it feels like not having a clue why things are the way they are? Living with questions like, 'Why is Mum so sad?' or 'Why doesn't she love me any more?'"

He halts on the threshold, and turns to face me, agonizingly slowly.

"I always wondered what I might have done wrong." My voice trembles. "What I did to make her stop loving me."

Rule number one. No tears shall fall, I tell myself. I will not cry.

"Every single day, I asked myself why Daphne wouldn't look at me. She wasn't always like that, you know—she adored me when I was little. We slept in the same bed, she'd hug me, brush my hair, put my socks on. She loved me."

"Stop," Muzaffer grunts.

"No," I snarl. "You will listen to me. You will hear me. I'm not a piece of furniture left by Daphne that you can lock away and ignore."

"I—" He quivers. "I didn't—"

"You can't avoid me like Mum did." I stomp over to the drawer and pick up the letters and photos, thrusting them at him. "Just because I look like Iris!"

The echo of my scream withers between us. My rage remains.

"You *do* look like her," Muzaffer says at last, eyelids twitching as if he's holding back tears. "Some nights, I can convince myself that you are Iris. It's not easy, looking at you. It wouldn't have been easy for her either."

"Just tell me what happened," I demand, furious. "You were angry with Daphne, weren't you? Because she was pregnant and unmarried?"

Muzaffer grumbles inaudibly, fueling my suspicions.

"I read her letters," I insist. "I know she hid the b-baby. I know she had a lover, and you didn't approve of him."

Muzaffer shakes his head, his mouth tightening in dismay.

"He's here in Istanbul, isn't he? My f-f—" The word balls up in my mouth, like food I keep chewing but can't swallow. "My father."

The word *father* momentarily petrifies him, a fleeting cloud of panic crossing his face.

"You have no father. Do you understand?" His voice bellows between the walls. "I had made it clear, Sare—I told you my rules, and yet you're defying every single one of them."

A flush of shame washes over me. A part of me knows that he's right: it's his house, his rules, his past.

His Defne.

And then I feel the fluttering. A persistent melody of drums playing inside my ribs. Faint and entombed. Did it start just now, or since he walked in? I have no idea. But I'm not going to let it possess me.

Twenty, nineteen, I breathe. *Eighteen, seventeen, breathe. Sixteen, fifteen, breathe.*

Breathe, Sare, breathe so everything you have been burying inside, everything you ignored won't kill you as you dig it all up.

"What are you waiting for?" Muzaffer's face is blank. "Out."

But how can I? All I want right now is to curl up on the floor and cry. I wish there was a way to tell him how I'm only trying to save myself from the curse, but there's none. My nails dig into my palm.

Fourteen, thirteen, breathe. Twelve, eleven, breathe. Ten, nine, breathe.

"Arda Banguoğlu," I whisper. "Is he my father?"

Eight, seven, breathe. I command myself. *Six, five, breathe. Distract yourself. Do something. Be angry. You can't give up. Not when you're so close to the truth, so close to breaking the curse.*

Four, three, breathe.

Two, one. I reach zero.

My heart is silent.

"She could have told you, if you had a father." Muzaffer's breath is ragged. "Respect her decision."

"Don't worry," I scream. "I'm leaving. I'm going to find Arda. He might tell me your secrets."

"You're not going anywhere." He grasps my arm. "Azmi!" he yells, his clutch on my wrist stronger than I anticipated. "Azmi!"

I must be an idiot, for I'm too afraid to pull back to free myself, too frightened to hurt him.

Outside, I hear footsteps, groaning floorboards, and then Azmi's head appears around the door.

"Escort Sare to her room," Muzaffer tells him.

"What happened here?" Azmi scans the room.

"I'm . . . not feeling well," Muzaffer says. "Take Sare, keep her in her room."

"Azmi." I am breathless. My eyes drift to Muzaffer, to his pale face. "Please let me go."

"You must go to your room," Azmi says slowly, staring at me as though I might crumble.

"Bathroom," I plead. "I need to go to the bathroom first, please."

To my relief, he nods and gestures to the door.

In the bathroom, I stare at myself in the mirror as the tap runs.

I need to distract myself, wake up from the shock, but I'm too stressed that something will happen to Muzaffer.

What if he dies? I grimace in panic. It will be because of me, my questions, my unyielding desperation to find the truth.

What if *I* die?

I've experienced more fluttering in one week than I have in a whole year. I worry that my heart is getting weaker.

You're doing well, I reassure myself, as I finally splash water on my face. *You survived losing Daphne. And then Munu. You can survive anything.*

"Canim," says Munu's voice in my mind. *Why do I keep hearing her?* As if everything isn't difficult enough already.

"Canim," the voice says again. It sounds so close that I lift my head and am startled to see her reflection in the mirror.

"You—" I gasp. "What the fuck are *you* doing here?"

"I'm frightened, Sare," she says from inside the mirror.

"Oh, please." I back away. "Just leave me alone, will you?"

The impact of seeing Munu again is harder than I imagined. Where has all my love for her gone? Only rage remains.

There's no way we could go back to being Munu and Sare again.

Because she's not Munu, is she? She's Eudokia. She's the reason I'm cursed.

"I always thought I'd be pleased if you were cruel, cold, heartless. How wrong I was," Munu whispers. "You must stop digging. You're heading into darkness."

"Why would I listen to your advice?" I snap. "Wait and see. I'll find out what happened to Mum."

"Sometimes it's better not to know. It's a wicked thing, knowledge," Munu says. "Without it, you're blind. But with it, you may become a part of the shadows you sought to chase away. Haven't you suffered enough already, canim? Haven't we all?"

"Just go away," I say through clenched teeth.

Munu disappears so fast I almost assume I imagined her.

I mull over her words. *Haven't you suffered enough already?* I stare at myself in the mirror. Perhaps I should give up, and just let the curse break me. I won't feel this pain when it takes my heart. I will be free of sorrow.

But my reflection shakes her head.

You will not give up, she says. *Not until you break the curse.*

When I finally compose myself, I retreat to my bedroom to get organized. But any hope of solace shatters as the telltale click of the lock pierces the silence.

"Hey!" I rush toward the door, but it's already too late. The sound of heavy footsteps fades as I grasp the doorknob, realizing I'm trapped.

"Azmi!" I shriek. "Open this door! You can't keep me locked in here!"

"I'm sorry," Azmi's voice comes through the door. "You're not allowed to leave today."

"Are you serious?" I scream, my frustration bubbling over into despair. "Why? This is insane!"

"It's best, for everyone's sake," Azmi replies, and he sounds sorrowful. "Mr. Gümüşhuş will come around tomorrow."

With these words, I erupt into a frenzy—pounding, kicking and screaming for freedom. Despite the weeks I've spent in relative confinement in this room, a sense of claustrophobia ensnares me now. I'm held captive when I need to get out, to go to that island and find Arda Banguoğlu. My desperation transforms into a wild fury. I'm a wolf trapped in a cage.

But Azmi has already left, and nobody comes to my aid. There are no other sounds in the house except mine.

I lean on the door and think of the only way I can escape—the one that's a possibility thanks to Leon, because if he's done it, I can as well.

The balcony.

Perhaps desperation works in my favor, because I climb down the woody wisteria without falling or being spotted, and dash out of the metal gate, straight to Leon's apartment across the street.

To my surprise, Pelin opens the door.

"What are you doing here?" She scowls at the sight of me. "I thought we had an understanding."

"I'm sorry. But I really need a word with Leon. Where is he?"

"He's out." The door creaks open wider, and Harika's voluminous hair appears behind Pelin.

"Out where?" My eyes dart from Pelin to Harika.

"Look, missy," Harika huffs. "Whatever's going on between you two is beyond my capacity to comprehend. And to be fair, I'm not the least bit interested. Leon isn't here but it won't require clairvoyance to find him. Check the tower, or the seafront."

"He has to leave this Saturday," Pelin warns me. "Don't you forget."

"And they blame my generation for being dramatic." Harika rolls her eyes, watching Pelin. "Darling, what did I tell you? Relax. Leon will remain where he's meant to stay—until he's sent, against his will, to a place he's not meant to stay. But in the end, he'll end up exactly where he's supposed to be."

"And what's that supposed to mean?" Pelin looks as baffled as I feel at Harika's cryptic remark.

"My dreams never lie," Harika says with a casual shrug, as if the confusion is entirely our failure to comprehend and offers no further explanation. And then she extends her hand to me, motioning toward my palm.

"Everyone comes here seeking answers," she says. "But the question is—are they brave enough to face them?"

I recoil. "I-I don't understand what you mean."

"Let me have a peek." Harika grabs my hand. I have no choice but to push through her performance. "You . . ." She begins but then her mouth falls open, and she closes her eyes. "But how? Wait." Slowly, her frown softens, and her eyes snap open again. "Ah . . . I see it now. Yes, it all makes sense. Exquisite."

It definitely doesn't make sense to me.

"What's going on?" Pelin asks. "What have you seen, Harika?"

"You must promise me—" Harika ignores Pelin and leans toward me, a faint waft of rosewater brushing against me as she speaks. "When the time comes to make a decision: choose love and not hate. Choose hope, not despair. Choose life, not death. And choose courage, Sare Silverbirch. Courage will save you—and Leon too."

Talk about melodramatic.

"Fab, thanks." I force a polite smile. Not that I understand in the slightest. But even if I did, how can I make choices when they're always made for me?

"That was intense." Under the white glow of the fluorescent light, Harika lets go of my hand. "I've never experienced anything like that before," she says, panting. "Are you . . . a catalyst?"

"A what?" Pelin and I ask in unison.

"A catalyst, a conduit to the Otherside," Harika explains in awe. "An amplifier for those with the pure eye. Rare. Very rare." She scrutinizes me like I'm a precious artifact. "But not unheard of. Especially when curses are involved. Yes . . . Come and visit me again. I'd like to do a full reading for you. Yes, I'd like that very much."

Okay, this is officially getting weird.

"Alrighty," I manage, clearing my throat and stepping toward the stairs, eager to escape her enthusiasm. "I guess I'll see you guys . . . around."

And then I bolt away, as fast as I can.

I find Leon sitting on a bench overlooking the Maiden's Tower. I'm drawn to him as if we have an invisible thread that connects us.

He's eating a bar of chocolate, having clearly given up on his hunger strike. He doesn't notice me at first, and I savor the freedom of watching him unnoticed. Then he glances up to meet my eye, as if he sensed me.

"Silverbirch." He stands abruptly.

I gulp down a nervous breath. "Hey."

"Are you okay?" He steps toward me.

"I'm fine." There's no use in telling him about Muzaffer's punishment. Or his aunt's speculations. The woman is on another wavelength, anyway. "Listen, I need to go to the island, so I need that card with the address."

"But you don't want me to come with you?" He fishes it out of his pocket but doesn't pass it to me.

I hesitate, not because I don't already know the answer. Of course I want him by my side. But what if Pelin's right? What if this whole thing is a threat to him? The thought knots in my chest. I can't be a boulder standing between him and his future. He has an exciting path ahead, and mine is littered with death and heartbreak.

"I don't want you to skip your flight because of me," I confess after a long, uncomfortable silence.

Leon tucks a curl behind his ear as he considers my words. A gull swooshes past us to land near our feet. Its eyes are greedy.

"Look," he says at last, "if we can't figure out anything before Saturday, I can go another time. There's a plane to Peru every week. I told you, there's no deadline—I don't need to go straight away."

I can't argue with that. "Right." I drop my gaze to the sea. The waves brush the rocks on the shoreline like rhythmic dancers. "And one last thing. No more drinking salt water or starving yourself. And should you have any visions, you must immediately report to me. Deal?" I extend my hand, completely professional, pretending I'm not distracted by how breathtakingly beautiful he is.

"Deal." He nods, his hand enveloping mine.

Communication is classified as Top Secret.
Circulation strictly limited to correspondents.

Subject: Your True Nature

Date: 6 August 2025
From: Grey the Compassionate, Senior Cherub, Temporal Intervention Agency, Fate Adjustment Bureau, Mortal Affairs Commission
To: Five the Fifth, Angel of Death, Field Operations, Mortal Termination and Transition, Mortal Affairs Commission

Five,

I've often wondered what makes you so different from the rest of us. We are all mighty, and some of us—those who don't share my progressive views—are as indifferent to mortals as you are, but no one else carries your . . . attitude.

I've spent many hours reflecting on this during my walks through the rolling hills of the Heavens—after all, a stroll can be far more enlightening than flying, giving wings a rest and pushing the mind and legs to work—and I believe I've finally found the answer.

Pride and arrogance, comrade, sets you apart from the rest of us who serve in the Heavenly Governance. Thanks to my recent promotion—no doubt facilitated by your divine influence to buy my silence, proof of said pride and arrogance—I've obtained some rather interesting records from the Vault of Angelic Registry (VAR). For that, I offer my sincere thanks. You see, I never had access to these before.

And guess what I found, Five? You aren't originally from the Heavenly Governance like the rest of us. No, according to the VAR registrar, you were transferred—from the Infernal Dominion.

You're not made of light, but fire. You're an *ifrit*. A demon born of flames. They changed your name to Five, but it's a rather fitting one, isn't it, considering you're from the fifth circle of Hell?

I don't know who you bribed, manipulated, or blackmailed to slither your way up the ranks toward Our Boss Almighty's power, but rest assured, your days here in Governance are numbered.

It may surprise you—or perhaps not, given your inflated ego—that I found my answers in the mortals you so condescendingly despise. It seems, my dear comrade, that you are much more like them than you'd ever care to admit.

Perhaps it's a side effect of spending too much time in their realm? Either way, I've uncovered some intriguing evidence—unauthorized trips of yours to London, New York, Venice, Bangkok and Istanbul. Are there more? For a demon-turned-angel who claims to detest mortals, you're entangled quite deeply within their world.

You've left a trail, Five, one even a lowly *cherub* could follow. But rest assured, these revelations are only the beginning. The Governance will soon hear everything. More to follow.

Yours in eternal vigilance,
Cherub

CHAPTER TWENTY-ONE

The most profound wounds are often inflicted by those we hold nearest, leaving us vulnerable. Every harm they cause chips away at our fondness, until the person we once held dear transforms into our most daunting enemy.

Excerpt from *The Book of Heartbreak, Müneccimbaşı Sufi Chelebi's Journals of Mystical Phenomena*

Once we're on the ferry to Büyükada, I let my hair dance in the sea breeze, a wild cascade of curls that I struggle to tame.

"*Akide Şekeri.*" Leon fishes out a bag of candies from his backpack and offers me one. "An Ottoman delicacy—traditionally made for sultans."

He smiles, slow and easy, entirely disarming, spreading a warmth like sunlight across my skin. I let my fingers hover over the open bag before selecting one. The gulls, quick to notice the presence of food, start their aerial maneuvers, diving down and then soaring up again, though an unseen barrier prevents them from coming too close.

I pop the candy in my mouth and wonder if Munu is lurking somewhere behind the bird's beady eyes, watching me ignore her advice. *You're heading to darkness.* I recall her words, and the sugar fails to soothe me. The possibility that my biological father, whose identity had never been on the cards, might reside on the island sits like a stone in my stomach. None of this was ever part of the plan. Ever since I arrived in Istanbul, everything has seemed to spiral out of my control, and all I discover is deceit.

But then, I'm no stranger to lying. I've told Leon so many lies about the curse already. The guilt works like sea sickness, and I feel suddenly queasy.

"You're quiet," Leon says, tossing two candies into his mouth at once.

It's painful to sit this close to him and still be so distant at the same time.

"I just don't know what to feel any more." I stare at the sea. Forging ahead, the ship cleaves through the water, leaving a trail like a fresh wound.

"Focus on our goal," Leon says. "We're going there to find out what happened, and then you'll mend the errors of the past and break this curse."

Daphne's room flashes before my eyes. *I will not forgive you.* Written over and over.

"What if Mum did something unforgivable?" I lower my voice to a whisper, my fear palpable.

"Then it won't be your fault," Leon says, his voice is soft, almost tender. "We can acknowledge their mistakes, but we can't bear the guilt of our ancestors. We're different people, Sare."

I sigh with frustration, cradling my head in my hands.

It's not your fault, Muzaffer said.

He'd probably be petrified if he knew I was on my way to the island. Thankfully the ferries run past midnight, so I'll sneak back into my room before he notices I'm gone.

"Let's not be afraid to hope." Leon reaches out to gently shift a stray curl from my face. "You always say it's me who makes you hopeful. But I've never told you how you made *me* hopeful the first time we met."

"Me?" I frown, thinking of our first encounter, how we did nothing but fight.

"When you arrived—" Leon drops his voice—"I had been searching for the journal for almost two years with no possible leads. I was lost and hopeless, about to admit that the tower had been a waste of time, which is why I signed up for this training in Peru. And then—" He pauses, as if he's embarrassed. "I began to dream of you."

My heart leaps in my chest at the intensity of his gaze.

"You kept telling me something . . . which I've been telling you since." His eyebrows rise, as if he's inviting me to guess.

As much as I can't imagine myself saying it, I take a wild stab at it.

"Don't be afraid of hope," I say, blushing like an idiot.

He nods.

"But I lost the book," I add, recalling how stupid I was to let it be stolen. "Right after I found it."

"I'm writing a journal now," Leon says. "My own documentation for our endangered profession."

My stomach flips as I wonder whether my name will be in it or not. And how will Leon write about me—if he'll write about me at all.

"Plus," Leon continues, unaware of my inner turmoil, "my relationship with Grey has improved significantly after the . . . night in the tower."

How could I forget Grey? The angels—considering how terrified Munu was of her boss, Five, and how little they seem to understand about our feelings—don't seem the biggest fan of humankind, but Leon seems pleased to know Grey. He trusts the angel, enough to let him possess his body, but how can I? It's impossible to figure out whose side the angels are on, or what they're after, or where they stand in all of this. I can't shake the feeling that we've all been pawns in a game architected by these creatures.

"Do you really think it can be done?" I turn to him. "That there's a way to fix this ancient curse? A way out of . . . this mess?"

Leon smiles. "You know what I'm going to say."

I fill my lungs with the sea air as we approach the shore, and I hope—more than I've ever hoped in my life—that I can break this curse.

The island is in stark contrast to the bustling mainland. It's small enough to traverse on foot, and there are no cars here, no traffic. As we disembark, the enticing aroma of freshly grilled seafood wafts through the air. Under different circumstances, I could have enjoyed this trip.

We walk until we find the address on the card: Yaverbey Sokak, No. 128. Soon, we're standing in front of a two-story house painted in a pastel green, complemented by wooden shutters that add to its fairytale look.

I stare at the porch adorned with pots of blooming flowers, as Leon sticks his hands into his pockets.

Come on, Sare. Just get on with it.

We walk up to the door and I press the bell without a second thought.

A sulking tween appears at the door, lanky in a vest top and denim shorts, looking us up and down. "Yes?" Her eyebrows raise with interest.

"We're looking for Arda Banguoğlu," I say, as politely as I can manage.

"Arda'yı arıyoruz," Leon translates.

The girl blinks, considering our request.

Then, to my horror, she turns inside and calls, "Anne!"

I shiver as I recognize the word *mother*. For a moment, I'm petrified. What if this girl is my half-sister? What if the woman she calls is Arda's wife? What am I supposed to tell them? "Hi, I'm looking for my biological father?" I would drop dead.

But the woman clears up my panic and confusion as she arrives. "Merhaba, ben Arda." She frowns. "Siz kimsiniz?"

I know enough Turkish to understand—she just introduced herself as Arda.

As we explain the reason for our visit, and show her the card, Arda's face softens. Almost instantly, Leon and I are perched on a floral sofa, each cradling a steaming cup of tea provided by her less-than-enthused daughter.

I'd built myself up to meet with my possible father and so, for a few minutes, I gawk at the woman as she talks about Defne, unable to focus on her words.

"Oh my God, I can't believe you're Daphne's daughter," she repeats, her large eyes alight with astonishment. "It's been so many years. How is your mother?"

"Daph—Mum passed away earlier this summer." The words sting as they leave my lips, a sudden, acute pain. It's been months now, but the ache lingers, raw and unyielding.

The woman's face crumples at my revelation. "Poor Defne," she mutters, dabbing her tears with a napkin as I recount the details of the accident.

I can't offer her any comfort or condolences. Since Daphne died, I've worn my grief like armor, and the idea of exposing my emotions to someone else feels utterly foreign.

"Poor Muzaffer Amca," Arda sniffs. "I hope he's okay?"

"He's . . . fine." I force a smile as I picture Muzaffer's grim expression from earlier. The teacup is scorching hot between my palms. "I'm sorry to show up like this," I venture, "but I'm looking for information about my mother's past in Istanbul. She didn't tell me much about her family, or why she left." It's too embarrassing to confess to this woman that Daphne lied to me, and even more embarrassing to explain how her own father shuns her name. "I know there was some sort of feud between her and Iris, but no one has told me what or why."

"Ah." Arda sighs. "Of course."

Finally, I sigh with relief, someone who knows Mum and who is eager to talk. I stir in my seat and my legs brush against Leon's. It astonishes me how relieved I am that he's here with me.

"You look so much like Iris." Arda stares at me. "Yet you have Defne's gentleness. It feels like I'm talking to her again. So strange."

"Did Mum and Iris . . . get along?" I nudge, hoping it will give Arda a lead to start talking about the past.

"They did, until—" She pauses, glancing upward as if searching for the precise description. "It's . . . complicated. Iris and Defne were thick as thieves. I used to live just down the slope, across the road from your mum and Iris, and we were best friends. So many happy memories."

"And?" I ask, suddenly confused. This isn't the story I'd anticipated.

"And then he came along. Ah—what was his name?" Arda ponders. "Ozan, that was it. Of course."

"Ozan?" I take a sip of tea as Arda's words sink in; the heat burns the tip of my tongue at this new name.

"I think he was working in the Maiden's Tower. It was a restaurant back then. I can't remember, but perhaps his dad was the owner?" Arda sighs. "He was very good looking. Girls wouldn't shut up about him."

I feel the color draining from my face, realizing where Arda is going with the story.

"In the beginning it was just harmless flirting." Arda considers. "But then he and Daphne . . . They started going out. And it made Iris very . . . unwell."

"How so?" I set the teacup on the coffee table, as if to brace myself for what I'm about to hear.

"She stopped being . . . herself," Arda says. "She was like a different person. A person possessed—she was obsessed with Ozan. She turned against Defne, claiming she had loved Ozan before her, and she was quite awful to her, to be fair. Still not enough to convince Defne to end things with Ozan, though. We thought Defne and Ozan would end up together."

"But they didn't?" I frown, not getting where she's going.

"They couldn't," Arda said. "Because Ozan married Iris."

CHAPTER TWENTY-TWO

The burdens we carry sculpt our essence. Pain and loneliness are uniquely personal trials, impossible to share or divide among others. When a soul bears the weight of both, may Allah be compassionate upon them, for they' risk betrayal by their own minds or hearts.

Excerpt from *The Book of Betrayal, Müneccimbaşı Sufi Chelebi's Journals of Mystical Phenomena*

Arda's words hit me like a blow to the head. My brain whirrs as I try to digest the information.

"Ozan married Iris?" I repeat, still unable to believe it. "Daphne's boyfriend left her for her sister?"

"I don't think he separated from Defne." Arda leans forward, perhaps aware of my shock, but her flare for drama must be greater than her empathy. "Perhaps he dated both of them from the start. It happened so quickly and shocked everyone. Your poor, poor mother."

I feel queasy. *Iris, Iris, Iris,* Daphne's voice echoes in my head. *Why do you hate me so much? Why are you still haunting me?*

I glance at Leon, who looks equally taken aback by the news. He gives me a knowing nod. We both understand what this means. History repeated itself. Theodora stole Eudokia's lover, and Iris stole Defne's . . . Does that mean that Daphne *is* the one who said the beddua and triggered the curse?

I'm so distracted by the buzzing questions in my mind, I almost don't notice that Arda is still talking.

"Things got worse after the marriage, though. Daphne told me that Ozan told her that Iris was threatening to kill herself, and that's how she convinced Ozan to propose. I don't know if that's true, but everything happened with such haste, perhaps it was," Arda says. "I know Defne begged your grandfather many times to check Iris into some sort of care facility. But your grandfather was . . . traditional. He didn't believe in that kind of thing. Thought it would cause a scandal . . ."

Muzaffer's pride is the least of my worries. I still have no idea where the mysterious A, who wrote Daphne those passionate letters, may be, or what happened to my mother.

"What year—" I need to quell my nausea and compose myself. Outside, the wind howls like it's angry on my behalf. "What year did they get married?"

"Oh gosh . . . Let me think." Arda puts a finger to her chin. "My mum had a hip replacement the year Ozan and Iris tied the knot, so it must have been . . . 2004."

"Mum didn't leave immediately, then?" I'm thinking out loud, because nothing is making sense.

"Oh no, she didn't. And believe me, it wasn't easy for her, because they all lived in the same house. It was a total nightmare," Arda says. "Daphne lost so much weight that summer they married. She wouldn't eat a morsel. And the next spring I moved to the island, and we kind of lost touch. I hadn't heard from her, not until she wrote to me a couple of years later."

"She wrote to you," I say. "Before you sent this card?"

"Yes, it was out of the blue. She told me she was pregnant and asked if she could come and stay with us."

"And did you know who the father was?" I'm perched on the edge of my seat now.

"No." Arda shakes her head sadly. "She never told me who it was. She was worried about her father's reaction. Muzaffer Amca has a reputation, you know—he's old school and Defne getting pregnant out of wedlock would be . . . inconvenient."

"Right," I whisper. Of course, everything Iris had done would be dismissed without consequences, but the same rule didn't apply to Daphne. Why did Muzaffer even let Iris marry the man Daphne loved? I'm suddenly disgusted by everything and by myself for remaining under Muzaffer's roof. Where does "A" fit in this picture?

"Did she have another boyfriend?" I insist. "Someone whose name started with an A?"

"I don't know," Arda says. "I had moved, as I said . . . We grew apart."

"Do you at least know why Daphne left Istanbul?"

"Oh, I'm so sorry but I don't. I never heard from her again. She'd already departed when I finally managed to visit after I heard of Iris's sudden death. Muzaffer Amca was alone in the house. Poor man looked like he'd aged a hundred years since I'd last seen him. He told me that Defne had moved to the UK to raise the baby there." Arda blinks, as if she's only just realized what she is saying. "You."

"What about Ozan?" I ask, before she gets too distracted. "Did he die too, in the earthquake?"

"Last I heard, he moved to the European side of Istanbul." Arda sighs. "Disappeared after Iris died."

Another dead end.

"Mum?" Arda's daughter peeks in, craning her neck from the doorway without stepping inside. "They say there's a storm coming. The ferries to the mainland have been canceled."

"Shit." I bolt upright. "But we have to get back."

"You can't," Arda sighs. "They're tight on procedure when it comes to storms. You'll have to stay the night."

Arda serves us a humble dinner. Despite having no appetite, I don't refuse, just to be polite. Things take a mortifying turn when she leads us to the guest room though.

"I only have one room," Arda says. "Big bed though, so it should be okay."

When I glance at Leon, he looks as horrified as I feel.

"No problem." I smile, because I'd rather throw myself out of the window than cause more problems for this woman who has already shown more than enough kindness to two strangers turning up at her door.

When we're alone, an awkward silence sits between Leon and me, powered by the howling wind and rain outside.

Perhaps if I wasn't so disturbed by my mother's fucked-up family history, I'd feel a sliver of excitement at the prospect of spending the night alone with him, but right now I'm only numb.

"You take the bed," Leon says, breaking the awkward silence. "I'll sleep in the armchair."

We both avoid glancing toward the double bed, pretending it isn't the most prominent object in the room.

"No—I can make a bed on the floor for myself," I insist, gesturing at the blankets piled at the foot of the bed. "It's me who dragged you here, and I'll feel awful if you spend the night cramped up in an armchair." I refrain from pointing out the obvious mismatch of his towering height against the size of the chair.

"How about I'll let you set up a bed on the floor for me to sleep on," Leon proposes. "But you take the bed. I can't stand the thought of you sleeping on the floor, Silverbirch. My inner gentleman won't allow it."

"Fine," I sigh and grab the blankets, then crouch down to arrange them in the gap between the wall and the bed—a space that's hardly ample. As I smooth out the folds, it strikes me how close Leon and I will lay next to each other tonight, separated only by the height difference between the makeshift bed and the actual one. Barely an arm's length apart.

Fuck, what is wrong with me? I've just learned harrowing secrets about my mother and her sister, and here I am blushing like an idiot.

With each passing second, the silence weighs heavier on my shoulders. When I'm finally satisfied with the layers I've made on the floor, I rise to my feet again.

"You told me that all the women in your family are cursed to die young." Leon makes a face. "Were you entirely honest? Listening to Iris's and Daphne's story, it feels like it's more personal than that."

"I-I—" I stammer, plumping a pillow, then dropping it to the ground.

Leon watches me with that piercing stare again. "We're supposed to be in this together. You need to be truthful."

"Okay," I confess, my heart pounding in my chest. I just can't take it any more; I have no energy to tell another lie. "You're right. I lied."

This is the moment he'll abandon you, Sare, I ready myself. *He'll leave you now. He'll see how damaged you are, how broken.*

"You lied." Leon nods, seemingly surprised, although not with my revelation, but that I dropped my guard without a fight. He steps toward me so that we're only inches apart.

I lift my hand and press my finger gently against his mouth. His lips are soft, but his unshaven chin is prickly against my skin. His breath is warm and I feel it quicken. I distract him, just as he distracts me, I realize in that moment, as the air between us charges with the touch we both seem unable to break.

"I know you want to learn everything about the curse, so that you can understand it. But you must also understand—" I pause. "That I can't speak of it. I can't speak of what it does to me. No matter how much I want to, no matter how hard it is to bear alone—I just can't." I drop my voice to a whisper. "Please don't ask me to."

As I withdraw my hand, the warmth of his lips remains on my skin like a candle flame, not with the searing pain of the scars on my palm when they burn, but a gentle, inviting sensation that yearns for more.

"I'm sorry . . ." I back away toward the bed.

"And now what?" Leon sounds agitated. "You'll go to sleep to avoid me?"

"We need to rest," I say firmly.

Please, I pray. *Please don't ask me again.*

"Don't you think there's anything else we should discuss?" His eyes hold a peculiar glint. "After everything?"

I'm unable to look at him. I'm too ashamed of myself, of my lies, of my feelings.

"Silverbirch." He speaks through his teeth. "Look at me."

I shut my eyes. I'm exhausted. Not from running around all day trying to find answers, but from getting them. Just like Munu said, I headed into the darkness, and now I have no light. I shouldn't have disturbed Mum's past. But it's too late. I'm too deep in it, and it's all fucked up.

"I'm sorry. I messed up, okay?" I hate how weak I sound, as I step backward toward the bed. "I wish I could give you all the answers about the curse, but I can't."

But Leon seems to have other troubles. I hear him shuffle about and when I gingerly open my eyes, he's towering above me.

"Do you think that's my problem right now?" His jaw clenches. "Do you think that's what I care about? The curse?"

I stare at him, clueless. "What is it then, if not that?"

"Do you really not see what I've become around you?" He gives me that sharp, furious look again, as if I'm disturbing his peace. "What you reduce me to?"

"I-I—" My eyes escape his, inevitably remembering Sufi Chelebi. But Leon knows that I'm not the maiden, and he can't possibly feel the same way. "I'm not sure what you mean."

And the problem is, I don't want to find out. I want to pull away, but I'm cornered. Pressed against the bed's edge, my calves warn me that one more step back will send me tumbling onto it.

He slips a KitKat from his pocket. "Here." He hands it to me. "I figured out that sugar calms you down."

I stand frozen with the chocolate in my hand.

"For once, stop being so stubborn and eat it, please." Leon sighs.

The plastic wrapper crinkles as I tear it open, wishing he'd stop looking at me like that.

Liar, a voice whispers in my head. *You don't want him to stop staring. You don't want him to go to sleep. You want him to be awake, and to hold you in his arms and . . .* I take a deep breath to silence the intrusive thoughts.

"Happy?" I say when I finish eating. "Now go to sleep."

"You're a fool if you think I'll be able to sleep while you're here next to me," he whispers. He sounds just as he sounded that night in the tower when he kissed me.

For a second, I hear my pulse and nothing else.

"Not everything is as it seems, right? And I see you for what you are," he says. "So lonely that sugar has become a friend to you. It's the curse that makes you lonely, I get that."

"Leon—" As soon as I open my mouth, he lifts his hand to stop me.

"Let me finish," he says. "The burdens we carry sculpt our being. And your burden, whatever it is, has morphed you into the forlorn creature you are. But I'm no fool, Sare Silverbirch." He leans over. "I feel the connection between us, I see the way you look at me. Even if it's against your nature, I know you can feel the magnetism. And when I kissed you in the tower, I saw a darkness in your heart, and it burned brighter than any light. It blinded me, it consumed me, and yet I couldn't turn away."

"I'm sorry—" I rush to stop him. My ears are burning, my hands, my chest.

"Sare." He ignores my interruption. My name between his lips sounds like a prayer. "You can't not be feeling what I feel."

My eyes escape his. *Of course I feel it,* I want to say. *You have no idea how profound your influence is on me. My heart gallops like a wild horse in your presence. You make me forget otherwise unforgettable troubles.*

I close my eyes again.

He'll blow up your heart in five minutes, I hear Munu in my mind. *He's explosive.*

I was a fool to think that Leon wouldn't steal my heart. He already has.

"Look at me," Leon says. "Please."

As if I'm under a spell, I do what he asks.

Outside, the branches of a tree lash against the window. The wind howls so fiercely, part of me wonders if Munu's out there somewhere, trying to stop what's happening between us.

"I love you, Sare Silverbirch," Leon says. "Don't you get it? I've loved you since I saw you on that balcony with that silly lollipop. I love you no matter how cursed you are, or whatever the curse does to you. I love you even if it's contagious or possessive, even if it drives me mad, even if it ruins me, even if there's no cure. I love you even if you'll never love me back."

He cups my face in his hands, and the room shifts like a Salvador Dali painting, the pale furniture elongates, the world slips off its axis, my legs buckle beneath me. It takes every ounce of strength not to fall.

"I never loved anyone before," he says. "And it hurts me, keeping it to myself, keeping it a secret from you."

He loves me. Fuck. He said . . . he loves me.

He removed his armor, leaving himself exposed. Vulnerable. It's a gamble he plays with his heart and he knows he can lose everything, especially with someone like me. My first instinct is to run, but how can I? I can't turn away. I can't resist it. I'm not heartless, not yet.

"There, I said it," he says. "And I'm not sorry for saying it."

It dawns on me then, he expects me to say something back. I may not have the courage to confess it, but still I cannot deny it. I do love him. I know I do. Still holding me, his fingers stroke my cheeks, as if inviting me to speak.

This is dangerous—what he's doing to me. My heart has never beat faster, it's never wanted to speak so much, I've never wanted to lose control like this.

Love is a disease, Munu whispers in my mind. I try to ignore her.

"I-I—" It would be so easy to let it slip, to scream, to wake the whole island: *I love you!*

But I can't say it. I just can't.

Instead, before I can stop myself, I push up on my toes, and kiss him.

Communication is classified as Top Secret.
Circulation strictly limited to correspondents.
Note: This email will destroy itself once read and must be read as carefully as if your existence depends on it.

Subject: Re: Your True Nature

Date: 6 August 2025
From: Five the Fifth, Angel of Death, Field Operations, Mortal Termination and Transition, Mortal Affairs Commission

To: Grey the Compassionate, Senior Cherub, Temporal Intervention Agency, Fate Adjustment Bureau, Mortal Affairs Commission

Cherub,

Let me be clear: your insubordination is not just heresy—it's a fast track to becoming a fallen angel. One I can easily orchestrate. It will take me **one** email to the Head of the Divine Disciplinary Board.

It's not *what* you know, dear cherub, but *who* you know that matters.

The choice is yours. Would you prefer I crush your cute little head under my thumb and repurpose your wings as a duster for my office? Or will you seize your new job, be grateful for the opportunity, and leverage it to elevate yourself within the Temporal Intervention Agency?

Perhaps, with proper conduct, you might even earn yourself a halo someday.

Now, piss off.

Five
Fifth **Angel** of Death

CHAPTER TWENTY-THREE

Love is the greatest of the sacrifices, often demanding heavy costs. But the heart, unlike wisdom, heeds no reason, and it pays every price.
Excerpt from *The Book of Heartbreak, Müneccimbaşı Sufi Chelebi's Journals of Mystical Phenomena*

Our first kiss, though impulsive and rushed, was something both Leon and I managed to shove to the back of our minds. But the second changes everything.

I lose track of time as his lips press against mine, as my tongue slips into his mouth. It may be seconds or minutes—I have no idea, for time slows down and loses all meaning. When we eventually break apart, my lips still tingle, longing again for his. In that moment, I hug him, and he envelops me in an embrace I wish could last forever. His chest is firm against my cheek. This, I discover, must be what happiness feels like. This safety in the rhythm of another's heart.

And, fuck, I'm scared of losing it.

"I love you," he says again. "I love you, Sare."

Do it, I tell myself. *Say it.* The words form on my lips, but I still can't bear to speak them aloud.

We stand entwined: a boy doomed to madness should he fall for a cursed girl, and a girl who'll perish if her heart shatters once more.

It takes all my strength to slip away from his arms. Once the pull of his touch fades, clarity begins to seep in. This isn't just about saving myself any more—I need to protect Leon. He's already confessed his love, how little he cares about the doom it may bring upon him.

He doesn't understand how merciless the curse is. But I do—I've died four times already. I can't be selfish. I can't allow him to remain entangled in this mess. What will happen if I fail to break the cycle? I'll be heartless, a hollow shell, incapable of returning his devotion. I'll be his damnation.

"I'm sorry." I step away. "This is a mistake. I don't know what's got into me."

I see the fleeting surprise on his face. His brow furrows, and he opens his mouth as if he'll say something, but I escape his gaze and glance at the bedding.

"Look," I begin, ignoring the fluttering in my chest, "you and I are impossible. There's no way we can be together. Forcing this will only hurt us, and others."

"Is there someone else?" He looks miserable. "Back in the UK?"

For a moment, I toy with the idea of lying to him. If I say yes, he'd let go. But I can't lie after everything I've been through. My voice abandons me, and I shake my head.

"Am I somehow making things worse for you?" Leon doesn't give up. "Is this about the curse—what it does to you?"

I always underestimate how clever he is, how he reads me like an open book.

"Yes," I whisper. "The curse—" My throat dries. I can't tell him about the heartbreaks—not from shame or embarrassment, not any more, but because I fear it will only make him hold on to me tighter. "I can't get close to anyone."

"Sare," he says, and I wonder how I'll tolerate not hearing my name from his lips if I let him go. "We can go to Peru together. The master there is the finest of the curse-breakers. He can help us. Come with me, Sare."

"I can't." I drop my gaze. Kissing him was a mistake. I'm undone by the urge to hold him close, to bury my face in his chest and beg him to stay. And the fact that I can't slices me like a knife.

"Then tell me to stay," he says. My struggle must be evident to him. "Tell me that you want me to stay, and I will."

It would be so easy, so simple to say, *Stay*. He wants to hear it. *I want to say it.* We'll be happy, even if only temporarily. But if I can't break the curse . . . I would soon cease to be able to love him back.

"I'm sorry." My voice is a whistle in the wind. "I can't."

Pain flashes across his face. But this is for his own good—he will be safe. He won't leave me unless I strike a blow.

It's unfair. It's for the best.

"Read the room, Leon." I force the words out. "I don't want a relationship. I don't want any commitments. Peru? To save me? I'm tired of you acting like my savior. I tried to be subtle, thinking you'd take the hint, but maybe I need to spell it out. I'm perfectly capable of taking care of myself. Stop treating me like some damsel in distress."

That does it. I see the hope in his eyes flicker and fade, and I'm hit by a tide of self-loathing.

This time, there are no more words, no more candies or kisses to exchange. He retreats to his makeshift bed without any protest, ending this misery for us both, and I curl up in mine with the fluttering within my ribs.

My hands are on my lips, and I can still feel him, taste him, smell him—everything about him that momentarily shreds all my troubles into nothingness, distracting my cursed heart. He's a drug, a storm that rips everything apart and one I can't afford to be in love with.

Within my ribs, doves are trying to set themselves free.

I close my eyes. *Rule number three,* I recite. *Death is not an option.*

A boy can't break my heart. Not after everything I've been through. Not before I know what happened to my mother. Not before I break the curse.

I will not die.

I will not die.

I will not die.

When I open my eyes the next morning, the storm has at last fallen silent outside and I'm alone in the room. I nip to the bathroom, wondering where Leon is, and then I hear him.

"*Biliyorum,*" he says, gritting his teeth. It means, "I know." The rest, I can't decipher.

I follow the sound of voices into the living room and when I peek through the door, Leon finishes his phone call.

"We need to go back, right now." He's disheveled, unamused at the sight of me.

I glance at him warily. "What's wrong?"

"Your grandfather is very upset." He sighs. "They assumed we ran away together. Pelin is with them now, assuring them we didn't, but—"

With panic, I turn on my phone and ring Azmi.

"Please, Miss, come home," he begs. "Mr. Gümüşhuş is very concerned."

"I'm sure he is," I say coldly. The fact that I have Azmi's number instead of Muzaffer's on my phone says a lot.

"Miss, please, he isn't well."

I resent Muzaffer for abandoning my mother, for turning his back on her, for letting Iris have everything she had. The list grows longer when I think about how he's treated me—his cold stare, his harsh and irritated tone. He locked me in a room, for fuck's sake. He trapped me like an animal in a cage. Like the maiden in the tower.

But I must be an idiot because I still pity him.

He's just a sad, old man.

"Fine," I hear myself say. "I'm coming. I need to speak with him anyway."

Leon remains withdrawn as we thank Arda for the hospitality and begin our walk to the ferry. Our intimacy seems to have been left behind on the island.

Because I'm a coward who couldn't say the words, *I love you*.

We both retreat into our own silences on the ferry, maintaining a cautious gap between us. Despite the revelations about Mum's past, I can't stop myself obsessing over him, from wanting to hold his hand, to look into his eyes again and kiss him. But he's hunched over his phone, tactfully ignoring me.

A gull shrieks above us.

What is wrong with me? Leon should be the least of my worries now. I'm still nowhere near breaking the curse. Yet all I can focus on is him.

Love was madness for Chelebi and a disease for Munu, but for me it's a distraction. An endless yearning.

I love him, I whisper to myself. I shouldn't, but I still do.

As if he's read my mind, he moves his gaze to me, and a sad smile forms on his mouth.

"I'm leaving on Saturday," he says.

I'm startled for a second, unable to grasp what he means.

"For Peru," he clarifies. "Wasn't that what you wanted?"

I feel the fluttering again. My heart warns me—whispering the dangers of loving him, loving Mum, loving and trusting *anyone*—as if a hundred little thorns are pressed against my flesh.

"I'm happy for you," I hear myself mumble. There's nothing more to say.

When we arrive, Pelin and Azmi are waiting for us outside the house. Pelin spots us from afar and scurries down the slope to the shore—followed by a galloping Azmi—to hug Leon.

Leon says something to her in Turkish, and Pelin waves me goodbye before they turn their backs to head off.

My heart aches, watching Leon leave. But I pushed him, didn't I? I can't complain like a child now. At least I'm not fluttering any more—a silver lining to this nightmare. I shift my gaze and am greeted by Azmi's furrowed brow.

"Thank goodness you're here," he says. "Mr. Gümüşhuş has barely eaten anything since we discovered you'd gone yesterday. Do you know how worried he is? It's . . . It's almost like when . . ." He presses his hand to his chest, breathless as we climb back up the slope to the house. "Never mind," he says as I frown.

"I'm here now," I say. It takes all my willpower not to glance at Leon as he climbs the slope ahead of us.

He can be happy in Peru, I tell myself. *It's for the best.*

Him, away from me. Me, away from him.

For the best.

CHAPTER TWENTY-FOUR

The pain of a heartbreak is immune to the passage of time. No matter how many years drift by, or how many souls one seeks to heal it with, the ache resides deep within, ever enduring.

Excerpt from *The Book of Heartbreak, Müneccimbaşı Sufi Chelebi's Journals of Mystical Phenomena*

I find Muzaffer in his library, seated in the leather chair behind the mahogany desk, as pale as a sheet of paper. His hair hangs loose over his shoulders, unkempt. A wooden box sits before him, alongside a bottle of raki and a glass.

Has he been drinking already? It's not even noon.

"Why did you run away, Sare?" His breath whistles, as if he's having difficulty breathing.

"Why wouldn't I?" I can't believe he's genuinely asking me. "You locked me in my room!"

He sniffs. "I was trying to protect you."

"From what?" I scoff.

Muzaffer fidgets, pushing some papers away instead of responding, veins green and visible under his skin. "Have you found your answers, wherever you were?"

"I did." I pin him down with my gaze.

"And what have you learned?" He pours himself a drink. I wish he wouldn't.

"You let Iris marry Daphne's boyfriend." I clench my fists. "How could you do that to her?"

"You have brought more questions, then." He sips his drink. Then again. It sickens me how much he resembles Daphne. Numbing himself with alcohol.

"The past is made of regret," he says. "I wouldn't call myself a wise old man, but still, I suggest you heed my advice. You are young. You have a future ahead of you. There's no point in haunting yourself." He shakes his head. "Don't look back."

He has no idea how much I *need* to look back, to understand, to fit the pieces together, to break the curse. It's easy for him to dismiss everything. But not for me.

"Why drag me to Istanbul if you don't want to talk to me?" I challenge him.

"You're only a child." He frowns. "I can't expect you to carry these . . . burdens."

"I'm not a child." I barely stop myself from stomping my foot.

"You are the only one I have left," he mutters. "You are all that's left, Sare. You are important."

"Am I?" I let out a nervous laugh. "Then tell me what happened to my mother. Or I'll go and find Ozan, Mum's old flame. Or should I say Iris's husband? I'm sure *he* knows something."

At the mention of Ozan, Muzaffer's head snaps to attention. "Please," he begs. "Don't speak of him."

That hit a nerve, didn't it?

I take a step toward him. "Why shouldn't I?"

Muzaffer pours himself another glass. Then downs it in one shot.

"What did you do to Daphne?" I'm burning with anger, I don't even worry about the fluttering. "Did you throw her out because she was pregnant? Did you lock her in a room like you did to me?"

The air conditioning whirrs, filling the silence between us. Muzaffer's face slackens.

"Look at yourself." My voice trembles. "Shunning the mere mention of your own daughter for God knows how many years."

He reaches for the bottle again and, before I can stop myself, I charge forward and snatch it from him. "Haven't you had enough?"

The bottle is almost empty, but the smell of raki bites me, releasing a flood of memories. Empty bottles on the floor, on the counter, stuck between the cushions on the sofa, inside the bathtub. The smell of vomit. "You shouldn't drink."

"I'm already dying." His eyes are glassy. "Does it matter if I suffer one day less or more?"

I knew it, since Azmi revealed how sick he was, but still, hearing it from his mouth shakes me to my core. There's something familiar in the way he's ready to give up on himself to stop the pain. It makes me remember how I died last time. How I *almost* died last week. How Death is always one step away from me.

The fluttering soars within my ribs.

"What is *wrong* with you?" I clench my fists, unable to contain my emotions any more.

"What is wrong with me?" Muzaffer mirrors my words as he leans back, seeming to be genuinely thinking of an answer. "You lost your mother and became an orphan. I lost two children at once and became empty. I've been empty for so long, child."

"You didn't lose Daphne when you lost Iris." My voice trembles as the intensity of the fluttering increases. "My mother was alive. She needed you."

"She wrote to me." His head sways as he taps on the wooden box. "She kept writing."

"She wrote to you?" I gasp, unable to believe my mother reached out to him.

"I couldn't read them. I was afraid. I still am." Muzaffer speaks with the queasiness of a benign drunk. "But I couldn't get rid of them either. What do you do with it? They kept coming."

My knuckles turn white on the empty bottle I'm still clutching. I drop my gaze to the box. Dark wood, engraved with Turkish motifs. A key sits in its lock.

"I wish I could rip them apart." Muzaffer's cheeks are flushed, his aniseed breath unsteady. "I couldn't forgive her."

He begins to quiver, then drops his head, cradling his face in his hands.

I will not forgive you, the writing on Defne's room whispers.

"Why?" I'm overwhelmed by pity, not sure whether it's for myself, for him, or everyone who ever had the misfortune to live in this house. What use is there in asking him? Muzaffer isn't going to talk.

"You're headstrong like her, aren't you? You won't listen. Like she never listened." Muzaffer lifts his head. "I will tell you everything. But first you must promise me something."

"What?" I take a deep breath.

Focus on him and ignore the fluttering. Distract yourself with his misery and your anger, I tell myself.

"You will not seek him," he mutters.

"Who do you mean?"

"Ozan," he says. "Promise me, no matter what happens, you won't go looking for him."

"Why?"

"Because . . ." He sways. "B-because—"

"For the love of God," I say, wishing I could lunge forward and grab his shoulders to shake the truth out of him. "Say something!"

He stares at me, glassy eyed, disheveled.

"Because he's your father," he says at last. "Ozan is your father."

When I was little, I used to ask Daphne about my father.

"You don't need a father," she'd say. "We have each other. Isn't that enough?"

"But everyone else has a dad," I would protest.

She would deflect the question. She would hug and kiss me until I forgot.

I was fourteen when I fully confronted her—when I wouldn't let it go. I was angry with the way she'd begun to neglect me, the way her eyes slipped past me as if I was a ghost.

"I *must* have a father somewhere," I begged. "I just want to know his name. You must know his name."

Daphne stared at me with her doe eyes. She always looked frightened of me when she was sober.

"He doesn't have a name," she said firmly. The strap of her vest dangled on her arm, right above the scar she'd got from falling out of a window when she was little. "A father is not a necessity, Sare. Look at me, I don't have one. You're not losing out. Call him Jack. Or George. What does it matter?"

No tears shall fall, I recited silently.

But my mother didn't stop. "Some people don't have mums and some don't have dads and some, like me, have no one." I wanted to ask her why she didn't count me as someone, but she beat me to it, cold and sharp. "It's called life. This is your reality—get used to it."

And, just like that, I did.

Ozan.

The name fills the library.

Shock yanks me away from Muzaffer.

"Liar!" I scream. "She had a boyfriend. I saw the letters—he signed them as A. His name wasn't Ozan."

"He had a middle name—" Muzaffer says. "Azlan. That's what your mother called that sick bastard. As if a different name would make him a different man."

"No." I shake my head. "I don't believe you."

A.

Azlan, Azlan, Azlan.

When we're apart, Daphne murmurs from her letter. *I'm drowning in guilt and longing. Only when we're alone together do I feel alive.*

Mum, what have you done?

Perhaps they used the copy of *Doctor Zhivago* as a postbox, exchanging notes while they lived under the same roof. What a fool I was, treasuring it as a keepsake.

Defne, sweet muse of my cravings.

I hear my own laughter as I recall Azlan's words and press my hand to my mouth. Perhaps I'm losing it.

Suddenly, I feel uncertain about hearing the rest. I hadn't bargained for this. It's too fucked up. It's too much.

"What's wrong with you?" Muzaffer growls. "Weren't you begging me a minute ago to tell you everything?"

"I was," I reply, my hand above my heart. Perhaps I'm so used to shock now, so used to feeling numb, or perhaps my heart has given up on emotions already without waiting for me to turn eighteen, because now it feels insensate, frozen. Not even fluttering. "I want to know everything."

"Sit, then." Muzaffer nods his head, groggy, and I lower myself on the nearest armchair. "Where do I begin, though? How could one begin to explain his daughters' fight over a man? Are there words to describe how one sister destroys the other?"

I think of Eudokia's beddua creeping through the centuries as an unforgiving curse. How the writing on the wall triggered it again.

I will not forgive you. A voice buzzes in my head. *I will not forgive you.*

"Who wrote on the wall upstairs?" My voice is a croak.

Muzaffer lifts his head to the ceiling as if it's transparent.

"I remember finding the room in that state," he mutters. "I wish I could erase my memory of that night. No matter how many years pass or how old I grow, it remains at the center of everything. The dread of knowing something terrible happened." He pauses. "She'd told me only a day before that she was pregnant. I was angry, Sare. Do you blame me? She was out of her mind. She was going to confront Iris. She wanted her sister's husband for herself. I pleaded with her to stop. Iris wasn't well enough to deal with it. She couldn't deal with it."

Run, a voice hisses. *Save yourself.* But I cannot move.

"When I came home from work they were nowhere to be found. I pushed the door open, and then I saw the wall. I knew it, then. I knew she'd confronted Iris, despite how much I'd begged her not to do it."

She never listened.

Perhaps it's Munu speaking in my head. *You're heading into darkness.*

My teeth chatter. I'm already in darkness.

"S-she was not in her room. T-then the earthquake started and I . . . I bolted outside to search for them. I cut through the crowds. Couldn't find them anywhere. I couldn't find them." Muzaffer sways, elbowing the glass which tumbles from the desk and, without smashing, rolls across the hardwood until it reaches my feet.

I can't tell if he speaks to me any more, or only to himself.

"Sare. Canim," I hear Munu's voice, though I cannot see her. "Leave him. Walk out. This is not your tragedy."

Perhaps I'm going mad. Perhaps the curse plays tricks on me. Munu sounds so close, but I scan the library and there's no one other than Muzaffer and me here.

"I returned home—" A vein throbs in Muzaffer's neck. He's so pale, his skin almost transparent. "I climbed up to her room. She was there, alone. She wouldn't speak. I begged her but she wouldn't speak. Catatonic. What could I do? She was pregnant. I couldn't shake her. And then he came. He came. Ozan. Azlan—"

I move back and forth on my seat. Panic covers my mouth like a hand. Words won't come to my aid any more. The questions that burned me for months now lie dead at my feet, shot down by the answers. I want to shout at Muzaffer, tell him to stop. I want to walk out and leave him alone with his tragedy, but I can't move.

"He told me everything. He had been with them. Iris . . . Iris summoned your mother to the Maiden's Tower. They fought and he just watched without intervening. He was . . . wrong in the head. As if he wished to be two different men with my girls. I never understood what they saw in him. But Iris . . . she was so in love, so reliant on him—she needed him more than her sister did. Or so I thought. I didn't know what would become of letting her marry him. Didn't know he continued to string your mother along. He was always so . . . manipulative. He even fooled me. I was the fool, Sare." Muzaffer sniffs, tears now flowing down his cheeks. There's something soul-destroying in his silent cry. ""Not my fault," he said, the night Iris died. As if he hadn't played with my girls like a cat plays with mice. He didn't even try to comfort your mother. She was there, crumpled up, crying, while he just shrugged. "This was her fate," he said. "You can't change fate.""

Everything Muzaffer explains seems to make the air thicker and unbreathable.

My mother was there when Iris died on the night of the earthquake. She was fighting with her for my father. Fate—how convenient for him to blame something so untouchable, so impossible to fight back against.

There must be a splinter in my throat because I still can't find my voice.

"Iris died that night. She died and I died, and your mother died. You know who walked away alive? Your father . . . He left. Never to be seen again." Muzaffer pauses to wipe his tears. "Had your mother only listened to me, and left for the UK without confronting her sister . . ."

"You tried to send her away?" I can barely believe it.

"Before, yes. I wanted her out from under Ozan's influence. And away from Iris, at least until I could sort things out, remove that man from our lives. I bought her the house in Cambridge, set up accounts for her in the UK." His eyes sharpen but then quickly dull again. "But she thought I just wanted rid of her. She said she wouldn't leave without him. I tried to talk sense into her. But it enraged her. Do you know what she said to me? 'He loves me more than he loves Iris.' I couldn't understand what had got into her. How could a person do this to their own sister?"

"Liar." I lash out again. "Mum wouldn't have done it! She wouldn't sleep with her sister's husband."

But even in my denials, even though I cannot bear to admit it, I know he's telling the truth. Daphne's restlessness. The way she wanted to hurt everyone around her. How she punished herself. The life she lived in exile, alone, away from the home she missed so dearly. It wasn't only the curse. It was my mother's atonement.

Iris, Iris, Iris, Daphne murmurs in my head. *Why do you still haunt me?*

The fluttering spreads through my ribs.

Rule number three, I recite. *Death is not an option.*

I will not die, I reassure myself. *I will not die.*

Iris died. Daphne died. I will *not* die.

"You think she was a monster." My pulse pounds in my throat. "But she wasn't. She was sad. She was so sad."

"I never said she was a monster." The chair squeals as Muzaffer swivels it round to see me. "I never thought she wished for any of that. There were days I wondered if she was hypnotized, possessed— she wouldn't listen no matter how much I begged her. Neither Iris nor your mother . . . They didn't listen."

Channel sorrow into anger, I urge myself. But I find only despair in my heart. He's a frail old man, and I'm a fool.

"Sare," I hear Munu again. This time, she's more determined. "Look at me, Sare. Look down. I'm here."

I look down and see her on the floor, a reflection inside the glass Muzaffer dropped.

"Distract yourself," Munu says. "Walk out."

I shake my head. "Leave me alone."

"You don't like hearing the truth, do you?" Muzaffer, oblivious to Munu's presence, tries to rise, perhaps to challenge me, but his hands slide off the table's edge. "But it *is* the truth. She pressed Iris to divorce. She drove her sister to a breakdown. She had no shame in demanding him for herself."

He wavers, seeking support. I don't rush to his aid. His eyes are wild as he watches me, but, drunk as he is, he still recognizes me. The name "Iris" doesn't slip between us.

"It's *he* who is shameless. He's the one who favored one woman over the other." Munu's voice rises in vain to enrage me. "Your mother was only twenty-one years old. Who doesn't make mistakes at that age? Be angry, Sare. Do it for your mother."

"S-shut up!" I lash out at her.

"I told you, didn't I?" Muzaffer laughs, or cries, I can't tell any more. "You should've left it alone. We all made mistakes and we paid the price."

"What about Iris?" My voice is low. "Did she have any shame when she stole Daphne's boyfriend? Did *you* have any when you let them marry?"

"I didn't know. Do you think I'd have let it happen if I did? Your mother didn't say a thing until I figured it out. Still she wouldn't stop seeing him. He was a disease for her. I told her it wouldn't end well. But she wouldn't listen. She wouldn't listen." Muzaffer's eyes are red-rimmed from crying and still the tears slip down his pale cheeks.

"She has a name," I say. "But you don't have the guts to say it, do you?"

I brace myself for his wrath but he must have none left. He blinks, his chest rising and falling rapidly.

"Say her name!" I can't contain my scream. "Say it!"

"Defne," he groans in the end, as if he's just remembered her name. "Defne."

He says it again, and again, bolder, louder, agonizing, inhuman.

My mother's name elongates as he wails. Time stretches between us.

I'm stunned, recognizing something I know so well. Too well. A heartbreak.

It comes down on us both, pouring through his tears, punching my chest. How did I fail to see how much sorrow he contained? The mask he wears wasn't anger, it wasn't a grudge, it wasn't that he resented Defne. It was his broken heart and, of all the people in this world, it should have been me who recognized his burden, when I've lived all my life under the shadow of the very same thing.

Muzaffer, like me, tried to toughen himself with anger. But what use is there in being angry all the time?

The fluttering hits me like a current now.

Rule number three, I command myself as Muzaffer is lost to his own agony. *Death is not an option.*

I lean over his desk and pull the box toward me.

"Sare!" Munu's reflection hisses again. "Walk out of this room now!"

"Don't you dare talk to me," I whisper at Munu. "You've cursed us all with your bitterness, you blamed Mum for your own mistakes!"

Breathe, Sare, Munu says, or perhaps the voice is in my head. I cover my ears with my hands. *Calm down.*

"Calm down," Muzaffer repeats, caught off guard by my outburst, staggering as he steps forward.

"Stop!" Munu calls out, but Muzaffer unknowingly kicks the glass away in trying to reach me. Munu shrieks as it rolls across the floor. I ignore the rest of her pleas and focus on the box.

Muzaffer halts abruptly as I turn the key and lift open the lid. Letters. The familiar return address scribbled in Mum's handwriting. I count five, transfixed. Unopened, unreturned, unforgotten. I don't have the guts to tear them open to see what words Mum poured into her seventeen years of silence. I can't bear shouldering the weight Muzaffer avoided carrying.

Yet, abandoning them feels unfair. She had something to say. I need to know what.

"Please," Muzaffer begs again. "Don't."

I stare at him, unmoving. I want to open them. I want to dismiss him and do what I need to do. But the sting of ignoring his first warning presses down on me, making me falter. It's unstoppable. It's relentless. It's cowardice—what I know the best. Slowly, I take a step back. Then another. And another. Until I'm running—from the old man, from the room, from the house and everything that binds me to the haunting past.

Subject: Bestest News!

Date: 7 August 2025
From: abettergreyforabetterworld@gmail.com
To: leon.dumanoglu@gmail.com

My dear and most hardworking partner Leon,

No matter how this message finds you, I guarantee it will leave you better!

M1274856567048112—the poor, plagued soul—finally agreed to meet me, and once I tell her the truth about my discoveries, she will surely agree to cooperate against he whose name I cannot type in an unencrypted email.

Unfortunately, I can't share the explicit details with you, not yet, as it is against the Fate Adjustment Bureau policies. The last thing I need is the Compliance Office on my back!

More information to follow.

Your passionate partner in crime (this is what you mortals say, isn't it? Not that we're committing any crimes, of course!),

Grey

CHAPTER TWENTY-FIVE

Forgiveness stands at the core of healing. Only the misguided seek solace in wrath.

Excerpt from *The Book of Revenge, Müneccimbaşı Sufi Chelebi's Journals of Mystical Phenomena*

There's only one person I have yet to meet: the one who witnessed what truly happened between Mum and Iris that night. Even if it feels like a betrayal after Muzaffer begged me not to seek him.

I leave Muzaffer buried in his sorrow, before he can lock me away again, and storm out of the house, as if my father will just be standing there, waiting to absorb the full force of my rage.

I follow throngs of people on the seafront. Swimming among their faces in my sorrow. I don't know how long I walk. I'm numb, wordless. Must be a couple of hours of trekking when I arrive at a bazaar. It's an expansive, exotic place. The air is a heady mix of spices and leather, the din of haggling and murmurs. As if in a dream, I weave through the maze of stalls and passageways, looking at each face as if one of them will be Ozan and I'll recognize him.

I don't even know how to address him.

Ozan belonged to Iris, and Azlan to Defne. He's no one to me.

Because of him my mother and aunt are dead. Muzaffer is living in his own hell. Yet my father lives as if nothing ever happened. He got to move on.

Anger clutches at my throat. But my fury is fickle. It's no remedy. It never has been, I realize now.

Like a fool, I end up getting lost. I walk aimlessly around the bazaar, letting the crowds drag me like a current. If I can walk for long enough, perhaps I can forget everything.

Tragedies befall the ordinary, often arising without a hint of malice, says Sufi Chelebi.

I think of Muzaffer, how he buried himself alive in that dark house, trapped by his memories. Defne, who drowned in guilt. Iris, and Munu, who both pledged not to forgive their own sisters, despite how it ruined them all.

What is the point of being trapped in sorrow, rage or fear?

I pause in a narrow passage beside a shop selling frames and mirrors, the air thick with smoke hissing from a nearby grill, building steam on the glass. I stare at myself in a gilded circle.

Is this the life you want to live, Sare? I ask myself. A life of sorrow and longing, hate and grudges. It's so easy to store away all the anger I have for Ozan, to keep it with me like a family heirloom and let it grow inside me.

But I don't want it. I have to leave it behind.

"Let it go," I tell my reflection. Only cowards seek the remedy for their pain in anger and fear.

I look up to see the seller inviting me inside the shop. I shake my head, yet my eyes remain fixed on my reflection. The girl staring back at me from the mirror is transformed beyond all recognition. She is no longer a coward.

I take a taxi back to Üsküdar, but I can't bring myself to go home. Instead, I stand by the rocks across from the Maiden's Tower, where everything started, watching the sea welcome rain and wind like old friends. Unlike me, it remains peaceful and oblivious on its tiny island.

And I . . . I have never felt more alone in my entire life. Never more forlorn.

Despite my newfound courage, I remain isolated, with no one to share the struggle or confide in about how difficult it is to keep from crying.

If only I could pick up the phone and call Leon, stop him before he leaves . . . It would be so easy to say, *I love you. Please don't go.* It would be such a relief. But how can I? I'm no longer scared to say it, but it would be so selfish. Leon deserves better than someone who, in a few months, will lose the ability to love him back, because I haven't managed to break the curse, even though I know now where it started.

I gaze at the tower, everything I've unearthed whirring around in my head.

I was a fool, thinking Muzaffer was the villain, convincing myself he hid everything out of guilt. He tried to shield me from the truth. It was my mother who wronged him, pursuing an affair with her own sister's husband. Whatever Daphne's reasons were, whatever obsessive love or longing drove her to that relationship, she betrayed her own family. Iris did the same. Just like Theodora— and Eudokia.

Do I have the courage to forgive any of them, especially my own mother?

I have to read her letters to find out. I have to hear what she had to say to Muzaffer.

"You're putting yourself at risk." I hear Munu's voice.

Summer rain crashes down on me as I turn to see her mid-air, braving the storm. I'm too broken to push her away.

"I found out who my father is today," I tell her, as fat drops of rain soak into my vest, sending a chill through me. "Or should I say, Mum's biggest mistake? She fell in love with the wrong person. He promised to love her for eternity—sounds pathetic, doesn't it?

I guess his heart was too big . . . big enough to fit Iris in as well. He married her, and had Mum on the side."

"What?" Color drains from Munu's face.

"I'm pretty sure he was a psycho. Who calls his wife's sister 'sweet muse of my cravings'? They had an affair living under the same roof. He made them call him different names. What sort of sicko does that?"

"Y-your father?" Munu shivers. "Boss Almighty . . . No, it can't be true."

"Finally, something I know, and you don't," I say.

A gull cries a deep, sad shriek above us. Munu, deflated by my revelations, hovers in the air like a broken ornament.

"What's so hard to believe?" I scoff. "Don't you always say people are disgusting? Some lower the bar, that's all."

"Sare . . ." Munu's voice is a whisper. "I know what I did is unforgivable. But I was scared to tell you the truth. Scared you would hate me for it. Scared to hurt you." Her wings beat against the torrent. "All I want is to protect you. You're special, Sare. You're too kind and gentle for this ugly world. You don't deserve the torment of love. You can't trust a heart that's not yours."

I feel like crying again. It's the third time in one day, and surely not a good sign.

"I was wrong about so many things. Perhaps I still am." Munu looks away from me, her gaze fixed on the horizon. "I know you'll never trust me again, but I will try everything within my power to correct my mistakes. I swear. But you must stop digging . . . That boy, Leon, has good intentions, but he . . . he doesn't know how dangerous this is for you. Perhaps I should warn him."

"You're a fan of his now?" I laugh. "After all these weeks calling him the devil?"

"He and Grey saved me from—" Munu trembles. "A certain punishment."

I think of the angel, Grey, and how he offered a "rescue" to Munu. It's ridiculous—why would he care after all these years, after all this suffering? The thought of questioning Munu on how this supposed salvation is meant to work crosses my mind, but I stop myself. Why should I care? Angels and their agendas always seem crafted to serve themselves, not the living. They don't give a shit about all this suffering.

"And he is in love." Munu pulls a pained face. "He suffers for it."

"We're not meant to be," I assert. "He'll be on a plane to Peru on Saturday. Away from me. I drove him away. Be proud of me, Munu, you've taught me well. It hurts like hell—no, it hurts like fuck—but I didn't die. Maybe I'm becoming heartless. Just like you always wanted."

"I—" Munu says, pouting. "I'm sorry."

"Why?" I ask. "Shouldn't you be happy?"

"You're alive, Sare. Still alive. You won't be another victim. That's all that matters."

I glance away, wondering how close, or how far, I stand from another heartbreak. There's a constant, heavy ache in my chest since losing Leon, but I try to endure it.

What is more unbearable is the wreck awaiting me at the place I can hardly call a home.

My grandfather's heartbreak. The shadows of Iris and Defne.

"Stop investigating," Munu pleads, as if she's reading my mind. "You learned everything. You survived it. Don't push it any more."

"There's one last thing," I tell her. "One more knot to unravel."

Those unopened letters.

The evening prevails over the house when I finally find my way home, drenched and trembling from the storm. Shivering, I creep back into the library. I'm cold and battered, but there's no rest for me before I read Daphne's letters.

In the dim light, there's no sign of Muzaffer, but to my relief, the box of letters remains on the desk, as if he's left it for me. Perhaps he wants me to be his courage.

But what if, the voice in my head whispers, *they break* your *heart?*

"I'm not a coward," I reply as I rip open the first letter and start to read. "Not any more."

15 January 2008

Baba, I know you don't wish to hear from me any more. You made it very clear on the day I left that you will not have me back if I walk out.

If the letter returns to me, I promise I will never write to you again.

I had a baby girl, born on 10th December. She won't cry or scream like the other babies. Perhaps I've done all the crying on her behalf. I've shed so many tears there are none left for my child. Some nights, I imagine she stares at me in the dark. Some mornings, I wake up and she lays in silence, awake. There's something wrong with her, Baba. Or perhaps I'm the one who is wrong. I'm broken, after all, and perhaps I've broken her too.

I don't know how to be a mother. I don't know how to live any more.

Write to me, Baba, please. Tell me you forgive me.

defne

2 March 2009

Baba,

I'm trying to put my life back together, but it's not easy. I couldn't have survived without the house or the money you gave me before I left Istanbul, and for that I'm grateful. But I want to speak with you, Baba.

You can't know how many times I've picked up the phone, only to put it back down, afraid you'd hang up on me. I'm holding on by a thin thread, and your rejection will snap it.

You know where I live. You're reading my letters—you can't be cruel enough to throw them away—yet you remain silent. This silence paralyzes me. Write to me, Baba. I'm begging you. Forgive me.

Tell me I can come home. I want to come home.

In this foreign country, in this strange bubble, I look back and feel the deepest shame. I don't know why I did any of what I did. I don't know who that person was. If you're reading this, know that it wasn't me. I swear I'm not her any more.

defne

23 April 2013

Baba. Everything is harder when you're alive.

You're alive, I'm alive, though we both pretend otherwise. Your silence torments me. You won't forgive me, I know. I'm not begging forgiveness any more. But I need you.

Write to me. Even if only to say that you hate me. Blame me. Curse me. Shame me. Just write something. Anything. I'm made of sorrow and longing. I'm made of regret.

defne

17 August 2019

I should've listened, Baba. But I never wished to harm her. I never wanted to hurt her.

defne

10 March 2025

Baba, this is my last letter. Call it pride, call it guilt or shame—but I know you won't have me back. Why would you? I don't deserve it.

What was it that you said? "You died for me with your sister." You are a man of your word, Baba.

Perhaps you moved on, but I never stop thinking about the past. My soul is tethered to Istanbul, trapped in that moment at the tower, unable to move forward.

There are so many things left unsaid between us. You never met your granddaughter, Sare. She holds a wisdom most adults don't possess. You never set eyes on her to see how much she resembles Iris. I never told you how she has become my punishment. A reminder of my mistakes.

It's taken me eighteen years to build the courage to write about that night.

If I tell you what happened, will it end your silence? Or will it deepen the fractures between us?

No matter what, here is the truth you deserve to know.

Iris summoned me to the tower, and like a fool I went. I found her on the terrace with Azlan. I'm not going to lie to you, Baba. I said things to my sister that can never be taken back. I was consumed by a darkness in my heart. In Azlan's presence, I wasn't myself but a shell, and that shell told Iris to show dignity, to step aside, because Azlan and I were to have a child.

"I will never forgive you," was all my sister said.

I can still hear her voice, even as I pen these words.

The earthquake began as we argued. In the chaos, I didn't notice how Iris climbed on to the other side of the railing until it was too late. I begged her to stop, screamed until I had no voice left, but Azlan held me. He urged Iris to come back, to stop being childish, but Iris wouldn't budge. And that made him furious.

"Do you even love me?" Iris asked, but Azlan was . . . so detached. So cruel.

The things he said to her . . . Eighteen years have passed, and I remember every word.

"Will you jump if I don't? I'm sick of this, Iris. Sick of your whimpering. Go ahead, then."

Iris shook her head. Silent and defeated, she turned to climb back over the railing. Then the earthquake roared again, the ground lurching beneath us. Her footing slipped, and her hands shot out for the railing— but the tremors wrenched her away.

I tore free of Azlan's arm and lunged toward her, desperate to pull her back, but she was already falling. All it took was a second, and she was gone. I heard her scream as she fell—she didn't want to fall, she didn't want to die—and the sickening crash. Since then, every single day, every hour, every minute, I've lived with the weight of that one fleeting moment.

Azlan said it wasn't my fault or his, that we couldn't have saved her. I don't know why I didn't have the guts to confront him. He was an ocean, and I was a sandcastle against his waves.

But whatever hold he had over me crumbled with that earthquake. The love I had been so desperate for, so reckless to chase, died with Iris. He didn't pursue me after that night, perhaps because he recognized how my sister's death broke me. Even if he had come after me, I could never have been with him again. Not after what he did. Not after what it cost.

And I regret it. Every moment, every word, every lie, every promise. I regret it with my whole being—with my exile, with my solitude.

I'm not seeking your mercy. I was a fool, and fools aren't worthy of forgiveness.

But you are, Baba. I blamed you for favoring Iris, when it was my own faults that destroyed us.

I love you, Baba. I miss you. And I finally set you free from myself. I forgive you.

defne

CHAPTER TWENTY-SIX

Pain, for its sojourn within some, forges a fork in the path ahead: toward wisdom or cruelty. The choice rests upon the inclinations of one's heart. Wisdom asks naught but a willing mind, yet cruelty always exacts its toll from the soul. Only the wise can offer true forgiveness.

Excerpt from *The Book of Betrayal, Müneccimbaşı Sufi Chelebi's Journals of Mystical Phenomena*

Defne's letters pierce me like a sword. I breathe through her sorrow, her guilt, her regret. Funny, what pains me the most is how she signed each note in small, diminished letters, as if she relinquished her right to the name she abandoned.

And Iris . . . I tremble, imagining those last moments Daphne described.

Perhaps it was Azlan's cruelty that made Daphne hide him from me. I should be thankful I never met that sick fuck. But still, she let it happen, she let it get to that point.

The world falls silent as I close my eyes, only the rustle of papers in my shaking hands remains. It takes a lot for me not to cry. A lot more not to die.

I lost two children. Muzaffer's words echo in my mind. *I became empty.*

Perhaps that's exactly what I've become—empty.

With trembling hands, I tuck the letters back into the box.

It must be a miracle that I stay alive. A miracle, that Daphne doesn't kill me a second time.

A fever overtakes me before midnight, drifting like a dream but spreading like a nightmare. Soon, I'm no more and it's all that remains. Perhaps it's the hopelessness that makes me shiver beneath the duvet, the despair of admitting the curse might win. How can I possibly fix such a tragedy? Mum's gone, Iris is gone, and now I'll be the sacrifice to end what they started. My teeth chatter, my body aches with thirst. I need water, but instead of forcing myself out of the bed, I fall into a deep sleep.

In my dream, I'm staring at myself in a gilded mirror, brushing my hair. My features begin to blur and shift. My nose grows larger while my mouth shrinks and my eyes darken with hatred. My hair is the last thing to change, deepening into a bolder shade of chestnut.

Soon, my reflection isn't mine any more.

"Iris," I whisper.

In response, she extends her arm through the mirror to grab my wrist. Her touch sears me.

"I will not forgive you," Iris tells me, and her face rots until her skin is gray. Now, seaweed is entangled in her wet hair. "I will never forgive you, even if the earth splits open to swallow you," she spits between her teeth, morphing into Munu.

I hear my own scream piercing the night. Buried within the sheets, I'm a creature of sorrow. I want my mother, who I mourn, and Munu, who I cannot trust, and Leon, who I hurt. But they're not mine any more.

Perhaps they never were.

When my eyes flutter open, daylight streams through the curtains. I straighten up in bed, my body aching as I check my phone to see if there are any calls or messages. It's 2 p.m.

It takes all my energy to scramble out of the bed, but when I do, I meet with parchment, neatly rolled in a pencil-sized shape and secured with the evil-eye pendant I cast aside on the night I banished Munu. I pick it up. The gemstone is whole again, no longer broken. I untie the pendant, then carefully unroll the paper, which reveals itself to be a strip torn from a larger page.

It takes a few seconds to grasp what I'm looking at, but when I recognize Sufi Chelebi's scribbles, it feels as if I've received a letter from an old friend.

Forgiveness stands at the core of healing, it reads. *Only the misguided find solace in wrath.*

But the journal was destroyed. Wasn't it? And then I recall what Munu said yesterday.

I will try everything within my power to correct my mistakes.

Did Munu leave it here for me? Did she somehow manage to rescue pieces of it? I flip the page over, and read it again. And again. But there's no answer.

I sink on the bed and fix the necklace around my neck. The gold chain dangles on my chest. I shiver despite the warm day and bury my head on the pillow once more.

The night becomes cruel. Led by the fever, I wander between nightmares again. My head is hot and heavy, my throat rusty with thirst.

Sometime after midnight, the balcony door clicks open. Someone steps into the room.

"Silverbirch."

Leon.

I'm not sure if it's a dream, or if he's really here.

"Sare." Leon creeps closer. "Munu told me everything. She told me what the curse does to you."

He *is* here. I'm not hallucinating. Slowly, I drag myself to sit up in bed.

"I'm sorry," I whisper. "I couldn't—"

"Here—" he reaches for the cup on my bedside table— "drink."

Between my dry lips, I feel the cool, soothing touch of the water.

"I love you, Silverbirch." He sets my head on the pillow. "And I'll be damned if I break your heart."

I love you too, I whisper in my mind. *Please stay. Please don't go.*

But my lips won't move.

I wake to the smell of toast and butter. When I open my eyes, the day is bright and I'm not alone.

Leon sits in the armchair.

Leon. He didn't leave.

"You . . ." I struggle to sit up. "You're here?"

"If you thought even for a second that I could leave you," he says, "you are an idiot."

I pause, my eyes lingering on the tray on the bedside table: two slices of buttered toast, a Snickers bar, a cup of piping hot tea. "Did Munu really tell you everything?"

Leon nods. "Everything."

I should feel furious at her for not keeping her mouth shut. But part of me is relieved I wasn't the one who told Leon, and comforted by the fact that he finally knows.

"But what if . . ." I swallow hard. "What if you become like Sufi Chelebi?"

"Chelebi gave his heart to someone who didn't belong to his world. But you and I . . . We belong together, Sare. It's like destiny has bound us with an invisible cord—I can't pull myself away from you. All I can think of is the feel of your skin under mine, your scent, the weight of your gaze. The way you walk. The way you tuck your hair behind your ear. The way you blink. Your glow. How your lips move, how they curl up on the rare occasion of your smile—it drives me mad." He pauses. "And if this is madness, then I own it. It's mine, not Chelebi's, and I call it love."

The bond between us, I think silently. It is indeed a tight and unseen cord. He can move about the house now, and I could tell where he is. If he goes to Peru I'm certain I'd still be able to find him—that I could take a map of the world, close my eyes and pin my finger to where he lives.

He belongs to me.

"I was a fool, not telling you to stay." My throat runs dry with his confession. "And I'll forever regret hurting you."

I reach for the tray and take a hungry bite of toast. When I next seek the aid of tea, the liquid touches my tongue, warm and sweet. How did Leon prepare it exactly how I like it? Two spoonfuls of sugar, no milk.

"I'm sorry I lied to you when I was angry with others for deceiving me." I savor my confession. "I've died of heartbreak, and a fifth will be the end of me. I was frightened. I've spent my whole life feeling frightened. And suddenly *you* appeared and promised a—" I take another sip of tea—"solution. It confused me."

"I know." Leon smiles, eyes full of compassion. "I know how much strength it takes to survive a curse like this."

"You know what will happen to me?" My voice is a croak. "The curse will claim my heart if I don't win against it. And then I won't be able to love you back. What will happen, then?"

"I don't care, Sare." Leon's jaw tightens. "I don't need you to love me, but I need to be near you. Unless—" He pauses, voice faltering. "Unless you don't want me at all. But *I* want to be with you, no matter what."

A smile tugs at my lips. It must be contagious, because he mirrors me. What a miracle it is to say yes with a mere glance into his eyes, without the use of words at all.

"And there's still time. I know how stubborn you are, and I know you'll break the curse. Didn't I always say? Sufi Chelebi's book chose you for a reason." He grins.

I gasp, suddenly remembering the fragment I found the night before. "There's a piece of it here. On the desk."

"Munu retrieved it," Leon says. "Her boss, Five, tried to destroy Sufi Chelebi's journals, but it seems indestructible."

Forgiveness stands at the core of healing.

I retrieve the torn parchment. Outside, a motorbike with a wailing exhaust pipe runs along the street.

"They underestimate us, these celestials. Mortals can be immortal too." I brush the paper with my thumb. "Look at Sufi Chelebi—he perished long ago, but he's still here."

Leon's eyes narrow.

"If this tiny piece has chosen not to be destroyed . . . It may be the key to breaking the curse." My voice pitches, hope stirring in my chest. "I found out what happened between Iris and Defne," I continue. "What my mother did."

"Your mother?" Leon frowns. "She triggered the curse?"

"It was Iris who said the beddua." I swallow hard. "She awakened the curse."

Don't cry, Sare.

I tell him everything. Not sparing a single detail, despite how much it hurts me to speak.

"There's a box of letters." I can't stop. I need to get it all out. "Mum wrote to Muzaffer. He never opened them. But I've read them. Mum begged his forgiveness."

Leon stares at me, speechless.

"My grandfather has to read those letters, he needs closure. He needs to understand how desperately Mum sought his forgiveness, the extent of her regrets, and the depth of her love. He needs to forgive her, for his sake and for mine." I reach out and place my hand on Leon's. "What else is there left to do to break this curse? Think about it, Leon. History repeated and they all made the same mistake—they never offered any forgiveness to each other, living in grief, regret or anger."

"I don't know." Leon's eyes escape me. "It's so risky. What if . . . What if he says something that hurts you?"

"I'll be okay," I mutter.

It's not exactly a promise.

I knock on the door of Muzaffer's study, my heart pounding in my chest. The curtains are drawn to contain the afternoon heat, and the room is shrouded in shadows, the only light coming from the glow of a laptop screen. I hesitate, my hand trembling on the doorknob.

Finally, I gather my courage and take three steps, the box of letters in my hands.

Muzaffer looks up from his computer. His red-rimmed eyes are hollow, and his skin pale and clammy. Böcek lies on his lap, swooshing her tail, as if she too realizes how sad her owner is.

"I'm sorry," I stammer, my voice barely a whisper. "I was cruel to you. I was so angry."

He looks at me, speechless. A thousand doves flap their wings inside my rib cage.

Still, I propel to the desk and place the box on it.

"I read them—" I pause, fighting with my own tears. "I thought you too might want to hear what she had to say."

He remains still.

"She deserves it," I whisper. I've never been so close to giving in to my urge to cry. The warmth of tears is a distant feeling, like the hum of a half-remembered song.

He nods. A tear rolls down his sunken cheek.

I place my hand on his. It doesn't sting like a stranger's any more. His fingers fidget lightly, offering a fragile truce. Perhaps in time, we will heal each other, the fragments of a family stitched with the invisible thread of our pain.

I always wondered if the hurt would ever fade, when what I should have asked was whether I'd ever grow strong enough to carry it.

"What happened to Mum wasn't your fault." I'm strong enough to say it. "I'm not going to blame you, or her. Not any more. And I promise, I will not look back."

When I return to my room, Leon's is pacing, restless.

"What's wrong?" I ask.

"We have to go," he says.

"Where?" I blink, taken aback by the sudden shift in his mood.

"I-I had a message. Munu is in the tower," he says, almost breathless.

My lips part to ask why he'd be so compelled by Munu's whereabouts, but he beats me to it.

"Grey's called a meeting, and we have to be there."

Communication is classified as Highly Confidential.
Circulation strictly limited to beings of celestial origins.

Urgent Meeting Request

From: Grey the Compassionate, Senior Cherub, Temporal Intervention Agency
Required Attendees: Five the Fifth; User15963318 (Temporary Ethereal); M939274856567048343; leon.dumanoglu@gmail.com
Place: The Maiden's Tower / KIZ KULESI (Earth, 41°01'16.2"N 29°00'15.3"E)
Time: 15 August 2025 6 p.m.
Subject: CID-1010834556

CHAPTER TWENTY-SEVEN

Reader, as my chronicles repeat within these pages, the fundamental laws of our realm present two ways to lift a curse: through a sacrifice deemed worthy, or by rectifying the misdeeds that ensnare those entangled by the curse.

Excerpt from *The Book of Heartbreak, Müneccimbaşı Sufi Chelebi's Journals of Mystical Phenomena*

We climb up to the tower just after the museum closes. The rotunda is eerily empty, with no sign of Munu or the book. Leon holds my hand tightly, as if he's afraid I might vanish at any moment.

We step onto the terrace, where Istanbul sprawls beyond the sea—a chaos no one seems to mind. The salty breeze uncorks a bottle of memories from the night I almost died here, and I wonder if returning to the place where the curse originated is a mistake.

"Canim." Munu emerges before us, cradling a bundle of yellowing parchments.

"You brought the surviving pages," Leon gasps, lunging toward Munu, tugging at my arm, unwilling to let go.

Munu's eyes flicker to our clasped hands, and her lips part as though she's about to speak, but she holds back.

"Please." Leon stretches out his free hand, palm open, waiting for the journal.

Munu hesitates, her gaze shifting between us. After a few seconds, she gives a small nod, seeming to convince herself, then drifts toward us.

"Not so quick," comes a voice from behind us.

We whirl around to find a man standing on the terrace behind us. Where did he come from?

His handsome, sun-kissed face is framed by dark, sleek hair, swept back as if even the wind wouldn't dare disrupt his features. His dark brown eyes are cold with a blend of disdain and arrogance.

I swear I haven't seen him before, but he feels oddly familiar.

"You." Leon frowns.

"You," Munu echoes.

It throws me off guard how they both seem to know him. Tall, broad-shouldered in a slick black suit, and far too large to have been hiding when we arrived, the man holds himself with an aura of power, as if the world itself tilts slightly in his direction.

"You will pay for your disobedience," he roars, jabbing a finger at Munu. His anger ripples through the air like an electric storm.

My jaw drops. Is he another seer? How can he see Munu?

"You can . . . see her?" Leon asks, just as stunned.

The man's gaze shifts to Leon, sizing him up with a thin-lipped scowl, then to our linked hands, and his expression hardens even more, the temperature around us seeming to drop.

"Get out, you two," he barks, a hundred thunderbolts crashing at once. It's not just a command—it's a force. "Now."

"Who the fuck are you?" I demand before anyone else can speak. There's something deeply unsettling about the stranger, an energy so oppressive it seems to paralyze both Leon and Munu.

"H-he's the historian I told you about," Leon declares, but the man remains unfazed, folding his arms with an air of indifference.

"Professor Arman Aziz—I didn't know he was involved in the craft—"

"Shut the fuck up," the professor snaps, then his gaze whips toward Munu. Her wings start flapping wildly, as if in agitation. "I didn't expect you to act so vulgarly, Munu, not after everything I've done for you," he says, shaking his head in disgust. "How could you betray me?"

The weight of his voice sends a chill through me, and for a moment, I can't clear my thoughts enough to realize he's accusing Munu. And is it just my imagination, or is Munu . . . growing?

"How do you know him?" I turn to Munu.

"I used to think I knew him," Munu says, her lips trembling. "But I'm not sure I do any more. I don't know if I ever truly did."

"Stop being hysterical and hand those papers to me," the professor demands, his voice a harsh growl. "Do you no longer fear my wrath?"

"No, Lazarios," Munu replies, her grip on Sufi Chelebi's pages tightening as she grows taller with each word. "It's time you pay for what you did."

It all unfolds in a blur as Leon and I watch, transfixed.

Professor Aziz—or Lazarios—groans before lunging at Munu with an inhuman speed. The gust of wind from his movement nearly knocks us off our feet and I wrap my arms around Leon.

Lazarios. The name rings in my mind as I watch him grapple for the papers in Munu's hands. Lazarios, the man both Munu and her sister Theodora once loved. But how could he still be alive? I glance at Leon, searching for answers, but he looks as shocked as I am.

"You worthless harpy! The beggar of my love. I told you not to call me by that name. Are you attempting to punish me for denying you my company?" Lazarios shouts as Munu wrestles for the parchments. "Give them to me!"

"You are damned! You are done for," Munu hisses, clinging on to the papers for dear life. She grows taller with every passing second, her form expanding. "I know everything you did. You treacherous, lying, cruel devil. I don't love you, and neither am I scared of you any more."

"You don't love me any more?" Lazarios laughs. "Impossible, Munu."

Munu spits in his face, then backhands his arm with fierce defiance. She's now as tall as I am, her form almost human except for the giant, gray wings on her back.

The contempt in Lazarios's face is also growing.

"I will show no mercy this time," he sneers. "You will beg at my feet like the wet mop you are, pleading for my affection once again, but I will have none of it. You ruined everything, you miserable wretch."

He yanks at the parchments, but Munu holds firm. "Never!" she shouts defiantly. "I will never beg again."

"Enough!" Leon shouts, diving into the fray to join the struggle over the papers, leaving me behind. I step back, gripping the railing tightly, and watch the three of them tussle for the parchments. The commotion halts abruptly when a sharp whistle slices through the air, freezing everyone in their tracks.

"Oh my," cackles a dreamy voice.

That laugh, like the sound of children giggling in unison. I remember it from the night he bent Munu. How could anyone forget it?

"Am I late to the party?" Grey steps into view. His body is lean and muscular, almost naked save for tight leather briefs, a belt with dangling handcuffs, and a policeman's hat perched on his head. His strange attire stuns me for a moment, and it takes a few seconds to register—he's not a real policeman. He's a stripper.

"Who the fuck are you?" Lazarios yells at him.

"Didn't you get my meeting invite?" Grey frowns, twirling a whistle in one hand while pointing a baton at Lazarios with the other.

"I'm not here for your stupid meeting, cherub."

"So, you do know who I am, dear comrade." Grey chuckles, not a single drop of enthusiasm lost.

What the hell does he mean by addressing Lazarios as *comrade*?

"Hello, Sare Sıla Silverbirch, my second favorite mortal." Grey beams as he spots me. "It's so wonderful to see you again."

Baffled by everything going on, I can't seem to voice my confusion.

"Partner." Leon nods at Grey. "If you know him, does that mean . . ." Leon trails off, glancing at Lazarios. "He's one of your kind? He introduced himself as a historian to me."

"He likes this handsome mortal face. I have evidence that he uses it every single time," Grey sighs. "Lazarios for Eudokia, and Professor Arman Aziz for you."

It dawns on me all at once.

Lazarios is a celestial in human form. Munu's lover was an *angel*.

"You're crossing a dangerous line, cherub," Lazarios snarls at Grey, his eyes burning a blazing orange now. "Piss off before I crush you."

"Where's the fun if I leave now?" Grey retorts, waving the baton. "Why do you think I chose this particular attire? I'm here to enforce the law, defend the innocent! Finally serve justice to all these poor, tormented souls."

Perhaps I'm too shaken to point out the obvious, but Lazarios isn't.

"It's not a real police uniform, dimwit."

"Is it not?" Grey blinks with sheer innocence.

If I wasn't so confused by everything unfolding, I'd be laughing—or maybe even hugging Grey.

"But the guy I have borrowed—he was . . . orchestrating chaos into harmony, and people were watching him, mesmerized." Grey lifts up his whistle. "He even had this horn to blow. I thought he was someone important."

"Umm . . ." I wonder how I can explain without offending him, not sure why I'm bothering. "He was a . . . dancer."

"A stripper, you idiot," Lazarios yells at him. "You assume you understand mortals? You have no clue, you low-ranking buffoon. Crawl back to your archives, now, before I shred you into pieces. Even my mercy has a limit."

"For the record, I no longer work in *those* archives. And let's be real—your mercy has always been sub-zero, which is why we're here today." Grey holds his fist out defiantly. "I'm sorry, but police officer or dancer, I'm not going anywhere."

Lazarios finally abandons his attempt to seize the parchments from Munu and towers over Grey, grabbing him by his throat.

"Will someone please explain what's going on?" I demand, watching Lazarios seize Grey.

"Hmm," Grey puffs nonchalantly as Lazarios shakes him. "Where does one begin with the misdeeds of this one?"

"Go on, then," I challenge him, and my words draw Lazarios's attention to me. "What has he done?"

Lazarios drops his hold on Grey and sashays over to me like a panther approaching its prey.

"Are you going to join this parade of ungrateful, reprehensible heretics, Sare Sıla Silverbirch?" He smirks.

I don't know what stuns me more, that he knows my full name, or the gentle tone he speaks to me with, a politeness he doesn't seem to have for anyone else.

Leon puts himself between us. "Don't touch her."

"Go to hell, Lazarios." Munu follows Leon.

"Why, Munu? Why did you turn against me?" Lazarios moves back to her. "What have they promised to you?"

"Don't you dare call me Munu again," she replies. "That name is a lie. I know everything. A fool I was, never once suspecting your sudden mercies. I condemned my poor sister because of you!" She slaps him again. I'm too stunned to move, and Leon's protective hold pins me to the spot anyway. "It's only when she said it—she said what you called *her*." Munu's lips tremble with a fury I've never seen on her before. "How could you do this to us? How could you do this to Sare?"

Me? I stand confused, as everything Munu told me about Lazarios plays in my head. "What does he have to do with me?"

The sun sinks slowly toward the sea, its fiery glow shimmering on the water's surface, casting tense, restless colors over the old, fragile tower.

"Enough," Lazarios demands. "Sare and I will have a word, in private."

He flicks a finger at Munu, and she grabs her own throat and begins to wriggle before disappearing with a loud crack, leaving the parchments in her hands drifting in the air. Instead of saving the fragments of the journal, Leon shoves me behind his body in a desperate attempt at protection. When Lazarios's murderous focus shifts to him, I'm more terrified for him than for my own safety.

"Leon is under my protection!" Grey's fingers hook on Lazarios's shoulder. "Your divine debt is too high already. Spare yourself from more ill! You owe these people justice."

"How dare you presume to give me orders." Lazarios stares at Grey's hand as if there's a fly on his shirt. He doesn't even seem angry. "I am Five the Fifth, Angel of Death."

Five the Fifth, I repeat. *The angel of death?*

Lazarios is Five . . . Munu's boss?

"I am the most impeccable, unblemished," Five announces, his voice emboldened with authority. "I am the might of the light, the fire of the stars. I am the ultimate superior." He snaps his fingers again and Grey disappears with a loud sizzle, leaving behind a swirling vortex of smoke. "And I don't owe anyone shit."

"Stop," Leon protests, but it doesn't save him from vanishing too. He departs in a flash, leaving behind a ripple of disturbed air.

I claw the empty space where Leon stood a split second ago, my heart sinking.

"Bring him back!" I scream at Lazarios—or Five, whatever his real name is. "What have you done to him?"

"Oh, calm down, he's *fine*. Still in one piece. I zapped him back to the mainland." Five rolls his eyes. "All that fuss, for one mortal boy? I felt quite proud with the way you had him under your finger. Don't tell me you actually *like* him."

A lump forms in my throat. "I love him," I confess.

"Well, that's a pity." He leans down to collect the remains of Sufi Chelebi's journals, scattered on the stone tiles. "I hoped you'd be different from the rest of these fools."

"What do you want from me?" My voice trembles.

"The real question is—" he looks up at me, bemused—"what you will want from me."

His smile, empty as it is, sparks that sense of recognition in me again. I've definitely seen this smile before.

Where though?

"I'm leaving," I announce. There's something unsettling in the way he looks at me, and I want nothing to do with him. Besides, I need to find the others, wherever he's sent them to. I hurtle toward the exit, panic rising within me.

"Running into the arms of that stupid boy?" Five laughs, a mocking, cruel sound. "After everything I've done for you? All the risks I took to save your worthless life?"

"What the fuck do you mean?" I turn to him with a dizziness that makes me stagger.

"Watch your tongue." Five rises to his feet, crushing the poor remains of Sufi Chelebi's legacy in his fist. "I will not be dishonored, Sare. Not even by my own child."

"W-what?" I try to make sense of his words as a cold gust sweeps at me.

No, I tell myself. I must have misheard. He can't possibly mean that. But then the memory surfaces—him, tall and striking in that old photo from Mum's room. His face younger, eyes bright with the same confidence, his arm wrapped around Iris.

Ozan. Azlan. The man who ruined my family.

"W-who are you really?" My knees buckle as Five takes a step toward me. Then another. I shiver, unable to peel my gaze off him, unable to make a move.

"I thought you'd figure it out sooner," he says. "I'm your father."

CHAPTER TWENTY-EIGHT

Fortune is forged by the valorous.

Excerpt from *The Book of Revenge, Müneccimbaşı Sufi Chele-bi's Journals of Mystical Phenomena*

Growing up knowing I was cursed, I was a strange, shy creature even her own mother didn't want to look at. A glitch in the world's order.

I always assumed I was just . . . an odd child.

Beneath the gray cloud of a curse hanging over her like a noose. Forced to mature earlier to look after her own mother.

I was someone peculiar, someone alone.

My father was just a hole—not even a hope. A shadowy figure. Mum's mistake. A nobody. I never dared to imagine him. I never even tried to sketch his face, unable to find an expression, a pair of eyes, a nose or mouth for him.

Perhaps that's why I feel so crushed by Five's revelation, and I finally grasp how little I had truly understood.

We stand beneath the relentless heat that the evening fails to scrub from Istanbul.

The angel of death and I.

Even the gulls seem to have withdrawn from their hotspot.

"W—who?" I ask, the world reeling around me.

"It seems you've inherited your aunt's wits as well as her looks." Five's eyes narrow. "Your lack of intelligence is truly disappointing. How many times must I say it? I am your father."

The pieces of the puzzle lie around me, finally starting to slot together. They are the same person. They always were. It was always *him*. The same man.

Ozan.

Azlan.

Lazarios.

"I saw you—in a photograph," I mutter. "With Iris."

He makes a pained face. "Iris was quite the headache. Weak but disobedient . . . the worst combination. I had to come up with that stupid marriage plot to control her. Merciful, wasn't I? Even though she hardly deserved it."

I can't process this. I can't escape. I'm a candle flame in the wind.

"She died here." My voice is a whisper, thinking how we're standing right in the place where Iris died. "She died because of you."

"You make it sound like I killed her," Five says. "Didn't your mother tell you? It was an accident."

I don't even know how to respond to his cruelty. My heart pounds as I glance around, desperate for an escape, but he shifts, blocking my path with an unnerving calm.

"Iris's death reminded me that it was time to end things and move on," he muses, without an ounce of guilt, shame or emotion. "What's the point of wasting my existence on mortals without pursuing new names—and new lovers?"

"What the fuck is your real name?" I lash out, fury bubbling under my skin. "Do you even have one?"

He pauses to think, and then when he speaks again, his voice drips with disdain. "I was once renamed by beings far beneath me, beings who fancied themselves superior. Five the Fifth—a name I was forced to endure, one I never truly accepted. So, I found other names, ones more to my liking, daughter."

"I'm not your daughter!" I scream, repulsed by his twisted logic.

"Oh, you are. First, I'll rename you myself, as I had no say in the pitiful choice your mother made. I was thinking, perhaps to honor our connection, I can rebrand you as . . . Asre?"

I almost falter, unnerved by the uncertainty of what he plans to do with me—how he presumes I'd ever want anything to do with him. The psycho.

"Names hold immense power." His eyes gleam as his tone grows ominous. "They're the simplest tools to charm and control mortals. With each name, you forge a unique bond, and with each bond, mortals will worship you in a million ways. It's pleasantly entertaining. Be patient and I'll teach you how to master this skill."

The games he played with these so-called names, the way he assumes I'd even want to learn—it's nauseating.

"Your mother adored *Azlan* the moment I revealed it to her," he says, a grin spreading on his face. "She was grateful to have Azlan all to herself, never once complaining like the others. But all my names lead back to my true self. Azarel."

Azarel. Lazarios. Azylios. Azlan. Ozan. Aziz. I shudder as I recall Munu's memories, how Theodora revealed to her that Lazarios forced her to use a different name. How did I not notice the pattern? How blind was I?

Five studies me, expectant, as if waiting for a compliment, but I offer none. I have only disgust. Only repulsion.

There's no way Daphne loved this . . . thing.

"Mum wouldn't fall for someone like you." I shake my head, refusing to accept it. "She wouldn't."

"Perhaps you're not as dim . . ." He tilts his head, as if recounting an amusing anecdote. "Yes, I was the one to woo her. She used to sit and paint on the seafront, like a mermaid fresh out of the sea.

A flawless beauty, and she smelled divine. Irresistible . . . What was her name again?"

It's unbearable to imagine Daphne in his clutches, but what makes it worse is that he doesn't even remember her name.

"I'm only joking." Five chuckles. "Of course, I remember Defne. Do you think I father children with any random mortal? No, I truly liked her. She didn't need much charming to devote herself to me. She was pure. Submissive. Always trusting," Five says with the same nonchalance as if he were raising a toast at a family reunion. "I liked her enough to let her keep . . . you."

My hand flies to my mouth as the truth hits me like a punch to the gut. "You ensnared her. It's why Daphne thought she was bewitched." Mum, Iris, Eudokia, Theodora—they weren't just in love. Whatever spells or enchantments Five used, they had no chance. They couldn't resist him. They were his victims. "They all fell for you, like moths to a flame!"

"Is it my fault that I am the most flawless creation of the Boss Almighty?" Five shrugs with infuriating ease. "One kiss is all it takes to bring them to their knees. The rest is easy."

"You ruined them." It takes all my willpower not to strike at him. "You self-centered piece of shit!"

"I don't like repeating myself, Asre." His face twists with a venomous pleasure as he spits out that wretched name he invented for me. "I will not be dishonored. I refuse to be blamed because mortals are so fragile, so shamefully weak-willed and quick to crumble."

I shrink away, trembling—whether from terror or fury, I can't comprehend—and he misreads me entirely.

"Ah, but you have nothing to fear," he says, a smirk curling his lips. "You're only half mortal. Once that weak heart is eliminated, snuffing out that damned curse for good, you'll be stronger than ever. Worthy of standing by my side for eternity."

My breath catches as his words settle over me, each more shocking than the last.

My heart. The sacrifice.

"You," I hiss, my hands balling into fists. Is there a limit to his evil? "You orchestrated the sacrifice. That's why you were after *The Book of Heartbreak*. You're worried it would help me break the curse in another way."

"Of course it was me." He chuckles. "Who else has the intelligence to craft such an impeccable plan?"

"Did Munu know any of this?" I demand, dreading the answer. I can't bear the thought of her conspiring with him.

"She, like everyone else beneath me, knows only what she needs to know." Five shrugs. "Do not mistake me for mortal half-wits, Asre. I don't share my agendas with anyone."

The sky above us darkens, and I darken with it. Stars flicker to life one by one as I fight the urge to close my eyes, hoping to wake and discover this is nothing but a nightmare.

But it isn't.

"You seem . . . upset." Five steps closer, his height suffocating. "Shouldn't you be rejoicing in the revelation of your divine parentage?"

"Stay away from her," someone interrupts.

I recognize my grandfather instantly. As I turn to face him, looming by the door, I see the loathing in his eyes as they lock on to Five.

"I swear I will kill you." Muzaffer stands straight, tall as a reed, pale as paper. "I will, if you touch Sare."

I go numb when Muzaffer clutches Five's arm, dragging him away from me. I watch him attack the angel while I stand helpless, stunned, speechless.

"Go back to where you come from." Muzaffer's rage is raw and unhinged. "Don't dare think you can become a father after all this time. Sare doesn't need a loathsome waster like you."

It hits me then. Muzaffer doesn't realize what Five is. He has no idea. He strikes him, once, twice, thrice. All in vain—Five doesn't even flinch. Muzaffer can't win against him. I shut my eyes, unable to witness this scene. My heart pounds in my chest as if it wishes to get out. But then I hear Muzaffer's yelp and force myself to look.

My throat runs dry at the sight of him.

The angel of death.

My father.

A normal man would have ended up with a bleeding nose after Muzaffer's blows, but he stands eerily unharmed, without even a scratch—taller somehow. But it's the black wings now arching above him that takes my breath away, each feather jutting out like a needle.

"Isn't it funny that I'm actually here because of your nearing end, dearest father-in-law?" Five snorts. His remark erases all the woes in my head.

He's here because of . . . Muzaffer?

"No," I protest, dumbfounded. "You're here because Grey summoned you."

"Petty little shits like Grey hold no sway over me, daughter." Five laughs, a cruel, heart-wrenching laugh, igniting a ring of fire above his head. A halo of flames.

"What are you?" Muzaffer stands, panting, hands still in fists, as he looks upon Five's true form.

Five grins. "I am your death, old man."

"No," I say again. "You can't take him from me." I wrack my brain for a way to stop him, but I'm just . . . blank.

"I see that you two bonded well despite your condition, daughter." Five snorts. "We'll have to get rid of these delicate mortal tendencies, as well as your name."

"*Kovulmuş şeytanın şerrinden Tanrı'ya sığınırım,*" Muzaffer mutters in Turkish. Five grabs him by his shoulder, staring down at him with a blank expression.

"Atta boy," Five says. "Pray all your prayers. Now's the right time."

"Take your hands off him," I yell. Muzaffer glances at me, and for the fleeting second our eyes meet, I swear there's pride in his face.

"Go," he mouths at me. "Run, Sare."

But I can't. I can't leave him with Five.

"To be fair," Five muses, oblivious to Muzaffer's warning, "your grandfather has my respect. Of all the mortals I've met, he is the only one who proved impossible to truly break—but his . . . kidneys are finally beating him, I reckon? Or—" his eyes narrow, as if he's thinking hard—"is it the heart?"

"Let Sare go." Muzaffer's face crumples. "You have no right to see her."

"Oh, I'll see her alright," Five teases. "Besides, she's the one who turned up here. She's the one who sought me out. Mine, old man," he whispers to Muzaffer. "She is mine."

"I'm not yours!" I lunge forward, tugging at Five's wings, but he doesn't even budge as his black feathers pierce my skin like razors.

He shoves Muzaffer away then, and the old man lets out a strained gasp, slumping, hand on his chest.

"*No!*" I scream as I watch him. Muzaffer wavers a moment, then drops to his knees, his face distorted with pain. I run to my grandfather's aid, throwing myself to the ground next to him, distracted from my own distress entirely. My hands tremble as they helplessly cling to Muzaffer's arms, then his neck, his face.

"Please—" Muzaffer is dying, and I can't do anything to save him. "Please, don't leave me."

"I was a fool to blame Defne," Muzaffer mutters. "And it was my own guilt that barred me from seeing her. That I didn't do better by her, or her sister. I didn't protect them. My girls. When . . . When I saw you . . . S-Sare. How much you resemble I-Iris . . . I knew, then. I should've reached out. My silence was a mistake. Forgive me."

"There's nothing to forgive," I rush to soothe him.

And how do I break the curse, if there's nothing to forgive?

The fluttering pounds against my heart. It's a miracle that I've kept going this far without yet succumbing to tears. A sob catches in my throat. I burn to let it go. For what's the point in holding back the tears any more?

"Rule number one, dear daughter: no tears shall fall," Five cautions me. "You are my child. You do not cry like a weakling. You do not beg or bestow forgiveness."

"Fuck you," I snap at him.

And just like that, crying becomes my rebellion. A drop runs down my cheek. Another follows. Then another. And instead of making everything worse, they start to calm me down, as if my heart isn't dented, as if my lungs aren't deflating. I should be panic stricken, helpless, defeated. But I feel empowered. I'm driving toward an end, I realize.

The curse's end.

"I'm s-sorry. Promise . . . t-to . . ." Muzaffer's eyes seem to wither like petals in his face. "Look . . . ahead."

I position his head on my lap to offer him comfort, uncertain if he can feel it.

I'm sorry. His regret drums a rhythm. *I'm sorry. I'm sorry. I'm sorry.*

The fluttering surges in my ribs.

What should I do? I can't recite those rules. They belong to Five, and to the world of celestials who never cared one jot for any of us.

They were never mine.

I can't break the curse by following someone else's rules. I have to abandon them to save myself.

"I promise," I reassure Muzaffer, "I'll look ahead."

He brushes the scars on my palm.

"Enough," Five says flatly, cracking his fingers. I watch as a plume of silver smoke rises from Muzaffer's chest, coiling like mist before rushing to Five's open hand. He clenches his fist, and Muzaffer's hand goes still beneath mine.

"Get up," Five orders, his voice devoid of empathy. "He's gone."

"He's gone," I repeat as despair swallows me whole. "He's gone . . ." My sobs turn ragged, raw, almost animalistic.

My grandfather's face is peaceful on my lap. The last victim of the sorrow and grief that made me.

No matter how far I run, Death always follows, because I am its child—the child of a man with no heart.

"Stop wailing," Five grits out.

A fire erupts in my chest, flames fluttering in defiance, none of them obeying him. Is that why the burning doesn't hurt this time? Or have I grown so numb that pain has forsaken me?

Then it comes—I let it come—an impact from deep below, rattling the tower as if it's nothing more than a toy.

The earthquake.

"Not this shit again," Five growls.

The earth groans in response, as though the land weeps with me.

I can't breathe. Strange, there is still no pain. Yet I feel all the past fractures in my heart, all at once.

I'm going to die.

"Look at me," Five commands, and my neck snaps upward, my body no longer mine to control. "Stop pitying these worthless mortals. You will not die."

I feel his intention slithering beneath his words—he's trying to distract me.

"Wouldn't it be better," I challenge him with defiance, "if I die, and the curse dies with me?"

"You foolish girl," he groans. "You will apologize once you realize how much I've risked for you. It would've cost me nothing to crush you before you were even born. You'd have perished, and the curse would've been erased, freeing me of my troubles. But I chose to let you live. I wanted more, something that even angels can't possess. You will be my prophet. The Almighty has countless prophets, why shouldn't I?" He leans closer. "Together, we will build my kingdom on earth."

His face shifts then.

I place a hand on my chest, forcing my eyes shut so I don't have to witness Five's full transformation—but no matter how hard I try, I'm forced to stare at him. He morphs, face paling, wings rising. He grows larger, impossibly so, until all traces of facial hair vanish and his skin turns translucent, ghastly pale. His wings loom over me like haunted hills. Only the ring of fire remains the same, above his head, soaring as he glares at me.

"I've never shown my true form to any mortal," he declares, towering like the monster he is. "Not when they're alive. But you are mine and you deserve to see me. You and I will share an eternity. A destiny. We will be invincible, wrathful, unforgiving."

I should feel small, powerless, but I'm emboldened by his failure to understand me. I'll never willingly abandon the emotions that make me human. I'll never belong to him.

"Never," I spit the word, refusing to be cowed. "I'll never stand by your side. Not after what you've done to Mum and Iris."

"It's my fire glowing in you, my mercy that saved you from the curse's reign," Five speaks softly, as if singing a lullaby, but his eyes gleam with pure wrath. "Stop being an ungrateful brat and celebrate your glorious lineage."

"It breaks my heart that you're my father." I pause as my breath scrapes against my throat. I wait for the lacerating pain to seize my chest, but despite the raging earthquake, it still won't arrive. "Y-you break my heart."

He looks into my eyes, his chest heaving, as if he's truly hearing me for the first time. He leans down and grips me tightly, lifting me as though I weigh nothing. For a split second, I think he might kill me right there.

"I think you're angry because I never showed up," he mutters to himself, as though trying to understand. "But I was going to. On your birthday, when you finally lose the heart. 10th December— I had it jotted down in my diary. I could show you."

"Do you think I care? Well, fuck you, because you can't control me. I will let my heart destroy me rather than live for you."

I tremble and Istanbul trembles beneath us, the earth shifting with the quake.

"Your heart will crack if you don't stop this tantrum," he warns. "And I can't save you this time. Even *I*, the most supreme, have limits. Pull yourself together! Aren't you hungry to live?" Even in my poor state, I notice how his confidence falters. "I can give you wings. I can give you gold. You'll always be young, powerful." He pauses, searching my face. "You can have that boy seer, and as many other lovers as you desire, all at your mercy. You can make anyone love you."

Love.

It's what killed me with heartbreaks, but it is also what kept me alive. No matter how hard I shunned it, I realize, love never abandoned me. I feel it inside my ribs, resting warm against the icy darkness of the curse, seeping through the cracks in my flawed heart.

There is no anguish in its imperfection.

Five leans toward my face. "I will not beg forgiveness, if this is what you're after."

Forgiveness. He makes it sound like an insult.

And right then, as I stare at his bone-white facade and glowering eyes, I grasp exactly what I need to do to break the curse.

"Aren't you frightened?" Five's grip is a shackle on my arms.

I almost laugh at him. Fear left me long ago. Heartbreaks may have destroyed me, but they forged me into someone far stronger.

Someone who's not afraid of Death.

"I'm not a coward any more," I challenge him. "I'd rather die than live without love. But I won't die without breaking the curse."

"Fool," he grinds out. "How could you do that?"

"All these years, I allowed only fear and anger in my heart." I waver, weakened, it takes all my remaining strength to speak. "You were the architect of the rules I lived by. You tried to make me . . . like you. But you failed. I hold nothing but love and forgiveness in my heart. Even f–for y—"

"No!" he roars. "I shall not be insulted like this. Your human heart only knows hating me. You cannot say it."

I *can* say it. I pity him so much, despite the deep hatred, I can forgive him.

"Even for you—Azarel." I cough, wheezing, my soul draining as a fracture begins to etch itself in my heart.

"Silence!" he bellows and, for a moment, I fear the tower might crumble—not from an earthquake, but under the weight of his fury. "Don't you dare speak those words. I will not have my pride crushed."

"Father," I call him, and he stiffens. "What a wretched state you're in. How hollow your existence must be. I pity you, for you will never understand how beautiful it is to be human. You are blind to the joys of a heart you deem weak—and to its power to forgive."

Something flickers in Five's eyes—hurt, mingled with contempt.

"I forgive you, Azarel." I close my eyes. "I forgive you."

It breaks my heart to forgive him. But I do. The forgiveness is my sacrifice, and his punishment.

The sound that follows is different—still loud, deafening, not a crack, but a deep rattling.

Strangely, I don't fall. Not this time. Perhaps, because I'm already in Death's arms, there's nowhere left to go.

CHAPTER TWENTY-NINE

Life unfolds as a journey of decisions, devoid of clear right or wrong, without truly missed opportunities. Serenity awaits only those who pursue it.

Excerpt from *The Book of Betrayal, Müneccimbaşı Sufi Chelebi's Journals of Mystical Phenomena*

Murmurs. Darkness. Shadows.

Is it death that makes me feel lighter? I taste something like freedom. It's soft, tender. Not the light at the end of the tunnel, but something deeper, quieter—a release more amplifying than fading.

I don't know if I'm awake or adrift in dreams, alive or beyond life, but my consciousness tunes in to a voice, clear as a radio signal breaking through the static.

"Listen," it says, determined. "There are minutes and then seconds. There's a difference between points of time—hey, are you with me?"

It's a genderless voice. Almost a chorus of chirping birds, reminding me of Munu, I remember, with a stab of longing. It's not her, but still familiar. Grey?

"For the sake of Boss Almighty," another voice replies, exasperated. "Cut the bullshit and let me move on with the mortal. As if you know the workings of Death!"

I immediately recognize the cruel, capricious *Five*. Azarel. *My father.*

"I have to take her to the Otherside," he asserts. "She died. She lost."

I've died, I recall. I embraced the heartbreak, I forgave Five, rather than allowing him to control me. And . . . the weight of the curse isn't tied around my neck any more.

I didn't lose. *He* did.

"Well, you can't, because she broke the curse. I'm telling you, mortal time moves forward, like an arrow, and she died a few seconds after the curse was broken. First, the old man died, then the girl's heart shattered but it beat the curse by seconds, hence the girl shouldn't die." Grey snorts. "You are the angel of death, surely you understand this!"

I broke the curse.

Suspended in the air, I drift like a wisp of smoke, weightless. Perhaps I've become a particle. A piece of dust. A ghost.

"Do I get it? Yes." Five sounds fed up. "But do I care? Not really."

"Excuse me—" Another agitated speaker pipes up. "But this matter sounds like something Afterlife Admissions should handle. As a senior angel of the Fate Adjustment Bureau, I fail to see how this falls within the scope of my duties."

"Let me explain, dear Nine." Grey clears his throat. "The curse records were modified without necessary authorization from Sacred Systems."

"I completely understand, but that would be of interest to the Celestial Compliance Office, not us." Nine sighs. "Or Afterlife Admissions. Definitely not my department. Look, I'm rather busy."

"I already summoned Chief Executive Celestial and Archangel Absolute Gabriel. He should be here in no time—" Grey pauses, and I hear the rustle of papers. "Listen, CID-1010834556 was first activated when you used to work under Prayer Fulfillment. You were the Curse Remediation Officer who dealt with it, weren't you? You must understand this is a disastrous consequence of Five's actions. He likes taking human form, and has seduced many mortal women, ruining their lives, spawning these curses and undoubtedly many more consequences besides."

"Did he, now?" Nine bites out. "Amusing, how he always claims quite the opposite—that it is the mortals who seek him."

"Shut up," Five snarls.

"If I'm going down, then you're coming with me," Nine retorts.

"Fantastic," Grey chuckles.

As my vision clears, I brace myself for the Inbetween, only to find myself in what appears to be an office. It stretches out like an airport hangar, seemingly endless, with towering shelves lining both sides, packed with folders upon folders. Papers protrude like tongues from many, while others are secured with locks.

It doesn't smell of anything, and the light glows eerily.

"Now if you'll let us get moving, I need to escort the mortal—"

My vision is still blurred, but I feel Five's pull in my very being. I try to lift my hands, or lean down to see my body, but I have no control over myself. My mind is whirring as if a vacuum cleaner rolls through my head, then I see them.

Three figures, the source of the neon glow in the gloom.

Five is unmistakable in his angelic stance and there's another like him—but with gray wings and a feminine form. The third looks like a child—fluffy white wings and a chubby body.

A *cherub.*

Grey in his true form.

Before I can say anything, a loud hum echoes through the air as another angel arrives. The newcomer is even taller than Five, with a crescent-shaped light glowing above his head. He shines so brightly that just looking at him stirs something within me—an almost fleeting sense of . . . serenity.

"Archangel Absolute!" Grey clasps his hands to his chest, quivering with either terror or joy, I can't tell. "You read my email!"

"I hope you have a good reason to cc Mikhael and I at the same time." The archangel frowns. "Now explain yourself, and prepare for a punishment if you're wasting our divine time."

"Of course!" Grey chirps, his eyes bright with ambition. "This is Sare Sıla Silverbirch. Please let's take a moment to extend our deepest sympathies for her victory: she has just broken an almost thousand-year-old curse. We are the most delighted!"

"It's not *sympathy*, you idiot." Five rolls his eyes. "It's *congratulations*. If you're really that fond of mortals, at least be decent about it and learn their language."

"Semantics." Grey flaps his wings. "I'm sure the mortal doesn't mind."

I don't mind, of course, but I can't find the voice to communicate.

"Let me kick off with intros. Most Holy Archangel, and Sare Sıla Silverbirch, these are Five the Fifth and Nine the Ninth. We'll return to them in a minute." Grey gestures at the taller, sulking angels. "And I'm Grey the Compassionate, currently a Senior Cherub of the Temporal Intervention Agency. Here's my card." With a sweep, Grey offers a business card to Gabriel, then his small body folds into a bow, his wings poking forward.

Five snorts. "Are we bowing down to mortals now?"

"First and foremost, let's focus on how Five refuses to respect mortals!" Grey turns to the archangel, who looks like he's about to doze off. "As I previously explained in my email, Five isn't a real angel—he is in fact made of fire, and not light. His true name is Azarel and he comes from the Infernal Dominion. And so is Nine, whose real name is Belzeren."

"Ah, yes," Gabriel begins nonchalantly. "Heavenly Governance used to run an infernal rehabilitation program back in the day. We sourced talent from the dominion, rebranded and reused them. There are hundreds in service, cherub."

"B-but how can they tend to mortals?" Grey looks mortified. "It's their demonic nature to divert people from the designated path of righteousness."

"Do you know how much angels cost? Demons are a cheaper workforce. We assigned them unbiased numerical identifiers as names. Automatically, of course, since we don't have time to bless each one with a new title. They've been fully trained, salvaged and now report to the relevant department heads."

"Precisely," Five cuts in. "This is blatant discrimination, warranting immediate disciplinary action. Now, may I please proceed with the mortal? I have a job to do!"

"Likewise," Nine grumbles.

"Please, listen!" Grey leaps forward to the archangel's feet. "I have proof that they have sinned!"

Five and Nine both look like they're going to rip Grey apart when Gabriel commands, "Proceed."

"Nothing Five does seems to follow our rules. For instance, this curse was broken just before this mortal died, but he still took her beyond the border—even though Death now has no claim on Sare Sıla Silverbirch."

"You degenerate, pitiful imbecile," Five snaps. "Sare is mine. Mine to take, mine to drag over whatever border I want."

Something clenches in me, hearing my name from his lips.

Grey hastily jots something down on a notepad.

"And what exactly is your relationship with this mortal?" The archangel raises an eyebrow at Five, showing the first flicker of real interest since his arrival.

"Nothing." Five holds his chin up, the flames on his round halo emblazoned.

"Is that so?" Gabriel hums.

"Ah, we'll get to debunking that lie soon, but first I'd like to invite my witness to testify," Grey asserts, and with the crackling sound I have heard thousands of times before, Munu appears.

"Munu." My voice is faint, but she still glances at me, giving a nod, as if asking me to stay calm.

"Mortal ID 1274856567048112, Eudokia Doukas," Grey rushes to explain. "Turned into an ethereal and renamed as Munu by Five."

"Enough," Five protests.

"I'm afraid it's not up to your discretion, Five. Need I remind you I'm your superior?" Gabriel seems unfazed, but his eyes are ablaze. "I'd like to listen to what the ethereal has to say—the cherub has gone to a great deal of trouble, after all. Talk, please, but be brief. I don't have much time."

Munu looks down at the floor. "I met Five in Constantinople in 1052. He introduced himself as Lazarios, the son of a nobleman, and he swore his eternal love to me."

"Lies," Five grates out.

"Silence!" The archangel's crescent halo glows brighter. "Continue."

"I didn't know he was courting my sister at the same time, I didn't know he was charming us both, and I ended up cursing my family when I died. Then Lazarios arrived . . . and he—" Munu swallows a sob. "He revealed his true nature. He told me he was an angel, and he convinced me that Theodora and her seer tricked him to abandon me, and the fool I was, I believed we were finally united. But another angel landed with us before I could rejoice my false happiness. This one." Munu points to Nine. "Nine the Ninth. She was angry with me for the curse I'd released. I had prayed for help for years," Munu mutters, "and found none in her wrath."

"Prayer fulfillment requires funding," the archangel sighs. "Which the Fate Adjustment Bureau rarely has."

"Pardon me, but I am the obvious victim here!" Nine cries. "This morbid minion of Five spawned the curse, and Five tricked me into modifying the record, as the department was too occupied to respond to the prayers or deliver any hope. And then he blackmailed me!"

"I object—" Five howls. "This is heresy."

"Zip it, you two," Gabriel commands. "Speak, Munu."

"Lazarios protected me from Nine, or at least I thought he did. He shrank me in size, claiming it was necessary so I couldn't drift between realms. At first, he kept me in a bell jar on his desk, but soon he grew bored. I wasn't enough for him, so I became his employee, running errands for the office."

"Et cetera et cetera," Grey interjects. "Please, let's fast forward to the present era."

"I was always loyal to Lazarios," Munu explains. "I never doubted him, even when he sent me on a mission across the globe, which I later discovered was nothing more than a ploy to keep me out of the way while he pursued another mortal. When I was tasked with protecting Sare upon her birth, I had no idea what he'd done . . . It was only after Sare found the artifact called *The Book of Heartbreak* that my suspicions arose. Lazarios never cared about mortals—why was he suddenly interested in this book?"

"Let's also note that he used Munu to steal this rare relic," Grey interjects.

"Yes." Munu nods. "And when Sare revealed to me that her mother's lover switched between names, that he called her 'sweet muse of his cravings.' Then I understood. H–he used to say the same to me. I never imagined—never thought—that Lazarios, who once pledged his undying love to me, could have seduced all of us. We were just victims of his cruel sense of entertainment."

"Objection!" Five folds his arms. "My private affairs are not open for judgment. I am the most flawless."

Gabriel rolls his eyes. "He's quite high in rank and we need solid evidence to take him to the Divine Disciplinary Board." His gaze darts between Munu and Grey. It's almost as if everyone has forgotten that I'm here. "Do you have any physical proof?"

"We do," I say at last, before anyone else can speak. My voice comes out loud and bold, echoing in the great hall we drift in. "I'm the proof. His daughter."

CHAPTER THIRTY

Your ancestors don't have to be your legacy. Have the courage to honor their memory, but reserve greater courage to walk your own path. Only the brave accept themselves for who they truly are.

Excerpt from *The Book of Betrayal, Müneccimbaşı Sufi Chelebi's Journals of Mystical Phenomena*

Everyone remains speechless after my confession. Grey is the first to break the silence.

"Let me get this straight," he says, scratching his head. "You essentially had your ex babysit your own child? I have to hand it to you, Five—your cunning knows no bounds. Deception at its finest! I've never encountered such a masterpiece of malevolence. If there were wickedness awards in the Infernal Dominion, I'd gladly nominate you."

"Piss off, cherub," Five hisses, and then he turns to me. "Is this how you repay my mercy? You'd be long dead as the child you were with that cursed, pathetic heart. I kept you alive with those resurrections. I deserve your loyalty."

"Never," I mutter. "You're nothing to me. You deserve nothing but punishment."

"Do you understand the consequences of this, comrade?" Gabriel says, voice steely.

"I have a child from a mortal." Five shrugs. "So what? Stop pretending as if I've summoned the apocalypse."

"And you blackmailed me into changing the curse records!" Nine shrieks.

"Yet, instead of coming forward," Grey sighs, "you did exactly what he asked."

"I didn't want to lose my job and end up back in Hell," Nine defends herself. "It's too hot there, and the pay's shit. Archangel—" she drops to her knees—"have mercy! At least I only manipulated documents, not mortals!"

"You have a point," the archangel says. "You still deserve punishment, though. I'll reassign you to . . ." Gabriel pauses, thinking. "Department of Research and Divine Development. As a test subject. No powers. No pay or benefits. Not until they figure out what went wrong with that ill-fated rehabilitation initiative."

"Archangel, mercy!" Nine roars, but with a dismissive flick of his hand, Gabriel banishes her without a second glance.

"You, however, will be dealt with by the Divine Disciplinary Board," the archangel declares, turning to Five. Then he cracks his fingers, and the fiery halo on Five's head diminishes.

"You cannot." Five trembles as though he's about to combust.

"I can, and I will." Gabriel shrugs. "A tribunal will likely send you back to Hell. To the lowest rank. You'll suffer for an eternity."

"No." A tremor runs through Five's voice. "I am Five the Fifth! I slaved away for the Governance. I spent years on your woeful tasks—"

"Oh, spare me." Gabriel snaps, and in an instant, Five begins to shrink, dwindling until he's no larger than a pinkie finger. His outrage dissolves into a faint buzz.

"You can't get rid of me like this!" he squeaks out.

Grey crouches down and scoops Five up in his palm. "What was that? Can't hear you."

Munu and I watch the scene with cold detachment. Five has finally grasped how much trouble he's in, but his terror leaves me unmoved. I don't hate him—not any more. Yet, even as pity stirs faintly within me, I know no punishment could ever suffice for the devastation he's caused.

"Canim," Munu calls to me. "You broke the curse. You did it."

"Yes," Grey says, handing Five, who is now no larger than a fly, to Gabriel. "And so, as I was saying, Sare must go back to the world to continue her . . . worldly things."

"I guess she can." Gabriel shrugs. "And after all this—" he eyes Five—"malarkey . . . I'd say the mortal deserves some compensation. A blessing. Perhaps she can choose if she wants to go back to her miserable life, or float to the Heavens for a perfect eternity with her ancestors, including you, Munu."

"Eudokia," she corrects. "I'm Eudokia Doukas, not Munu. Not any more."

"Splendid," Gabriel says flatly. "Sare, the choice is yours."

I consider the offer. Mum is there in the Heavens, and Muzaffer. I didn't even call him grandfather, not once. I didn't even hug him.

"I-I—" I stammer. It would be so easy to let them have me, unite with my family. Meet Iris. I'm almost ready to give up, to forget life and its troubles, but then I remember Harika's advice.

When the time comes to make a decision: choose love and not hate. Choose hope, not despair. Choose life, not death. Choose courage, Sare Silverbirch.

She must have warned me for today, I realize in astonishment.

Look ahead, Sare, Muzaffer's voice lingers in my ears.

Behind me lies a ruin, a life I never had the courage to truly embrace.

"I want to return," I declare. I won't look back. I will live. A surge of longing for Leon fills my being. I can't abandon him. I haven't even told him how much I love him.

"Of course you do," Gabriel says, casting me a downward glance. "These mortals!"

"Archangel, may I have a word?" Grey whizzes over. "I was thinking if we had stronger ties with mortals, things could be different? Say, we throw a few kiosks in some of their cities or open a social media account, that sort of cost-effective thing to promote our holy efforts. Why is our hard work always hidden?"

"I need you to sign an NDA." Gabriel grimaces, ignoring Grey's enthusiasm.

"Please forward it to my assistant, Deidre, and I'll have a look."

"They gave you an assistant, cherub?"

As they continue their banter, Eudokia and I gravitate toward each other.

"Farewell, canim," she says.

"Is there no way I can still see you?" I feel devastated to lose her now. My only friend for all these years, her absence in Istanbul has troubled me more than I admitted to myself. Letting go of her is almost as hard as giving up my life.

Eudokia's face radiates as if she is wrought from silver, a vision of strength. She carried the burden of cursing her own family, of being tormented by Five's cruelty. But now, at long last, her imprisonment ends.

"It's time to part ways," she declares, her tone bitter-sweet. "You don't need me any more. And I have waited a thousand years to ascend to the Heavens. I must find Theodora, my poor sister, and apologize to her for everything I've done. I can only hope she will forgive me. I didn't know, Sare. I had no idea how wicked Lazarios was."

"Theodora will forgive you," I reassure her. "Just like I did."

And then I do something I've always yearned to do, had she not forbidden it.

"I love you," I announce. "I will miss you so much."

She frowns at me, wide eyed, but then her face smooths into a proud and peaceful smile.

"I l-love you too," she says. "You're the bravest girl I've ever known. Take care of your heart, okay? Don't let anyone break it."

"I promise." I laugh. "I'll take care of my heart."

"And don't you dare forget me, Sare Sıla Silverbirch."

"As if that would be possible," I say. It's strange to accept my emotions without fearing them. But, like Eudokia, I am unshackled, liberated at last.

"Until we meet again." She stares at me, eyes like goggles. And then she pulls me into a hug.

"Until we meet again," I repeat, wrapping myself around her. What will I do without her?

"Are you ready?" Gabriel looks at me wearily.

"I'm ready," I confirm.

"Then by the authority of the Governance, in the light of Our Boss Almighty's blessing, I weave you back to life."

And I shut my eyes, ready to be reborn.

People compare death to sleep, but death is a river. It flows in the dark, eager to pull you into its current, away from the life you lived, which could be a drop of water, or an ocean, depending on how brave you are.

The life I return to isn't what I left behind. It's not a drop of water but an ocean without the barriers of fear.

My eyes flick open and I see that I'm in hospital, lying in a bed.

A small room with a window too large, filtering the broken light of a late afternoon.

I feel my arms and legs, my stomach, mouth, fingers, knees.

This isn't a dream, or a trick. *I am alive.*

"I survived." My voice is a croak.

"Sare?" Leon hovers above me. "By all that's sacred, you're awake."

"My heart—" I place my hand on my chest.

It's here, it's mine. And it's not my enemy any more.

It beats without the bitter curse. A pulsing chorus of emotions surge between my ribs: grief, relief, longing and the joy of being free. They stir, sharper, freer, more powerfully than ever. Sorrow is the first to overtake me, a blue tide, cold and warm at the same time. I hug it and grieve for Muzaffer.

But I still breathe. There's no fluttering.

"I broke the curse," I tell Leon. "I won."

"I thought you were gone." Leon holds my head in his hands. "I found myself back on the shore after Five's trick, and I took the boat to the tower, and found you lying there."

"It's okay," I fumble. "I survived."

I survived death. I survived my father.

I survived the curse.

There's a completeness in its absence. I'm whole. I'm myself.

I'm Sare Sıla Silverbirch, four months shy of eighteen, five times heartbroken. And still alive.

No matter how much a heartbreak might hurt me, it will no longer kill me. Not any more.

Despite the release of embracing all the emotions I had long suppressed; grief still overwhelms me. In mourning for Muzaffer, I think I also allow myself to finally grieve for Mum. And even for Iris, who I never met.

I cry three times, shedding all the tears I'd held back in life until his death. There's a liberation in crying. A power in letting go.

The first flood comes in tides while I'm still in hospital, trying to come to terms with my grandfather's sudden death and everything I discovered about my lineage.

I sit up in the bed, tugging at the IV in my arm, and give into ugly, trembling sobs. I weep for Muzaffer, for Mum, for Iris, myself, for the fact that I have no family left any more.

And no Munu.

Leaning on Leon's shoulder, I let the tears flow.

"It will be okay," Leon comforts and I know it's true. "I'm here." He feels like home.

The second episode of tears arrives on the morning of Muzaffer's funeral, in a place called Gasilhane, where the Turkish wash their deceased before laying them to eternal rest. The room is like a hotel bathroom; white marble, pale as Death itself.

It's only Azmi, the washer and I who are present. Perhaps there is also Allah, because the name is on everyone's mouth, but even if Allah is present, they remain unseen.

"Mr. Gümüşhuş is with Allah now," Azmi keeps saying. "We come from Allah and Allah is where we end."

Muzaffer lies on a slab covered by a towel, his thin face in peace now, finally free of his sorrow and grief. His pain has come to an end.

The washer, Gasal, is clad in white robes with a face bearing the numbness of a lifetime spent washing the dead.

He pours a jug of water over him, and Azmi's whimper echoes between the walls. We cling to one another, and I can no longer tell who trembles, or if we're both quivering as one in our grief. My cries are silent, but Azmi howls like a giant child.

The third time I weep is when I say my goodbyes to Muzaffer.

The Turks don't have large funerals, it turns out. They don't have caskets or fancy cars like the British do; people don't dress up. But they weep, and mourn, and swear oaths to remember. There are some things, then, where every culture is the same.

A small crowd is gathered: Azmi, Gökhan, Leon, Harika, Pelin and myself huddle together in the graveyard.

The imam is a middle-aged man with black hair and a gray beard. "*El Fatiha*," he begins to pray.

Death isn't forgetting, Munu echoes somewhere in my mind.

My grandfather is enshrouded in a thick, white cloth, and they lift him from the crude casket to lower him into the earthen grave. It's too soon, and I will miss him too much.

"*Hamd, Alemlerin Rabbi Allah'indir,*" the imam intones. Azmi whimpers, his arms limp by his sides. Leon and Gökhan throw spades of dirt to cover his body. With buckling knees, I walk up to look down into the grave.

He looks shrunken somehow. Shorter.

This is the moment I begin my third and longest cry.

"*O Rahmân ve Rahîm'dir,*" the imam says.

I think of Mum's funeral, how it changed my life and brought me to Istanbul, where I finally managed to break the curse.

This funeral marks another end.

But this end, I feel in my bones, is also a beginning. Perhaps all ends are.

Still, I weep. My balance tilts, and I drop to the ground above his grave. My palms graze the damp dirt, my wail lifting the birds from the branches of the cypress tree.

My cry is no cloud. It's a storm. One to wash away everything that came before.

EPILOGUE

Fate belongs to victors.

Excerpt from *The Book of Betrayal, Müneccimbaşı Sufi Chelebi's Journals of Mystical Phenomena*

It's a balmy September morning when Leon asks me to come to Peru with him again.

We're already planning a trip to the UK, paddling through the bureaucratic swamp of his tourist visa application. We filled out what feels like a thousand pages of forms, so that I can show him what life in Cambridge was like for me—the cobbled streets, the timeless buildings of the university, the riverbanks where I used to sit all alone. But more importantly, I need to visit Mum's grave and lay flowers there, finally, without the weight of the curse pressing down on me.

"There's nothing to keep us here," Leon says, as if I need convincing. "And I wrote to the master in Puerto Maldonado. I told him about you and your five encounters with Death."

"You did not," I tease him. "Did you?"

Ova Ceren

Across the sea, the Maiden's Tower stands bright under the morning sun. I might be imagining it, but since the curse has been broken, the gulls seem to cruise more lazily around it, contrary to their usual aggressive, whirling dances.

"You're one of a kind, Silverbirch." Leon pulls me close. "The girl who cheated death five times."

"I wouldn't necessarily call it cheating," I say, enjoying the quickening of my heart. "I had some help."

The truth about my parentage didn't stay a secret between us for too long. Perhaps one day I'll forget him, but Five's shadow still lives in mine, as I too have been blessed—or stained—by a pure eye. It turns out Leon wasn't imagining the glow he claimed to see around me. My presence has a strange effect, amplifying both his and Harika's abilities. A "catalyst" they call me. A half-celestial with a human heart. Perhaps there's much more about myself I'm yet to discover.

"I bet *you'll* be a master one day," Leon says. "And teach people how to make bargains with Death."

I laugh. "I hope not."

"Come with me to Peru," he says.

I consider it, my cheeks flushing with sun rays and the excitement of his company.

"I'm not sure about Böcek, but Azmi will miss me dearly," I say at last.

"That isn't the right answer." He leans down and whispers in my ear. "Say yes."

I study his face, his faint freckles, his bright dark eyes, his high cheekbones. Good fortune must be loving someone without fear. And finally, for the first time in my life, I feel lucky.

"You're so beautiful," I tell him. "I can't believe you're mine."

"I guess I can accept 'beautiful' as yes too?" He mocks me.

"Yes." I nod. "I'll come to Peru. I'll go wherever you go."

He turns me around in his arms, and we almost collide with a dog-walker who tuts at us disapprovingly.

"But I have one condition." I pause. "You must promise me—if it's anything less than what we have here, I don't care what your master says, we'll come back."

He turns to look at the Bosphorus, the sea, the Maiden's Tower, and the Istanbul skyline beyond.

"I promise," he says. "I love you."

"I love you," I reply.

And I'm no longer scared.

Communication is classified as Highly Confidential.
Circulation strictly limited to beings of celestial origins.

Subject: A Divine Thank You

Date: 17 September 2025
From: Grey the Compassionate, Head of Curse Assessment and Remediation Panel, Prayer Response and Fulfillment Division, Fate Adjustment Bureau, Mortal Affairs Commission
To: Fate Adjustment Bureau—ALL Angels
CC: Archangel Absolute, Head of Mortal Affairs Commission

Dearest and Holiest Angel superiors,

I pen this missive with my new halo brimming with gratitude.

Thanks to your legacy of neglect and your unparalleled commitment to ignoring the mortals most in need of our grace, I have been fortunate to address such celestial oversights, thereby earning the prestigious Divine Excellence Award. This honor elevated my position within our sacred hierarchy, and I have only you to thank for my promotions and the blessing of a halo!

I want to repeat what I profoundly believe: you save just one mortal, and you change the world and the realms beyond it.

With sincere appreciation and celestial camaraderie,
Grey the Compassionate
Doctorate of Angelic Scholarship (Hons)
The Esteemed Winner of the Divine Excellence Award

ACKNOWLEDGMENTS

They say everything happens for a reason, and perhaps it does. The year I lost my left ovary, I started sharing daily musings on Instagram. Before long, my account grew, and people were telling me I should write a book. At the time, I was just a software developer, an immigrant in the UK, navigating menopause twenty years earlier than expected, writing code instead of fiction. It took me a long time to believe I could do it in a language that wasn't truly mine. But here I am, after some blood and tears, writing the acknowledgments. I did it!

Now I made it sound too easy, didn't I? Honestly, *The Book of Heartbreak* wouldn't have happened without the support of some incredible people.

A huge thank you to:

My brilliant agent, Elizabeth Counsell, for championing this book (and my fragile writer heart). I'm never good at giving compliments, so I'll simply scream: You're the best!

My UK editors, Ruth Bennett and Ella Whiddett, for making this story better with every thoughtful suggestion. I'm so fortunate to work with such intelligent women, and I love their brains!

Acknowledgments

My dearest friend Menna Van Praag, for telling me that it would be a tragedy if I didn't pursue writing. I couldn't have done it without your encouragement.

The rest of the wonderful team at Hot Key: Jas Bansal, Sarah Lough, Pippa Poole, Kate Griffiths, Melissa Hyder, proofreader, thank you for your dedication, expertise and for making me feel so welcome at Bonnier. Will Speed and Kailey Whitman, thank you for creating a beautiful cover that reflects the soul of this book.

The Alcove Press team in the US—my wonderful editor Jess Verdi, and the fantastic team: Thai Fantauzzi Pérez, Rebecca Nelson, Dulce Botello, Mikaela Bender, Stephanie Manova, Megan Matti, Doug White, Matt Martz. Thank you for your hard work, enthusiasm, and for giving my book a home in the US.

The amazing team in Northbank Talent Management, for being so lovely and supportive.

My incredible writing friends Sylvie Markes, Victoria Lancaster, and Jennie Boyes, for reading countless drafts, listening to my ramblings, bouncing ideas with me, and inspiring me with their beautiful writing.

Çiğdem, Arife, Hatice, Aslıhan and Ani for looking after me. Soraya, for giving me hope when I needed it most. Emily Winslow, Alison Stockham, Alice McIlroy, and Amy Crawford, for being so kind and supportive.

All my followers, for being there, for telling me you want to read this book. Besties, I couldn't have done this without you.

U, whose heart I was so foolish to break and who, I know, will never forgive me. I am sorry that a mother dies in this book. I thought of you often while writing Sare, and I miss you.

Kibariye, for singing Sil Baştan (Start from scratch). Girl, I took your advice.

Readers, for giving this book a chance. I hope you like it!

Boss Almighty—Teşekkürler Allah'ım. Sen konuyu biliyorsun . . .

Acknowledgments

And last but not least, my family. My son, the beautiful product of a long-lost ovary, the light of my life. My parents, my sister, and my husband Mehmet, for the endless patience, love, and faith. Where would I be without you? Nuray, for being so sweet. Nathan, Jane and Tony, for giving me a family in the UK.

Thank you to each one of you. Teşekkür ederim hepinize.